PRAISE FOR ANIA AHLBORN

"…genuinely scary…damn good..."
-Cemetery Dance on *Apart in the Dark*

―――――

"…good, spooky stuff."
-Jack Ketchum on *Within These Walls*

―――――

"…creeps under your skin and stays there.
It's insidious…"
-The New York Times on *Within These Walls*

―――――

"For fans of sleepless nights."
-Portland Monthly Magazine on *Within These Walls*

ANIA AHLBORN

ANIA AHLBORN

If You See Her

Born in Ciechanow Poland, Ania has always been drawn to the dark, mysterious, and sometimes morbid side of life. Her earliest childhood memory is of crawling through a hole in the chain link fence that separated her family home from the large wooded cemetery. She'd spend hours among the headstones, breaking up bouquets of silk flowers so that everyone had their equal share.

Ania's first novel, *Seed*, was self-published. It clawed its way up the Amazon charts to the number one horror spot, earning her a multi-book deal and a key to the kingdom of the macabre. Eight years later, her work has been lauded by the likes of Publishers Weekly, New York Daily News, and the New York Times.

She lives in Greenville, South Carolina with her family.

If You See Her is her tenth published work.

WWW.ANIAAHLBORN.COM

ALSO BY ANIA AHLBORN

Seed

The Neighbors

The Shuddering

The Bird Eater

Within These Walls

The Pretty Ones

Brother

I Call Upon Thee

The Devil Crept In

Apart in the Dark

If You See Her

ANIA AHLBORN

Baby Bird, I love you. Look at me, Baby Bird.
It's all for you.

ANIA AHLBORN

And as to being in a fright,
Allow me to remark
That Ghosts have just as good a right
In every way, to fear the light,
As Men to fear the dark.

———

Lewis Carroll, *Phantasmagoria*

ANIA AHLBORN

PROLOGUE

MAY 2000

BY THE TIME Jesse realized where they were heading, it was too late to object. He had been absorbed in his new Nokia 3310, long-coveted and so fresh out of its box that it still had that new plastic smell. It was a luxury he'd spent months saving up to buy; a damn fine high school graduation present if he did say so himself. And quite frankly, he was obsessed with it, which was why—lounging in the back seat of Casey's beat-up Honda Civic—he hadn't been paying attention to the conversation being had between his two closest friends.

But now, glancing up from his game of Snake II, he knew where they were. It was pitch dark out there, but that made no difference. There was no mistaking the area, and the butterflies that had been slumbering in the pit of his stomach exploded into a frenzy of undulating wings.

With his phone clenched tight in his right hand, he forced himself to lean forward, positioning himself between the two front seats. Eminem was cranked to nearly full volume. He wasn't sure how it was possible, but it was exponentially louder in the front two seats than in the back. Reed was obsessed with this damn CD, and while the songs were getting tiresome, it wasn't hard to understand Reed's infatuation. Sure, Michigan had its share of breakout stars. Alice Cooper. Stevie Wonder. Madonna. Al Green. But none hit as close to home as the no holds barred rapping white kid with 8 Mile roots. The guy had come out of nowhere and from nothing. It wasn't tough to imagine that dead-end existence had been had in Warsaw rather than Detroit.

1

Casey was driving way over the limit, his head bobbing in time to every bass beat, the ruts in the road threatening to shake that shitty Civic to pieces. Not that it mattered. Casey had a habit of trying to destroy his ride for God only knew what reason, taking it out to empty fields, doing donuts at full speed.

Reed, who was sitting in the passenger seat, was rapping along with the music. He'd burst into laughter every now and again, stumbling over the lyrics despite knowing them by heart. The trio had heard every song on the Slim Shady EP about a hundred thousand times, but it didn't make the lyrics any easier to master, and it didn't lessen Reed Lowell's infatuation with the man himself. But that was Reed for you. A little obsessive. A little over-the-top. Jesse's best friend since elementary school.

"Hey," Jesse said, reaching between Casey and Reed to turn the music down. He was trying to keep from sounding too concerned—too chickenshit—but he had to say *something*, because this was a field trip he hadn't signed up for. "What the hell are we doing out here?"

Jesse's cohorts glanced at each other. A moment later, they were cracking up at their oblivious backseat passenger. Reed twisted in his seat and peered back at him. Casey's upgraded stereo—the only upgrade that car would ever get—illuminated the contours of his face in a pale and ghostly glow. His mouth twisted up into his signature grin. It was the kind of smile that made you feel simultaneously stupid and too amused to care.

"Dude, are you drunk?" Reed asked.

Casey fell into a fit of poorly suppressed laughter.

It was true, the car *did* smell like a mixture of booze and Cool Ranch Doritos. And from the tinkle of glass that sounded every time Casey hit a particularly jarring pothole, there were plenty of empties rolling around beneath the seats. But Jesse was far from drunk. Yes, he'd had a couple of beers before the trio had crawled into Casey's car for a late-night drive, but both Casey and Reed had imbibed way more than he had. Not that *that* mattered, either. Warsaw had all of six cops and not many obstacles to hit while inebriated. Especially not past the buckshot-riddled city limit sign.

"He's drunk," Casey ascertained from behind the steering wheel.

"I mean, he *must* be," Reed said. "Maybe we should hit up Speedy's for some hair of the dog to sober him up. What do you think?"

Speedy's was Warsaw's only alcohol-licensed convenience store. It was a real shit-show of a place with a bathroom so dirty even a junkie would think twice to use it. But it was open twenty-four seven, even on Christmas, so the grime was easily overlooked. Rumor had it the guy who owned the business was a Buddhist, which didn't sit particularly well with the older blood-of-Jesus locals. But anyone under thirty? They couldn't have cared less. What they *did* care about was that the guy didn't card; a nightmare for any God-fearing teetotaler trying to raise upstanding young Michiganites, but great for business, and great for getting tanked.

Some would venture to say that Warsaw High's seniors were the only reason Speedy's had stayed open so long. There had been some town counsel hubbub about shuttering the place a while back, but the outrage petered out. Even the cops hadn't been for it. After all, Speedy's may have been making underaged sales, but they had powdered doughnuts—three fifty a dozen—and the coffee was surprisingly good, even at three AM.

But Casey and Reed's back and forth was doing little to soothe Jesse's nerves tonight. It was nothing but darkness and wheat fields and a two-lane highway beyond his window, but there was no mistaking their destination. The trio had taken this drive a countless number of times, and the trek never failed to make Jesse squirm.

"Why the hell are we out here?" Jesse asked again, turning away from Reed's buck-toothed smile to stare at Casey's hands on the wheel. "We aren't seriously going back to that place again, are we?"

That place was a house, crooked and abandoned, sitting lonely on a spent plot of land that had once been used for one crop or another— soy beans, or maybe wheat. It was a place Reed had visited as a kid while he and his older brother rode dirt bikes along back-country roads. A place you could reach on a pedal bike in about half an hour if you were fueled by old-fashioned pre-teen hopped-up-on-sugar gusto. A place that had always been there. Always. Since the beginning of time.

"No," Reed said, turning back to face the windshield. "We aren't going back there *seriously*. We're going back for shits and giggles, man."

Except, Jesse didn't buy that. Shits and giggles? No way. Reed had been infatuated with that house since they'd first ventured inside it at eleven years old. Ever since then, it's like it called to him, forcing him back, over and over.

"Calm yourself," Reed said, "before you bust a vein."

Casey found this commentary just as funny as Reed's other lines.

With Jesse's trepidations ignored, the car kept rolling forward. As a matter of fact, it accelerated rather than slowed. But that was Casey's style. He was always one to exacerbate the situation, especially when it came to stuff between Jesse and Reed. Sometimes, Jesse was convinced that Casey's ultimate goal was to push the trio's friendship to a breaking point. He'd almost managed it a few times, too. First, on Halloween night of 1993. And just recently, when he started dating LouEllen Carter.

Both Casey and Reed knew that Jesse had been pining for LouEllen since sophomore year. He'd been talking about asking her to prom for months. Then Casey swooped in and beat him to the punch as if to say *too slow, sucker*. Now, LouEllen was up in her room on Westmont Road, gazing at whatever frilly prom dress she'd picked up at a Detroit department store, thinking about Casey Ridgemont. And Jesse was here, in the back of Casey's car, possibly sitting in the spot where Casey would pull down LouEllen's panties and—

"Hey." Reed regarded Jesse with a new level of suspicion. "You aren't going to freak out, are you?"

No, Jesse wasn't going to freak out. What was there to freak out about? Skipping prom so as not to see Casey and LouEllen slow-dance to the sappy Savage Garden billboard hit the student council had chosen as the class's graduating anthem? Or the fact that, despite getting into MSU, Jesse had just gotten a Dear John letter about the scholarship he'd applied for? Denied despite his grades. And there was no way his folks were going to throw their money at an English degree—a *useless* degree if you asked them—when there were "perfectly acceptable" community colleges in Detroit.

Or maybe he *should* freak out because Casey was pulling off the highway and onto a dirt road that would take them to the house that gave him massive anxiety; a place that had haunted him since the night Casey and Reed had hidden his bike in an utterly hilarious prank.

"No," Jesse said. "I'm not going to freak out." But he felt on the verge of doing just that, tiptoeing along the edge of panic as Casey's Civic plowed over potholes and loose gravel.

Jesse's response made Reed narrow his gaze even more. Clearly, Jesse was less than convincing.

"It's just for fun, dude," Reed said. "Besides, Casey's got a new camera." And when Casey had a new toy, there was no use fighting it. Reed loved that house, and Casey was obsessed with abandoned America.

They called it a farmhouse, but there was nothing farm-like about it. It must have been built by some weird eccentric because the place was taller than it was wide. It reminded Jesse of something out of a Hitchcock film, or maybe he was thinking of the Addams Family. Either way, it was bizarre sitting out there the way it was; nothing but it and ancient trees lining a road that cut through a desolate field. He was no architect, but the style struck him as Victorian, like something out of a twisted fairytale. The front door was at the base of a tower that shot four stories up. The roof was so steeply pitched it was eerie, and the fancy gable and delicate-but-rotting woodwork only made it that much more macabre. What must have once been a remarkable home of gleaming white intricacy was now a boarded-up skeleton of broken glass, the mangled porch steps leading to little more than a front door hanging from a single hinge.

Casey pulled into the overgrown roundabout in front of the place. There was a dead spot in the center, surrounded by flat stones someone had stacked as a planter border. What had once housed the likes of coneflowers and daffodils was now littered with empty bottles and crushed beer cans. Because when you live in a town as small as Warsaw, abandoned places like this have a strange sort of pull.

"You think there's a mattress up there somewhere?" Casey asked, leaning his chest against the steering wheel and peering up the turret.

"A mattress?" Reed asked. "Like, for…" He paused, thinking better of extrapolating the obvious. But if he was doing it for Jesse's sake, it was a wasted effort. Jesse rolled his eyes and surprised himself by shoving open one of the Civics' back doors. Because standing out in the darkness was better than listening to Casey go on about his prom night plans, even if it did mean standing alone in front of that house.

Yeah, he thought. *A mattress.* If Casey wanted something covered in mold and infested with chiggers, he'd score big. A goddamn mattress. *How romantic.*

Reed eventually exited the car and wobbled in front of Casey's headlights. He'd never been one to hold his liquor well, and tonight was no different.

"So," he said, "are you super-pissed or what?"

"Super-pissed?" Jesse asked, reaching into the pocket of his sweatshirt for a pack of cigarettes. "Super-pissed about what?"

"You always get super-pissed about LouEllen," Reed said, then motioned to the house before them. "About this."

Jesse shrugged, trying to look nonchalant. He pulled a cigarette out of the pack and pressed the filter between his lips—a rebellious act that would have set his mother's hair on fire had she known. "Whatever," he murmured. "We've all got our hang-ups, right?"

This reply seemed to satisfy Reed. He gave Jesse a swift few slaps on the back as if to say *'atta boy*. A moment later, the driver's side door swung open and Casey met them next to the car's dented quarter panel. He held a flashy new SLR camera in his right hand.

Jesse eyed the camera. There was no doubt it cost a pretty penny, and he was sure Casey hadn't spent a dime of his own money on it. It was the same with his car. It was used, sure, but also a far cry better than most of the teen-owned lemons rolling around town. Casey's parents had bought it freshman year, and Casey didn't even pay for his own gas. Jesse had noticed him using plastic at the pump on more than a few occasions—the credit card was in Mrs. Ridgemont's name, no doubt.

Don't count other people's money, Jesse's mom would have warned. But the benefit of growing up as the town's rich kid was impossible to ignore. There was a tinge of jealousy, sure, and how could there not have been? Ninety-nine percent of Warsaw made less than forty grand a year, and here was Casey Ridgemont, walking around like he owned the place. Swooping in like a raptor. Plucking LouEllen up and carrying her off to his nest.

"You two done dicking around out here?" Casey asked, slipping the camera strap marked NIKON around his neck.

"Yeah," Reed said. "But I need another drink." He lifted a hand into the air and spun his wrist around. *Bring on the booze.*

"What happened to the rest of that forty?" Casey asked, suspicious.

Reed lifted his shoulders and gave Casey a virtuous smile. "Vanished," he said. "Like some sort of Criss Angel voodoo. Swear to God."

Casey snorted and moved to the trunk of the car, pausing to get an eyeful of the unlit cigarette balancing upon Jesse's bottom lip. Their eyes met, and a second later, Jesse was pulling a lighter from his pocket. Because that was the power of Casey; the guy who could persuade without even trying, the guy who got the girl.

Casey popped his trunk and brought out another bottle, this one whiskey.

"I'm saving this for prom, man, so if it *vanishes*, you owe me a bottle of Beam." He tossed it at Reed, who just barely caught it before it went crashing into the wild grass and dirt. Reed uncapped the bottle, took a swig, and offered it to Jesse, who shook his head in refusal.

"I'm good," Jesse said, only to be met with another drink. Then a third. "You want to slow down, maybe?" Jesse asked. This time he was the one to watch his friend with cautious skepticism. It felt like Reed was psyching himself up for something, like he was trying to settle his nerves.

Reed capped the bottle and slid it atop Casey's roof, then clapped his hands. "Okay," he said, "let's go." And then he set off for the house's front door. He didn't bother glancing over his shoulder to make sure his two friends were in tow.

Casey didn't hesitate. He fell into step, his SLR held fast in his hands. Jesse watched him for a moment, not sure what Casey saw in taking photos of places like this. But he supposed everyone had a hobby. Reed memorized intricate rap lyrics. Casey took pictures. And Jesse? Jesse spent most of his time in his room writing fiction and fantasizing about becoming an honest-to-goodness pay-the-bills kind of author. Perhaps for a magazine. Maybe for a newspaper. Hell, if he got lucky, he could write novels like the big guys, do press tours and sign books for fawning teens. Whatever. If it got him out of Warsaw, it would be good enough.

But as for now, most of his free time was spent behind a greasy grill at the local Mister Frosty, and he had the burns to prove it. But he also had a new phone, so it wasn't all bad.

"Hey." Reed nodded at Jesse from beside the house's front door. "Are you coming or what?"

Going inside that house was the last thing Jesse wanted to do. But it was also only six weeks until graduation, and something had been "off" between the three of them for the past few months. There were Casey and LouEllen, the thought of which turned Jesse's stomach. There was Reed and his occasional mumbling of taking off to Detroit to do *whatever*. Because, as he had put it, *any place is better than* this *shithole*. Jesse, of course, whole-heartedly agreed.

And then there was the fact that, when Jesse suggested he and Reed split a crappy apartment in Detroit—because, hey, maybe he *would* take some classes at the community college after all—Reed had been less than enthusiastic. Almost as though he didn't want Jesse to tag along; as though he was quietly plotting some sort of exit. Leave the old life and friends behind. Start a new life somewhere else.

When Jesse had questioned Reed's lack of eagerness, Reed had just shrugged and dropped the subject. It had been weird. Disheartening. Something was definitely up, and it made Jesse feel like this part of his life—this friendship—was nearing its end, and that made him infinitely sad. Because he didn't know why it was happening. He didn't understand it. Didn't know what to do.

"Yeah, I'm coming," Jesse said, took a drag off his cigarette, and tossed the smoke to the ground before mashing it into the dirt. It tasted like shit. It always did. He didn't know why he bothered. Maybe he was searching for something to make himself feel more grown up, more in control and less insecure.

Reed ducked around the skewed front door before either of the guys started their trek toward the house. Casey reached the porch first, watching Jesse from the steps for a few beats as if to make sure he wasn't going to chicken out. Eventually, Casey grew tired of waiting for Jesse to catch up and followed Reed inside.

Jesse hesitated. It didn't feel right. He craned his neck to look up the length of the house's turret, his gaze pausing at the double side-by-side windows at the top. He shuddered and turned away.

By the time he stepped into the dusty foyer, Casey was snapping photos of moonlit spiderwebs stretched between the broken spindles of a zig-zagging balustrade. There was a full moon tonight, bright enough to light up the place in a pale blue glow. Casey continued clicking away, murmuring things like "this is so fucking cool" beneath his breath, his artistic eye roving every corner, every potential capture.

Reed, on the other hand, was merely standing at the base of the stairs, staring at Jesse as if surprised he had decided to join them at all. When they regarded each other, Reed cracked his signature grin. But there was something strange about it, something not quite right. It almost didn't look like Reed's smile at all. Or maybe it was just a trick of the light.

"Hey," Reed said, "I want to show you something." And then he began to climb those rotting, dangerous risers without so much as a care in the world.

Jesse blinked at Reed's back, then turned to Casey, who had glanced up from his camera's viewfinder. Casey was now looking up at Reed with a similar dose of fascination.

"Reed, wait…" Jesse protested, but he was cut off by a more assertive objection.

"Are you *crazy?*" Casey asked. "Those stairs are going to collapse, man. You're going to kill yourself."

Reed paused half-way up the first staircase to shoot them a look of feigned terror.

"Zoinks!" he said, then beamed down at them. "Haven't killed myself yet, have I?" he asked, then continued his upward trajectory toward the second floor.

"What?" Jesse looked from Reed to Casey and back again. "You've gone up there before?"

There was no way those stairs were safe, no way he was going to risk his neck so that Reed could *show him something*. Show him what? An old TV? A busted transistor radio? A crappy, dust-covered room crawling with spiders and maybe a dead bird or two? Yeah, like *that* would be worth it.

"Sure," Reed said, stopping at the first landing to grin down at them. That tower went all the way up, four stories high, the stairwell creating a perfect square as it spiraled past each floor. "It's fine," Reed insisted. "They don't even creak." He jumped up and down a few times to prove his point. *See?* But all his convincing did was give Jesse a heart attack. Because clearly, his best friend had lost his mind.

"You want some kickass photos of a spooky old house or what?" Reed asked, shifting his goading toward Casey. "Come on, already."

Casey considered his options. For a moment, Jesse was convinced he would wave his hand at Reed's batshit crazy antics and tell him to screw off, then go back to shooting spiderwebs and cracked floorboards and peeling paint. Casey's attention shifted from Reed to Jesse, as if to ask, *are* you *going to go?* But that questioning glance quickly morphed into something darker, something more akin to a challenge.

"See you at the top, man," he said, then stepped around Jesse to ascend the stairs himself.

Jesse was left to stand alone in a skeleton foyer, watching his friends climb the ribs of the house toward its cadaverous heart, listening to Reed's aimless chattering and Casey's nervous laughter. Just like seven years ago. Just like when they had ridden off on their bikes without him, leaving him alone in the dark, surrounded by nothing but the sound of his own thumping pulse.

He stood motionless for a long while, contemplating whether to throw caution to the wind and follow both Casey and Reed up to those abandoned floors. But the moment his sneaker hit the first step, a wave of dread hit him square in the chest. It was as if that sense of eeriness resided up there somewhere, oozing down from the top floor like a rust-colored leak along the wall. Jesse looked upward, his attention pausing on fingers dragging along the handrail. Casey was at least holding on. Meanwhile, it sounded like Reed was taking the stairs two at a time, bouncing around like a freaking Muppet. When Reed reached the third-floor landing, he peered down at Jesse again.

"Still alive," he announced, sounding victorious.

"Great," Jesse called back. "Congratulations."

"You really aren't coming up?" Reed asked. Apparently, Jesse's refusal to take part in this act of comradery was suddenly dawning on him, offending him. Because if you couldn't count on your best friend to venture up a treacherous set of haunted house stairs with you, what *could* you count on? "Dude," Reed said, "are you serious?"

"I'm going to go screw around on my phone," Jesse said, hooking a thumb over his shoulder toward the front door.

"But I want to show you something, man," Reed protested. "It'll change your goddamn life."

"Yeah," Jesse murmured to himself. "I'm sure it will." Then he raised his voice, speaking upward into the house's tower. "Show Casey. Have him snap a picture."

Jesse couldn't see it, but he was sure Reed was rolling his eyes. It didn't matter, though. There was no way in hell Jesse was going up there, and it wasn't even because he was sure he'd break his neck. No, it was that feeling. That awful, murky sense of heaviness pressing down onto his chest.

There was, however, no stopping Reed and Casey. The duo continued their upward climb while Jesse showed himself out. He'd wait by Casey's Civic, and a few minutes from now, there was no doubt Reed would be yowling down at him from those top two turret windows.

Hey, check me out! Hey, still alive! Hey, you're a real shit of a friend! But at least Casey's here. He's always been a better pal.

Jesse stepped off the front porch and made his way to Casey's car, then glared at the bottle of Jim Beam that had been left on the roof. He swiped it by its neck, uncapped the bottle, and took a swig. It made no difference how innocent their visit was—just three bored high school seniors seeking adventure in a no-hope town. He didn't like being here. He hated this house. Hated every excursion he'd been made to take here in the name of solidarity.

Pulling open the back door, he sat sideways on the seat, his sneakers still out in the dirt and Casey's bottle of Beam in the footwell. He could hear them in there; two guys strengthening their friendship while Jesse sat alone.

Tweedle Dee and Tweedle Dum.

Scooby and Shaggy.

The Skipper and Gilligan.

Beavis and goddamn Butthead.

Whether it was the emptiness of the place or the broken windows, that house formed a strange sort of echo chamber. Every laugh and whoop was amplified as though broadcast via megaphone. Seated with his left shoulder pressed flush against the back of the seat, Jesse fished his phone out of his pocket and pulled up his address book. He had precisely one number inputted into his contacts list. It belonged to no other than Casey's prom date.

LouEllen had scribbled her digits in his yearbook beneath her inscription the year before. *Stay cool, Jesse Wells.* Maybe, sitting there in the darkness, already feeling edgy and left out, he'd finally swallow his nerves and call her. Perhaps, sitting alone out there, he'd be bold enough to tell her that the limerick he'd written for the Warrior Wrap-Up last month had been part of his master plan to eventually ask her to prom. But that was B.C.; before Casey. Before he'd ruined everything.

Jesse stared at LouEllen's name glowing on the tiny phone screen and shook his head at himself. "Some master plan," he murmured, then jumped, just about dropping his cell when that ghost of a house shuddered from the inside out.

The bang was enormous, as though the boys had found a grand piano and, on a whim, had pushed it down the stairs. Jesse jumped to his feet, shoved his phone into his front pocket, and took a few tentative forward steps.

"Guys?"

That was another thing. There was no more chatter. No more whooping or laughter. There was suddenly nothing but silence, dead and hollow.

Jesse stood between the car and the house, unsure whether to go inside or to call out again. Surely, they would hear him if he did. But his throat seized up at the worst-case scenario that unfolded like origami inside his head.

Those stairs. They had given way.

Those fucking stairs had collapsed, just as he had feared. And now there was silence because both Reed and Casey were buried beneath thousands of pounds of splintered lumber. They had gone up there like a pair of idiots, and now...

No.

Footsteps.

Someone was running down the risers, taking them two-by-two.

Jesse watched the front door, waiting for his friends to come blasting out of there, pale-faced and jacked up on adrenaline. He was sure they'd cackle their heads off at whatever had just gone down as soon as they verified all their limbs were still intact. Whatever had happened, it had been epic, and Jesse had missed it. He'd never hear the end of it. It's all they'd talk about for weeks.

He waited, but his friends didn't surface.

"...guys?" He meant to yell it, but the word came out weak and warbled.

He was eleven all over again, and maybe that was the point. Perhaps this was another prank. A final send-off. An ode to the inevitable dwindling of friendship just as soon as diplomas were grabbed and Warsaw High was put in the rearview. Sayonara to the good ol' days.

"Oh, screw you guys," Jesse hissed. If they thought this was funny, they were bigger assholes than he thought. Maybe this time he wouldn't keep his anger bottled up. No, *this* time he'd finally tell them where they could shove their stupid jokes.

It was then that Casey came stumbling through the front door and onto the porch, ashen, just as Jesse had expected. Whatever the punchline, Casey was really selling it. He was grasping the front porch balustrade, his chest heaving as though unable to catch his breath. His shocked expression actually looked genuine. Jesse couldn't help but be mildly impressed.

Finally, Casey glanced up. "We've got to go," he said, then just about tripped down the porch steps, his SLR hanging heavy from around his neck.

"What?" Jesse frowned as Casey approached.

"We've got to go," Casey repeated. "Now." Reaching the Civic, he jerked open the driver's side door.

"Where's Reed?" Jesse asked, pivoting back to the house.

"Get in the car," Casey instructed, sliding behind the wheel.

"You know what? I'm tired of this crap," Jesse said. "It isn't funny. Where the hell is Reed?"

That was when Casey shot Jesse a glare he hadn't seen coming. It was a look so vicious, so deadly serious, that it left him feeling disoriented, unsure whether to panic or laugh.

"Get in the fucking car, Jesse!" Casey bellowed.

It became clear, then, that Casey wasn't screwing around.

But Jesse wasn't just going to get in the car. That was ridiculous, because...

"Where the hell is *Reed?*" He turned back toward the house, ready to march in there and figure out what was going on. He wasn't getting in the car, not so Casey could blast off down the road and leave Reed behind the way they had abandoned him so long ago. He remembered how bad it had felt. How scared he had been. How it had seemed like such a betrayal. It had taken Jesse months to forgive them.

Sure, they were older now, and Reed loved this godforsaken place. But even if Jesse's participation in such a half-witted prank was coerced, he didn't want to be 'that guy.' No, he'd go inside, he'd find out what was going on. And if he chickened out at the door, whatever. He'd just stand out there and wait for Reed to resurface. If Casey wanted to leave, so be it.

But before Jesse could step away from the Civic, Casey grabbed him by the wrist to hold him back. Jesse looked over his shoulder, and for the first time since he'd known him, he saw genuine hysteria creeping across the contours of Casey's face.

"Casey?" Jesse furrowed his eyebrows. He slowed his speech. Maybe careful annunciation would warrant a reply. "Where's Reed?"

Casey's bottom lip began to quiver.

"We've got to go," Casey whispered, allowing Jesse to pull his wrist free of a weakening grasp. And then, with that camera still around his neck, Casey lifted his hands to his face and emitted a sob into his palms.

Jesse's stomach flipped.

He felt his head go light, like sucking helium out of a balloon.

Before he knew it, he was sprinting up those warped front steps and shoving himself through the small space between the front door and the jamb, not giving himself enough time to consider the possibility that now he'd *have* to run up that four-story staircase. Now, he'd have no choice.

But that possibility was quickly extinguished because Reed wasn't hiding on any of the top floors.

He was right there in the foyer.

Motionless in the moonlit dark.

ONE

JESSE COULD HEAR LouEllen and Ian from across their tiny two-bedroom house. They were in the kitchen, Lou singing John Mellencamp's *Small Town* and Ian babbling in his high chair, probably throwing Cheerios onto the floor for Winston to Hoover up with his tongue. In the past ten months, that dog had eaten everything from chocolate to avocado; every food that should have killed him. And yet, despite all those forbidden foods, the worst thing to ail the old Basset Hound was a few extra pounds and a wicked case of gas.

Jesse glanced to Winston's dog bed beside the TV and then regarded the papers in front of him. They were scattered across his scarred-up desktop like a haphazardly shuffled deck of cards. He readjusted his task lamp, though it was useless. The hinge was loose and the thing continuously drooped. But there was no money in the budget for a new one, which wasn't the least bit surprising. Warsaw High was like every other school in the country. The job was thankless and the pay was absolute crap, but at least he and Lou had been able to afford their own house before Ian had come along. It needed a ton of renovations, but a house was a house.

The neighborhood was a constant reminder that many were in far worse shape than Jesse and Lou, whether they had a budding toddler or not; trailers that were beaten down by endless Michigan winters, countless lots where houses had once stood but were now long gone. Most were little more than foundations surrounded by prairie that, in the summer, grew wild and knee-deep. They were properties that nobody would build on again because nobody in their right mind moved *to* Warsaw, Michigan. If anything, folks were wracking their brains on how to get the hell out.

Jesse clicked his red pen as he tried to concentrate on a sorry excuse of an English essay. That was when Winston came barreling into the living room, his nails clicking against the floorboards and his stubby legs scrambling like a Saturday morning cartoon. Jesse squinted out the window in front of him, then leaned forward to push down one of the plastic blind slats to get a better look.

A black Impala came to a jarring stop along the broken curb—the kind of tire-squealing halt that's only made in emergency situations or crime investigative sitcoms. Jesse grabbed his phone off his desk and looked at the screen. The Nokia he'd started out with during his senior year was a far cry from the Android smartphone in his hand now.

No texts. No missed calls.

With Winston's butt on the front door rug and his droopy ears vibrating with exertion, the hound began his sorrowful howling routine.

"Easy, Dubs." Dubs was short for Dubya. It had been Ian's first word to LouEllen's chagrin.

Jesse leaned back in his chair and crossed his arms over his chest, watching Casey Ridgemont march around the front of his car and up the snow-covered walkway. Jesse had shoveled it an hour after he'd gotten home from school, but it was coming down hard tonight. He wasn't sure why he'd even bothered. It was only the start of January, but over a foot of fresh snow had buried Warsaw since Christmas Eve.

A knock sounded at the door. Winston jumped up as if spooked, then scrambled backward, still howling but far more pensive than before.

"Way to guard, Dubs," Jesse said, rising from his seat.

"Jesse?" LouEllen's voice rose from the kitchen.

"Got it," he called back, then moved across the room to the front door.

When it swung open, Jesse was taken aback by Casey's haggard look. LouEllen and Casey's wife, Blaire, were best friends; they had been since high school. Had it not been for the girls, Jesse wasn't sure he and Casey would have ever seen each other again after that awful night. But Lou and Blaire were always up to something. Jesse and Casey had been strong-armed into staying in each other's orbit. There was the occasional backyard barbecue. Sometimes, the girls would arrange a movie night, complete with pizza and wings.

But now, a typically clean-cut Casey stood there in shambles—nothing but a wrinkled T-shirt and pair of jeans he'd clearly fished out of the hamper before jumping into his car. And he wasn't there for pizza, that was for sure.

"Casey?" Jesse raised an eyebrow at the odd sight, but he took a backward step to let Casey pass. It was freezing out, and Casey had forgotten his coat.

Winston sniffed the knees of Casey's jeans, then bared his teeth, leaving Jesse to blink dumbfoundedly at his dog.

"Woah," he said, "stand down, Dubs." He grabbed the hound by his collar and pulled him back, baffled by Winston's reaction to their visitor. Because Casey was no stranger. Winston had met him dozens of times, and there had never been a problem before.

Casey held up his hands, as though waiting for Winston to strike. But Winston eventually backed off, wandering out of the room with a huff.

"Hey, sorry about that," Jesse said. "Not sure what's gotten into him."

"It's fine," Casey murmured.

"You look like shit, man," Jesse quipped. "And how are you not freezing?" The gusts coming off Lake Saint Clair were cold enough to crack bones. And there was Casey, standing bare-armed on Jesse's doorstep, wearing little more than a short-sleeved White Stripes concert tee.

"Can we talk?" Casey shambled half-way into the living room, shoving his frozen fingers deep in the pockets of his jeans. His gaze wandered the place as if waiting for Winston to come barreling back into the room.

"Casey, is that you?" LouEllen filled the kitchen doorway with Ian on her hip. She wore a wide and easy smile but was quick to catch on to what Jesse had already noticed—there was something wrong—and her smile disappeared.

"What's up?" LouEllen asked. "Are you okay?"

"Yeah," Casey said, "yeah, how's it going Lou?" But he wasn't convincing anyone. He seemed just about ready to crawl out of his skin.

"Um…" LouEllen gave Jesse an unsure glance, then turned to Casey. "Everything good with Blaire?"

"Yeah, yeah, she's fine," Casey said, shoving his fingers through his hair. "Gotta head home in a minute. I'll tell her you said *hi*. Sorry, I know it's late. Just had to talk to Jesse really quick."

LouEllen turned to her husband, both eyebrows raised.

What the hell?

Jesse shook his head just enough for her to read his response.

Clueless, same as you.

It was enough to have LouEllen retreating into the kitchen with Ian in tow, and Jesse was thankful for that. He'd never admit to it, but he was always a little uncomfortable when Casey and LouEllen were in the same room. Nearly nineteen years and that pang of jealousy still lingered. It didn't matter that she and Casey had never gone to prom. It didn't even matter that, when he'd asked years later, Lou insisted that she and Casey hadn't ever officially been a couple. *We didn't even go on a single date.* And yet, there was something about the idea that they *would* have gone to the dance, that they *would* have been an item if what had happened to Reed hadn't happened at all.

And then there was the fact that, after that evening, Jesse couldn't bring himself to completely trust Casey again. Jesse had demanded to know what had happened while he and Casey had waited for the police to arrive. *What happened to Reed, Casey? What the hell happened inside that house?* And yet, even with the cops pulling up with their red and blue lights turning the darkness into a circus show, all Casey did was mutely shake his head. Jesse never did get his answer, and he still held that grudge. That animosity had seemed reasonable at the time. Hell, it still seemed reasonable now.

"Sit," Jesse said, motioning toward the couch. Casey did as he was told, wringing his hands all the while. Jesse grabbed his desk chair and pulled it over, the chair's legs hissing across the floor.

Casey sat soundlessly for a long moment, head bowed and hands clasped as if summoning God. Finally, he forced a painful smile.

"How're you doing?" he asked. "You okay? How's school? What're you making those little shits read now?"

Jesse did the guy a solid and replied, but he was sure his face said it all. *What the hell is going on?*

"Sinclair. *The Jungle.*"

"Oh yeah?" Casey shrugged. "I don't know that one, man."

And there was no reason he should have. Back in their day, Casey and Reed had done more screwing around than studying. Jesse's love of English and literature had pushed him to be the outsider of their group. Now, Jesse was a teacher making a next-to-nothing salary while Casey's passion for abandoned buildings had led him to a successful YouTube career. Casey was about as famous as anyone in Warsaw could get. He lived in the biggest house in town on what must have been ten acres of land. And he could have had more, but he was no rancher. All he did out there was roll around on a four-wheeler while his videos racked up views. And then he'd find another abandoned barn to explore or another dilapidated building to break into in Detroit and the ad money would come pouring in.

Don't count other people's money, Jesse.

Right. He knew. Resentment wasn't a good look. But it was hard not to hold it against him because of Lou. Because of Reed.

"Cut to the chase, Casey," Jesse said. "What's wrong? You look spooked."

"I do?" Casey attempted to eke out a laugh, but it came out weak and unsure. He leaned forward, elbows upon knees, and covered his mouth. "Fuck," he whispered. "Fuck, man, I feel like—" He stopped, then glanced up at Jesse. "I feel like I'm losing my fucking mind."

Jesse didn't want to speak the name, but it was automatic, like a reflex.

"Reed?"

Because no matter how much time passed, what happened back at that farmhouse felt like just yesterday, and Casey's flinch said it all.

Jesse waited, his eyes fixed on his old friend's hands. Somehow, he knew what was coming, knew what Casey was about to say. He could sense it like a psychic premonition, could almost hear the words forming across the surface of Casey's tongue.

"I need to go back there," Casey said. "But I don't want to go alone."

Jesse gave him an incredulous look.

"I know," Casey said. "It's crazy, but..." He shifted his weight upon the couch, then reached into the back pocket of his jeans and pulled out a piece of paper he'd folded into eighths. "Look," he said, handing the square of printer paper over. "I was on my computer, and I found this. I just… I got into my car and I drove over here. I didn't even tell Blair where I was going. I just left."

Jesse took the paper from Reed's hands and slowly unfolded it; cautious, as though whatever was printed there held the key to the rest of his life.

"It's like…like, I couldn't breathe," Casey continued. "I mean, I travel the country searching for places like this, you know? I've seen hundreds, maybe thousands of these types of old houses. But then I found this…" He motioned to the paper. "…and everything just froze. All I could think was, *I have to show Jesse. He has to see this before it's too late.*"

Jesse leaned back in his seat, peering at the headline: OLD MILL HOUSE SET FOR DEMOLITION.

"They're going to raze it, man," Casey said. "They're going to bulldoze it to the ground."

Jesse squinted at the date. It was old news, published months before. Since then, nothing had happened to the farmhouse. Jesse knew that because he drove by it every so often if only to make sure it hadn't somehow crept closer to his own home.

He looked up from the article, his attention settling on his friend.

"How is going back there going to change anything?" he asked. "This isn't like one of your old Detroit car factories, Casey. Why would you ever want to set foot in that place again?"

Casey shook his head the same way he had when the cops had pulled up behind his old Civic. He didn't have an answer, just like he hadn't had one that muggy summer night. But Jesse could tell there was a reason behind Casey's weird request. Everything about Casey's posture screamed *don't ask questions you don't want the answers to.* From the tension in his features to the wringing of his hands, all of it assured Jesse that this wasn't some left-field desire. This was purposeful. Thought out. Casey had spent countless nights thinking about this moment, this exact sequence of events: sitting on Jesse's couch, handing over the article he'd conveniently "found" on his computer, pleading with Jesse to hear him out.

The article was published in August. There was no way Casey hadn't heard about the Old Mill house being put on dilapidated death row until just now. Hell, that was Casey's passion. His business.

He probably had Google Alerts set up for that sort of crap. No, Casey had been thinking about this for a while.

Jesse slowly extended his arm, holding out the article for Casey to take back.

"There's a reason they're going to demolish that place," Jesse said. "A reason nobody has bought it, and why kids still park out there to scare themselves shitless. There's something wrong with it, Casey. I don't want to go back."

It was then that Casey looked up, imploring.

"I know you don't," he said. "But we have to."

Jesse frowned at that.

"I just need an answer," Casey finally admitted. "Before it's gone, you know? Before we *can't* go back. I just want to know why."

Except, the house held no such answer. Only one person truly knew why, and Reed had been unavailable to chat for a while.

All Jesse knew was, Reed had become obsessed with that old house. He'd visited it countless times, both with and without his friends in tow. And then, one night, he leaned over a rickety banister and fell four stories to his death. At least that's what Casey had told the cops. It's what the local paper had printed, though in not so many words: SUICIDE AT LOCAL WARSAW HANGOUT.

Jesse had spent years asking himself why his best friend had done what he'd done. But now, there was no why, there was only *I wish I had known*. He'd read plenty of articles on the topic after the fact and now knew depression was a mysterious beast. Hell, he'd felt it plenty of times himself. And he knew that, sometimes, even those who seemed to be stable struggled with dark tendencies. For some, there was no why, there was merely a question of when.

Casey turned away, using the back of his hand to take a rough swipe at tears that were threatening to fall. Meanwhile, Jesse said nothing. For nearly two decades, Casey had looked to have coped with Reed's death pretty well. But now, seeing Casey so broken made Jesse wonder; maybe Casey was just as good at hiding his true self as Reed had been.

Jesse, on the other hand, was terrible at it. He'd drowned his sorrow at the bottom of any bottle he could find, and at eighteen years old, he'd been a bonafide alcoholic. It was why it had taken him and LouEllen two years to get together. He'd been a wreck, and she'd kept him at arm's length until he was under control. She'd helped him more than anyone else. Sometimes Jesse was sure LouEllen had saved his life.

Maybe Casey had been haunted by Reed's death far more than he had led on. And in a way, that made Jesse feel better. Not the idea of Casey's suffering, but the fact that his stiff upper lip had been little more than an act. That, at least, made Jesse feel a little less pathetic, stronger than he was accustomed to.

"I was there," Casey finally muttered.

"I know," Jesse said softly.

He'd spent years replaying Reed asking *him* to go upstairs and recounting his own refusal. Maybe if Jesse hadn't said no, Casey would have stayed downstairs, clicking away on his camera. Then, it would have been Jesse witnessing Reed's great leap instead.

"I'm sorry that you were," Jesse said. "But going back to that house isn't going to change anything. Sometimes, we just have to deal with not knowing."

"No." It was then that Casey met Jesse's gaze, a newfound determination crossing his face. "You don't get it. You think Reed killed himself." He issued a soft laugh. "That's my fault, I guess."

Jesse narrowed his eyes, not understanding.

"I told them he jumped because…" Casey hesitated, then stared at his clasped-together hands. "Because the word *fell* didn't make sense. Because *pushed* made even less."

Jesse's muscles tensed. His stomach twisted—a reflex to strange and unexpected news.

"I told them what I did because if I hadn't, they'd have thought it was me."

That desk chair was suddenly the most uncomfortable piece of furniture Jesse owned. He shifted his weight, unsure whether to stay where he was or rise to his feet, whether to keep his post or start to pace.

Pressing his hands against the wood beneath him, he coiled his fingers and spoke. "What do you mean they'd have thought it was you?"

What the hell was Casey trying to say? Sure, he'd never been able to tell Jesse what had happened up on that top floor, but foul play? Murder? Was this some sort of confession?

"…what are you saying?" Jesse asked again, trying to keep his voice from trembling.

"I've replayed it so many times in my head," Casey said, "over and over, and at first I thought I was just driving myself crazy. But the more I did it, the more I saw. The more I remembered. So, I started replaying it on purpose. These days, it's all I fucking do."

Jesse shifted his weight again, unease settling into his bones.

"Reed didn't kill himself," Casey said. "There was someone there."

Jesse's response was something between a squint and a wince, partly because he didn't get it, partly because he was sure he was about to throw up.

"A shadow. A figure," Casey clarified, but that only intensified Jesse's malaise. "A girl," he said. "It was a *girl*, Jesse. The more I replay that night, the more I'm sure we weren't alone."

That did it.

Jesse was up and shoving his fingers through his hair. He turned away, staring at his cluttered desk. His desk lamp had drooped so low that the lightbulb was touching the varnished wood beneath it. For a moment, his cheeks flushed hot. He felt lightheaded, as though he was going to topple over where he stood.

He knew who Casey was talking about.

He'd seen her himself, seven years before Reed's final hour. She'd been standing up in that fourth-floor window, staring out at him as he screamed for Casey and Reed to come back, for his friends not to leave him there in the dark all alone. She'd stood there, staring down at him, and for a moment he hadn't been able to catch his breath. When he had finally turned to run down the tree-lined drive toward the highway, he had been gasping for air between inconsolable sobs. By then, he didn't know whether he was running in some feeble attempt to catch up with his friends or to just put as much distance between himself and that house as he could.

Reed and Casey had been waiting for him at the intersection, dicking around while leaning against the handlebars of their bikes. Jesse remembered they had been laughing when he finally saw them. But their grins shifted to concern when he skidded to a stop on his hands and knees. He collapsed onto the broken pavement, the October air already so cold it had stripped the leaves from the trees and frozen the ground. It was there that Jesse succumbed to a full-fledged anxiety attack, trying to scream but not having the air.

Reed had been the one who had apologized for their stupid prank. *Oh man, sorry Jesse. We didn't mean it like that, you know? We thought it would be funny. I'm sorry, man. Are you okay?* He was the one who had given Jesse a ride back to the house on the front pegs of his bike. Casey had stayed a good few yards behind. *It was just a joke, man,* was the only thing Casey had eventually said; a fauxpology to excuse himself of any responsibility. A classic Casey Ridgemont move.

And now, rather than a joke, it was a girl.

It hadn't been that maybe Reed had been depressed and that Jesse and Casey should have seen the warning signs. It wasn't that Reed had been acting weird for years and, perhaps, he'd been planning to off himself all along. It had nothing to do with the fact that Reed had been dealing with something neither one of his closest friends had understood. And that was fine. They'd just been kids. But they *had* both known about Reed's bizarre infatuation with that place. They knew something had been off. But they had gone there with him anyway.

In fact, it had been Casey who had ushered them there. *He* had driven while Jesse had been oblivious for most of the ride. And when Jesse had finally realized where they were headed and protested their destination, what had Casey done? Accelerated. Because he had wanted to go there to take his precious photos.

And now Casey was here, slashing open old wounds, rehashing feelings Jesse had worked so hard to suppress. Now he was here, talking about a girl Jesse had convinced himself had been a figment of his imagination.

Because that place had been empty.

There had been no girl.

"Have you forgotten that I was there, too?" Jesse asked, pausing his pacing to shoot his visitor a dubious look.

"No," Casey said. "I know you were."

"Then you understand that I *know* we were alone," he said. "Maybe you've gone to too many of these places…"

"Look, I know it's—"

"Maybe it's finally gotten inside your head." He tapped his temple.

"Jesse, if you just—"

"I think you should leave," Jesse said, cutting him off. Because the longer Casey sat on Jesse's couch, the longer Jesse had to consider that what he'd seen as a kid had been real. And he wasn't willing to do that. No goddamn way.

"What?" Casey actually appeared surprised. He hadn't expected the anger that was flashing across Jesse's face.

"Leave," Jesse repeated. "Get up and go, man, because I'm not listening to any more of this bullshit."

"But it's not—"

"Haven't you had your fun?" Jesse asked. "Wasn't it enough, you two constantly dragging me out there? You, driving Reed there whenever he wanted, even though it made no sense? Even though you knew something was up, that he'd been acting weird?"

Casey blinked. It was his turn to stand. "Are you saying this is *my* fault?"

"I'm saying it doesn't matter anymore, Casey. Reed is dead."

Casey winced. He took a backward step, his palms pressed flush against the thin cotton of his T-shirt in a self-soothing sort of way.

"I just don't want to go back there alone," Casey said, his head bowed. "It might not matter to you what really happened, but I *was there*, Jesse. Maybe you can live without knowing, but I was standing inches from him, okay? And it messed me up."

Jesse turned away. He wanted to tell Casey to get the hell out of his house again, but he knew that confession was big. Casey wasn't the type to admit how he felt. The fact that he was doing it in Jesse's living room said something. He still felt the ghostlike thread of a bond between them, regardless of how forced the past two decades-worth of interaction had been. What had once been the three musketeers was now just a sad excuse of a duo. Two friends that were hardly even acquaintances anymore. But they still had history. They still had all those years. And they'd always have Reed.

Jesse shut his eyes, the thud of his pulse mellowing with each measured intake of breath. He turned, not sure what he was going to say, but it didn't matter in the end. By the time he looked Casey's way, Casey was breezing past him toward the front door.

"I just need a friend, man," Casey said. "I know I wasn't the best back then, and I'm sorry for that. But right now, I just need someone to have my back, someone who understands."

Jesse swallowed against the lump in his throat, watching Casey pulled open the door.

"Just think about it, alright?" he asked, then let himself out into the cold.

Jesse moved to the front room window and with his arms crossed over his chest, he watched Casey's Impala pull away from the curb. The way Casey had carried himself, the way he'd been talking, it was like someone who'd finally come unglued.

Jesse considered asking LouEllen to call Blaire before Casey got home, wondering if he should stick his nose in or whether an intervention would make things worse. Not that he'd have to say anything for Lou to do whatever she deemed fit. In a house that small, it was impossible to play deaf.

He nearly jumped when he felt a hand slide up his back and across his shoulder.

"Hey." LouEllen gave him a faint smile. "It's just me."

Jesse exhaled and looked out the window again. He half-expected to see Casey's Impala squeal back into its previous parking spot, for Casey to come ambling out of the car to plead his case one last time.

"You want to tell me what that was all about?" Lou asked, cocking an inquisitive brow. "I mean, I heard most of it. But you've got to admit, that conversation was a little hard to follow."

Jesse pinched the bridge of his nose, not sure how to explain it without making Casey sound like he'd gone insane. Except, maybe he had. Perhaps not having Lou call Blaire was irresponsible. Hell, Reed had killed himself without so much as a warning, but Casey? Casey was throwing up red flags left and right.

"I think he needs help," Jesse finally said. "You should have seen his face."

"I think you're right," LouEllen said. "But he also sounded pretty determined."

"Yeah, determined to carry out a pointless plan."

Jesse could hardly believe Casey was serious about going back to the farmhouse. He was finally taking his love of abandoned America to a twisted extreme.

"But *he* doesn't think it's pointless, right?" LouEllen asked. "He's convinced that whatever answer he's looking for is there?"

Jesse turned to her. Was she serious? She thought going back was a good idea? And there it was, that pang of unrequited jealousy rearing its ugly head. Jesse wanted nothing to do with this plan, and here she was, standing behind Casey's appeal.

LouEllen held up her hands in surrender as if reading Jesse's thoughts. *Don't shoot the messenger.* "All I'm saying is, maybe if he realizes that there are no answers there, he'll be willing to get help elsewhere."

"You *want* me to go with him?" Jesse asked.

She sighed. "Of course I don't *want* you to go with him. For all I know, you'll come home with a pair of broken legs and a case of tetanus. But he's your friend." She pushed a dark curl behind her ear, then placed a hand against his chest.

"Is he?" Jesse asked.

"Cut him some slack, okay?" she said. "He admitted that he's been hurting. You know Casey. That couldn't have been easy for him."

Jesse frowned and reached up to the center of his T-shirt, his own hand curling over his wife's.

"All I'm saying is, Casey's experience was different. I know you were there, too, Jesse. But..." Her words trailed to nothing. She didn't have to finish her sentence for Jesse to know what she was getting at. Jesse hadn't been upstairs with Reed. He hadn't watched it happen. In essence, he'd lucked out. There was a big difference between witnessing a suicide first-hand and seeing the result of one after-the-fact.

"And if I don't humor him?" he asked.

LouEllen offered him a pensive smile.

"You know me," she said. "I'm no Judge Judy." She turned away from him, then. "Ian's finally asleep. I'm going to waste some time on my phone and go to bed. I left your dinner in the oven."

Jesse nodded, though she didn't glance back to see it.

No, Lou wasn't the type to judge, but she had a way with words, a way with influence. An hour before their wedding, LouEllen's step-father had laughed and patted Jesse on the shoulder while giving him a grin. *You're marrying a psychoanalyst, you know that, right?* Jesse was, in fact, marrying an office administrator turned stay-at-home mom, but he knew what the man had meant. Had they lived someplace else, someplace bigger, LouEllen would have made an incredible therapist.

"Though..." Lou paused just before disappearing down the hall. "I think you could probably use some closure, too," she said. "A place like that would be pretty incredible for some inspiration, don't you think?"

Inspiration.

Jesse had been muttering about writing a book for what felt like a decade, but he always found some excuse. He had homework to grade or class agendas to sort out, a problem student to deal with or parent-teacher conferences coming up. But the truth of the matter was, ever since losing Reed, that spark of imagination had vanished, eaten away by grief and alcohol. It had left him with nothing but dead-end ideas and a blinking cursor on a blank word processor screen.

Lou's suggestion gave him pause. Because could that house really help him rekindle his long-lost creative spark? Did he have the strength to draw inspiration from tragedy?

She was still hovering between the living room and hallway when he finally looked up at her.

"But I'm not the artist," she said, pounding the final nail into the proverbial coffin. "So, what do I know?" And then she ducked out of the room.

TWO

IT WAS NEARLY two in the morning when Jesse readjusted his task lamp and rubbed his hands against his face. He still had half a stack of essays to sift through before first period English; but he'd been staring at a single one for what felt like an hour, his red pen not making a single mark. He couldn't focus no matter how glaring the grammatical errors, his thoughts a good nineteen years removed from where he sat now.

When he tipped his chin up from his work and looked out the window past his own reflection, he swore he could see that house. And standing in front of it was Jesse as a kid, his neck craned back, staring up the length of that looming tower.

He'd wracked his brain all night, and after hours of consideration, he was reasonably confident he hadn't told anyone about the girl. But there was still an inkling of doubt that maybe he was wrong. He remembered the panic he'd felt as a child, the sense of suffocation. Even after Reed had pulled Jesse's bike out of the bushes with an apologetic look, Jesse hardly managed to ride it. The pedals felt like they'd rusted to the chainring, and no matter how hard he forced his sneakers against the pedals' metal teeth, the bike seemed to hardly move. The world had gone fuzzy around the edges, as though a fog had descended upon that empty field. Jesse knew he hadn't been himself just then. He had been crushed by the weight of his own fear. So, despite not remembering, it *was* possible that he had mentioned the girl to Reed.

And if Jesse had told Reed, Reed had definitely told Casey. *Dude, you won't believe what Jesse thinks he saw...* Maybe Reed had relayed the story, and the idea had planted itself within the deepest reaches of Casey's subconscious. And that's where it had sat, dormant, only to be germinated by Reed's suicide years down the line.

Turning away from the window and back to his grading, a sickening thought twisted deep within Jesse's chest. What if he *had* told Reed, and that's why Reed kept going back to that place; what if it was Jesse's panic-riddled imagination that had driven Reed to that strange and eventually deadly obsession?

And if Reed had told Casey, perhaps that's why Casey was now convinced he'd seen exactly what Jesse remembered—a phantom occupant living in a dead and empty farmhouse.

It was possible. So very possible. Quite frankly, it was the only thing that made sense. His story had spread between the three of them like a virus. His two closest friends had been infected by the product of his own fear.

Which meant that Reed's death was Jesse's fault.

The idea nauseated him. He dropped his pen atop one of his student's incoherent ramblings and leaned back in his chair. When his gaze flitted back to the window, that house continued to loom just beyond the glass. It was as though his own home had been placed beyond the soy bean fields and town limit sign he'd driven past so many times. The house remained there as if calling out to him.

I want to show you something, Jesse. Are you coming or not?

THREE

THE NEXT DAY was Friday, and Jesse couldn't have been more thankful for it. The night before had left him a tense and sleepless mess. Sure, he was used to losing plenty of rest due to Ian's middle-of-the-night wakeups. But there was a big difference between grabbing a three AM bottle and reliving the worst night of his life.

For the first time in years, Jesse snoozed his alarm. He rolled out of bed half an hour late and shamble to the shower. Before he knew it, he found himself standing over a toaster with a jar of Nutella close at hand, peering bleary-eyed across the tiny backyard at his dog. Winston was ambling up and down the length of the chain-link fence with his nose buried deep in the snow, as if smelling something suspicious. And while Jesse knew it was ridiculous to entertain such a thought, he couldn't help but wonder if the farmhouse had been out there after all.

Jesse ate his chocolate toast during his ten-minute commute to Warsaw High. The school was a squat red brick building that—had it not been for the five cathedral-like windows between both front entrances—would have resembled a prison more than an institution of learning. Regardless, those windows had done little to keep Jesse and his classmates from calling the place Warsaw Pen. And who could blame them? The inside was no better than a Supermax; nothing but white-painted cinderblock and scuffed up linoleum floors. The endless banks of fluorescent lights gave off a constant buzz, as though a colony of killer bees had created a hive within the hallway walls. That lighting didn't do the place any favors, either. It lent the banged-up hallway lockers a sickly tint and highlighted every scuff mark along the rubber baseboards and dirty tile.

There were student-made posters and fliers taped to the walls to break up the monotony; stuff about basketball games and student council meetings. Once, there had been drama club ads for upcoming productions: *Death of a Salesman* and *The Crucible, Romeo and Juliet* and *Macbeth*. Those had always been Jesse's favorites, but the drama club had disbanded years ago. Lack of funding led to a lack of interest, and there were only so many four-person plays a thespian group could perform.

Despite the missing theater placards, the other posters made Warsaw High seem like a relatively normal school. But the graduation rate told a different story. When Jesse had been a Warsaw Warrior, nearly forty percent of the student body didn't make it through senior year. Now, the dropout rate was even higher, and it wasn't hard to see why. There wasn't much need for a high school diploma in a town like Warsaw. Most of the kids who *did* graduate only pushed through so they could get the hell out of Dodge.

Jesse knew his hometown wouldn't be able to sustain his son. Just as any kid with potential was better off leaving, he had to get himself and his family out, too. The students of Warsaw High were proof positive that the town didn't have a future. Most days, Jesse felt like he was teaching a room full of ghosts.

Those phantoms happened to be juniors, and the dropout rate left Jesse's classes small. On top of the fact that a good chunk of his students weren't interested in reading anything beyond listicles and celebrity news, the job was made tougher with no money for books and no earmarked funds for much-needed renovations. Jesse was sure the place was in violation of at least a dozen building codes. Last year, the wall-mounted heater in his room had spent half the winter on the fritz, and summers weren't much better. Every so often the air conditioning would shut off, and while the maintenance guy claimed the unit was old and needed replacing, the rumor was that the administration simply turned them off to save a few dimes. After all, the old Xerox machine in the teacher's lounge only printed terrible quality copies. It did not, in fact, print hundred dollar bills.

The kids that did do their work were disillusioned, distracted by thoughts of *just one more year*. They were the same thoughts that had pushed Jesse through those halls when he was their age. *Just get through this and get out.* And the kids who didn't apply themselves? Some would say they were problem students while others would argue they were playing it smart, because you didn't need a GED to work the register at the local ThriftMart. You didn't need to ace a physics test to do an oil change. Understanding the symbolism in *Of Mice and Men* wasn't going to help you swap out tires at a car repair shop.

Despite all of that, Jesse did his best to keep his kids engaged, and his efforts didn't go unnoticed. Most of his students liked him. But there were still nights when Jesse would sit at his desk with his head in his hands and wonder what the hell he was doing with his life. That, however, was par for the course. He'd been wondering the same thing when he had wobbled across the auditorium stage, so drunk he had hardly heard his name when it was called.

Jesse.

Jesse Wells.

"Mr. Wells."

Principal Garvey was a tall mountain of a man in a perfectly pressed suit. The man prided himself on looking like a million bucks, hoping to set a good example for the students who did make it to their last semester. His demeanor said it all: *this could be you.* And while Jesse respected him for the effort, in his opinion, Garvey was selling an empty promise. Because when it came down to it, Garvey was the principal of a high school in a town of less than eight thousand. How, exactly, was that the picture of success? Jesse couldn't quite figure it out.

"Morning." Jesse greeted his boss with a nod.

"TGIF," Garvey said, forcing a toothsome smile onto his face. The man knew how to dress, but he resembled a grimacing alligator whenever he tried to play nice. "You all doing anything fun today?"

"Taking a surprise quiz," Jesse said, giving the man his own version of an over-the-top grin. Because at least with a quiz, Jesse could try to get the rest of those essays graded.

"Fantastic," Garvey said. "God speed to you, then."

And yet, despite the relative silence of each of Jesse's classes, he still couldn't concentrate. The longer he sat there, trying to focus on anything beyond Casey's visit, the more he found himself stuck in an endless loop of uncertainty. He wasn't sure whether to let it lie or whether to give in and go back to that damn house one final time. Because no matter how much he tried to reason it away, no matter how much he denied it or how anxious he felt, he had become a little obsessed with that house, too.

It had started at age eleven, after Jesse had been abandoned by his friends. That girl, he hadn't been able to get her out of his thoughts for months. Eventually, those obsessive thoughts had faded until he'd convinced himself what he'd seen had been nothing more than a manifestation of his own fear. But that fixation reared its head again after Reed had died. It had come back more vicious and unapologetic than ever before. The only difference between Jesse and Reed's monomania had been that instead of physically going there as Reed had, Jesse revisited that place in his mind every night for what had felt like years.

And now it was back, looming large enough to break his concentration. It was standing outside his front room window, occupying one of the many empty lots across the street. Smiling at him through the darkness. Happy to have found its long-lost friend.

Jesse managed to get through a single essay by lunch. Ready to admit defeat, he tossed his grading pen onto an ever-growing pile of student quizzes, grabbed his now-empty insulated mug, locked his classroom behind him, and headed to the teacher's lounge for a much-needed refill. No matter how burnt and bitter the breakroom coffee was, he wouldn't turn his nose up at a fresh cup.

When he arrived at the teacher's lounge, Sam Wilson greeted him with an easy-going smile. Sam was a few years older than Jesse—he'd been a senior at Warsaw High when Jesse had arrived as a freshman. The age gap never gave them the chance to become friends until they found themselves working side-by-side. Sam taught US history and could recite every constitutional amendment and rattle off every critical date of the Civil War faster than his students could spell 'Confederacy.' When it came to friends, Sam had become Jesse's closest. Not that it had been difficult to win such a status. Jesse never did make friends easily, and making them in adulthood had proven next to impossible.

"Hey, man," Sam said.

"Hey," Jesse greeted back, lifting his empty travel mug in a salute. "How's the coffee today?"

"Terrible, as always," Sam responded.

"Just the way I like it." Jesse pointed himself to the counter where the Mr. Coffee sat.

It wouldn't have been so bad if the school supplied little buckets of creamer, but those weren't in the budget. Hell, sometimes the *coffee* wasn't in the budget. When Garvey had announced cuts the previous year, the teachers who couldn't live without caffeine had taken turns buying giant containers of Folgers to share.

"Plans for the weekend?" Sam asked.

"Grading papers," Jesse said. "I'm behind."

"But..." Sam raised an eyebrow, then shook his head. "Didn't you give the kids a pop quiz today? I heard a few of them groaning about it before the bell."

"I did." Jesse lowered his voice, muttering to himself. "Because I'm a genius."

Sam scoffed at that in a story-of-my-life sort of a way. When Jesse turned back toward him with his fresh mug of caffeinated dreck, Sam closed the book he was reading—something about John Adams—and leaned back against the lounge sofa. That piece of furniture was a thing of pure beauty; tattered, stained, and smelling a bit like Corn Nuts. Jesse would have bet an entire paycheck that brown, plaid thing had been in the lounge since both he and Sam had attended school there.

"New subject?" Jesse asked, nodding to the tome.

"Mmm. You know what one of our astute young academics said today about John Adams?"

"Couldn't guess if I tried." Jesse took a seat next to his coworker.

"I don't need to know about John Adams, Mister Wilson. I've already got my signature all figgered out. She was talking about John Hancock," Sam clarified. "John *Hancock,* Wells. You know, the guy who's only famous for his signature? *That* guy."

"I once had a kid ask me how Mark and Shaina Twain were related," Jesse mused.

"Did you know Abraham Lincoln faked his own death?" Sam asked. "It's true. He got tired of all the attention. Also, he wasn't all that into top hats."

"Why would he be?" Jesse asked. "He was already tall, so..."

"Jesus," Sam whispered, then bowed his head and squeezed the bridge of his nose. "Some days, you know? And now Stella wants to go to some fancy place out in the city."

Stella was Sam's wife. Definitely not LouEllen's type. The woman was a romance novel-loving Hallmark Channel addict with a Shih

Tzu named Ronald Reagan. She walked old Ronnie around the neighborhood and let him crap on random lawns. Jesse knew this because LouEllen had watched it happen the only time she and Stella had hung out. It was during an afternoon when Sam had invited Jesse and Lou over for a Super Bowl viewing party on his new big screen TV. That first encounter had staunched Jesse's idea of easing up on their Blaire and Casey hangouts by throwing another couple into the mix.

"A restaurant?" Jesse asked.

"I said to her, *fancy? Should I break out my monocle?* Fancy." Sam smirked. "I didn't realize there *were* such places in Detroit."

Jesse snorted.

"Promptly got smacked, of course," he said. "I was expecting a downright beating, but I think she's still holding out hope. If she kills me, who would drive?"

Beyond Stella's quirks, Sam's marriage sounded a lot like Jesse's. There were places that LouEllen loved in the city, too; places they rarely went, especially after the cash ran out.

"Hey, you two want to come with?" Sam asked, looking hopeful. "We can carpool. Stella will *probably* want to do carpool karaoke, but just let her get through one round of *Don't Stop Believin'* and she'll let it go."

"Oh my God." Jesse couldn't help it. He chuckled at the thought.

Personally, he would have loved to have blown off Casey's request and ditched town for a handful of hours, even if it meant listening to Stella belt out monster ballads the entire time. It was so tempting that he found himself genuinely considering it. But Lou would have never gone for it. He'd have to ditch her with Ian on a Friday night, and that was guaranteed to buy him an entire weekend in the dog house, maybe more. He wouldn't have been able to enjoy himself, anyway. He'd just keep thinking about Casey's visit, his weird request. Jesse was crap at putting on a game face when something was bothering him, like now.

"What's up?" Sam asked. It was only then that Jesse realized he was scowling at the steam rising out of his unlidded cup.

"No, nothing," he said, attempting a half-way convincing shrug. "Just some weird shit from my past coming back to haunt me."

Sam quirked an eyebrow at that. "History?" he asked. "That's my specialty, you know."

"Yeah," Jesse said. "I know. But I've already got my John Hancock down pat, Sam. I have for years."

"And it's lucky we don't have a communications class at this prestigious academy of learning," Sam said, thoughtful. "Because you'd have scored an F for that conversational dodge."

Jesse nodded toward Sam's book. "You can't help me. Not unless you've got a book about Reed Lowell stashed away among those countless dead presidents."

Sam immediately recognized the name. After his suicide, Reed had become a postmortem Warsaw celebrity, and the stardom hadn't been limited to the dead. When the news hit the halls, the student body's morbid curiosity was turned onto the two remaining Musketeers. Jesse had never been much of a social butterfly, so most questions were tossed at Casey's feet. The way girls had flocked to Casey's side had turned Jesse's stomach. They had been vultures hungry for carrion, and Reed's death had made Casey more popular than the star quarterback. And whether it was his way of coping with his own grief, or whether he had really been indulging in all that fawning, Casey hadn't waved the popularity away. All of that dead-friend exaltation was the reason LouEllen had turned her back on the guy that had asked her to prom and sought companionship elsewhere.

Not that she found a great friend in Jesse. At least not at first. If anything, she stumbled onto nothing short of a train wreck. When Principal Herman had announced Reed's name at the commencement ceremony and offered Reed's devastated parents their dead son's diploma, Jesse had nearly puked into his lap. That nausea was more than likely caused by a crippling wave of emotion, but it could have also been the booze. Only an hour beforehand, Jesse had pilfered a good three fingers of Jameson from his father's liquor cabinet. Because if anyone expected him to feel emotions that afternoon, they were out of their fucking mind.

"Wow," Sam said. "Reed Lowell?"

Jesse nodded, then capped his travel mug and allowed himself to collapse back into that smelly couch. Yeah, Reed and Casey had become household names—the guys that had *been there when he jumped*. Hell, people *still* talked about it. He'd overheard kids muttering about *Mr. Wells and the suicide house* on more than a few occasions. Because after that dark summer evening, whatever had made the farmhouse spooky before had been erased by the blood Reed had left on the foyer floorboards. And because of that, Jesse had become a piece of the myth itself.

"So, what's going on?" Sam asked. "You want to talk about it?"

What Jesse wanted was to shrug it off and say *not really*, because no, he honestly didn't. And why would he have? Lou's distaste for Stella and that yappy Ronald Reagan forced both Jesse and Sam to keep their distance. If Sam and Stella picked up and moved out of Warsaw, that would be the end of that. Sayonara. Have a nice life. And yet, something about keeping Sam at arm's length gave Jesse comfort. It was almost as if—since he and Sam hadn't been buddies in high school—Sam was less likely to judge him if he talked about the past. Or about Casey acting nuts at his house last night. Or the fact that he hadn't actually watched Reed jump like everyone assumed.

"You know Casey Ridgemont?" Jesse asked. Sam did, of course. "He showed up at my place yesterday. Out of the blue, talking about Reed."

Sam frowned but didn't speak. That was the thing about Sam; when he asked a question, he listened, refusing to interject until all the cards were on the table. And even then, he had a thoughtful approach.

"He was pretty upset," Jesse continued. "He showed me an article about that house out on Old Mill where...you know."

Sam nodded.

"I guess it's finally up for demolition, and something about that has Casey flipping out."

Jesse sighed and finally took a sip of coffee. For once, he wished Sam would say something, anything, even if it was as benign as *wow, that's crazy* or *interesting, tell me more*. But of course, Sam held his silence, and it left Jesse lingering on the memory of Casey's strained and imploring countenance. It had been a mask of emotion so foreign it had rendered Casey's face almost unrecognizable; like he'd changed on a molecular level, like there had been a shift in his DNA.

"Anyway." Jesse lifted his shoulders to his ears, ready to dismiss the whole thing.

"So, what did he want?" Sam finally asked, surprising Jesse by pressing him further. It wasn't typical of Sam to push for more. Then again, this was Warsaw folklore. He supposed that even a guy like Sam wasn't immune to its mysterious pull.

"He wants me to go back there," Jesse said. "He says he doesn't want to go alone."

A suspicious look crossed Sam's face.

"Lou thinks he's just looking for closure, which, maybe he is. I don't know." Jesse shifted his weight forward, forcing himself out of the spongy cushions beneath him. "I mean, it's nuts. Who in their right mind would go back to a place like that?"

He scowled down at his hands, falling silent as he considered his own questions. Because it *was* crazy, right? Or was he just bending beneath the weight of his own fear again?

"Anyway, I should go," he said, hooking a thumb toward the door. "I need to get back to grading."

"Sure," Sam said. "I should do the same." Only ten minutes until the bell, kids would be hopped up on their lunch and excited for the weekend. The last few hours of Friday were always chaos.

"Have fun wearing your monocle into the city." Jesse toasted Sam with his mug.

"You sure you don't want to come?" Sam asked, tucking his book beneath his arm.

"Yeah, I'm sure," Jesse said. "We don't have a sitter, so..."

"Gotcha. That, and I shouldn't have mentioned the carpool karaoke thing," Sam mused. "There was no coming back from that, was there?"

"Not when Journey is involved," Jesse said. And while he flashed Sam a good-natured grin, he suddenly felt a pang of sadness, reminded of all the Eminem karaoke sessions Reed had instigated way back when. *May I have your attention, please?*

They both walked to the door, where Jesse would go left and Sam would go right. Their classrooms were clear across the building from one another. The breakroom was the only place they ever really got a chance to talk.

"See you Monday," Jesse said, giving his coworker a ghost of a smile. Then he pivoted out the doorway and began to make his way along linoleum that hadn't been waxed since the previous year.

"Hey, Jesse?"

Jesse stopped, turned, and glanced back to Sam, who was standing where Jesse had left him.

"Maybe you should go," Sam suggested.

Jesse couldn't help but furrow his brow. Sam was on LouEllen's side? They were both in agreement that Casey's plan wasn't as crazy as Jesse thought?

"I mean, it isn't my call," Sam said. "But LouEllen might be on to something."

"What?" Jesse asked. "Closure?"

Sam lifted his shoulders up to his ears, not wanting to step on toes. But he spoke a few seconds later anyway. "It's just that you were there too," he reminded Jesse. "I'm guessing that's why Casey is asking *you* to go rather than asking someone else, right?"

Jesse said nothing, not because he didn't want to respond, but because he didn't know what to say. He merely stood there, his hands wrapped around the aluminum body of his travel mug, wondering if it was wrong to protect himself from reliving something that had almost destroyed him.

"My grandmother," Sam said. "I was in college when she got sick. We were never close. She had a lot of issues." Sam shook his head as if to clear his mind of the memory. "Anyway, she had a stroke. Her condition kept getting worse. First, she was in the ICU. Then she was in recovery. But then she lapsed into a coma, and the whole family congregated in her hospital room. There was talk of funeral arrangements. My mom kept calling me: *Sam, you have to come. Sam, she's your grandmother.*

"My family wasn't dirt poor or anything, but my parents weren't exactly swimming in savings either. And me, going to college out in Pennsylvania, I was already up to my eyeballs in student loans. I didn't have the time or the cash to drop everything, hop on a plane, and fly home. Especially not on short notice. But my girlfriend at the time...she told me to go *because you might regret it if you don't.*

"My initial reaction was, *yeah right.* I mean, this woman was not your standard chocolate chip cookie-baking cheek-pinching lady. She was mean as hell. She'd scream at us kids throughout the entirety of all the summers we were made to stay with her, which was relegated by our parents as *Grandma Time.* She chased us around the house with kitchen utensils, waving them over her head like clubs. She beat my kid brother so hard with a metal spatula he had bruises up and down his back for a month."

"Jesus," Jesse murmured.

"Yeah," Sam said. "Exactly. So, regret? I doubted it. The woman was an abusive old hag."

Jesse shifted his weight from one foot to the other. He could tell where this story was going.

"And yet," Sam continued, "after my girlfriend brought up regret, I couldn't get it out of my head. Like, was it possible that I *would* regret not being at the hospital with my family? Maybe I wouldn't care about not seeing my grandmother alive again, but I might feel bad for not being there for everyone else. I mean, how would that make *me* look, you know? What kind of a person would that make me? And so..." He paused, allowing Jesse to respond.

"You went," Jesse concluded.

"I went," Sam said. "And you know what? I'm glad I did. I expected to get there and sit in silence for a few days, but that didn't happen. I saw my brothers and my cousins, my aunts and uncles that I hadn't seen in forever. I felt closer to my family than I had in...maybe ever. Hell, some of them even had pleasant memories of my grandma, which was eye-opening. Despite my own version of her, it helped me see her in a different light."

He pulled the book from beneath his arm, glanced at the cover, then looked back to Jesse. "She died the day after I got there. I can't say that I felt much of anything when I heard her flatline from down the hall. And I doubt you'll miss that house out on Old Mill once it's gone. Hell, you'll probably be relieved. But what you might regret is not going back there with your friend, if not for yourself, then to at least lend him a shoulder."

Jesse grimaced at his shoes.

"Or, hey, maybe I'm totally off-base," Sam tossed in. "I'm just playing devil's advocate. You know what they say..."

Yeah, Jesse did.

You will be more disappointed by the things you didn't do than by the ones you did do. So, throw off the bowlines. It was precisely why he and LouEllen had decided to get married after years of dating. It's why they had thrown caution to the wind and had a kid. Those two impulsive decisions ended up being the best things in Jesse's life. So maybe going back to the house with Casey would pan out. Perhaps it would finally allow Jesse to move on. And hell, maybe he'd get a book out of it, too.

"But, man." Sam emitted a nervous laugh. "I'm sorry. I don't know where that diatribe came from. It's not my place. I've said way too much."

"No, it's fine," Jesse said. "You're probably right."

"I'll see you on Monday." Sam tapped his fingers against his book. "You've got my number. Call me if you need me, huh?"

"Thanks," Jesse said, watching Sam turn to walk down the hall. A moment later, the bell screamed through the empty hallway. The sound of kids began to flood in from a distance. Soon, the building would be swamped with teens.

Jesse turned in the opposite direction, making his way to his own classroom. Once he got there, he collapsed into his desk chair, placed his travel mug next to the pile of ungraded essays, and pulled his cell phone from his pocket. He scrolled to Sam's number, then backed out of it and began to crawl through his contact list. When he found Casey's listing, he stopped. And then he closed his eyes and sighed, muttering a quiet "shit." Because, while he and Casey had grown distant over the past nineteen years, it didn't change the fact that they had once been close.

Jesse tapped out a quick text onto his screen and hit SEND before he could think better of it.

OKAY,   it   said.   I'LL   GO.

FOUR

CASEY WAS a married man, but his Impala resembled a bachelor pad. The stench was a miasma of stale pizza and old takeout boxes poorly disguised by a tree-shaped air freshener. It was a faithful reflection of Casey Ridgemont circa 1998.

Sliding into the passenger seat was like stepping into a time warp. That, however, didn't make it any less baffling. The guy lived in a perfect house with an impeccable lawn. That YouTube money paid for a couple of housekeepers who—from what he'd heard from LouEllen—cleaned the place twice a week. And yet, there was Casey's car. If Oscar the Grouch had a license, Casey's Impala would be his trashcan on wheels.

"You ever clean this thing out?" Jesse asked, craning his neck to take in the junk filling the footwells of the back seat. There were bags from Shake Shack and White Castle, a box full of cables Jesse assumed Casey used to hook up recording gear, empty paper cups with lids and straws still intact, old circulars and store receipts. When Casey didn't respond, Jesse shifted his weight and looked out the window, but he could only maintain the awkward silence for so long.

"So," he said, "I mean, I don't want to make you talk if you don't want to, but...I guess I'm still a little unclear about what we're doing."

"What do you mean?" Casey asked, but he didn't look away from the road. There was nothing but snow and black asphalt out there. No streetlights. No oncoming traffic. Just darkness so bleak it felt like a void.

"Well…" Jesse paused, then looked out the window again. "You said you needed an answer. I'm just wondering what that answer might look like."

Casey narrowed his gaze at the windshield. He didn't reply, just stepped on the gas as if worried that too much thinking would result in second thoughts. Jesse decided not to push it further. At least not yet. He chewed on a nail and watched frostbitten trees speed by his window, lit by nothing but a slash of high beams.

Part of him wanted to pull an encore from nearly two decades ago. His anxiety was stirring at the pit of his stomach, imploring him to sit up straight, blink at his surroundings, and demand to know why they were going back to that creepy house. But he'd signed himself up for this imbecilic adventure and Casey had the text to prove it. Backing out would make him an ass.

"Does Blaire know where we're headed?"

Had Casey informed his wife of his weird plan to visit where Reed had died, or was this act two of Casey's stopover to Jesse's house a few days before? It was possible Lou had called Blaire after Casey had shown up at their place that night, but it was unlikely. Lou knew how to keep her mouth shut. Blaire did not. If Lou had ratted Casey out, there was no doubt Jesse would have heard about it by now.

"Blaire?" Casey echoed the name as though never having heard it before.

"Yeah, Blaire," Jesse said. "You know, your wife?"

"Yeah," Casey smirked. "I know my wife."

"So?" Jesse asked. What was with all this evasive dodging? Why was Casey being so cryptic? "Does she know about this, or…?"

Casey's mouth tensed into a tight line. That's when Jesse knew he had hit on something Casey didn't want to discuss.

"Hey, can you just talk to me?" Jesse asked. "I didn't want you coming out here on your own, but it's like…" He hesitated, searching for the right words. "It's like you're shutting me out. I don't get it. I thought you *wanted* me to come."

"I did," Casey said. "I do." Finally, he shot Jesse a brief look. "I'm just edgy, I guess. Amped up. I don't know."

"Amped up about what?"

But the conversation ended there. Casey just stared ahead. Meanwhile, Jesse struggled with the ever-increasing trepidation he hadn't felt in years. It was the same anxiety that had welled up inside him the evening Casey had driven the Three Musketeers to the place they were heading to now. *Shits and giggles*, Reed had said. But this wasn't that. Casey had a motive. Despite the darkness of the Impala's interior, it was easy to see the determination pulled taut across his face.

When Casey slowed the car and took a turn onto that all-too-familiar road, Jesse bit his tongue. He'd seen the house so many times, but it didn't make a difference. His heart jumped into his throat when that building finally came into view, crooked and strange, standing alone on a plot of land that stretched for God only knew how far. It seemed to smile at them against the glare of Casey's headlights. But there was a new addition to the landscape: a sign.

NO TRESPASSING
PRIVATE PROPERTY
VIOLATORS WILL BE PROSECUTED

"Wait, we're not allowed to be here?" It was a stupid question. Jesse should have considered that this place was off-limits, especially after reading the article Casey had found.

"Relax. There's nobody out here," Casey said, failing to slow the car as they continued their approach.

Jesse swallowed, his spit having gone acrid in his mouth. He leaned back in his seat and tried to stay calm. Sure, it was easy for *Casey* to relax. He got paid to break into places like this. But Jesse? He was pretty sure an arrest wouldn't look good on a teaching record.

Casey eased the Impala up to the front of the building, then guided the car around the circular drive they'd parked on so long ago.

"Christ." Jesse croaked out the word. He'd seen the place a thousand times while driving by, but he'd never dared get this close again.

"What?" Casey asked.

Jesse let his hands fall to his lap and drew in a deep breath. "I just feel like I'm going to puke, that's all."

"I know this car is dirty," Casey said, "but if you're going to spew..." The old *Wayne's World* joke had never failed to get a laugh when they were in high school, but it now fell flat. Jesse glanced up in time to watch his friend unclick his seatbelt and push open the driver's side door. He eyed the keys, which Casey left in the ignition.

"Wait," he said, reaching over to catch Casey by the arm. At least Casey was wearing a jacket tonight. Had he come here wearing nothing but a t-shirt, Jesse would have been completely unnerved. "I'm not going in there," he said. Maybe it was better to back out of this half-baked plan after all, promises be damned. "At least not until you tell me the real reason we're here. And I don't mean the cryptic *I need answers* stuff you've been feeding me up until now. Why are we here, Casey? If you can't at least tell me that, I'll just wait for you outside."

Part of him hoped Casey would snort and get out of the car, just leave him to sit there on his own. Or maybe he'd sigh and realize just how creepy this whole idea was. Because what was he expecting to do, summon Reed's ghost? What did he think they'd find in there, a long-overlooked suicide note?

"Wait outside?" Casey tone was tinged with anger. "Like you did that—" He stopped himself before finishing his thought, but he didn't need to. Jesse should have seen that one coming.

Jesse turned away, waiting for Casey to let fly. *I was up there alone with him because of you.* But rather than getting angry, Casey leaned back and kept his eyes forward. Jesse frowned as he pressed his hands between his knees. He dared to look out the window and back to the entrance that waited for them, not quite open, but not entirely shut.

"I've been back here a lot," Casey finally confessed, drawing Jesse's attention away from the crooked front porch balustrade. "Most of the time I just sit here like this," he said. "I guess a part of me feels this is like visiting Reed's grave or something." He shrugged. "It's stupid."

Jesse shook his head as if to say, *it isn't stupid, it makes sense.* Hell, he had had his own share of rough nights. Sometimes, he'd considered coming out here with a bottle of booze, standing out in the dirt driveway, and staring up at the top tower windows while pouring one out for his fallen comrade. But Jesse wasn't ready to bring that up. He didn't want to say anything that might stop Casey from finally spilling the truth about tonight.

"It's, like, ever since then, I can't get this place out of my head."

"That isn't surprising," Jesse said. "After what happened, I couldn't get it out of mine, either."

"Yeah, but you also haven't been out here time and time again," Casey said. "It hasn't pulled you back the way it's been pulling me."

That, Jesse assumed, had to do with the difference of their experiences. Casey had been inside, Jesse had been out. Maybe that's why he had never wanted to go in, had never wanted to come back enough to turn onto the road and drive past the no trespassing sign. He'd been on the outside, and as cowardly as it sometimes felt, the outside was exactly where he wanted to stay.

"And what's the difference tonight?" Jesse finally asked. "Why are we both here? How is this going to break the cycle?"

Casey went quiet again, and Jesse looked away. His breath fogged the passenger window. The interior of the car was as cold as the outside, now. Casey's door stood fully open, inviting them both to step toward the inevitable.

Meanwhile, a question balanced on the tip of Jesse's tongue, yet refused to tumble. *What about the girl?*

It was his chance to finally get the whole story. Had Jesse, amid his childhood panic, sworn to his best friends that he'd seen a figure in the highest window of the house? Had Reed mentioned a girl to Casey? Was *that* where all this was coming from?

And what about what Casey had said about Reed not jumping but having been pushed? An ugly sense of doubt pushed against Jesse's chest as he sat there, peering at the gear shift between them both.

Did Casey have something to do with what had happened that night?

The three of them had been drunk. Was it so impossible to think that—

"I don't know about breaking any cycles, but you know what I know for sure?" Casey asked.

"What?"

"You were right about what you said. This place? There's something wrong with it. It's infected. Or maybe it's just cursed."

Casey got out of the car and slammed the door behind him, and Jesse's mouth went dry. Suddenly, he found himself wishing it was summer again, that this was Casey's Civic instead of the Impala. He wanted all the trash in the back seat to be gone, replaced by the bottles that had rolled around on the floor so long ago. Because at least then, he could steel his nerves with a few swigs of alcohol. At least then, he wouldn't feel so goddamn scared.

FIVE

JESSE TRAILED behind Casey as he crossed the farmhouse's threshold, but he wanted to turn back. Because this was a bad idea; a terrible, awful, stupid thing to do.

He was struck by the scent right away. It was a dank, wet smell of soil and decay, and he couldn't help but think, *it reeks of an open grave*. He didn't dare look to his feet. He knew if he did, he'd see the broken floorboards Reed's body had left behind.

And yet, despite his trepidation, he found himself fascinated by the way the moonlight came in through the windows and spilled onto the staircase. He was oddly transfixed by the way it danced along the peeling wallpaper and filth-covered floors. He felt himself taken by the strange beauty of the place, the rusty wheel of creativity slowly beginning to creaking upon its axle inside his head. As peculiar as it was, he suddenly understood Casey's addiction to these types of spots. It was beautiful in its dust and decay. A monolithic memento mori reminding him that he, too, would one day find himself where Reed was now.

His eyes dared to wander. Beyond the foyer was an empty room with a massive fireplace centered against the wall. It didn't match the scale of the place, much too big for the room; eccentric, like the house's exterior. And the mantel was just as curious, made of marble that must have once been white but had turned ivory with time. A shadow of a large cross hung above it as if burned into the wallpaper. It was upon seeing that ghost of an outline that Jesse's heart thumped hard against his chest. Despite his sudden fascination, that familiar sense of foreboding hit him all over again.

Because they shouldn't have been there.

They needed to leave.

"Hey, I think we—" He turned to speak to Casey, but Casey was gone.

Again, his heart thudded against the curve of his ribs. Because what if Casey had brought him here as a joke? What if, during Jesse's momentary lapse in focus, Casey had ducked out of the house and was crawling back into the driver's seat of his car? Was that why he left the keys in the ignition, to make a quick getaway?

Don't be stupid, he thought. *He wouldn't do that. There's no way.*

But something about the possibility, no matter how implausible, poised him on the edge of panic. His pulse continued to race, speeding up enough to trigger a sudden, spinning sense of vertigo.

I'm okay, I'm okay. Jesse's brain switched to autopilot, playing the mantra he'd taught himself after he'd discovered that fear could feel like dying. But that half-assed mantra wasn't doing anything for him now. He reached for the closest wall to steady himself.

"Casey?" He called out, but the name left his throat weak and strained. "Jesus, *Casey?!*" Was this really happening again? Was he really here, back in this nightmare place?

"Up here."

Jesse craned his neck to find Casey on the second-floor landing. Seeing him brought immediate relief. *Thank God.* At least he wasn't alone. But that consolation was short-lived, wiped out by Casey's next appeal.

"Come on," he said. "I want to show you something."

Jesse's foreboding became darker, more urgent, because there was something off, something *wrong*. He winced at the sound of Casey's ascending footstep. The panic that had stirred at the pit of his stomach began to rise up in his throat. Because why would Casey have said that? Surely, he must have remembered the dialogue from that summer night as vividly as Jesse did. Christ, Jesse could recall it as if it were yesterday. Sometimes, it replayed itself inside his brain on a neverending, torturous loop.

Or maybe it was a coincidence. Maybe Casey *didn't* remember. Hell, he'd been busy taking photos of random cracks in the wall with that fancy Nikon. It was possible he hadn't been listening, that he'd been too busy fumbling with aperture and shutter speeds to hear

Reed at all.

He wouldn't bring you here to scare you, Jesse told himself. *He wouldn't do that. You're okay.*

"Hey, Casey?"

The sound of footsteps stopped.

"Maybe it would be better to come back here during the day?" Because really, what was this? It was clear Casey intended on climbing to the house's top floor for God only knew what reason— and that was fine, whatever. Lou would have encouraged Jesse to cut him some slack. *Let him do what needs to be done.* But this—Casey's words, the darkness—it was too much. It felt like deja vu.

"We don't even have a flashlight," Jesse protested, searching for anything that might convince Casey to turn back.

"Don't need one." Casey murmured from overhead, disappearing into the shadows once more. "Just come on. We're already here."

Casey began climbing again. When he didn't stop to see if Jesse was coming, Jesse knew something was seriously off. This felt bad. Like a huge mistake.

Then again, this was Casey. Back in high school, he'd have kept climbing upward just as he was now. And no, he wouldn't have looked back. He knew Jesse wouldn't turn around and leave him there on his own, knew there was no way in hell he could handle feeling as though he betrayed his oldest living friend *yet again* because he was chickenshit.

Don't be a jellyfish, Reed would have told him. *Grow a backbone. Find your balls.*

"Shit," Jesse whispered, then began his own reluctant ascent. "Shit, shit, *shit."* A new mantra, because he was sure those stairs would crumble beneath his feet. And yet somehow, even after all these years, they continued to hold.

"Are you coming?" The question drifted down to him, chilling in its monotone.

"I'm coming," Jesse responded, but his anxiety kept him from quickening his steps. He met each riser with hesitant suspicion, refusing to trust a single one, sure that as soon as he did, his foot would punch through rotten wood and he'd be done for. Ignoring the spiderwebs and dust, he white-knuckled the banister. Eventually, he reached the first landing. Then the second. Thank God for small miracles. At least he was still alive.

He tried to ignore the shadows along the stairwell, stains that matched the one above the fireplace downstairs. It was as though the eccentric that had once lived here hadn't just built a strange house in a strange place, but had also lined the stairs with dozens of holy relics. He couldn't make it out too well by moonlight alone, but he could swear he spotted a faint patchwork of squares beneath those cross-shaped ghosts. There must have been a gallery of family photos hung there at one time, each picture replaced with a religious symbol, regardless of placement and position. It left that wall of silhouettes looking haphazard and disorganized. In some spots, large crosses were crowded next to one another. Meanwhile, a cross as small as the palm of a child's hand hung alone in an otherwise empty space. He counted nearly twenty of them before pausing upon the third-floor landing, where he blinked at an armchair left to decompose in an empty room.

"Where are you?" Casey's voice drifted down.

"Here," Jesse replied, tearing his gaze away from that chair and turning back toward the flight of steps.

There was a smell, now. Like urine and vomit, as though a handful of Warsaw Warriors had drunk themselves into oblivion and gotten sick in every corner of the house.

"Casey," Jesse said, feeling wobbly despite his firmly planted feet. The stench was overwhelming, so strong that it made him wonder what a decomposing body smelled like. Was it possible there was one hidden somewhere within one of those upstairs rooms? "I think we should go," he said.

"But we've come too far," Casey responded. "And besides..." His words faded to nothing, though Jesse swore he could hear a whisper.

"What, besides?" Jesse asked, unable to keep from clenching his teeth. "Don't you smell that?" He covered his mouth and nose with his free hand, the other remaining steadfast on the handrail. "What *is* that?"

"Besides," Casey repeated from overhead but said no more.

"Besides *what?*" Jesse just about barked the words. He was losing patience. If Casey was trying to freak him out—

"Tell me if you see her," Casey said.

A moment later, Jesse was stumbling sideways.

He nearly lost his footing as his shoulder crashed hard against the wall.

Because that's when Casey rushed past him so quickly he was nothing but a blur.

That's when Casey fell.

Jesse didn't scream because he couldn't catch his breath.

He stood frozen in place—a misplaced statue forgotten in the tomb of an old house—his shoulder pressed against disintegrating wallpaper. He stared wide-eyed and petrified at the swaying and spinning body before him.

The rope creaked in the silence, rubbing against old flooring and balustrade spindles. Casey floated mid-air, his body swinging in a gentle cadence, suspended between the third and fourth floor.

All at once, that stench became so overpowering it wrapped itself around Jesse's throat, stealing his air. The cold that lingered inside the house bore down on him, cutting through his coat. It bit at his skin, threatening to snap his bones. And then there was the panic. What had once been yielding now became unfettered.

"Holy shit…"

Those three words were all Jesse needed to kickstart the uncontrollable tumble of his own delayed panic.

"Holy shit."

He veered away from Casey's body. His foot slipped along the edge of one of the stairs, which sent him stumbling headlong down to the third-story landing. He caught himself against the adjacent wall once he got there, then zeroed in on the empty room, on the armchair that sat inside it, as if beckoning him to take a seat.

Stay a while, Jesse, it said. *You're okay. You're okay. You're okay.*

He turned away and bolted down the stairs, his dread so all-encompassing it was blurring his vision. He gasped and choked past the sobs he couldn't hear but knew were tearing themselves from his throat.

By the time he hit the second-story landing, he was sure something was snapping at his heels. Something was crawling up his fucking back. His footsteps felt slow no matter how fast he tried to move. Each footfall was like stepping in ankle-deep snow. It was the same feeling he'd had when he'd run from this place as a child. Terror. Hysteria. He'd been without his friends then, and he was without his friends now.

Déjà vu.

When he reached the foyer, he froze, because there it was, the mark Reed had left on the house so many years before. Directly above it, Casey's body swung like a pendulum. And as Jesse glanced up the hollow center of the turret, it was then that he saw it. A strange, swirling mist as dark as an inkblot was twisting away from Casey's dangling feet and through the empty space of the stairwell. It was a mist that moved slowly, deliberately, offering Jesse plenty of time to either get a good look or run like hell. And yet, all Jesse could manage to do was stand there, his eyes silver dollar wide, his hands balled into stone fists at his sides. He was clenching his teeth hard enough to make his molars creak.

Move. The single syllable presented itself, the only guidance his lizard brain could muster. *MOVE!*

But he continued to stand there, rooted in place until that mist came low enough to drifted around him. It was the source of the stench, that foul smell now coiling up his nostrils, coating his tongue.

It felt like an eternity, but his feet finally became unstuck. When they did, Jesse didn't stop to marvel at his sudden ability to move again. He bolted out the front door, tripped down the crooked porch steps, and crashed into the side of Casey's car hard enough to rattle his teeth.

He fumbled open the driver's side door and threw himself behind the wheel.

This place. There's something wrong with it.

Jesse pressed his cold hands to his face.

It's infected. Or maybe it's just cursed.

Except it couldn't be. That was nonsense, and he knew it.

It couldn't be, because he'd convinced himself as a kid that such things were implausible and absurd.

There was no such thing as a cursed house.

There was no such thing as ghosts.

SIX

JESSE WAITED for the police to arrive while sitting in Casey's car with all the doors locked and his cell held tight in his hand. When they finally came, three cruisers drove up the rutted drive in silence. No sirens. Just whirling red and blue lights sending carnival shadows across a frozen, snow-covered field.

Jesse eventually found himself standing outside with chattering teeth. He was trying to answer questions he only half-heard and hardly understood.

An ambulance came. It shook its way up the road at an almost leisurely pace, in no hurry to arrive at its destination. A stretcher appeared. The paramedics had to remove the house's front door from its busted hinge to squeeze the gurney inside.

When they came back out, a zippered black bag accompanied them.

Seeing it brought everything full-circle. It assured Jesse that this wasn't some incredibly vivid dream from which he couldn't wake. Casey was really gone.

Before the paramedics had a chance to load Casey into the ambulance, one of the attending officers tucked Jesse into the back of his squad car.

At the precinct, they ushered him to a featureless room; just a metal table, a few chairs, and cinderblock walls. Jesse looked down to his hands, which were folded before him atop cold aluminum. He couldn't help but wonder how long it would take the coroner to place Casey's body on a table exactly like the one he was sitting at now.

"We're going to get to the bottom of this," an officer said, pulling Jesse out of his thoughts. Jesse looked up and squinted against the glare of the fluorescent lights. He could hear the tubes buzzing overhead, just like they did at school. It was an ugly, unnerving noise, like a gnat trying to wriggle its way into his brain.

A second cop stepped forward, placed a pair of plump hands onto the table, and leaned in just enough to assert his authority. And then he spoke.

"I'm just gonna ask what we're both wondering, bud. You one of them demon worshippers, aren't ya'?"

Jesse blinked.

He remembered the details of the evening, but he had no idea how long ago they had happened. He had no clue how long he'd been sitting where he was now, or how much time had passed since he'd last spoken with Casey. Had it been an hour? Had it been a day? Had these officers called LouEllen? Did she know what had happened, where he was?

"*Hey.*" The looming officer snapped his fingers in front of Jesse's face. It was clear the man had little patience. He was short, stocky, stuffed into his uniform, which was sausage casing-tight. Those fingers snapped mere inches from the tip of Jesse's nose again. "I asked you a damn question," he said.

"Sorry," Jesse muttered dryly. "What?"

"The devil. Satan," the cop said, slowing his words and annunciating each syllable as though confronting the village idiot. "Do. You. Worship. Him?"

For a moment, Jesse wanted to laugh. He wanted to say, *yeah, of course I do. Who doesn't?* Because the inquiry was so half-witted it was actually funny. It was a question only a Podunk hillbilly cop would pose in all seriousness and expect a genuine answer. But that was the trouble with Warsaw. Podunk was the gold standard. It was why Jesse had to get his family the hell out of there. He had to save Ian from cops who avoided walking beneath ladders and blamed broom-riding witches for unsolvable crimes.

"No," Jesse finally replied.

"Took you an awfully long time to answer," said the looming cop.

"Hey, Mel?" The seated officer chimed in, looking up from some papers attached to a clipboard he'd been perusing. "This guy...he's a high school teacher out in Warsaw."

"That right?" Bad Cop Mel squinted at Jesse.

"It's what it says, Mel," Clipboard Cop said, then reached across the table for a Styrofoam coffee cup.

"Well, good thing we aren't in Warsaw," Mel muttered. "I'm not so sure I'd be wanting some devil worshipper teaching *my* kid about anything."

"Wait, sorry." Jesse straightened in his seat. "We aren't in Warsaw?"

"Zion," Clipboard Cop said. "County picked up the call."

Jesse swallowed. He assumed he was under arrest. Maybe they thought he had killed Casey. Hell, if they searched hard enough, they might have even found a motive, and LouEllen was the link. Perhaps she and Casey had been getting a little too close, cozying up behind Jesse's back. Maybe Jesse found out and decided to take care of the problem. It was a classic crime of passion. One guy ambushing another in the middle of nowhere, tying a noose around his neck, and giving him a firm two-handed push. *Stay the fuck away from my wife.*

Jesse knew the law. At the very least, he'd be taken into custody for trespassing. He'd gone through trespassing convictions with a couple of his students when they had broken into some guy's barn on a dare. As far as minors went, they got slapped with a misdemeanor and a fine, sometimes probation, maybe community service. But that was kid stuff. This was not. There was no telling what type of conviction a judge would bring down on Jesse's head, especially when there was a dead body involved.

"There's something else on here, Mel," Clipboard Cop said, tapping the page with his pen.

Mel squinted at the document as if having a hard time understanding. Or maybe his eyesight wasn't what it used to be. *Perhaps he's illiterate,* Jesse thought. *Wouldn't that be priceless? Wouldn't that just be the best?* But Mel could read, and he eventually turned his suspicious glare back on Jesse.

"You have got to be *kidding* me," he said. "You were there when the Lowell kid committed suicide, too?"

The point-blank question sent a shudder down Jesse's back. Was that on his record?

"And now you happen to be there when *this* fella hangs himself from the fourth floor?"

Jesse didn't respond, because it looked bad. *Really* bad. Anyone would have been dubious. Because what were the odds?

"And you mean to tell me this whole thing is a *coincidence?*" Mel asked, so incredulous that he snorted.

Jesse leaned into the table and pressed his hands over his mouth. Here he was, way out in Zion. Casey's car, he assumed, was still parked outside the farmhouse. LouEllen would have to pick him up from the precinct. The idea of explaining to her what had happened struck him about as bad as her inevitable decision to never see him again. He couldn't imagine the look on her face, couldn't fathom the sorrow, the disgust. Because soon, LouEllen would be at the Ridgemont place trying to calm her hysterical best friend, trying to explain how in the hell something like this could happen under her husband's watch. Soon, Blaire would know that Casey was dead.

And Jesse? He should have been able to stop Casey from doing what he did, right? He should have picked up on the clues during the drive over. Clearly, something terrible had happened inside Casey's mind. Unless...

Cursed.

No. He wouldn't allow himself to entertain even an inkling of such an illogical idea. Because it didn't make sense. It couldn't be real. That place wasn't cursed or haunted, no matter what Casey had claimed. What had been haunted was Casey—haunted by guilt, by grief for his long-lost friend.

"Can you tell us again what you were doing at the location? Why were you there?" Clipboard Cop asked.

"We went back for Reed," Jesse said softly, his gaze once again fixed upon the table's scuffed top.

Mel shifted his girth from foot to foot, impatient as ever, as though they'd asked Jesse these questions a dozen times before. And maybe they had. Maybe Jesse just couldn't remember.

"Reed Lowell?" Clipboard Cop asked. "Is that right?"

Jesse issued a weak nod.

"You went back for your dead friend?" Mel asked, not buying any of it. "A guy who's been dead for how long now...?"

"Can you tell us what happened to Mr. Lowell, Mr. Wells?" Clipboard Cop asked, keeping up the good cop routine. "Back in 2000."

Jesse winced at the question. They knew what happened to Reed. Mel had made that clear. He wasn't sure why they needed him to rehash the details, but he was in no position to argue, so he just let it tumble past his lips.

"He killed himself, same as Casey."

"Sounds like some sort of a pact," Mel said gruffly. "Like I said, devil stuff."

"A pact?" Jesse asked, swallowing the sour-tasting spit that had collected at the back of his throat. "What do you mean?"

"A suicide pact," Mel clarified. "You think we don't watch horror movies out here? Think we haven't heard of that dark stuff you freaks get into?"

"You wouldn't know anything about that, would you, Mr. Wells?" Clipboard Cop asked.

"What?" Jesse's eyes drifted from one officer to the other.

"The pact," Clipboard Cop repeated. "Did you know about it?"

"No, I—" So, there *was* a pact? Jesse squinted, confused. "I don't understand."

The officers exchanged a glance.

"You realize you're in a crap-ton of trouble, right?" asked Bad Cop Mel. "You know there are laws in this state against assisting a suicide?"

"I didn't—"

"You know there are laws against cult stuff? Against human sacrifice? Is that what this was, Wells?"

Jesse opened his mouth to speak, but all he managed was a blank-faced grimace. Before he could say anything in his own defense, Mel pushed on with his insane line of thinking.

"We should arrest you on the grounds of being one of them Satanists," he murmured. "Freedom of religion my ass."

"Okay," Clipboard Cop cut in, eager to nip Mel's grumbling in the bud. "I think we have enough to go off of. You understand that none of what we've discussed takes into account any trespassing charges that may be filed against you?"

"Am I under arrest?" Jesse asked.

"Not yet," Mel muttered. "Soon, though. You can count on it."

"Not at the moment," Clipboard Cop followed up.

"But don't leave the state," Mel said, his tone gruff.

"You can call your ride from the front desk," Clipboard Cop said. "I'll show you to the phone if you'll just follow me."

"What about Casey?" The question slithered past Jesse's lips, though even *he* didn't quite understand what he was asking.

"What about him?" Mel asked, daring Jesse to come clean about something that had been left unsaid.

"Where is he? We aren't from here, we're from——"

"We have him at our morgue, Mr. Wells," Clipboard Cop explained. "We'll be able to transfer him to Warsaw as soon as the paperwork is in order. But for now, he stays here."

Jesse nodded as he rose from the table. He shuffled toward the door that Clipboard Cop was now holding open for him. "Okay," he whispered to himself after slinking past the officer. "Okay," he echoed, wringing his hands. "I'm okay," he told himself. "It's going to be okay."

SEVEN

JESSE COULDN'T remember what he'd said to LouEllen when he called, but whatever it had been, Lou arrived at the Zion police station red-eyed and pale. She said nothing while waiting for him to be released, and she didn't meet his gaze to assure him that things would be okay. She didn't even look at him to communicate that she no longer loved him, that this was it for them, that they were done.

He followed her out of the police station and into the biting January wind. Watching her climb behind the wheel of their Altima, he matched her silence while slipping into the passenger's seat. Once inside, LouEllen sat motionless for what felt like an eternity, her attention fixed on the center of the steering wheel. When she did finally move, it wasn't to acknowledge him but to shove the key into the ignition.

She sniffed and wiped at her cheeks with the back of her hand, then shoved the car into reverse and backed out of the space a little too quickly. Guiding the vehicle onto the road, the Altima's back tire hopped the curb. She was heading toward the highway that would take them back to Warsaw, and Jesse had no clue what to expect when they got home. It wouldn't surprise him to find a pre-packed suitcase waiting for him at the front door. Hell, maybe the damn thing was in the trunk and rather than heading to the house, she intended on ditching him at the Greyhound station or a cheap motel.

He managed to hold his tongue for a good five minutes, but his willpower eventually gave way. "I don't know what happened." It was a confession made of desperation. Because if he was going to get through this, he needed LouEllen's help.

But she didn't respond, at least not right away, and not with words. Holding fast to her silence, another minute went by before she pulled the car over onto the shoulder of the highway. She slid the gearshift into park and pressed her hands to her face. Jesse stared into his lap as Lou's sobs nudged him toward his own emotional breakdown.

"What is this?" she finally asked. She took a rough swipe at her eyes, angry at herself for being so weak. "What the hell *is* this?" she repeated, shooting him an imploring look. "How can this have happened, Jesse? *How?*"

His mouth went bitter at her questions, because she was asking the same things Bad Cop Mel had been firing off at him all night long. They were inquiries that pointed the finger, that said *this makes no sense, there must be something more.*

"I don't know," Jesse said softly. "Casey just..." He hesitated, not sure where that thought was going, afraid of where it might lead. "I don't know, Lou. I really don't."

"Blaire," LouEllen said, and then burst into tears again.

Yes, Blaire. Straight-forward, sophisticated, not-belonging-in-Warsaw Blaire. She and Lou were as close as sisters, and both were small-town anomalies. Neither one of them should have existed in a place so bleak, so dead-end. But now, Blaire would change. Bleak was what she would become. Warsaw would swallow her whole, and she'd let it unless Lou could keep it from happening. And Jesse knew better than anyone that Lou would fight for her friend until she had no fight left.

Fighting for friends: it's what Jesse should have done for Casey after Reed had died. Regardless of their differences, he should have fought harder for an answer. It would have been easy to say that he should have helped Casey more, but that would have been inaccurate, because Jesse hadn't helped him at all. He'd turned away not only from Casey, but from everyone. He'd zeroed in on the bottle and, rather than being strong, attempted to drown himself instead. Selfish, as though his pain was paramount above all else; as though nobody could have possibly understood how he was feeling, because nobody the world over had ever experienced the suicide of a friend.

Back then, LouEllen had pulled him out of his self-made mire.

But now, he was sure she'd let him sink down into it until he was hopelessly stuck. Both Ian and Blaire would keep her busy and her rage would keep her at a distance. She'd have no time left for him. No patience for any more of his bullshit. No desire to fix what she no longer wanted to keep. Eventually, he'd be up to his chin in sorrow. And then, one day, that misery would render him invisible.

"Is this some sort of weird…" She searched for the right word, but she couldn't find it.

"Some sort of weird what?" Jesse asked.

"I don't know," Lou whispered down to her hands.

"Pact?" Jesse asked, tossing Bad Cop Mel's word choice into her lap.

She fell into another bout of silence, but for Jesse, it was enough of an answer. He turned, focusing out the window and into the darkness. This was a rural highway, one that folks didn't often take after dark. He and Lou had yet to see a single car pass them from the time they'd pulled onto that ribbon of road. He considered getting out, telling LouEllen to leave him there, and walking down the broken center line. He'd spot headlights after a while, and he'd see them long before they ever saw him. A sixty mile per hour impact would obliterate a human being. Chances of survival: zero.

The idea of it made him go numb, because here he was, thinking of repeating the cycle mere hours after Casey had erased himself. It was a thought that, up until that moment, hadn't ever crossed his mind before. Not even during the summer after his senior year. And yet, somehow, it struck him as both insane and enticing. There was something seductive about the idea of being strewn across a dark and lonely highway, surrounded by blood and snow.

But that would be suicide, he told himself. *That would prove that Bad Cop Mel was right, that there was some sort of dark deal.*

"You think I'd sign a goddamned suicide pact?" he asked, the words sounding far harsher than they had inside his head. But really, what was this? Was she seriously asking him if he'd made some sort of death deal with Casey and Reed? And was he genuinely imagining himself smeared onto the pavement?

Lou began to cry again. But this time, rather than breaking his heart, all it did was make him grit his teeth. Because she hadn't responded with a clipped and immediate *of course not*. She was asking him a preposterous question, suggesting he was involved in some bizarre blood bond with two now-dead guys, a bond that trumped his love for her, for their son. And she wasn't reassuring him that everything was going to be okay, that they just had to get through this and things would get back to the way they'd once been.

"I didn't want to go," he told her. "*You* told me to."

"I know." She said sharply. "I *know*, Jesse. Don't remind me."

"Then why would you think—?"

"I don't know!" She just about screamed the words. He winced and turned away. "All I know is that both Reed and Casey are gone, that they both killed themselves in the same house, and that you were there both times, okay? All I know is that you're the only one left. So, what now?" she asked. "Are you next? Is *this* what I have to look forward to? Should I worry every time you come home late from work? Should I wonder if—"

"Okay, enough," Jesse said. Sure, he'd been thinking the same thing just a few seconds prior, Lou just had the guts to ask the question out loud. But hearing those words was too much right now. "You sound like that cop back in Zion," he said. "He asked me if I was a devil worshipper. A *Satanist*, Lou. Is that what you think, too? Has this place warped your mind so thoroughly that you—"

"Warped my mind?" She twisted her face up, appalled at his suggestion.

"I told you, we need to get the hell out of here," he said, because that's what it came down to. The place. The town. "Places like this are toxic," he told her. "You start thinking dead-end thoughts in a dead-end town, and before you know it, you're just like them."

"Like *them*..." LouEllen echoed.

"Ian can't grow up here. Not with these people. Not like this."

"Like what?" she asked, her tone sharpened to a razor's edge. "Like how *we* grew up around *these* people? Because *we* ended up so terribly? Is that it?"

Jesse exhaled a breath.

"And even if I did say *fine, let's go*, how?" she asked. "How is it that you propose we get out? With what money? The millions of dollars we have in our savings account? The fortune they're paying you at the elite institution of Warsaw High?"

That stung, but she wasn't wrong. They had less than six hundred bucks saved for a rainy day, and Jesse's job was a joke. Their house was a money pit that nobody would ever consider buying without serious renovations, which they couldn't afford. And even if they could, who the hell was moving to Warsaw? Nobody. Until they had some cash-in-hand, they were stuck.

But it seemed that the only way to make real money in a place like Warsaw was to look past the town like Casey had. And while Jesse wasn't about to try his hand at social media stardom...

"I can write that book," he said. "Write it, sell it, use the advance to get us out of here, even if it's just to Detroit."

LouEllen curled her fingers around the steering wheel and shut her eyes. He'd seen her do the very thing when Ian—wailing and thrashing and strapped into his car seat—refused to be consoled.

"Writing and selling a book isn't easy, Jesse," she said evenly—an adult explaining the ways of the world to a naïvely optimistic kid. "You know that."

"I know," he said. "But what else is there?"

It was then that she looked at him, and that's when he saw it: the hurt, the fear. She was scared for them, afraid of what the future held. Less than a year ago, pregnant and excited, things had been brighter than ever. Now, they couldn't have been more different.

"Look, I know my job sucks," he said. "I can't keep teaching at that place forever, not if we ever want to send Ian to college. Hell, at this point we can't even afford daycare."

Lou smirked down at her lap in agreement. She knew as well as he did that their finances were in shambles.

"You know we can't stay in Warsaw much longer. But moving will take time. Maybe I'd be able to get a degree if I drove out to the community college and took classes part-time, but that means I'd have to work part-time, too, and we can't afford that."

"No," she murmured. "We can't."

"And I *could* study in the evenings after I've graded papers, but we sure as hell can't afford to pay tuition to one of those online schools. You've got your hands full with Ian. But me, I may as well try to do *something*, Lou."

"And what are you going to write about?" she asked, turning back to the steering wheel.

He didn't respond for a long while, not sure what he'd do if she threw her hands up and told him she found the whole idea disgustingly morbid. He didn't know what he'd say if she accused him of trying to cash in on the deaths of his two closest friends. But he didn't see the point of keeping it a secret, either. Eventually, she'd read the manuscript. She'd know.

"The house," he said.

She glanced up. But rather than the scowl Jesse was expecting, her face was nothing short of a mask of frightened hesitation. The question flickered across her features, plain as day. *Are you sure?*

"You're right about the closure," he told her. "I've needed it for a long time."

She looked down again, frowning at her lap. He reached across the center console and took one of her hands into his own.

"Lou," he said. "It's going to be okay."

And it had to be. He didn't know how, but he had to make it so.

EIGHT

JESSE SPENT the next few days floating from one tiny room of his house to another. LouEllen called the school, and Garvey insisted on a full week of emergency family leave. The principal didn't want Jesse there as much as Lou didn't want him going in. It would have freaked out the students; a zombie roaming the halls.

LouEllen dedicated most of her daylight hours to either Blaire or Carrie Mae. Blaire was in shambles, and Lou spent a lot of time making tea and sitting on one of Blaire's many couches while watching *Real Housewives* reruns.

Carrie Mae was more for Ian's benefit. The kid had a lot of toys at his aunt's place. There was even a Pack n' Play he was happy to nap in when he wasn't terrorizing Carrie Mae's cat, Alabaster.

Either way, LouEllen wasn't home much in those first few days, and she always took Ian with her. It left the house hauntingly quiet. Nothing but Jesse sitting at his desk for hours, staring at the pulsing cursor of his word processing program. Sometimes he'd actually try to write. But mostly, he'd peer out the window and fixate on the spot where Casey had parked his Impala the night he'd stopped by.

When his back started to ache from sitting in his wooden desk chair, he'd move to the couch and fixate on a blank television screen. Sometimes he'd fall asleep. Other times he'd blink and it would be three hours later—everything the same save for the light outside. No LouEllen. No Ian. Just an unnerving silence so loud it made his ears ring.

And the idea of losing time? It made him want to crawl out of his own skin. He tried to get out of the house every now and again, if only to keep his head on straight. He'd bundle up and take Winston for a walk along their unplowed road. But by the time they'd reach the end of the block, Jesse would be half-frozen and didn't feel much like walking anymore. And even though Lou stocked the fridge with leftovers and pre-made casseroles, he subsided on little more than chocolate toast and pitchers of coffee so burnt it put the stuff in the teacher's lounge to shame.

It was on Friday—close to a week after Casey's death—that LouEllen came home sans baby. She held a sack of Mister Frosty burgers instead, four words that could damn any marriage dripping from her lips.

"We need to talk."

Sitting at the kitchen table across from his wife, she passed him a hamburger wrapped in red-and-white gingham-checked paper. It was the same design the restaurant had used since he was a kid; the same stuff he had slapped around sandwiches coming off the grill during his high school days.

He stared at his dinner, wondering how different his life would have been had he made more of an effort, if he had found a few more friends. If he hadn't chickened out of joining the drama club his sophomore year, perhaps he wouldn't have been in the backseat of Casey's car the night of Reed's suicide. Maybe he would have been playing *Vampire the Masquerade* in some drama geek's basement. Or, perhaps, he would have been home in his room, bleeding onto the keys of his desktop computer, going over his prose with meticulous precision, maybe even writing a play. If he had focused on his writing rather than dicking around with Reed and Casey, he might have made something of himself by now. He'd at least have had an easier time of filling the page now, that was for damn sure. Writing would have been a nice change of pace from sitting in front of his laptop with absolutely nothing to show for it. Being able to focus on something creative rather than replaying Casey's suicide on a loop would have been great. Hell, if Jesse had the opportunity to turn back time to that fateful summer night, he'd have erased himself from the equation entirely. Instead of finding Reed dead in the foyer and watching Casey fling himself over the same goddamn banister twenty years later, Jesse would have simply lost their friendship in one fell swoop. Like ripping off a Band-Aid.

"So, Blaire…" LouEllen said after a long while.

That name made Jesse's stomach sink. He let his elbows hit the table top and pressed his face into his hands. A moment later, LouEllen's fingers grazed his arm.

"She doesn't blame you, Jesse," she said. "If anything, Blaire blames herself."

"Why?" he asked. "She wasn't there. I was."

"She said Casey had been acting differently. I mean, we all noticed it, didn't we? The way he showed up here unannounced, or how quiet he was the past few times we had gone over to visit. Something was bothering him for the past couple of weeks."

The truth of it was, Jesse hadn't noticed. Had anyone asked, he would have answered with absolute certainty that Casey was the same Casey he'd always been. He had only become aware of just how disturbed Casey had seemed when the guy had literally knocked on his door asking for help. How was *that* for a good friend?

"She's asked if you'd say a few words at the funeral," LouEllen said.

Jesse shook his head. "No." It was an immediate, knee-jerk response.

"Jesse…"

"We weren't even that close anymore," he said. "He just asked me to go with him because of that night, because of Reed."

"I don't believe that," Lou said. And neither did Jesse, no matter how much he wished he did.

The more he mulled it over, the less sense it made. Casey *must* have had a reason for wanting Jesse to go back to that house with him. Jesse's presence had meant something beyond Casey not wanting to go alone. And yet, the more Jesse sought answers, the foggier everything became. It was easier to shrug it off, to forget there must have been some hidden link, to blame it on Casey—little more than a guy at the end of his rope, driven to kill himself by the memory of a dead best friend.

"You didn't know him the way I did," Jesse murmured.

"Maybe not," LouEllen said, pushing the Mister Frosty bag away from them as if suddenly disgusted by the idea of food. Winston, on the other hand, was a champion stress-eater. Patiently sitting on the kitchen rug, he was wondering if maybe LouEllen would forgo the bag and dump the whole shebang into his bowl, which was appropriately marked DOG FOOD.

"But you went to that place with him, anyway," Lou continued. "You did what only a true, good friend would have done. He was searching for something, some magical answer, a silver bullet—the thing you say doesn't exist, remember?"

He remembered. Jesse used the silver bullet metaphor in class all the time.

There's no ultimate solution. No perfect way to solve your problems.

And if there was no panacea, no cure-all to *any* of life's quandaries, then it meant there was no answer to why Reed and Casey had done what they had.

"You went there with him to show him that he had to move on," LouEllen reminded him, but was *that* why he had gone? "If that isn't being a friend, I don't know what is," she said. He knew she meant it to be a comfort, but all it did was leave a foul, penny-like taste across his tongue.

"It doesn't matter," he finally said. "It was too late."

I want to show you something: Reed's words, Casey's voice, both of which were now but a memory.

"That wasn't your fault," she said, squeezing his hand in reassurance. "You tried, you did what you could. He's gone, you're right. But it's time to stop thinking about Casey and start thinking about the people who are left, and one of those people is my best friend. Blaire asked if you would speak, Jesse. Consider it a favor."

"A favor to her?" Jesse asked, continuing to frown at the table top.

He could just barely make out a small, sticky handprint against the varnish. It made him miss Ian. It also made him wonder what phantom reminders of Casey Blaire was coming across every minute of every day while locked inside that big empty house. Jesus, he hadn't even bothered to offer his condolences to Reed's parents after-the-fact. Undoubtedly, those two had been finding reminders of their son for the last two decades.

"A favor to me," LouEllen said. "You said you're going to write to find closure. I think that's a good idea. But use your gift to help Blaire find closure, too."

And to that, Jesse could hardly say no.

NINE

THAT EVENING, LouEllen spent the night at Carrie Mae's. Ian had been there all day, and before Lou had a chance to pick him up, he'd fallen asleep for the night. So, she packed a small bag, grabbed her toothbrush, and drove to her sister's place, leaving Jesse alone in the house yet again.

The previous couple of nights hadn't been easy. Jesse had loaded up on Tylenol PM to knock himself out, which had resulted in dreamless sleep—a restless unconsciousness that left him in a mental fog. But LouEllen had promised to bring Ian home the next morning, and Jesse didn't want to be half-doped when his son arrived. Tonight, he skipped the meds and laid down in the bedroom, leaving himself open to the full sting of any nightmares that may have been creeping around the perimeter of his subconscious mind.

And oh, did they creep.

He found himself standing on the road leading up to the farmhouse, staring at the cockeyed shell of a building just as he had as a kid. His Schwinn was there, propped against the broken front porch steps. It was next to two bicycles he would have recognized anywhere: Reed's red Huffy and Casey's black BMX.

Someone yelled his name.

Jesse!

His chin jerked upward, and his gaze climbed the tall turret to the house's towering roofline. It was there that he saw both Casey and Reed precariously balanced upon the roof's steeply pitched top ridge. They were tiptoeing along the seam, their arms jutting out and their legs wobbly. They came off like a couple of amateur tight-rope walkers waiting for little more than a gust of wind.

Come on up! An eleven-year-old Reed yelled down to Jesse.

We want to show you something! Casey said.

Both their tones were cheerful, as though they were having the time of their lives up there.

Don't be a chicken, Reed said.

Don't be a drag, Casey told him.

It's just for shits and giggles, Reed explained.

And for her, Casey added, pointing down at Jesse from high above.

Jesse looked down at their bikes, then back up at his two friends. For her? What did he mean by that?

For who? Jesse yelled up at them.

For her! They replied in unison, now both pointing at Jesse.

That was when he felt it—that skin-prickling sensation of someone standing behind him, of boring a hole into the back of his neck with an unwavering stare. He swallowed against the thudding of his heart, because surely this was the part where he turned and saw whomever they were referring to. This was the part where he saw some terrifying figure lurking behind him.

But before he could glance over his shoulder, his attention snapped back to the roof just in time to see Reed and Casey leap from their perch.

Jesse screamed as he watched both his friends fly through the air. Screamed as a noose Jesse hadn't noticed until then yanked Casey back, snapping his neck with a wet sort of crack. Screamed as Reed hit the ground next to their bikes, head-first in the dirt. He cried out as he turned to run down the road and away from that place. But rather than falling into a sprint, he froze instead.

Because there she was. The girl in white.

Her face rotten and fetid.

Her smile a black crescent moon.

Jesse screamed and bolted upright, sure he'd see that terrible countenance snarling at him from the foot of his bed.

But there was nobody there. Just him with the blankets pooled around his waist and Winston giving him a dubious look from his dog bed in the corner.

"Jesus Christ," he whispered. "Jesus *fucking* Christ." His pulse was pounding hard enough to make him queasy. He shut his eyes and tried to find some equilibrium, attempting to curtail his unease. "You're okay. You're okay." He was fine. It was just his mind trying to purge itself of all that trauma. Just his psyche trying to heal.

He grabbed his cell off the bedside table and checked the time. It was Saturday morning, just after three AM. He had one day to get his thoughts together and compose himself before Casey's service, and he had yet to write a single word of the eulogy.

He got up, went to the kitchen, put on a pot of coffee, and collapsed onto the couch with his laptop across his knees. Staring at a blank Word document he'd left open on his machine, the cursor blinked at him without remorse.

My friend killed himself because he was haunted: he typed it out, then deleted it.

My friend killed himself in front of me. Delete.

My friend killed himself in front of me because my other friend failed to kill himself in front of me. Delete.

My friend killed himself because of her.

The coffeemaker beeped. Jesse pinched the bridge of his nose, tossed the laptop onto the couch cushion beside him, and got up to pour himself a cup.

Winston wandered into the living room and curled up on his second dog pillow, which had been relegated to the corner next to the TV. It had been LouEllen's idea. Winston needed a bed *and* a 'couch' since he wasn't allowed on the furniture. She spoiled that dog, not that Winston was undeserving. He was a good boy, comfortable now, upside-down with his long ears flopped outward like Dumbo the Flying Elephant. He served as a reminder that some things were still the way they'd always been, that the daily grind—like endless naps and sleeping with four paws straight up in the air— would prevail. Jesse just had to get through this. He had to press on.

He retook his seat, took a sip of his coffee, and pulled his computer back onto his lap. Turning back to his screen, he clicked out of the word processing program and found himself typing CASEY RIDGEMONT into Google's search bar. It brought up links to Casey's website, his YouTube channel, his Instagram account, and a Wikipedia page. There was a short profile on the right, complete with Casey's portrait, his birthdate, and the day he had died. Jesse frowned at that last bit of information. Clearly, someone in Warsaw had taken it upon themselves to tell the world Casey had passed away, and it didn't feel right, like an invasion of privacy. Casey's funeral hadn't even happened, and yet there it was, splashed across the Internet.

Then again, Casey had probably provided most of the information on that page himself, from his height and weight to his spouse's middle name. Everything except for the date of his death.

Unless he had known.

Unless he'd updated the page before he had...

Don't be an idiot, Jesse thought. *There's no way. No possible way.*

Looking away from Casey's smiling photo, Jesse moved his cursor over the YouTube link and clicked. There were hundreds of videos. Casey's name was featured in bold at the top of the page, right below a beautiful header image of an abandoned building located somewhere in Detroit. The last video he had posted was titled MICHIGAN FARMHOUSE, PART FOUR.

Part four?

As far as Jesse understood, Casey had a strict policy of one-and-done. *You'd be surprised how many people you'd swear have ADHD,* Casey had explained during a celebratory backyard barbecue. He had just reached over a million subscribers. *They're click-happy. Hell, posting a video longer than ten minutes is treading into dangerous territory. Revisiting the same location and posting multiple videos? Not a chance.*

Casey had known the importance of novelty. He had understood that sequels weren't as successful as the original. And then there was the fact that this was a farmhouse, which wasn't typical of Casey's industrial locale. But that was all rendered irrelevant beneath the veil of a single, disturbing detail. Casey had posted the video days before he had shown up on Jesse's doorstep, practically begging Jesse to go with him to that house. He had said he hadn't wanted to go alone, but he'd gone by himself on four separate occasions. Which meant it had all been bullshit.

Casey had been lying.

Jesse had been duped.

A spark of anger ignited behind his breastplate, but it wasn't enough to quell his hesitation. His pointer hovered over the video link. *Don't be so yellow.* Eventually, he clicked it.

His heart stuck in his throat at the opening montage. There were a few gorgeous shots of the spent field surrounding the house. It glowed in the warm light of a Michigan sunset. There was the rutted road, golden-cast despite the tell-tale signs of winter. And then, of course, there was the eerie exterior of the house itself, all taken by drone. It was like watching the opening credits of a horror movie, complete with ominous music and slow panning shots.

The images then shifted from the exterior of the house to the inside, which had been taken during the day. The dusty light caught walls of peeling paint and the rickety staircase was almost romantic as the shot panned upward from the first floor to second to third, slow and steady like a flawless dolly zoom. And finally, there was Casey, sitting on the broken front porch steps.

Hey explorers, he began.

Jesse had seen some of these videos before. In them, Casey had always been witty and charismatic, just the way he tended to be in person. But in the footage Jesse was viewing now, Casey looked tired and anxious.

I know it's weird that I'm back here again, Casey told the camera, *but sometimes a place grabs hold of you, and this one's got me in a vice grip.*

But Jesse couldn't concentrate. He kept looking away from the footage to the post date beneath it. He clicked out of the video, suddenly feeling unsure. Twisting his fingers around his mouth, he shot a look toward his sleeping dog, then turned back to the screen again. If it hadn't been the middle of the night, he would have grabbed his cell and called Lou. She had followed Casey's stuff more regularly than Jesse ever had. Did she know about this farmhouse video series? Was she aware that Casey had been filming there for nearly a month before he had ended his life?

Doubtful, he thought. Ian was a handful, toeing the line of toddlerhood. Lou had complained more than a few times about how the kid was starting to test her, beginning to push boundaries. Meltdowns were Ian's new normal, and his naps were terrible—forty-five minutes at best. It left LouEllen with little time for anything but motherhood. *You know, maybe it makes me a bad mom,* she had complained, *but sometimes I just want to sit down and catch up on my shows. Sometimes, I wish I could take the damn nap for him.* No, Lou didn't know about this footage. She would have said something. And she certainly wouldn't have pressured Jesse to go back to that house.

He didn't want to, but he clicked on the video labeled PART ONE anyway. Because, maybe if he watched the entire series, it would all make some kind of sense. The ten-minute clip opened with the same drone footage. When it circled back to Casey, it became clear just how fast he had spiraled downhill. In the previous video, Casey had been hollow-eyed and pale, but in the first clip—filmed only three weeks before the last—Casey was lively, if maybe a little manic.

Hey explorers, he began. *Today we're at an abandoned Michigan farmhouse. This place has been a part of my life for as long as I can remember. I rode my bike up here with friends as a kid, and I lost a friend just inside these walls during high school. It's haunted me ever since, haunted me beyond what you'd expect. This isn't just grief I'm talking about. This is something else.*

Casey's narration played over an image of him ducking past the farmhouse's broken front door. It continued over slow, sweeping shots of empty rooms that Jesse had never been brave enough to explore. There was the living room, which he'd caught a glimpse of from the foyer. The massive fireplace and silhouette of a missing crucifix above it was like something out of The Exorcist. That view lingered long enough to make Jesse squirm in his seat; a purposeful choice by the filmmaker, no doubt. Nobody could say that Casey didn't do his job well.

There was a kitchen which, to Jesse's surprise, still housed a few items the former residents had left behind. Rusty metal containers labeled SUGAR and BREAD. Stacks of unopened tin cans inside mold-ridden cabinets. There was a round breakfast table that reminded Jesse of the one in his own kitchen, surrounded by wooden chairs. Some of them were upright, and some had been toppled, as though pushed over in a rush.

You guys know this isn't a ghost show, Casey explained while moving up the staircase. *And you all know I'm a skeptic.* The camera zoomed in on a couple of phantom crosses, their impressions forever burned into the house's brittle wallpaper. *But man,* he said, *the energy in this place is something else. There's something—*

His words stopped short. The camera swerved around, quick and jostled, completely unlike Casey's smooth and deliberate filming style. First, the shot panned down the stairs to where he had come from. Then the lens tipped up, as though searching for the source of whatever it was Casey had just heard. The video caught the sound of his breath hitching ragged in his throat.

I don't know if you were able to hear that, he said after a while. *It sounded like... like footsteps, I guess? Like someone running from one room to the other.* He paused as if listening again. A few beats later, he continued to move up the risers, continued to speak. *Every time I come back here, I feel like I've had...I don't know,* he stammered. *I guess all I can call it is an "experience."*

Jesse narrowed his eyes at that statement. *Every* time? How many times had Casey gone back to that house, exactly? Sure, he'd admitted to driving there on more than a few occasions. He'd confessed to sitting in his car and staring at the house's empty windows the way one would fixate on a name etched into a gravestone. But the idea of Casey just hanging out in his junk-riddled Impala didn't sit right. That wasn't Casey's style.

This house is like nothing I've ever felt before, Casey continued. *It's terrifying and addictive, which is why I keep coming back. At first, I couldn't stop thinking about it because of what had happened here. But now, I can't get it out of my head, period. I think about it. I dream about it. All I do is sit in the library or on my computer looking things up about it. It's like I'm...I don't know. Obsessed.*

It's like he was Reed.

Nothing significant happened in the video beyond Casey's sudden pause. Nothing save for the fact that Jesse now understood what he previously hadn't. Casey had been visiting the farmhouse on the regular, even before he'd filmed his first video. And then he'd been bold enough to post them onto his channel, somehow sure that neither Jesse, LouEllen or Blaire would catch him in his lie.

Because nobody paid attention, Jesse thought. *We all should have known.*

Perhaps it had been a test, a silent question: *should I go through with it?* Had someone noticed, there would have been a discussion. Casey had sounded alarms. He'd been foreshadowing his final curtain call for weeks.

Jesse twisted the fingers of his left hand against his mouth, his right guiding the pointer over the video titled PART TWO.

According to the post date, Casey had waited two weeks to go back. The second video was even less remarkable than the first. And yet, he had filmed part three and four in rapid succession, as though he couldn't have stopped himself from returning even if he had tried. By the fourth installment, it was obvious: if this escapade had started out as a test to see how long it would take anyone to notice what he was doing, it had morphed into an assessment of how far he could push himself. It was clear that Casey didn't want to keep wandering through those rooms. He seemed genuinely spooked, his breathing rapid and the camera-work less than stellar. And yet, he kept going, as though something was drawing him further into the house, further up the staircase to the uppermost floor. He kept going until, to Jesse's horror, that fourth story landing came into view.

I don't know why I'm here, he kept saying. *I don't know why I'm here.*

Jesse felt nauseous when the camera panned to Casey's feet. Casey pointed the lens down over the banister. It was the very place from which he had jumped.

At first, there was nothing to see at the bottom of the stairwell. Evening had fallen and the spotlight on Casey's camera wasn't powerful enough to cut through four flights of darkness. It was only when the view switched to that off-putting white-and-green night vision that Reed's broken foyer floorboards came clear.

"Jesus Christ," Jesse murmured, his pointer hovering over the PAUSE button.

But then, there was a blip of something else.

Something white darting out of the shot.

What the hell was that? Casey jerked away from the banister with shaky steps.

It could have been anything, and the lengthy comment section below the video made sure to hammer that point home. Animal. Vagrant. Nothing but a setup to attract more views. Or, hey, maybe it really was a ghost. Some commentators loved it while others were less than amused.

I thought you were the real deal, Ridgemont, one person wrote. *But you're nothing but a ghost hunter sellout. Way to ruin a good thing, bro!*

Wow. Just wow, wrote another. *I know those haunted places shows are popular, but this is something else. Unsubscribing!*

Jesse reversed the video, replaying the rush of that mysterious white streak over and over despite his own malaise. He tried to slow it down, tried to pause it at just the right moment to make out what the hell that flash of white had been. And then he remembered Casey's last words.

Tell me if you see her.

Jesse suddenly sat up straight as a rod. He snapped his laptop closed.

...if you see her.

The girl in the upstairs window.

The girl in his dream, standing right behind him, as if waiting for the third musketeer to arrive.

"Bullshit," he whispered, then shoved his laptop aside. He grabbed his coffee mug, threw back the cold and bitter dregs, and rose from his seat. He wasn't sure why, but he was suddenly angry—mad enough to smash something. Peering at his mug, his fingers tightened their hold around its handle. He considered hurling it to the floor if only to hear the ceramic explode.

He made his way back to the kitchen, slammed his mug against the base of the sink, and gripped the counter as he glared out the small window overlooking the backyard. All at once, he was compelled to get the hell out of the house, to throw on his shoes and coat and go somewhere. Anywhere.

The bar.

His mouth went dry at the thought of a drink. He needed something to take the edge off. Just one shot. Hell, he'd even take a lousy Busch or Keystone Light. Anything was better than nothing at all.

He marched out of the kitchen and to the bedroom in search of his sneakers. It would be a quick trip. Half an hour tops.

Except, as soon as he stepped into the room, Ian's bassinet caught his attention. Ian no longer slept in that thing, but it remained in the master bedroom as a catch-all for LouEllen's discarded clothes. In only a handful of hours, Lou would be back with the baby and finally, *finally*, they would try to get back to the way things had been.

But not if Jesse fucked this up.

Not if he undid all the hard work he'd put in so long ago.

He exhaled a shaky breath. "You can do this," he told himself, then crawled back into bed and pulled the sheets over his head. It was doubtful he'd be able to get back to sleep—not after that nightmare, and definitely not after the realizations he had made. But it didn't matter. Like a kid hiding from the boogeyman, he pulled his pillow to his chest and shut out the world.

Because if he could just hold out until sunrise, he'd be safe.

That was, after all, how nightmares worked.

TEN

CASEY'S FUNERAL felt just as alien as Reed's had.

Jesse sat in one of the front pews with LouEllen's hand in his, staring down at his lap while a pastor gave a sermon about everlasting love and the joy of happy memories. He could hear people sniffling, some of them weeping into crumpled wads of Kleenex. Meanwhile, Blaire sat stoically on LouEllen's opposite side. There had been an open casket viewing an hour before the service, but Jesse hadn't been able to stomach it. He'd done it for Reed, and he refused to ever do it again.

Reed's viewing had been held in a room just big enough to stuff twenty people in at a time. Cramped with strangers at his elbows, Jesse had looked down at what had appeared to be a wax figure lying where his best friend should have been. He remembered concentrating on the strangest, smallest details, like the fact that he could see where Reed's hands had been glued together, one on top of the other. The funeral director had given a strange, powdery look to Reed's hair, as though it had been dusted with talc before Reed was put on display. Jesse's mother had encouraged him to go to the viewing in case he regretted not doing it later. That day, Jesse learned that when it came to Reed's lifeless body, the only regret he ended up with was that he'd listened to his mom.

The pastor ended Casey's sermon by playing a Jack White song through the church's PA system. It was a lullaby-like melody that tore sobs right out of a few ladies' chests. When the song came to an end, LouEllen clasped Jesse's hand and gave him a brave smile. *You can do this.* After a beat of hesitation, Jesse rose from where he sat and approached Casey's casket. It was so laden with flowers it just about disappeared beneath sprays of white lilies and gladioli.

He had crushed the paper he'd brought with him in his fist during the pastor's prayer. Now, he smoothed it across the podium, cleared his throat, and kept his gaze averted. And that was it. One minute he was up there, nervous and wondering if the folks in the back could hear him. The next, he was sitting beside LouEllen again, his head feeling buoyant like a child's balloon.

"You did great," she whispered, assuring him that he hadn't, in his torpor, gone completely off the rails. But Jesse couldn't remember any of it. He'd lost time again, just like at home.

After the service, a woman Jesse didn't know caught his hands in hers and patted him with bony, bird-like fingers. "Wonderful speech, dear. Thank you," she said. "You're a wonderful writer. You should write a book."

Jesse forced a smile and murmured his thanks, wondering if she was making the comment because she knew he had cribbed the entire eulogy off a random website. In the end, he'd gone looking online for something that sounded nice, something that he modified to make it more like what he would have written. He had tried to compose the speech himself, but words failed him, as they always did these days.

He waited outside the funeral home while LouEllen chatted with a few of the guests. He could hear her offering sweetly-worded condolences to people she hardly knew, patting folks on their backs and giving hugs to those who needed one.

Jesse spoke to no one. He just stood there, bleary-eyed and shivering, watching the woman who had told him he was an excellent writer make her way to a vehicle that didn't match her slight physique. Rather than driving a boat of an Oldsmobile or Buick, the woman stopped next to a beat-up Ford pickup truck. It was old, probably made in the '50s or '60s, and cherry red. Before she pulled out of the parking lot, she met Jesse's stare. The glare of the sun coming off her window blinded him, making what Jesse was sure was the old woman's smile look like a tooth-bared snarl.

When Blaire finally surfaced in her black dress and matching hat, she was flanked by a couple Jesse assumed were her parents. They escorted her out of the place and to an awaiting car without Blaire ever glancing up. LouEllen reappeared at Jesse's elbow a moment later and sighed.

"We'll see her at the wake," Jesse told her. "Just give her some room."

"Yeah," she said, nodding in agreement. "I guess you're right."

Jesse considered asking her who the old lady had been but decided against it. Instead, the two trekked to their car in solemn silence. Once inside the Altima, Lou looked at him from the passenger's seat and spoke.

"Christ, I feel terrible," she groaned.

"I know," he said.

"No, I mean..." She fidgeted. "I didn't eat breakfast, did you? Do you think there will be food, or should we stop and get something first?"

She was so sincere that Jesse actually laughed. It was his old LouEllen; a brief glimpse of his past life flashing before his eyes. And he couldn't have been happier to see her.

Of course, there was food. A ton of it.

As soon as they arrived, LouEllen gave Jesse's hand a squeeze and wandered off, desperate to check on Blaire. That left Jesse in front of a table full of meats and cheeses, which was fine by him. He lingered there, if only to avoid conversation, then took his plate and found a place to sit.

He ate his cheese and crackers and eavesdropped on conversations. There was a story about how Casey had broken his arm while rollerblading as a kid, a joke about how terrible he had been at math, a memory of his awful stint at driver's ed, and a recollection of the time he'd lost his pizza delivery job because he'd gotten hungry and eaten the order. Someone brought up the fact that, as a child, Casey had dreamed of becoming either a bus driver or a garbage man. Photos were circling the room, snapshots that someone had blown up to five-by-sevens for the occasion. Casey's YouTube videos streamed onto a large television in the living room, muted. No doubt his last four entries were left off the rotation.

Occasional bouts of laughter were peppered by sobs and muffled *I'm sorrys*. Jesse searched the crowd for the lady who had squeezed his hand and thanked him for his speech, but he didn't see her; missing, just like LouEllen and Blaire.

"Hey, you're Jesse, right?"

Jesse blinked up at a guy who had stopped a few feet in front of him. He didn't recognize the stranger until the guy pointed at him with two fingers, like a pair of loaded guns. *Pow*. The gesture matched the guy's classy getup; a blazer tossed over an Affliction t-shirt, acid-washed jeans paired with Timberland boots. It took a moment, but it eventually came back to him. Suddenly, Jesse knew exactly who this guy used to be.

"Rick Marshall," Jesse said. "It's been a while."

"Nineteen years, man!" Rick said, as if Jesse could have possibly forgotten just how much time had passed. His enthusiasm felt inappropriate, as did the energetic extension of his right hand for a pseudo-high-fiving handshake. Jesse gave in and slapped Rick's palm anyway, if only to avoid an awkward moment of *thanks, but no thanks*.

Jesse had never liked Rick. Back in high school, Rick was the type to have an insult for every person and every occasion, even for those he considered friends. He was the dude who would call a girl fat and then get pissed that she couldn't take a joke. And yet, for whatever reason, he and Casey had hit it off. They hadn't been super-close, but close enough for Rick to watch Casey be put in the ground.

"So, what's up, man?" Rick asked, his inquiry as casual as if they'd run into each other at a grocery store rather than a wake. "How've you been?"

"You mean, other than this?" Jesse asked, motioning around the room, unable to keep the edge from creeping into his tone.

"Yeah, man." Rick shrugged as if to say *what's the big deal? People die all the time*.

"And other than Reed?" Jesse added, unabashed.

"Shit," Rick said, as though having altogether forgotten about Reed Lowell. "What the hell, right? Is everyone jumping off buildings or what? Who's next, you know? Not *me*, that's for sure." Rick grinned, but Jesse grimaced rather than laughed and Rick quickly raised his hands. "Hey, don't get pissed, man," he said. "Sometimes you've gotta look at the bright side. Silver lining and all that crap. Otherwise, you'll end up choking on the fumes."

Jesse didn't know what that was supposed to mean, but he assumed it was some deep and meaningful Rick Marshall truth.

"Yeah," Jesse said. "Right."

"Damn," Rick said, as if realizing where he was for the first time. He then turned back to Jesse, changing the subject to lighten the mood. "So, you still living in this shitkicker town? What do you do, man? What's your job?"

Jesse hesitated, unsure whether to continue this conversation or cut it off at the knees. But it was either that or excuse himself and aimlessly wander around the place. Inevitably, someone else would start the same sort of chitchat, and he'd find himself here all over again, wondering how to escape.

"I'm a teacher," Jesse said.

"A teacher." Rick took a long pause as if considering that response. A moment later, he was raising a skeptical eyebrow. "You mean, like, at *Warsaw?*"

"The very place," Jesse said, peering at his plate of cubed cheese and sliced salami.

"Wait." Rick squinted as if trying to remember something. "Weren't you, like, going to be a journalist or something. Or, no. No, hold on." He held up a hand as if to say *wait, it's coming back to me.* "A world-famous writer. Like, the next Stephen King."

Jesse smirked.

It was weird to Jesse that Rick remembered anything about him. They had, after all, never been friends. But he supposed there were stranger things than remembering details about the guy who'd been there when one of Warsaw's own had killed himself. And then there was the fact that most Warsaw Warriors were just happy to be done with school; forget college plans. But Jesse had been different, never quiet about his intention of getting out of Warsaw, of possibly getting the hell out of Michigan altogether. But even best-laid plans had a tendency of getting derailed, which was why Jesse wasn't signing hundreds of copies of a bestselling novel in every bookstore across America or giving a TED talk on the magic of fiction. It's why he was here, at Casey's funeral, talking to Rick goddamn Marshall.

"You were going to put Warsaw on the map, man," Rick said. "Take the world by storm."

"Yeah, well…" Jesse frowned down at his plate, not sure how to respond. He wasn't about to lay out his life story to this guy, wasn't planning on telling him that rather than moving to Ann Arbor to study writing, he had gotten piss-drunk off vodka spiked with Gatorade right here at home. And then there was the simple fact that Jesse no longer needed to put Warsaw on any map at all. Casey Ridgemont had taken care of that for him.

"Things don't always work out the way we plan," Jesse finally said.

It was, in his opinion, a perfect segue back to the situation at hand. The ball was in Rick's court, and his options were wide open. He could have said anything, from *yeah, no shit,* to *at least you aren't dead.* But instead of taking that route, Rick gave Jesse a weird sideways smile.

"You know what they say about teachers, though, right?" he asked. Had Jesse been standing rather than sitting, there was no doubt that Rick would have nudged an elbow into Jesse's ribs. "Those who can't do, teach."

Jesse's mouth went sour. For a second, he felt like launching out of his chair and punching this guy right in the teeth. Because who the hell did he think he was, anyway? But before he could squint in anger and come up with an appropriate response, his attention wavered. Blaire was making her way through the room, dodging condolences with her head tucked between her shoulders.

"Great talk," Jesse said, rising from his seat and brushing past Rick without a second glance. At that moment, approaching Blaire was an act of survival, an exit out of a painful tête-à-tête. But by the time she noticed him moving toward her, Jesse felt like it was a mistake. Because what was he supposed to say to her? *Hey, I know you're feeling lousy, but why don't you distract yourself from your grief for a minute and save me from the asshole behind me?* Or, no, even better. *Shit, I'm sorry I let your husband hang himself. Hope you aren't mad.*

"Blaire." Jesse managed an unsure smile.

"Jesse." Bundled in a pea coat Lou would have killed for, Blaire leaned in and gave him a light hug.

"Are you..." he hesitated, "I mean..." Jesus, this was a disaster. He closed his eyes and winced. "I'm sorry," he murmured. When he felt her hand land on his arm, he looked up at her again.

"It's fine," she said, her gaze meeting his. "I told Lou that I don't blame you, you know." She lowered her voice. "I'm just sorry you were there. I don't know what's wrong with this world anymore."

Jesse peered down to his feet, unsure of what to say. Before he could stop himself, he blurted out the first thing that came to mind.

"Do you think we could talk?"

Suddenly, it wasn't Casey who was seeking that nonexistent silver bullet. It was Jesse, searching for how it all could have been possible; how could two of his friends have killed themselves the way they had?

"Give me a moment?" Blaire asked.

"Sure," he said, taking a step away from her to give her room.

"Let's talk outside," she told him. "Five minutes."

Jesse nodded and then watched her duck out the front door.

When he finally stepped outside, he found her sitting on the front stoop, cowering against the wind. At first, she seemed not to notice him standing there as she smoked a cigarette. Her hand trembled against the cold. Meanwhile, her sockless feet were stuffed into a pair of black ballerina flats—about as appropriate as being barefoot in the snow. When she finally looked up, she motioned for him to take a seat next to her. He did as she requested, pulling his own coat high against his neck.

"So, this is pretty fucked up, isn't it?" she asked, breathing out a plume of smoke.

Of all the years he'd known her, he wasn't sure he'd ever heard her swear, and he'd certainly never seen her light up. Blaire peered out toward the long drive leading up to the house for a moment, both sides of the street lined with parked cars.

"I'll just come out and say it, because I'm sure you're wondering," she finally said, looking his way. "I spoke to the police. They aren't going to bother you about this."

Jesse shifted his weight upon the step, silent.

"I mean, they *might* bother you about the trespassing thing." She shrugged. "But I told them that was all Casey, that he was the one that dragged you there. Not like there isn't proof, you know? Just look him up online and there you go."

Jesse nodded, still hesitant to speak. But saying nothing felt inconsiderate, unappreciative. "You didn't have to do that," he finally told her.

"Yes, I did," Blaire said, taking a deep drag off her cigarette, then exhaling the smoke into the wind. "He pulled you into this. It was probably the most selfish thing he could have done to another person, let alone to a friend. But leave it to Casey…" She shook her head, then glared at the burning tip of her cig. "I have to at least try to make it right for you and LouLou, especially since I have no answers as to *why* he would have done what he did," she said, taking another pull of nicotine. "So, yeah, I *had* to do it."

"So, you know about the videos?" Jesse asked.

"The ones he took at the farmhouse?" She waved a hand, dismissing their existence.

"Did you know he was going there?" Jesse asked. "Did you see the posts before, you know…?"

"He'd mentioned it," she said. "But it wasn't like it was anything new. I don't know what it was about all those stupid abandoned buildings, about that house in general. He saw something in them, I guess." She shook her head and turned away. "I always hated him going to those places. The homeless. The asbestos. Just the general danger of it all. But you tend to shut up about those things when it pays the bills, and it certainly did that."

Jesse ducked his chin against his coat collar. He wasn't sure why, but he was tongue-tied by Blaire's sense of guilt. He had expected her to point the finger at him, to scream and pound her fists against his chest. *How could you let this happen? How?* But instead, here she was, protecting him from prosecution, whittling the situation down to the love of her own comfortable lifestyle, to her pretty shoes and fancy coat.

"I *did* tell him I thought his going back there was morbid," she said. "But he made it a project, and it had never been my style to get involved in any of that. He seemed unnerved, though," she said. "Something was bothering him. I asked him about it, but by the time he went to you he was hardly speaking to me anymore."

"Why is that?" Jesse asked.

"I don't know," she said. "He'd just gotten distant in the weeks before. When he wasn't visiting that godawful house with his camera, he was on his computer, or at the local library. He even drove out to Lansing. I guess they had some old papers and articles out there that he couldn't access online. He wouldn't even sleep upstairs anymore," she confessed. "Of the little sleep he did get, he'd just pass out on the couch. Sometimes, he'd wake up screaming."

Jesse frowned. "Screaming?"

"The first few times I ran downstairs thinking something had happened, you know? But every time I did, he told me to go back to bed. I'd ask him if he was okay and he'd get angry, as though he was insulted that I'd dare think he might need help." Blaire shrugged again, regretting that she brought it up. "I know what you're thinking," she said, the wind stealing some of the volume from her voice. "Why didn't I do anything? A man wakes up screaming from his sleep, he spits venom and tells you to screw off, you should look for a shrink, right?" She paused, took another drag. "But by then, he was different."

"How?" Jesse asked.

"It's hard to explain," she said. "He was just spooked all the time, like he'd seen something he couldn't shake."

They both went silent, then—Blaire recalling how her husband had changed, Jesse remembering how odd Casey had behaved when they'd stepped into the house together. He'd been almost loopy, like he hadn't been fully awake.

Jesse could sense that Blaire wasn't telling the whole story, however. He could feel that maybe—by the way she was weighing her words—she didn't want to flat-out admit that she'd been afraid of who her husband had become. Perhaps part of the distance had been created not just by Casey's bizarre behavior, but by Blaire's hesitation to confront him. She had been protecting herself, and nobody could blame her for that.

Blaire finally broke the silence. "Look, like I said, I don't have the answers. But I do have some advice, if you want it."

Jesse nodded. *Sure.*

"Move on," she said. "I know it sounds harsh, especially so soon after the fact, and it's definitely easier said than done. But don't dwell. Just...*move on.*"

What was she saying? For Jesse to forget about what had happened, forget what Casey had forced him to live through?

"Look," she said, "after what happened with Reed, Casey couldn't let it go. I know you were there, too, and now you have *this* to deal with. It's a lot. Nobody would say otherwise. But Casey couldn't move past it, and here we are." She motioned to the line of cars parked along the drive. "You know LouLou would die if something happened to you, right? She won't admit it, but she's terrified. As long as you push forward, things will get better for you. Move past this, Jesse. For your family. Forget this nightmare even exists."

"And if I can't?" he asked.

"You have to," she said. "Channel your energy. Distract yourself. Hell, take up smoking." She glanced down to her cigarette. "It tastes terrible, but believe it or not, it does wonders for the nerves."

Jesse nodded, worrying his bottom lip between his teeth.

"It's freezing out here," she said, flicking her cigarette aside. She rose to her feet and gave Jesse a thoughtful smile. "Just do me a favor, okay?" she asked. "For LouEllen?"

He craned his neck to look up at her.

"Don't start believing in ghosts," she said. "And whatever you do, don't do what Casey did. Don't ever go back to that house."

ELEVEN

WHEN JESSE finally went back to work, his classes were subdued. It was as though Principal Garvey had gone out of his way to tell Jesse's students to take it easy on him. Then again, there had been plenty of time for everyone to have heard about Casey's passing. A week of playing high school hallway *telephone* would inevitably result in twisted versions of the story, versions even darker than reality. And the only kernel of truth that would be left? That Jesse had, once again, been present at the scene.

From the look of a few of his students, those stories had spread fast. With their backs pressed flush against their lockers, their eyes were wide as Jesse walked down the hall that morning. It was as though they never expected to see their English teacher again.

Just before lunch, the secretary's student aid stopped by class and handed Jesse a note. Principal Garvey wanted to see him in his office for a quick hey-how-ya-doin', a little one-on-one to kick the tires of his mental state. Jesse knew he needed to convince the head of the school that he wasn't teetering on the edge of some sort of existential crisis. And if he couldn't? He didn't even want to think about what that would mean.

When he stepped into Garvey's office, the man wore a look of concern. "Jesse, how are you?" he asked.

"I'm all right," Jesse said. "Glad to be back to a normal schedule. I think it'll help."

"Do you need anything?" Garvey asked, and Jesse shook his head in the negative. "You'll let me know if you do," Garvey said.

"I will," Jesse assured him.

"Good." Garvey folded his hands over his desk blotter, seemingly satisfied. "I'll let you get on with it, then." And that was it. Conversation over.

Garvey didn't push as hard as expected, and Jesse was thankful for it. He only hoped Sam would be as easy on him. After retrieving a bowl of school mac and cheese from the cafeteria, Jesse found him in the teacher's lounge.

"Wow," Sam said as soon as Jesse stepped into the room. "Some lunch. What'd you do, rob a five-star restaurant?"

Jesse took a seat next to his friend, peering at a few other teachers milling about. They were giving him the side-eye, probably wondering if that second suicide had pushed him over some invisible edge. Jesse turned away, his gaze pausing on Sam's new reading material. It was a bible-thick book about the history of the Civil War, the tome marked *Volume One*, which meant there were others. He glanced back to his bowl of food. It had congealed since he'd first retrieved it, more orange now than it had been a few minutes before. He squinted up at the lights.

"No," Sam said. "It really does look *that good*."

"Looked better on the line," Jesse murmured.

"And it'll look even better on the way out," Sam assured him. "Michelle Obama would be appalled."

Jesse stuck his plastic fork into his elbow mac and took a reluctant bite. Sam said nothing as he balled up a piece of aluminum foil and tossed it into a paper bag he'd brought from home. He then pulled a package of peanut butter crackers out into the open.

"Got anything to trade?" Jesse asked.

"Yeah, but you don't," Sam said, then tore open the plastic bag and offered Jesse a cracker anyway. "On the house, all things considered."

Jesse took it and held it up in a toast of thanks.

"I feel partly responsible, you know," Sam confessed. "I told you to go. I even told you that story about my grandma. Completely unnecessary and totally out of line. I'm a jerk."

"You had nothing to do with it," Jesse told him.

"Yeah, but I *feel* like I did. When I found out..." Sam's words trailed to nothing. He shook his head a moment later. "I'm just really sorry, man. If you need anything..."

"Thanks," Jesse said. "Maybe one more cracker."

Sam exhaled a dramatic sigh and offered up another one. "You're a lousy son of a bitch, you know that?"

Jesse cracked a smile.

"Anyway," Sam said, grabbing a cracker for himself. He slid the rest of the pack Jesse's way, as if in apology. "How're you holding up?"

"Haven't crumbled yet," Jesse said, though he refused to make eye contact as the words left his lips. Because the keyword was *yet*, and every day that passed felt like a day closer to a stumble. But that was the thing about Sam; at the end of the day, he was a work friend. His and Jesse's relationship wasn't the type where Jesse could just come out and confess, *Hey, I've been thinking about hitting the bar a lot, lately.* They weren't the type of friends who could shoulder such burdens. As far as Jesse was concerned, those friends had effectively wiped themselves out.

"Do you want to talk about it?" Sam asked, though it took him a beat. It was clear that he was just as reluctant to broach the subject, but Sam was a better man than Jesse. He, at least, was willing to give the hard stuff the old college try.

"I mean, you don't have to," Sam said. "If you want to forget it, I understand. I just want you to know that I'm..." He paused, testing the weight of his words on his tongue. "Don't think you don't have anyone to talk to, okay? I'm a good listener."

Jesse looked up at his friend and offered him a nod.

"You're a good guy, Sam," he said.

Sam lifted his shoulders in dismissal, then mercifully changed the subject.

"How was the substitute?"

Jesse groaned and took another bite of his lunch.

"That good, huh?"

"When are they not?"

"I know," Sam said. "When Stella had that ulcer last year and I had to miss a couple of days?" He snorted at the memory. "Would have been easier to just cancel class altogether than deal with cleaning up that mess."

"Speaking of," Jesse said, shoveling another forkful of overcooked pasta into his mouth. A moment later, he was pushing the Styrofoam bowl away, deciding he'd rather spend the rest of the day hungry than finish his food. "I've got a stack of ungraded homework the height of a toddler on my desk."

"You *could* just give everyone an A," Sam suggested. "Cut your losses?"

Jesse rose from his seat. "Oh, they'd love that," he said. "But I need something to focus on." He tapped his forehead—the first and only suggestion Sam would get that not all was well inside Jesse's head. The childhood memories, seeing that house outside his window, the nightmares…

"If you need help, I'm just down the hall," Sam said. "I've got red pens and everything. Pretty sure I can get through grading a lousy book report."

"Are you saying you can do my job?" Jesse asked, feigning offense.

"I mean, it *is* just English," Sam mumbled. "Isn't that, like, the easiest teaching degree to get?"

Jesse snatched the remaining peanut butter crackers off the table. "I'm taking these," he said, crumpling the thin cellophane in his palm. "And I'm stealing your lunch for the rest of the week." He grabbed his half-eaten mac and cheese off the table and stepped toward the trash bin.

"Jesse," Sam said. When Jesse turned, Sam appeared far more somber than he had a moment before. "I'm serious about what I said. If you need anything…"

"Sure," Jesse said, and before he could stop himself, the words rolled off his tongue. "I've got something. Find me an answer, Professor Wilson."

"An answer?" Sam asked.

"Yeah," Jesse said. "Because everything happens for a reason, right?" It was the exact opposite of his own philosophy—the fact that no, not everything had to make sense. Sometimes, shit just happened. But the more time that passed since Casey's suicide, the more not seeking out a reason felt like self-sabotage. Because maybe LouEllen worrying about Jesse being next wasn't as crazy as it seemed. Maybe Bad Cop Mel was on to something and there *was* a pattern beyond the obvious. Perhaps Jesse was involved in something he didn't know about, that he didn't understand.

Except, that was silly, wasn't it? It was the exact line of thinking that Jesse had warned LouEllen about—that toxic small-town superstition that reduced well-meaning, intelligent people to Podunk hillbillies without a clue.

Jesse smirked.

"What?" Sam asked.

"Nothing," he said. "I just really hate this town," then lifted his hand in a silent *later* before stepping into the hall.

TWELVE

THAT NIGHT, after sitting through a dinner of meatloaf and mashed potatoes, Jesse retired to his front-room desk while Lou put Ian down for the night. With the house quiet, the lights low, and a mug of coffee close at hand, it was the perfect setup to bang out the first few pages of the story he was determined to dedicate to his two lost friends.

It should have been no sweat, no big deal. He'd spent his entire high school career typing out various novel manuscripts and still had them on a USB drive, which was floating around in a desk drawer full of useless junk somewhere. Back then, there was no such thing as writer's block or seeking out inspiration. It was automatic. He always had an idea, and if he lost interest in what he was working on? He'd abandon ship and move on to something else. Ditching a project wasn't an issue because, back then, he'd never been short of ideas. Another bigger, better story was just around the corner.

But now, the action of putting words to a blank page felt foreign, and self-doubt was quick to creep in. After Reed's suicide, rather than writing to work through his grief, Jesse stopped writing altogether. He couldn't remember the last time he'd sat down at that desk not to grade papers, but with genuine intention. Rather than opening his word processor to bang out a lesson plan or type up a quick pop quiz, here he was, hoping to create something from nothing. But nothing was what he got, because the words refused to come.

He supposed that, in the end, Lou's efforts to keep him on track after helping him sober up had made little difference. Regardless of how hard she tried, he had become the stereotype he'd promised himself he'd never be. Washed up. Someone who had abandoned his dreams and settled. A creative who couldn't create.

Those who can't do, teach.

Jesse grimaced at the memory of that asshole Rick Marshall and his ever-so-charming funeral quip. He didn't know what Rick did for a living, but he doubted it was anything more significant than mall security or a self-storage rent-a-cop. The picture of success, right? Like Rick had room to talk.

Staring at the pulsing cursor on his screen, he took a deep breath and shoved Rick Marshall to the back of his mind. But just like with the eulogy, he ended up giving up without writing a single word. He instead spent a good half hour wandering from room to room, searching for things to do, wondering if he should reorganize his bookshelves. Maybe alphabetically. Maybe by color or genre. Digging through desk drawers that he hadn't opened in years, he found the USB drive in question, then plugged it into the side of his laptop and opened a document he hadn't read in ages. Perhaps he'd find inspiration there. Or maybe he'd just find a way to waste time.

He'd read an article about procrastination, once. It said that procrastination was the brain's attempt to shield itself from discomfort and anxiety, and indeed, Jesse had plenty of that to go around. His feelings of artistic inadequacy, of flat-out incompetence at how to be a good friend, of how to support his family and get the hell out of Warsaw—it was pressing down on his shoulders, refusing to let up. And that itch for a drink? It wasn't abating. If anything, it grew stronger with each passing minute—an old acquaintance reaching out from the past, whispering *hey, remember me? We used to be such good friends.*

He sat in his desk chair for what felt like hours, rubbing his hand over his mouth, his attention fixed on his coat, which hung to the right of the front door next to Lou's. He thought about how if he ducked out of the house for a minute, LouEllen would never know. She was fast asleep. Just a quick trip to Speedy's. Just a miniature of something. A single shot. What could it hurt?

The only thing that stopped him from sneaking out the door and to the car was the thought of coming home to find her on the couch, waiting. Because sometimes he swore that woman was telepathic. Sometimes, she just *knew*, and he didn't know what he would have said to her if he found her there. All he knew was that it would be a lie, and she would know he was full of shit before he ever spoke a single word.

But the fact he was staying put only because he was afraid of being caught wasn't lost on him. He wasn't doing it out of love or respect for their relationship, for his wife, for all the promises he'd made to her and the endless effort she'd put into his recovery. He was doing it to save his own neck, and he wasn't sure where that uncaring disregard had come from. All he knew was that ever since Casey's suicide, it felt like something was different, like *he* was different. Something had shifted, and it was scary as hell.

THIRTEEN

THE NEXT DAY followed the same sequence of events: school, a terrible cafeteria lunch, the inability to think straight, dinner with Ian and Lou, and back to the desk. And again, no words were written. Another bout of pacing was had. LouEllen kissed him goodnight. And an hour after she'd gone to bed, Jesse found himself standing out in a snow-covered driveway, chewing on his bottom lip, cowering against the wind. This time, he'd nearly gotten into the car.

When he came back inside, Winston barreled into the living room, barking his head off. By the time Lou dashed across the house to shut him up, Jesse had shrugged out of his coat and kicked off his shoes next to the door. He grabbed Winston by the collar, and when Lou came into view, gave her an apologetic look.

"I don't know," he said, shaking his head at the dog. "I guess he heard something outside."

Winston woke the baby. Ian cried for over twenty minutes before falling back asleep.

All the while, Jesse sat on the couch and stared at the blank TV screen, feeling like an asshole, but still wanting that drink.

FOURTEEN

DAY THREE brought the same routine. Except this time, when the words failed to come, Jesse didn't leave his computer. He found himself on YouTube, watching Casey's videos instead. Every time he saw that white ghost-like blip dash across the screen, he got thirstier. He ended up in the kitchen, chugging a glass of water, drawing the shades over the kitchen's window when he spotted it in the backyard: the house that shouldn't have been there. The hallucination that felt all too real.

By the time LouEllen woke up, he'd fixed bacon, toast, and eggs.

"How long have you been up?" she asked, baffled by the spread. "And since when do you eat an adult breakfast?"

Jesse gave her a faint smile. He'd let her think it was insomnia.

There would be no mention of the house.

It was just his brain purging the experience. His body's way of flushing grief and guilt and confusion from his system.

It would pass.

But there were no words that night either.

YouTube, yet again.

He was no longer just watching Casey's videos, but studying them, pausing and rewinding every few seconds to take in each murky detail. And again, thirst stirred in the pit of his belly, like a serpent rousing from a long slumber.

That night, Jesse dreamed a different variation of the same nightmare. He was eleven again, walking up the rutted road toward the farmhouse in the dark. But this time it was snowing. They were giant flakes that stuck to his hair, the kind that he used to love to catch on his tongue. And this time, Reed and Casey weren't on the roof. He only spotted them after sneaking through the crooked front door and casting a glance up the hollow core of that turret. Four stories up, both his friends were sitting on the top banister, their legs dangling over the edge.

Hey, check out who made it, Casey said, pointing down to Jesse.

About time, Reed chimed in. *Damn jellyfish.*

It was only then that Jesse realized it wasn't just snowing outside, it was snowing inside as well. By the time Reed hit the floorboards at Jesse's feet, the snow had risen past his knees. Above, Casey levitated like a wingless angel, glittering snowflakes spiraling past his body in delicate slow-motion. And standing behind the railing that both boys had dismounted in simultaneous leaps was the girl. Her eyes dark as an oil slick. Her skin as gray as an old daguerreotype.

But it was her mouth that held Jesse rapt.

Her mouth, twisting into a ghoulish grin.

He heard the words against his ear—a disembodied whisper.

Two down, one to go, it said.

And then came the titter; ominous, rumbling laughter. A sound so wicked it roused him from sleep.

He expected to wake in a dark bedroom with a yell tearing past his lips. Instead, he awoke to daylight and an empty spot where LouEllen should have been. Squinting at the brightness of the light that was creeping in from around the blackout curtains, he slid out of bed and pushed them aside, then winced against the glare. Outside, their unkept backyard had been cleaned up overnight, blanketed by a perfect covering of white. The snow wasn't surprising. It was Michigan in January. But he couldn't help but feel a looming sense of disquiet as he got ready for work.

Maybe he'd woken up in the middle of the night to roll over or adjust the blankets. Perhaps that's when he saw the snow had started to fall again, and that's how it had worked itself into his dream. But that couldn't have been, because the curtains had been drawn.

Maybe he'd heard a weather forecast, or one of his fellow teachers could have mentioned it in the lounge during lunch. *Looks like another storm is rolling in.* Hell, it could have been nothing but a coincidence, but that didn't feel right either. Even as he watched LouEllen bundled Ian to play in the front yard, Jesse couldn't shake his sense of dread.

When he arrived at school, he parked his car in his usual spot, grabbed his tumbler of coffee and his satchel of yet-to-be-graded essays, and marched toward the side entrance the teachers used. But as soon as he stepped inside the building, he stopped dead in his tracks, because there was snow in the hallway. It was scattered across the linoleum and rested atop trashcans. It was melting on top of lockers. Jesse blinked at the sight of it, unsure of what he was seeing; confused until a snowball whizzed by his ear and an audible gasp sounded from down the hall. The snowball exploded against the door behind him, spraying his back with a slurry of ice.

"Sh—sorry, Mr. Wells!" James Jones, one of his students from fifth period English, yelled the apology. He then ducked his head and pivoted on the soles of a pair of ratty Converse, disappearing into a random classroom. The Warsaw boys had brought freshly packed snowballs into the building and some were still flying down the hall like heat-seeking missiles. But Jesse was too unsettled to react. It was too familiar. Too much of an echo of the pictures in his mind.

The linoleum was so slick that Jesse had to press his hand against the cinderblock wall to keep his legs from shooting out from beneath him. Had it been any other day, he would have marched himself down the hall and demanded a cease-fire. Someone was liable to get hurt on the wet floor, and that someone very well may have been Jesse himself. He wasn't as young as he used to be.

But it was all just too strange, too disorienting. Another coincidence? Maybe. But it felt different. Heavier. More like déjà vu.

Garvey was down the hall, yelling at a couple of boys to get their butts into his office, ASAP. Jesse avoided eye contact and tried to make himself invisible as he shuffled past the principal's office. Garvey stopped shouting, taken aback by the fact that Jesse was going to let this chaos unfold without putting a word in edgewise. But Jesse was as ill-prepared to defend his lack of action as he was to scold students. With Garvey to his back, Jesse risked twisting an ankle and walked a little faster. He ducked into his classroom the same way James Jones had bowed out of the hall.

Of course, he couldn't concentrate. Every time he glanced up from those essays, his gaze wandered to the window and the snow beyond it. Either that, or he'd catch something darting out of his periphery. Something quick and blurry. Something gauzy and white.

At lunch, he avoided the cafeteria and the teacher's lounge. He didn't feel like talking, even if it was to Sam. But he knew Sam would seek him out, so rather than hiding out in his classroom—a place Sam was sure to check—he locked himself in his car. It was there that he considered pulling a move from his own high school playbook and ditching the rest of the day.

When he, Casey, and Reed would bail on classes during their senior year, they often ended up sucking down shakes in the Mister Frosty parking lot. But this time around, Jesse wasn't craving milkshakes. His tongue was fuzzy for something more potent, and his thirst wasn't letting up. But leaving would mean coming up with an explanation. It would mean suspension. Maybe worse.

He wasn't sure how he did it, but he managed to slog through three more classes. When the bell rang, he just about bolted out the door.

On the way home, he nearly side-swiped a barricade, not because the roads were slick but because he was distracted yet again. Because there, on one of the overpasses Jesse drove beneath twice a day, was a man standing on the railing with his arms outstretched. When Jesse realized what he was seeing, he was well beyond the bridge. But that didn't keep him from spotting a blur of something falling in his rearview mirror.

A minute later, he pulled the car into the parking lot of a defunct strip mall and pressed the palms of his hands against his mouth, as if stifling a scream. Because anyone else would have slammed on the brakes and spun their car around, but not Jesse. No, he had kept driving. If anything, he had accelerated. *Run.* It was the cowardly part of his brain crying out for Jesse to listen. *Run away, Jesse. Just like a jellyfish.* And it made him wonder, was that all that was left of him now?

Why a jellyfish? Jesse had asked Reed. It had been summer, right before their seventh-grade year.

Because jellyfish don't have spines, genius, Reed had said.

That memory was the only thing that pushed Jesse to head back. But when he reached the overpass, there was no one lying on the road beneath it. It was nothing but slush-covered tarmac.

No sign of suicide.

Not even an imprint in the snow.

FIFTEEN

JESSE WAS two hours late arriving home.

LouEllen met him at the door, giving him zero chance of escape. She grabbed him by his coat sleeve and pulled him close the way a girl would tug a boy forward in a romantic movie. But she had no intention of kissing him. Rather than showering him with affection, she leaned forward and took a deep breath mere inches from his nose. And then he saw it. Her expression shifted to maligned indignance. The smell was all the proof she needed. He'd been caught. He'd given in.

"I knew it," she said, then shoved him backward, as if disgusted that he'd bothered to come home at all. Stomping across the living room in her pajamas, she turned to look at him just before reaching the kitchen's threshold. "So, what's it been then, eighteen years, or nineteen?" she asked. "How much hard-earned success did you just piss away? Remind me, Jesse, because I've lost count."

Maybe she had lost track, but Jesse hadn't.

Eighteen years undone. And for what?

With Reed, it had at least made sense. Jesse and Reed had been best friends since the first grade. They had been as close to brothers as a pair of kids could have been, practically living at each other's houses during the summers, even taking family trips together to Mackinac Island, Chicago's Field Museum, and Cedar Point. But he and Casey? Jesse had been searching for excuses to avoid Casey for the past two decades. They had grown apart. Up until the night Casey had shown up at Jesse's place, Jesse hadn't been sure Casey even considered him a friend. And with what he had discovered about Casey's visits to the farmhouse, about the lie Casey had told to get Jesse to go with him that night, he wasn't sure that *friend* was the right descriptor.

That, however, was beside the point. Because back when Reed had erased himself, there hadn't been any dreams keeping Jesse awake at night. The house didn't appear across from his own. And there had been no blur of white. No looping videos. No proof that the girl he had been sure was a figment of his imagination was actually real.

"Are you going to answer me?" LouEllen asked.

Rather than speaking, he pressed a cold hand to his face.

"Jesse?" Her tone softened.

"I'm sorry," he said. "I fucked up. It won't happen again." Because it had just been one fumble, right? A single moment of hopelessness brought on by the guy he'd seen standing atop a bridge, his arms outspread; by the fact that Jesse hadn't slammed on the brakes and implored the stranger not to do it the way he should have begged Reed. The way he should have pleaded with Casey.

There had been no body. He kept reminding himself of that fact even as he had sat with his sternum pressed flush against the bar. But in the end, it didn't matter. Jesse had seen what he'd seen. Now, all he could do was shake his head and redirect himself. He turned away from Lou's glare and toward the television, grabbed the remote and began to channel surf, looking for the news.

"What are you doing?" LouEllen asked, her eyebrows knitting together, beyond confused.

The local news was covering some banal story. Something about a new Michigan tax law. No word on a jumper. But it hadn't been that long—only a handful of hours. And Warsaw wasn't exactly a place that made headlines. Maybe word hadn't yet spread.

Jesse moved to his desk, opened his laptop, and went to the Warsaw sheriff's website. But there was nothing there either.

"Jesse?" LouEllen pressed, urging him to cue her in.

"A man," he said. "I saw a man standing on the overpass. He was going to jump."

She gawked, not having expected that.

"And instead of stopping, I stepped on the gas," he said. "I didn't even look back. I just needed to get out of there."

Just like how he'd booked it out of that farmhouse foyer moments before his life had changed forever. Reed may have spread his arms in the same way the man on the bridge had. Hell, maybe Casey had, too. The motions that came before the act were a mere technicality. The act itself was what mattered. It's what couldn't be undone.

"But there's nothing," he said, snapping his laptop closed. And maybe there was a reason for that. He kept replaying it: for the blip of a moment he'd seen him, the guy had worn Casey's face. And maybe it was because it had been Casey—a carbon copy placed on that overpass to remind Jesse of just how rotten a person he was. Nothing but another hallucination. One as vivid as the farmhouse materializing across the street, as defined as the girl staring at him from the top turret window.

A hallucination, because it was impossible.

None of this is actually happening, he told himself. *None of this could possibly be real.*

SIXTEEN

THIS TIME, it was snowing outside, not in. And the farmhouse was no longer a crooked skeleton of what it had once been. It was a shining beacon of warm glowing windows at the end of a well-kept drive.

Jesse found himself standing at the end of that road, wondering whether the inside gleamed as bright and hopeful as the exterior, curious about who was living within those walls. With a single forward step, he was transported. The road and snow vanished, replaced by yellow damask wallpaper and gleaming hardwood floors. The scent of freshly baked bread coiled around him in a comforting embrace, reminding him of his own childhood, of Christmas, of spending snowy days in his pajamas curled up in front of the TV.

A fire roared in the living room's massive fireplace. Jesse could see the flames from where he stood in the foyer and could hear its cozy crackle. A family portrait hung above the mantel in a thick wooden frame. A man and a woman comparable to the couple from Grant Wood's *American Gothic* stared out toward the viewer while the girl between them smiled wide, disrupting the severity of her parents' looks. But the inviting atmosphere of the home was shattered just as soon as Jesse was able to take it in, displaced by a scream that came from upstairs.

His head snapped back to glance up. That grand staircase climbed four stories up with framed artwork and photographs lining the walls. The screaming continued, animalistic and tortured. There was something awful to that wailing, something that made his skin crawl. Because it sounded wrong. It sounded less than human.

Jesse was ready to flee. The tranquility he'd felt only moments before was now replaced by an almost suffocating sense of foreboding.

You shouldn't be here. You shouldn't be...

But the slamming of an upstairs door stalled his exit. There were footsteps, urgent as they came clacking down the risers. Jesse blinked at a woman's hand as it slid down the banister, from the fourth floor to third, to second, until the woman came into view. She was older, perhaps in her fifties, descending the steps in a frenzied rush. Her silver hair was pulled back in a thick top-knot and her dress was reminiscent of the Great Depression; a simple floral sheath with a full lace collar paired with clunky brown shoes. Wiping her hands on the apron tied around her waist, she blew past Jesse without notice. To her, he wasn't there; nothing but a ghost watching events unfold.

She rushed across the foyer to a small console table housing a black telephone. Grabbing the receiver off its cradle and pressing it to her ear, she tapped the disconnect a few times.

"Hello? Operator!" Tap tap tap. Her features were tense, impatient, waiting for someone to pick up the line. "Yes, get me Doctor Ladeaux, please." A pause. "Detroit." Another. "Michigan, yes. Please hurry!"

Another scream ripped through the house. When it did, the woman lifted a trembling hand to her mouth. Her fingers twisted and pulled at her lips as if suppressing her own agonized cries.

Jesse's attention shifted from the quivering woman to the stairs. A bang came from somewhere on the third or fourth floor. It was a familiar sound that reminded him of when Reed had gotten stuck in Warsaw High's broom closet. Someone was throwing all their weight against a locked door.

It came again and again; hard, rhythmic thumps maybe five seconds apart, so forceful that it seemed to vibrate the entire house. A framed photo fell from the wall and bounced down the stairs. The glass shattered, sending a spray of glittering shards across the hardwood floor.

"Oh my God..." The woman gasped into the palm of her hand. "Oh my—Doctor Ladeaux? Yes! It's Hannah Ecklund. Georgiana, she's—"

Another bang. It was followed by laughter; impossible laughter, because rather than coming from someone's physical form, it was disembodied, freely drifting through the air. As Jesse stood there, he could swear it had come from right beside him. From in front of him. From above. From all around him all at once, yet he stood alone.

"Please," Hannah whispered into the receiver, wide-eyed and ashen. "Please, come as quick as you can. It's here."

Those last two words sent a shudder down his back. His trepidation grew ten-fold, pushing against his chest, creeping into his lungs. It made it hard to breathe, forcing him to shrink back toward the front door.

You shouldn't be here.

He was sure now that this was a mistake.

Even if this isn't real, you really shouldn't be...

Hannah Ecklund hung up the phone. She paused, fumbling with a small silver cross hanging from around her neck, her lips moving in soundless prayer. A moment later, she was crushing shattered glass beneath the soles of her shoes as she dashed back up the stairs. Jesse had no intention of following her. He pivoted away, ready to make his exit. But as soon as he turned toward the door, the house's golden hues disintegrated into cold grays and blues.

The wallpaper shriveled and cracked and, within an instant, rendered the pretty damask design nearly invisible. The floor creaked beneath Jesse's weight, it's pristine gleam replaced by broken boards and dust. And there, standing between him and the front door, was the girl. Her white nightgown was filthy and tattered. Her face was smudged with grime. Her hair was a tangled rat's nest atop her head. And her smile...

Jesse screamed and backed away, but unlike the last time he saw her, she remained steadfast. This time, she didn't vanish. Canting her head to the side, as if fascinated by Jesse's horror, the distinct pop pop pop of her vertebrae set his teeth on edge.

"Two down," she said, her tone a nefarious purr. "One to go."

And then she lunged.

SEVENTEEN

JESSE BOLTED upright in bed, his chest heaving, his hair slicked back with sweat. It was still dark. LouEllen was asleep. But Winston, who was lying on his dog bed, was not. The dog was staring right at him, as though having experienced the same nightmare. His eyes shone in the soft blue moonlight that crept around the edges of the drapes. It was unnerving how still Winston was, unflinching in his focus, as if boring a hole through Jesse's chest, wondering if his master was still his master. If his master was gone, who the hell was this person sitting up in bed? Who had taken Jesse's place?

Jesse turned away, disquieted by Winston's stare. It was only when he threw the sheets back that Winston flinched. When Jesse swung his legs over the edge of the mattress, he blinked at the low rumble of a growl coming from Winston's throat. He shot the dog a glare.

"Don't even think about it," he hissed. If Winston burst into a fit of barking and woke the entire house again, LouEllen would have a fit. It had happened a few times in the past couple of months. Stray cats yowling outside. Some asshole honking his horn in front of a neighbor's house. The random creaks and pops of old pipes. An occasional scurrying inside the walls. It didn't take much to send Winston into a tailspin.

On his feet now, Jesse slid into his slippers and grabbed his sweatshirt from the foot of the bed. Winston settled as soon as Jesse passed, which was good because Jesse had more important things to attend to. Like, why the hell the house felt like a meat locker instead of its typically balmy seventy degrees. He stopped in the hallway and squinted at the thermostat.

"The hell...?" he murmured, because someone had turned it all the way down. *He* certainly hadn't done it, which only left LouEllen, and Lou reducing the heat was so nonsensical it was almost funny. She was perpetually cold and slept in socks even in the summer. He'd begged her once, *Lou, the heating bill.* She'd begrudgingly laid off cranking up the temperature for an entire week, but she'd complained about *freezing to death* every single day. On night eight, her cold hands became more critical than their budget.

Jesse adjusted the thermostat to its standard setting and moved to the kitchen. He put on a pot of coffee, sat at the breakfast table, and rubbed his forehead, unable to shake the dream images that were still flashing against the backs of his eyelids. It had been so vivid, so clear. The perfect movie intro. Or, perhaps...

The opening to a book...

Suddenly, he was rising from the table and rushing across the living room to his desk. He pulled out the chair and sat, grabbed his laptop and pushed open the screen. Bringing up his word processor, he typed a few quick reminders.

Frantic woman. Screaming. Doctor Ladeaux.

But when it came to forming those ideas into complete sentences, his mind went blank. Jesse was, it seemed, in the middle of a full-blown bout of writer's block.

"Goddamnit," he whispered, frustrated by his inability to produce something that had once come so naturally.

Sitting there for a few minutes, he eventually gave in. He brought up YouTube and searched for Casey's channel instead, pulling up part four of the farmhouse series. He knew the spot in the recording by heart, having watched it so many times he'd memorized the time stamp. It was toward the end, right before Casey had decided it was time to go.

Jesse forwarded the video and leaned in.

There was Casey, scared, his camera-work shaky. There was the staircase, the fourth-floor landing.

I don't know why I'm here, Casey repeated. *I don't know why I'm here.*

But he crept toward the banister's railing regardless, as if pulled to it by some invisible string. The camera panned down. It switched to night vision. A moment later, there was the blip, an unidentifiable blur of white darting out of the shot.

What the hell was that?

Casey teetered away from the balustrade with shaky steps. But this time, Jesse understood what he was looking at. This time, it all added up. It made sense.

Tell me if you see her.

He slammed his laptop closed.

He was the one who had put those crazy notions inside Reed and Casey's head when they had been kids. Now, it was Casey who had passed those stories back on to Jesse, the nightmare coming full-circle. The dark dream coming home.

The cops were right, it was all related. The story, these hallucinations, they had been passed from one friend to another. Like an illness. A disease.

Jesse opened his laptop again and brought up Google, then typed GROUP PSYCHOSIS into the search bar. The results were abundant: shared psychotic disorder, folie à deux. There were real-life cases, like Christine and Lea Papin, like Pauline Parker and Juliet Hulme and the entire Tromp family. Jesse read article after article, scribbling down details that harked back to both Casey and Reed. He paced the room, frantic and unsure of what to do. Because was this what it had come to? Was he some rare psychological case? Was he seriously losing his mind?

Except, no, that didn't make sense. Because hallucinations didn't show up on video. So, what the hell had Casey caught?

Jesse only realized what time it was when he heard Ian fussing and LouEllen getting up. When she came into the living room with their son on her hip, he swiveled around in his desk chair and gave her a weak smile.

"Hey," he said, his greeting little more than a dry croak.

"Hey," she echoed, a look of concern pulling her features taught. "What're you doing up?" she asked.

It was a question Jesse couldn't answer, not without making himself feel crazier than he already did. And so, rather than telling her what he was up to, he shrugged and shut his laptop screen.

"Writing," he said. "Had a bolt of inspiration, I guess."

Lou raised a suspicious eyebrow.

"It just came to me," he said. "Last night."

"What's it about?" she asked—another question he didn't want to answer, but her dubiousness wasn't out of place. She didn't trust him anymore. After coming home smelling of alcohol, LouEllen wasn't about to cut him any slack. But she didn't have to twist her face up the way she was now, like everything that came out of his mouth was bullshit.

"The house," he said. "I told you."

She frowned, as if having hoped that he'd changed his mind.

Writing about the place where two friends had committed suicide was bleak, he'd give her that. That house was a scar, not just on the landscape outside of their small town, but on Jesse's mind. But she didn't have to be so quick to discourage him. Hell, if he could create his own narrative for it, he could override the things that happened there, right? If he could make his fiction more vivid than his memory of reality, he could move on, just as Blaire had urged.

All things considered, writing about the house didn't strike him as such a bad idea. As a matter of fact, it felt like what he *should* have been doing, no matter what LouEllen thought.

"And you're *sure* you want that to be your focus?" Lou asked, sitting Ian down on the couch. "I know that was the whole point of you going out there, but..."

Jesse glanced down to his hands. She was testing his patience.

"I'm sure," he said, keeping that small flame of annoyance in check, refusing to let it grow into full-blown anger. "I need to get rid of this, slough it off. Put my energy into something creative."

A creative outlet was a hell of a lot better than what he'd gotten himself into yesterday. He couldn't let that happen again.

"And you don't think it's just going to get you stuck in some sort of loop?" she asked, skeptical.

She knew as well as Jesse that Casey had become preoccupied with that place. Blaire hadn't said it outright, but she had revealed enough; Casey had gone down a twisted, obsessive path, just like Reed had. Jesse could picture them now, both LouEllen and Blaire sitting in Blaire's living room, Blaire muttering about how Lou had to keep Jesse away from that house, no matter what it took. But this bolt of inspiration was too good to ignore. He couldn't walk away from the spark he'd been hoping would return to him since his college days, could he? And then there was Lou's doubtful tone—another jab at the aggravation he was trying to keep under wraps.

"You don't believe I can do it?" The inquiry tumbled out of him before he could drag it back by its question mark, accentuated by exasperation that was becoming harder to disguise.

"That's not what I'm saying," she told him.

"Then what are you saying?"

"I don't know if going there, creatively or otherwise, is the healthiest choice for you right now."

He turned away from her, rested his elbows against his desktop, and pressed the heels of his hands into his eye sockets. He wasn't used to feeling so irked by her. She should have been happy he wanted to get back to writing. She should have encouraged him instead of playing twenty questions, just like that cop in Zion.

"Jesse." He nearly recoiled when she placed her hand on his shoulder. "I just want you to be sure about this."

"I'm sure," he said, his throat dry, his tone flat.

It was a story he should have written eighteen years ago. A story that could have been his salvation then, but had been waiting in the wings to save him now. And he had to write it.

He *would* write it, no matter what.

EIGHTEEN

"MR. WELLS?"

Jesse sat motionless at his desk, transfixed by the pulsing cursor on his screen.

"Mr. *Wells?*"

He'd never brought his laptop to school with him before. Quite frankly, it was a risky move. If he didn't watch it like a hawk, there was a good chance he would be sans laptop by the end of the day. Not that the kids at Warsaw High were *that* terrible, but extra spending cash was hard to come by. There were only so many fast food joints that needed burger flippers or grocery stores that needed cart wranglers.

"*Mr. Wells?*"

But bringing his computer to school was worth the gamble, especially with his classes doing nothing but silently reading. And since it had become clear that Jesse couldn't pull off grading those damn essays, the least he could do was try to get some writing done. If someone asked what he was doing, he'd lie, say it was for class.

"Yo, Jesse!"

Jesse blinked, glancing from the screen to just above it. He spotted Shawn Gregory leaning back in his desk, his right arm folded over the top of his head. That arm was limp and tired, as though Shawn had been holding it up all day.

A couple of girls gasped at Shawn's unabashed attempt at gaining their instructor's attention. A handful of students suppressed their laughter. A few flat-out chuckled beneath their breaths. Jesse peered at the student in question. Shawn's brazenness made him feel awkward in his own skin. It was a feeling that was all-too-familiar, because he's spent his high school career with kids just like Shawn smirking behind his back, whispering as he passed them in the halls. Because Jesse asked too many questions in honors English. He left himself vulnerable by publishing short stories in the Warrior Wrap-Up. He'd always been the kid that had been not-quite-right with his ambition. With the fact that he'd rather have spent a Friday night reading a good book than getting wasted and doing donuts in an empty wheat field. With the desire to be bigger than himself, than the town of Warsaw would allow him to be. He was, as Rick Marshall had recalled, supposed to be *the next Stephen King,* and that kind of aspiration had painted a target onto his back.

And here it was again: that same feeling of inadequacy, of not fitting in. Twenty years later and the kids were virtually the same. Jesse was an adult, sure, but that just made the sensation worse.

But there was also something else. That morning's bristling seed of indignation was just waiting to combust. Earlier, he'd managed to keep his irritation in check because it had been LouEllen, because Ian had been sitting there, watching his parents interact. But neither Lou nor Ian were here now. It was just him and these know-it-all shit-stain kids he suddenly hated with every fiber of his being. And that little fucker, Shawn Gregory? He was a pain in the ass if there ever was one.

Those who can't do…

Jesse reached forward, snapped his laptop shut, and looked to the collection of faces staring back at him.

"Sorry," Shawn muttered. "But you were kinda zoned out, Mr. Wells."

"Was I?" Jesse asked, his tone sharp enough to make a few of the kids tense in their seats.

Shawn looked back to the open novel in his hands, as if having forgotten the burning question that had spurred his outburst. It would be a surprise to see Shawn graduate. He was a dimwitted good ol' boy in the making, a perfect representation of all the things Jesse considered wrong with his hometown. Shawn was a close-minded anti-intellectual replica of Rick Marshall.

Jesse's gaze flicked from Shawn to his closed laptop lid.

Rick Marshall, that prick.

Who was *he* to suggest that Jesse couldn't make it as a writer? As if becoming a teacher had somehow wiped out his talent. As if earning an honest living made him some sort of a chump.

Jesse glared at Shawn, his anger growing despite the kid having gone back to reading *The Jungle* in hopes of avoiding confrontation. But that wasn't going to happen. Because ever since that morning, Jesse had been itching for a fight.

"Shawn," Jesse said. The kid looked up. "Get your stuff." He nodded to Shawn's backpack next to his desk.

"Huh?" Shawn appeared puzzled as he lowered his book, most likely five chapters behind the rest of the group.

"Get your stuff," Jesse repeated, "and get out of my class."

Shawn gaped. As a matter of fact, a lot of the students did, surprised by Jesse's request. Because Mr. Wells was one of the "cool" teachers. He was younger than most, and he tried to keep his classes fun. Every now and again, he'd let his students watch a movie adaptation of the novel they were reading to spur discussions of how the film was different from the original text. If the movie was new, he'd give kids extra credit if they showed him their ticket stub. Most of his female students were boasting A's and B's based on their love of Elizabeth Moss and weekly episodes of *The Handmaid's Tale*.

And as far as discipline went, he didn't send students to Principal Garvey's office. But now, here he was, telling a kid to get out of his classroom for calling him by his first name. A minor infraction by Warsaw standards, but Jesse was beyond caring. He needed an outlet for his ever-growing ire, and Shawn Gregory would have to do.

Tag, you're it.

"Hey, Mr. Wells, I'm sorry, I just—" Shawn attempted to plead his case, but it only aggravated Jesse that much more.

Rather than repeating his request, he rose from his desk and crossed the classroom, stopping at Shawn's side. He stood there, curious as to what it would feel like to strike a student. How long it would take the cops to arrive and, in that time, would he have the strength and the nerve to beat this kid to a bloody pulp against the linoleum floor?

Turns out, he didn't have the nerve after all. He was the gutless wonder. A jellyfish. A guy who ditched his friends when things got spooky. A guy who drove a mile down the road after having sworn he saw a man jump to his death. And now, rather than pummeling

Shawn with his fists, he merely grabbed the kid's backpack off the floor and march it to the classroom door. Once there, he chucked it into the hallway, precisely the way he wanted to shove Shawn out of the room.

When he regarded his class again, he was met with a throng of startled faces. A few of the more dramatic girls had clamped their hands over their mouths to hold back mortified gasps. Because of course they were. This was Warsaw where, if someone dared to show how they truly felt about a situation, their honesty was met with the fanning of flushed cheeks and a request for a fainting couch. They thought the Republic of Gilead was dystopian? *Look around,* he wanted to tell them. *Wake the fuck up and look around, kids.*

"Yo, Shawn," Jesse said. "Go fetch."

It was then that Shawn went positively ashen. Whatever Jesse thought of him, Shawn was Mr. Popular. He played varsity basketball and was a team favorite. And as far as the hallways went, if anyone was doing the pushing around, it was Shawn's hands shoving a weaker member of the species into a locker; kids that reminded Jesse a lot of himself.

"Need I repeat it?" Jesse asked.

It took a while, but Shawn eventually closed his book, rose from his desk, and bowed his head as he marched past his classmates to the door. Once there, he stopped. He seemed surprisingly dismayed, not used to the humiliation that was flushing his cheeks.

"Where do I go?" he asked, and for a blip of a second, Jesse felt terrible for putting him on the spot. Because how many times had *he* felt exactly the way Shawn did now—out of his element, confused, unsure of everything? Jesus, how many times had he felt like that in the past week? But he couldn't let it slide. To back down now was to negate his authority, and there wasn't a chance in hell that was going to happen.

"I don't care, Shawn," Jesse told him. "Go see Mrs. Stowe."

Mrs. Stowe was the student counselor. She was a pudgy old woman who had a knack for calculating how Warsaw flunkies could still manage enough credits for May's commencement ceremony. It kept the school's graduation rate out of the toilet. It kept them accredited, which had become an open joke among the staff.

"Mrs. Stowe?" Shawn asked, realizing that if he went to see old Mrs. S, it meant Jesse didn't want to see Shawn in his class ever again.

But could that be? This was *Mr. Wells*. Only the toughest teachers permanently kicked kids out of their classrooms, and even *that* was rare.

But oh, it was happening. Because there was something noxious brewing in the pit of Jesse's stomach, something that made him feel simultaneously angry and intensely alive. For all he knew, if Shawn didn't step out of his classroom in the next few seconds, Jesse would grab him by the front of his Detroit Pistons jersey and shove him out there himself. Maybe he *would* land a punch square against the little punk's jaw. And then he'd quit this crappy job for good.

"Goodbye, Shawn," Jesse said, shutting the door in the kid's face. He watched through the long vertical window as a dejected Shawn gathered his spilled backpack off the floor. It was only when he heard the soft rustle of restless students behind him that he glanced back at the class.

"One down," he said, offering them a sardonic smile. "Now, who's next?"

His grin was short-lived, however, because as soon as the question squirmed past his lips, he remembered her face.

He remembered her words

One to go.

NINETEEN

THE ENTIRE school knew what happened to Shawn by midday, and Jesse felt guilty about putting the kid through the wringer the way he had. But when he got called into Garvey's office to discuss the situation, Jesse made quick work of the meeting, refusing to stand down.

"There are other English classes," he told Garvey. "I'm not going to tolerate disrespect in my classroom." Garvey could hardly argue, so he didn't. After all, juggling classes was Mrs. Stowe's specialty. Shawn Gregory would be nary a challenge.

By lunch, Jesse's anger had gone dormant. If anything, the place it had resided was now nothing more than an itching scab of remorse. He'd not only shown his class the worst side of himself, but he was now officially the teacher who had snapped after watching someone die. Small town legends had been created from less.

And yet, when he stepped into the teachers' lounge, that flame of annoyance leaped back into his throat. Because there, next to the coffee maker, was a small group of teachers talking amongst themselves in hushed tones; a conversation that came to an immediate stop the moment Jesse entered the room. They all looked at him and, seconds later, broke their huddle like an intrusion of roaches. Jesse regarded them for a moment, compelled to throw a verbal jab. But rather than spitting barbs, he moved across the room to where Sam was sitting, eating his lunch in front of yet another American history tome.

Sam stopped chewing as Jesse approached, resuming only after Jesse sat next to him with his tray of cafeteria food. Today's selection: something resembling meatloaf covered in a gelatinous brown goo, powdered mashed potatoes, and a tiny portion of boiled peas and carrots. Prison food would have been a welcome alternative.

"Hey," Sam said. "If it isn't Warsaw's own celebrity educator."

"Live and in person," Jesse replied, then stabbed a carrot with his fork.

"So, what happened?" Sam asked. "Or should I go by hearsay?"

"Do that," Jesse said, not in the mood to rehash the details. "I'm sure it's far more dramatic the way the kids tell it."

Sam frowned while Jesse popped the carrot into his mouth. It was flavorless. Unsalted and undercooked. Sam waited until Jesse finished chewing, then posed a predictable question. "Are you all right?"

"I'm fine," Jesse said.

"You sure?" Sam pressed.

Jesse let his fork fall from his fingers with a clang and leaned back in his seat, giving Sam a scowl.

"You just seem..." Sam searched for the right word. "Edgy."

"You think?" Jesse raised both eyebrows at his fellow colleague, then snatched up his fork again.

"Why is that?" Sam asked, "What's going on?"

Jesse motion around them, as if presenting the room for the first time. *Take a look around you.*

"Ah." Sam nodded, as if understanding, then grimaced down at his sandwich. "Yeah, I get it," he said. "It's not Harvard. But what're you going to do, leave?"

Jesse snorted.

"Maybe you just need more time," Sam suggested.

"More time for what?" Jesse asked, unable to choke back his aggravation. "To waste away in this shitty place?"

Sam went silent, picking at the crust of his bread. The teachers that remained in the lounge were just as quiet, clearly eavesdropping.

"To process what happened, maybe," Sam eventually said, though he was reluctant, worried that he was crossing another line.

"I know what happened." Jesse snorted, then poked at his meatloaf with the tines of his fork. "My best friend killed himself and I couldn't get over it. And rather than ending up where I was *supposed* to be, I ended up here." He tapped the table with his finger.

"I meant—"

"You meant Casey," Jesse interrupted. "Yeah, I know you did. But I know what happened there, too," he said.

"What?" Sam asked.

"Oh, come on, Sam. If anyone knows about history repeating itself, it's you. And you know what?" He shifted his weight in his seat, suddenly acutely aware that they weren't alone. The teachers who had been whispering when he'd come in were on pins and needles. Their ears were stretching to hear every word.

Jesse lowered his voice, his gaze shifting to Sam's face. "Sometimes," he said, "when history repeats itself, it wakes you the hell up."

Sam pressed his lips together in a tentative line. He peered at his pack of unopened peanut butter crackers, then looked up again. "Is that what this vibe is, then?" he asked quietly. "Your renaissance? An awakening?"

"What vibe?" Jesse asked.

"Umm…" Sam lifted his shoulders to his ears. "I mean, you're obviously angry. *Seething*, actually. It's kind of spooky. I've never seen you this mad before."

Jesse sighed and leaned back in his seat. Sam was right, Jesse *was* angry—pissed at the fact that he'd let his life become what it was. Incensed that Lou was discounting his desire to finally get back to what he loved to do. Raging that Casey had done what he'd done, that he'd decided to play God with Jesse's emotional well-being. And then there was Reed. But *Jesse* was the one who was gutless, right? Reed wasn't the coward despite having started this whole fucking mess.

Jesse shoved a hand through his hair and exhaled a breath. "I don't know," he finally said. "Maybe you're right. I came back too early. Maybe I'm not ready to be here yet."

Sam offered him a faint nod. "And you're still searching for that answer?" he asked.

Jesse looked away from his tray of food, not the least bit hungry anymore. He glanced to his comrade, realizing that of all the people in that nowhere town, Sam was the only guy he could honestly consider a friend anymore.

"Is there an answer, though?" Jesse asked. "Or is it possible that I just keep showing up in the wrong place at the wrong time?"

Sam went quiet for a beat, as if genuinely considering that possibility. And then he spoke. "If that's the case," he said, "you've got the worst luck of anyone I've ever met."

TWENTY

THAT NIGHT, Jesse managed to sit in front of his laptop for a good three hours before exhaustion hit him hard. Brushing his teeth, he stared at the dark shadows that had formed beneath his eyes. In the weak bathroom light, he looked like a boxer recovering from a fight. Or an addict in the throes of withdrawal which, he supposed, wasn't all that far from the truth.

He crawled into bed, determined to get in a few good hours of sleep before he had to start his day all over again. But rest wasn't in the cards. As soon as he shut his eyes, he saw the farmhouse again.

Its strange façade was stark against the snow. The windows were glowing beacons—the only light in an endless swath of dark. Jesse stood on the side of the road, staring at the house until the sound of rocks crunching beneath tire rubber drew his attention away. A black 1930's Ford eased its way up the road, the driver rolling past him without so much as a sideways glance. When the car stopped along the roundabout and the engine cut out, nothing but the muffled silence of winter remained. But only for a moment. Because even before the driver pushed open his door, a scream cut through the quiet of the countryside.

Jesse turned back to the house. Another noise came from within—the sound of rumbling thunder, or a bowling ball bouncing down a flight of stairs. Another scream followed, but this one was different from the last. This one was weaker, shriller, more terrified.

Jesse shot a look at the driver of the Ford. The man was now standing outside his vehicle, still protected by his open car door.

Perhaps he was reconsidering his visit, unsure of whether he wanted anything to do with what was happening inside. But the man—who was dapper in his black topcoat and matching bowler hat—didn't have the opportunity to retreat. The farmhouse's front door flew open, and a girl clothed in a white nightgown tripped and fell down the front porch steps.

Jesse's eyes went wide with recognition. It was *her*, except not at all. The girl from his nightmares was black-eyed and ashen with sunken cheeks and a skeletal sneer. This girl was nothing close to that, but he had no doubt: this was the same person, or at least the same body. The nightgown and the tangle of hair assured him of that.

A moment later, Hannah Ecklund stumbled through the front door and into the cold. She clamored down the stairs in her clunky brown shoes, her arms extended outward, ready to grab hold of the child that had careened bare-legged into the snow.

"Doctor Ladeaux!" Hannah squawked. Her urgent expression beseeched the doctor to intervene. It was enough to get the man to step out from behind the safety of his door. Despite his age—Jesse guessed he was in his seventies—the man was spry. He dashed around the car and reached the girl, whom he caught by the biceps and pulled up off the ground.

"What's going on here?" Ladeaux asked. When Hannah failed to respond, a third party spoke from the porch.

"We're hoping you can answer that question for us, Doctor."

The man who made the declaration looked tired. He had shadows beneath his eyes—a perfect match to the ones Jesse wore himself. His skin was sallow, and his hair was a mess. His dirty overalls made him appear thin and malnourished, and his body language spoke volumes. Whatever was going on inside that house, it was clear that it had pushed this man to the edge.

"We've taken her to every physician in the county, but nobody knows what it is," he said.

It was then that Hannah—having fallen silent—broke into the conversation. "Nobody but us," she said. "*We* know."

As soon as the words left her lips, the girl began to struggle against the doctor's grasp, desperate to get away.

"We don't know anything," the man in overalls said. "Hannah, we don't... It's her mind. We just don't understand it because—"

"It's not her mind," Hannah snapped. Her focus jumped from the man Jesse assumed was her husband to Doctor Ladeaux. "It's not her mind," Hannah echoed, quieter this time.

"What is it, then?" Ladeaux asked, genuinely curious. He continued to hold the girl's arms tight in his grasp.

"She's sick," Hannah said, "but not in the mind." She paused, wringing her hands, worried that speaking the words poised upon her tongue would somehow seal her daughter's fate. "She's sick in the soul, Doctor. I just know it."

"In the soul," Ladeaux repeated.

"Yes," Hannah said. "Joseph doesn't want to believe, but I know the truth. I can see it. I can *feel* it. I know my child, and I know that I'm right."

"And what is the truth?" Ladeaux asked. "Tell me, what do you think is wrong with Georgiana?"

Georgiana, Jesse thought. *That's her name. Georgi—*

"I don't think, Doctor," Hannah said. "I *know*. My daughter needs faith, not drugs. Not a hospital. *Faith*, Doctor. It's the only way to get the demon to go."

It was at that moment that Jesse was torn from sleep, not by his dream, but by a sound. He bolted upright in bed, staring into the darkness as a faint and distant scream filtered in through the bedroom window.

"Holy shit." He gasped, instinctively grabbing LouEllen by the shoulder and shaking her awake. "Jesus, what is that?"

LouEllen sat up with a start. "What?" she asked. "What? Is it Ian?"

It most definitely was not Ian, but Jesse didn't have time to explain. He shoved the sheets aside and rushed to the window, pushed the curtain away and found himself blinking at a moonlit silhouette.

Down the street, standing barefoot in the snow, was a girl in a white nightgown.

It was her, and she was screaming into the wind.

TWENTY-ONE

IT HAD BEEN too late to tell the police not to come, especially after Jesse's panicked 911 call. LouEllen had pried the phone out of his hand and taken it into the other room, where she tried to explain to the dispatcher that her husband had merely had a bad dream. *There is no girl. I didn't hear a thing.* But two outfitted officers showed up anyway, because when it came to Jesse Wells, there could have been a dead body involved.

The cops questioned both Jesse and LouEllen, though they did it in separate rooms. Jesse played it off as no big deal, just a hallucination, and the questioning officer made no attempt to conceal his suspicions as he leaned in, wondering how much Jesse had downed before ghosts had started wailing in the streets.

By the time the police left, Jesse was humiliated and LouEllen was red-eyed from crying. She said nothing to him before going back to bed.

Jesse thought about following her, but he sat down at his desk and concentrated on the glowing computer screen instead. And even though he knew it wasn't there, he saw it anyway. Outside his window, that farmhouse stood in the snow, beckoning him.

Come back, it said. *You belong here, Jesse. Come say hello to your friends.*

TWENTY-TWO

"JESSE."

LouEllen's tone forced Jesse's eyes open. Had he fallen asleep at his desk? He sat up, then turned to his wife. She was glaring at him from the kitchen's threshold.

"I've been calling you for the past ten minutes," she said. "Winston." She gave the dog a pointed look. Winston was sitting on the front door mat, whining and scratching the door's already scratched-up paint. "And then your son," she said, disappearing out of the room once more.

Down the hall and in his nursery, Ian was crying for a fresh diaper, or breakfast, or a cuddle. Jesse rubbed at his face and rocked himself to his feet.

He let Winston out into the yard, then went to Ian's room. The kid was wailing in his crib by the time Jesse arrived. After swapping a wet diaper for a fresh one, he hefted Ian up onto his shoulder and wandered into the kitchen in search of a bottle. When he arrived, LouEllen frowned at them both. She seemed tired as she stirred a boxed cake mix by hand. Her electric mixer had burned out its dinky motor during the previous holiday season and it had yet to be replaced. Jesse had meant to get her a new one, but it seemed like an odd gift; like getting a wife a vacuum cleaner or a microwave.

"We need to talk," Lou said. She pushed the bowl of chocolate mix away, deciding it wasn't worth the effort.

"What're you making?" Jesse asked, stepping past her to retrieve Ian's bottle from the fridge.

"Cake," she said. "For Carrie Mae's birthday dinner tonight, which you've clearly forgotten about." Jesse winced as LouEllen heaved an aggravated sigh. She was getting fed up with his weird behavior, and it was clear that the previous night had pushed her to her limit. "We have to leave at four," she told him. "So, you know…" She turned back to her bowl of cake batter. "Plan around it."

But what she meant was keep it together. Jesse allowed the nuance of her statement to roll off his shoulders. Sliding Ian into his high chair, he grabbed a bottle out of the fridge and tossed it into the warmer. His gaze fixed itself across the fenced square of land that made up their snow-covered yard as he waited for Ian's formula to reach the right temperature.

That house, it had been out there last night.

He'd seen it with his own eyes.

Right. Like you had seen her.

Shaking his head to himself, the warmer clicked off. Jesse handed the bottle off to Ian, then took a seat at the breakfast table and fixed his attention on his wife.

"You're right," he said. "We do need to talk."

LouEllen paused her stirring to glance his way. He assumed she was awaiting a discussion about the night before, about what the hell had freaked him out so badly; why he hadn't been able to control his panic to the point of calling the police. But that wasn't the topic Jesse wanted to broach. If anything, his choice of conversation was even more complicated than hallucinations and ghosts.

"This house," he said.

LouEllen arched an eyebrow.

"This town," he clarified, and she turned away from him with a glare. "I know you don't want to talk about it."

"That's right," she said, her tone clipped, her patience gone.

"But we have to, Lou," he told her. "If anything, this house is going to be too small for us soon. We're going to have to find a bigger place."

"You were the one who liked this house," she reminded him, then grabbed the mixing bowl again. She began to stir with newfound vigor.

"Yeah, but that was before Ian," Jesse said. "Before we had a family." It had been before Casey had dragged him back to the farmhouse. Before something dark had awakened, refusing to let

Jesse close his eyes without playing out imagined movie reels inside his mind.

And then there was a new worry, one that had struck him while he sat on the couch and tried to hear LouEllen murmured her side of the story to the police. Bad Cop Mel's line of questioning came back to Jesse all at once. Mel's suggestion of there being some sort of pact had seemed ridiculous at first, but it had somehow clawed its way inside Jesse's chest through the space between his ribs. Because, sure, Bad Cop Mel was little more than a middle-of-nowhere authority figure, but what if he was right? What if Jesse couldn't see what this really was because he was too close?

"So, you want to sell the house," Lou said, not looking at him. "You want to leave Warsaw. Leave everyone we know."

Jesse scowled at his hands. It would be an ordeal, that was for sure. Picking up and moving away from a hometown was never easy, but…

"And who will we sell to?" she asked. "Who's going to buy this place out from under us? And even if we did manage to sell it, where are we going to go, Detroit?" She scoffed. "How is raising a kid there better than raising one here?"

Because the girl isn't there, he thought. Because it's further, safer. But bringing up his delusions would have been a mistake, so he posed a question instead.

"Why are you so angry with me?"

That did it. Lou stopped stirring. She was either trying to come up with an answer or attempting to keep herself from flying off the rails.

"I'm angry with you," she said calmly, "because I feel betrayed."

"Because of the slip-up," he said.

"Yes. Because of the slip-up. Because ever since then, things have gone sideways. We had the police at our house last night, Jesse," she reminded him. "Because you thought you saw someone outside when there was nobody there."

"I know," he murmured.

"Last time, Reed was the trigger," she said. "And last time, it took over a year to pull you back from the brink, you remember?"

"Yes," he said, unable to meet her gaze.

"Now, the trigger is Casey. And I get that, Jesse, I do. What happened is awful, and if I could pull Casey out of his grave right now, I'd tell him that I hate him not because of what he did, but because he did it in front of you."

Jesse swallowed. His throat clicked. Every time Casey came up, Jesse was transported back to that staircase. He'd never unsee his friend swinging back and forth like that.

"But you cannot let yourself slide down that spiral again," she said. "You have a family now. A job. A son."

He nodded, understanding. Agreeing.

"And yet, you slipped up."

He pinched the bridge of his nose. "I know," he sighed.

"That's why I'm angry."

"I'm sorry," he said, finally glancing up at her. "I told you it wouldn't happen again."

"I know you did." She leaned down, opened a cabinet, and fished out a cake pan from a collection of kitchen junk.

"But you don't believe me," he said.

It was LouEllen's turn to sigh. She slid the pan onto the counter and finally met his gaze. "I just think there's more to this than you're telling me," she said. "But what am I supposed to do, pry it out of you?" She pivoted away from him again. He watched her in silence, a fast-growing lump forming in his throat.

"I mean, we all have our secrets," she said, speaking more to herself than to him. "It's just that most of us don't have secrets so goddamn dark."

Was that what she was, then? This girl...the fact that he was starting to believe she was real rather than imagined: was that his dark secret? Or was it that believing she truly existed meant something worse? Because accepting she was real proved that he'd lost his grip, that he could no longer differentiate between truth and fiction.

The mere thought of it had Jesse rising from his seat and excusing himself. He couldn't bear to sit there even a second longer. If he had, he would have ended up screaming the way Georgiana had the night before.

TWENTY-THREE

CARRIE MAE'S birthday dinner was an awkward disaster. Jesse didn't want to be there and it showed. He could see LouEllen casting sidelong glances in his direction as she stood in her mother's kitchen, talking to her sister in low murmurs so nobody would overhear what Jesse assumed were marital complaints. He could only imagine what she was saying about him. Unhelpful. Preoccupied. Plagued by nightmares that were now resulting in dead-of-night 911 calls. And, of course, the big bad slip-up—something for which Jesse had apologized but had been far from forgiven.

Carrie Mae, who was huddled next to her sister, eventually looked over to Jesse, though she seemed far more puzzled than outraged. It was as though she didn't believe what Lou was telling her—Jesse was, after all, a good guy. Nobody in the family had any complaints when he and Lou had decided to tie the knot. In contrast to his relationship with his own family, he'd always gotten along with Lou's parents and siblings without a hitch.

But Jesse wasn't a good party guest today. Rather than mingling, he sat on the opposite side of the couch from LouEllen's stepdad, Pop-Pop, and pretended to be interested in a football game he couldn't give two shits about all to avoid human interaction.

When the family finally sat down at the table, Carrie Mae posed a question that caught Jesse off-guard.

"So, Jesse," she began, "Lou mentioned you're getting back into writing again?"

Jesse blinked, surprised that LouEllen had brought it up at all. After all, she was entirely against the idea—or, at least his story concept. But he knew Carrie Mae well. The woman was as sweet as she was calculating. It was clear her goal was to make Jesse the center of attention, even if it was only for a few minutes. Perhaps she was doing it to get back at him for being a wretch of a husband. Or maybe he was being ridiculous again, too sensitive. Sure, Lou had probably vented to her younger sister, but that didn't mean she'd been malicious. A wife could complain about her husband without wanting a divorce, right? Of course she could.

Eventually, Jesse nodded in response. "That's right," he said.

"Writing?" Pop-Pop asked with genuine interest, though his concentration was never undivided on game day. He'd left the television on in the living room, albeit with the volume nearly all the way down. Regardless, the man's attention shifted from his plate to Jesse's face to the Detroit Lions piling on top of each other on the gridiron. "What kind of writing?" he asked.

"Fiction," Jesse said.

"Like the stuff you teach the kids at school?" Pop-Pop asked, his focus forever moving.

Pop-Pop, whose name was actually Dwayne, was typical of older Warsaw generations. He had completed school through the eighth grade, then dropped out to work on his dad's Christmas tree farm. Reading was not his forte, and writing was even further from his niche.

"Just like it," Jesse said.

"Well, I'll be," Pop-Pop marveled. "LouLou, you never told us Jesse was a writer."

LouEllen gave her stepdad a terse smile, which Pop-Pop completely missed—the Lions had just scored a field goal. Lou turned to Ian, who was holding a spear of broccoli in a single fisted hand, eyeballing the vegetable with skepticism.

"You did a lot of writing in high school, right Jesse?" Carrie Mae asked.

"High school." Pop-Pop looked back to the table. "That's ancient history, innit? Didn't you graduate along with LouEllen?"

"Lou was a year behind me," Jesse explained.

"And LouLou, you graduated in…"

"2001," LouEllen said.

"That long ago?" Pop-Pop asked, astonished by the passing of time.

Jesse chewed on the inside of his bottom lip, trying not to curl into himself. Yeah, it had been that long ago, which only made him feel that much more creatively inadequate. Did he even still have it in him to write anything? Lately, it didn't feel like it.

"Oh, stop." Missus Augusta finally spoke. "You're making me feel old." Age was a touchy subject for LouEllen's mother. Of all the years Jesse and Lou had been together, Miss Augusta had skipped every one of her birthdays. Buy her so much as a birthday card and you'd be on the woman's shit list for the rest of the year.

"Well, what're you writing about, anyway?" The question was posed by Thomas, Lou and Carrie's older brother.

Jesse and Thomas had ducked out of many a family event to hang out on Missus Augusta and Pop-Pop's back porch. He'd always been an ally when Jesse needed one. But this time Jesse hesitated in answering the question, because Warsaw folks knew that farmhouse. There was a dark superstition attached to it despite its lack of written history. One glimpse of its exterior stirred up thoughts of ghosts and ax murderers in every kid in town. It was a place you went on a dare, or a drive you took with a date so that she'd scoot up nice and close and cling to your arm. Hell, it's where Casey was going to take LouEllen after prom. The idea of them having sex on an old, rotting mattress had never entirely left Jesse's bank of imagined scenarios.

"Um." Jesse shifted his weight in his dining room chair. "It's about that old house, the one just north of town?" He posed it as a question, because maybe they wouldn't know which house he meant.

"Sweet Lord." Missus Augusta immediately crossed herself, then regarded LouEllen, her face a mask of worry. She knew as well as anyone that Reed had died in there. She also knew that, only two weeks before, Casey had pulled the same maneuver, and Jesse had borne witness to his final moment on earth.

Lou offered her mother a faint what-do-you-want-me-to-say sort-of look. It dripped with a strange sort of penitence, as though her inability to talk Jesse out of writing about that nightmare house marked her failure as a wife. Watching her grow uncomfortable in her own skin, Jesse glared at the untouched Caesar salad on his plate. Lou's expression made him feel dirty, like his interest in the farmhouse made him less of who he was *supposed* to be—a teacher, a smart man, someone who walked away from gross and glaring tragedy, not reveled in it like some sort of masochist. For a flash of a moment, he considered blurting out that the farmhouse had been LouEllen's idea. *She* had encouraged him to give in to Casey's request. *She* told him to go to that abandoned place, all in the name of inspiration. And now that he'd found it, Lou resented the whole thing.

"I thought you said it was fiction," Pop-Pop said, actually interested enough to keep his attention off the game.

"It is," Jesse said, his gaze remaining fixed upon his plate.

"But it's about a real place?" Pop-Pop didn't get it. Weren't books about real places history, not make-believe?

"It's inspired by a real place," Jesse explained. "I'll probably change the location of the building in the story..."

"There's something wrong with that house." Missus Augusta spoke, and all eyes—Jesse's included—turned toward her. His throat went dry at her words, because it was what Casey had said, too.

"Oh, you think I don't know?" A smirk rolled across the top of her lip. "I was young once, too," she said. "I had friends just like yours, folks who loved going to spots they didn't belong, messing with things they didn't understand. I heard about what happened to your friend, Jesse," she said. "And I've heard about what happened to the other one, too."

Jesse wasn't sure why it rattled him to hear both Casey and Reed brought up in the same breath. After all, they were the reason Ian had practically lived with Carrie Mae for the past week. It was no secret what Casey had done. And yet, Miss Augusta's frankness soured his stomach.

"You know I love you, honey," Missus Augusta said. "And I'm not nearly as smart as you are. But believe me when I tell you that writing about places where bad things happen only gives those places what my daddy used to call *favorable circumstance*. There's an old belief that the more you think about something, the more energy it takes from you. That goes both ways, Jesse, good or bad. And you—" She turned to LouEllen. "You know all this, yet you still let him toy with this nonsense?"

LouEllen frowned at her mother. "I've *tried* to tell him, Momma," she muttered. "Besides, it's just a story."

"I'll tell you one thing about stories," Missus Augusta said, her eyes coming back to Jesse. "Fiction is fantasy, but it comes from truth. Isn't that right?"

It wasn't a rhetorical question. She was waiting for Jesse to respond. He nodded but didn't speak. Yes, he supposed she was right.

"When you amplify that truth, it's like giving whatever truth it has a megaphone. Amplify the negative, and negativity is what you'll get. You stop this before you start it, Jesse," she said. "You step away before it goes too far, you understand?"

Jesse said nothing. Neither did anyone else. And for that he was grateful, because he already had LouEllen challenging his decision. Now, here was his mother-in-law, jumping on the bad idea bandwagon. If anyone else at that table spoke up with a *yeah, maybe write something else,* Jesse was sure he'd excuse himself and spend the rest of the party freezing his ass off outside.

"Well," Missus Augusta murmured. "I suppose you'll do what you want. You kids always do. But you heard what I think about it. The *both* of you. And that's all I'm going to say about that."

Missus Augusta was a woman of her word. She dropped the subject and the rest of Carrie Mae's birthday dinner was spent in relative silence. After the meal, while everyone waited for their food to settle and for the cake to make its grand appearance, Jesse pulled on his coat and ducked out of the house through the living room's sliding glass door. A few minutes later, Thomas joined him on the back porch. He was already fishing out a pack of smokes from the depths of a dirty Carhartt jacket before he ever slid the door closed behind him.

"You want one?" he asked, holding out a pack of Marlboros.

Jesse glanced to the pack held aloft by Thomas's scraped up hands, perpetually stained by motor oil.

"No thanks," Jesse said.

"Suit yourself." Thomas lit his cigarette as both men peered out across a floodlight-illuminated patch of snow. Missus Augusta and Pop-Pop had a lot of property—more than eighty acres if Jesse remembered right. Once, LouEllen had suggested they buy a piece of land out from under them. That way, rather than buying the house they were stuck in now, they could build a bigger one close to Mom and Dad. Jesse still worried about that idea every now and then, worried that if he didn't manage to talk Lou into moving away, that would be their inevitable fate: he, Lou, and Ian living out the rest of their lives way too close to the in-laws, bound to repeat the cycle of living and dying in a zero-opportunity town. Just like that John Mellencamp song LouEllen loved so much.

"You shouldn't listen to my mother," Thomas finally said, cigarette smoke spiraling past his lips. "You know how she is. Throw a black cat at her and she'll cross herself a thousand times and beg Jesus for mercy."

Jesse gave that a soft laugh, but he knew better than to talk badly of his mother-in-law. Thomas, however, was allowed.

"I mean, I get the appeal," Thomas said, taking a second drag off his smoke. "I imagine that place is a festering wound for you, isn't it?"

Jesse gave his brother-in-law a look. *It is that obvious?*

"I mean, hell, if it were me...?" Thomas shrugged, then shuddered, though Jesse couldn't tell if it was brought on by the thought of being in his shoes or the fact that it felt a few degrees below zero out on that porch. "I overheard the girls talking before dinner," he said. "You want to move away?"

Jesse winced. "Lou brought that up?"

"Don't worry," Thomas said. "I was eavesdropping. Nobody but me and Carrie know. Especially not Momma."

"For now," Jesse said.

"Right. For now," Thomas agreed. "But whatever, right? It's not Momma's life."

No, it wasn't. But it *was* her grandson, and Jesse knew Missus Augusta would throw a Grade A fit if she couldn't see Ian on the regular. Not that Detroit was that far away...

"Don't mention that I said so, but I think it's a good idea," Thomas continued. "I mean, you have a family. I wouldn't want to be here, either. Because *this* place? Give it another twenty years and it'll be nothing but a ghost town, man. Once the old folks die off, who will be left?"

"You," Jesse said, "if you stay."

"And even *I'll* be geriatric by then," Thomas chuckled. "Besides, if you and Lou take off, it'll be a hell of a lot easier to follow."

"She'll never go for it," Jesse said, looking back out across the snow.

"She will," Thomas said. "If you manage to sell that book you're writing."

"She said that?" Jesse asked.

"Nope." Thomas took another pull off his cigarette. "But I'd put money on it. Listen, you get serious about leaving, and I'll tell her I want to leave, too. The shop is on its last leg, man," he said. "Jax's been talking about selling off the stock for scrap and shutting the doors. You know where that'll leave me?"

"I can take a guess," Jesse murmured.

"Out of a goddamn job, is where," Thomas said. "Hell, I know Carrie wants out, too. She's been wanting to move to that fancy-ass Grosse Pointe for as long as I can remember. And she shouldn't be stuck here, either, you know? You tack the two of us onto the end of that deal, and how could Lou refuse?"

"And what about your parents?" Jesse asked.

Thomas waved a hand. "All they do is watch television, man. I swear, Momma is addicted to that Court TV crap. That and Hoarders. Have you seen that show?"

Jesse had heard of it.

"Anyway, they aren't exactly the eighth world wonder. Besides, it would do them good to load their asses into the car and—"

Their conversation came to a halt when the glass door behind them slid open. LouEllen popped her head out into the cold. "Cake," she said, then gave both her husband and brother a dubious look. "Also, it's freezing out here. What're you two doing?"

"We were just going in," Thomas said, flicking his half-smoked cigarette over the railing and into the snow. "Because you never know when Momma will start talking about black magic, do you?"

LouEllen narrowed her eyes at her sibling.

"Maybe she'll perform a Voodoo ritual before Carrie blows out the candles. She can chant a few incantations. Wouldn't want to miss *that*. And neither would you, right?" Thomas gave Jesse a wink.

"I wouldn't," Jesse said, but he couldn't quite get over Miss Augusta's claim.

There's something wrong with that house.

The woman was beyond superstitious, but this time Jesse couldn't help but wonder if maybe she was right.

TWENTY-FOUR

DURING THEIR drive home, LouEllen sat silently in the passenger seat and Jesse couldn't help but wonder, was she replaying the dinner conversation that had occurred a few hours before inside her head? The fact of the matter was, the more *Jesse* recounted it, the more aggravated he felt. Missus Augusta's lecture had been humiliating, and LouEllen had just sat there, allowing her mother to talk down to him as though he were a child.

"Are we on speaking terms?" Lou finally asked, as if sensing his anger.

"I don't know," he said. "Are we?"

She sighed toward the window, not liking either his answer or his tone.

Spurred on by his discussion with Thomas, he decided to pursue a conversation. "I just don't understand why you wouldn't defend what I want to do."

"Defend what?" she asked. "That damn farmhouse?"

"Yeah," Jesse shot back. "That damn farmhouse."

"Why would I do that?" she asked. "I told you, I don't like the idea. That hasn't changed."

"Because *you* told me to go there with Casey." His fingers tightened against the steering wheel. "You thought it would be great inspiration, remember?"

"Yeah, well, that was before—"

"Before," he said, cutting her off. "Who cares what it was before? What matters is that you wanted me to go and I went. And now that

I've found something to write about, you don't like it. Well, that's not how this works, Lou."

"Keep your voice down," she told him, glancing toward the backseat. Ian was sleeping. If Jesse woke him, there'd be hell to pay.

"You can't pick and choose someone's subject matter until your happy, alright?" he said, lowering his voice to an angry whisper. "And you certainly shouldn't just sit there when your mother lays into me about wanting to do something beyond wasting my life."

LouEllen brought her right hand to her mouth to keep herself from speaking. She continued to look out the window, leaning into the door—a blatant attempt at creating as much distance between them as she could in such a confined space.

That was it, then. Conversation over.

But after a minute of silence, LouEllen spoke again.

"Her point is that it's dangerous to dwell on the negative," she said, "And I didn't defend you because I happen to agree."

Jesse kept the car rolling for another ten seconds, but he finally lost his nerve and veered into a gas station parking lot. He hit the brakes and shoved the car into park while trying to keep his cool, but he could hardly believe what he was hearing. He was trying to better himself, trying to expand his horizons, trying to move past a tragedy in a creative way and, in the end, maybe have a book to show for his efforts. It was something that, if he was lucky, might dig them out of their financial hole. And yet, LouEllen was telling him it was a bad idea, that he should give it up, forget it, quit. Because it gave her bad vibes.

It was ridiculous; nothing but black cats and broken mirrors. Fucking Voodoo rituals. And then, out of the blue, he thought to himself, *she's just like her mom*. It was a betrayal he hadn't seen coming, which is why it was such a jarring sting. Why couldn't she understand why he had to do this? Why couldn't she just squeeze his hand and tell him she was proud of him for working through his grief, for wanting a better life for their family? *Because no matter how much you love her, she's just like the rest of them; a small-town girl.*

"You're right," Jesse finally said. "It's dangerous to dwell on the negative."

LouEllen exhaled a breath of relief—*thank God*—and reached for his hand. But he pulled away from her touch.

"Which is why I'm not going to dwell on the fact that you've turned your back on me," he told her, making her tense all over again. "The moment I need you most, Lou," he said. "And you aren't here."

TWENTY-FIVE

WHEN THEY pulled into the driveway, LouEllen said nothing. She unfastened her seatbelt and stepped out of the car, then pulled the back door open to retrieve Ian from his car seat. Jesse left her out in the cold while she struggled with the buckle. When he stepped inside, Winston glanced up from his pillow in the living room, then growled deep in his throat; either not recognizing his owner or sensing the oncoming storm.

"Seriously?" Jesse scowled at the dog. Winston remained on his pillow, tentative. But as soon as Lou and Ian appeared in the doorway, he jumped up and greeted them in his usual tail-wagging way.

Jesse rolled his eyes and moved into the kitchen. Lovely. Even the dog had forsaken him. Clearly, he was on his own.

Pulling open the fridge, he searched the appliance for something to drink. He eventually grabbed a bottle of water; though, what he really wanted was a goddamn beer. Twisting off the cap, he took a swig, then rubbed his face with a hand. He hated fighting with LouEllen. It wasn't like them to be at each other's throats, and it wasn't like him to be so quick to anger, so eager to speak up when she pissed him off, so willing to hurt her feelings. Hell, once upon a time, they were the perfect couple. They'd always been able to sort out their problems without so much as raising their voices. But their relationship no longer felt like it had in the past.

LouEllen came into the kitchen with a sleepy and whining Ian against her shoulder. She walked around Jesse as though he wasn't there, grabbed a bottle from the refrigerator, and dropped it into the warmer. She said nothing as she stood there, bouncing Ian on her hip, tempting Jesse to get it over with, to just apologize.

But even if he did try to salvage the crumbling bridge between them, would it matter? He wasn't going to change her opinion on his writing project, and he wasn't willing to give up the book. Not after how the idea of writing again had made him feel, if only for a moment—invigorated, creative, as though he'd rediscovered some sort of long-lost purpose. There was power in that black Ford rolling up the frozen drive. There was mystery in the panicked girl that had come flying down the front porch steps. She'd haunted him for so long, ever since he was a kid. And now, finally, she was coming to him after all this time, ready to reveal her tale. Perhaps, if he could uncover Georgiana's truth, he could start to understand what happened to Casey, what happened to Reed.

Jesse rose from the table, grabbed his water, and abandoned the kitchen for the living room, where he took a seat at his desk. Maybe LouEllen wouldn't understand why he needed to do this, but she would later, after he'd finished his manuscript. She'd read it, look up at him from the pages before her, and nod as if to say *I get it now. This is catharsis. You did what you had to do for yourself, for them, for us.*

He turned when he heard her step into the living room. She was watching him from the kitchen's threshold, possibly considering clearing the air herself. But rather than saying that she was tired of fighting, she just shook her head at him and pivoted away. Jesse wasn't sure how long he could handle being at odds like this, but he also couldn't abandon the Ecklunds. He needed to know what was happening to Georgiana. LouEllen would resent him for it, but only for as long as it would take him to finish.

And so, he decided then that he'd write as fast as he could. Because the quicker he got the story out, the faster he could let LouEllen read it. And the quicker that happened, the faster things could get back to the way they'd once been.

Or, at least the way he wished they could be, minus two. Because, despite his sudden surge of optimism, he knew one thing for sure. No amount of writing would bring Reed or Casey back from their graves. But this, at least, would maybe keep Jesse from digging his own.

TWENTY-SIX

THE BLACK Ford pulled up to the farmhouse just as Georgiana came flying through the front door and into the snow. Had she not stumbled down the front porch steps and landed on her hands and knees, any onlooker may have thought she was rushing not away from the house, but toward the doctor who had just arrived. With her eyes wide and her face full of panic, she stared at the man that now took her by the shoulders and held her in place.

Hannah Ecklund dashed into the cold after her daughter.

"Please," she said as she approached them both, her own frame shrinking against the biting wind. "Come inside." When she reached them, she paused as if to consider something, her gaze fixed upon her daughter. Then, rather than taking her child by the arm, she let Doctor Ladeaux's grip remain steadfast. It was as if she knew the moment she took Georgiana into her own care, the girl would twist away and run.

She followed Georgiana and the doctor up the stairs and into the foyer, then spoke again.

"Joe, show the Doctor to the great room." And then she turned her back on her guest and busied herself at the door, locking it behind them.

There were two deadbolts on the door, and a third lock that only worked with a key. Hannah tried to be discreet, but Ladeaux noticed her fish the key out of her apron pocket, sealing them all inside. He considered protesting, and perhaps he would have if Joseph hadn't stepped forward, inviting Ladeaux to join him deeper inside the house.

Elegant yet straightforward furnishings decorated the great room. There was a couch upholstered in a velveteen-like fabric, it's deep blue color almost shocking against the vibrant yellow wallpaper behind it. A couple of matching wooden-armed chairs sat near the sofa, angled away from the fireplace and its opulent white marble mantle. A family portrait hung above the roaring fire.

"Should I…?" Doctor Ladeaux nodded toward his hands, which were still upon Georgiana's shoulders. Joseph responded in the affirmative, but only after turning to his wife for guidance.

"The door is locked," Hannah said softly.

The Doctor's hands fell away from Georgiana's arms.

"I'll make some coffee," Hannah murmured, then disappeared into a separate room.

Georgiana failed to react when Ladeaux let her go, as if not feeling the release of his grasp. She stood in the center of the room, blank-faced until her father stepped forward and guided her to one of the armchairs across from the couch. Ladeaux took a seat upon the sofa near the fire, then removed his hat and placed it upon the curve of his knee. His focus lingered upon the family portrait, attempting to decipher what type of child Georgiana had been before the family had called on him for help. After a moment, he offered both father and daughter a brief smile.

"So," he said, pausing to watch Joseph with mounting curiosity. The man was backing away from Georgiana much the way an owner would back away from an unpredictable, untrained dog. He kept his wrists flexed at his sides as if to say *easy, easy now*. Eventually making it to the second chair, he took a seat, his eyes remaining steadfast on his daughter. It took him a moment, but he built up the nerve to look away from her, finally giving Ladeaux his attention.

Ladeaux cleared his throat. "What seems to be the trouble?"

"It started last September, in South Bend," Joseph began. "Hannah's niece was getting married, so we drove down for the festivities. It was nice." His gaze wavered, heavy with regret. "The weather was good. The wedding was on Hannah's brother's farm, with the ceremony held outside. There was dancing inside the barn afterward. Georgiana found it lovely," he said, his voice tensing at the memory. "She looked so pretty in her yellow dress and sun hat. Hannah had bought them at Hudson's."

Ladeaux listened patiently, nodding, then fishing inside the pocket of his overcoat with his right hand. He brought out a silver cigarette case and a small leather-bound notebook.

"Mind if I smoke?" he asked.

"Not at all," Joseph said.

Ladeaux pressed a cigarette between his lips, then opened his notebook to where he'd stuck a tiny pencil between its pages. "Tell me when the trouble started," he said. "When did Georgiana's behavior become..." He paused, looked at the girl, then turned back to her father. "...hysteric."

"Well, that's the thing, Doctor," Joseph said, wringing his hands. "Everyone's behavior became hysteric. What happened was a tragedy."

"And what was it that happened?" Ladeaux asked.

"I'm really not sure how she got there." Joseph's features became infinitely solemn. "Someone should have seen her climbing up there, yet nobody did."

"Climbing up?"

"Onto the roof of the barn," Joseph said.

"Georgiana climbed up onto the barn?" Ladeaux asked, his eyebrows raised.

"No, not Georgiana. Her cousin," Joseph clarified. "Little Emma. She was only seven. Georgiana was the first to see her up there, balancing along the roofline, her arms extended, the hem of her dress flapping in the breeze."

It was then that their conversation stalled. Hannah entered the room, a silver tray of cups and saucers rattling with each step. She paused, then nodded to a small side table pushed up against the wall. Joseph rose from his chair and moved the table in front of the sofa.

"Doctor Ladeaux," she said. "Please, your coat, your hat. Make yourself at home." She placed the tray of coffee onto the table, then motioned for him to hand over his things.

"It's fine," Ladeaux protested, but Hannah wouldn't hear it.

"I insist," she said. "You came so quickly, and all the way from the city."

Ladeaux placed his small notebook onto a sofa cushion, handed the woman his hat, and shrugged out of his coat.

"Thank you," he said, retaking his seat. Hannah rushed off with his things, and Ladeaux retrieved his notebook, glancing back to Joseph.

"I'm sorry," Joseph said, "I've lost my place."

"Little Emma," Ladeaux reminded him. "She'd climbed up onto the barn."

"Yes." Joseph heaved a breath, clearly not wanting to rehash the memory. "Many of us were scattered about the area. Some were inside the barn, enjoying the reception. Others were taking in the sun, leaning against the horse fences, watching the animals out in the fields. Emma yelled down to Georgiana, who was out on the grass."

"And what did she yell?" Ladeaux asked.

It was then that Georgiana looked up, speaking in a high-pitched little girl's voice, causing both her father and doctor to startle. "Hey, Georgie!" she squawked. "Catch!"

"Catch?" Ladeaux asked.

A smile did a slow crawl across Georgiana's mouth.

"Catch," Joseph said softly.

"Catch what?" Ladeaux asked, his stare still fixed on Georgiana. Because the grin she wore was shifting from pleasant to something different, something unhinged.

"Catch her," Hannah said, stepping back into the room, her hands clasped before her, as if in prayer.

Hannah's reappearance triggered something in the girl. The moment her mother returned, Georgiana began to laugh low in her throat.

"Catch *her*," Hannah repeated in a whisper.

"...and then what?" Ladeaux asked, sounding unsure of himself for the first time since he'd arrived.

"And then she jumped," Hannah said softly. "And nobody caught her."

"Georgie rushed to Emma's body," Joseph recalled. "She practically lied on top of her, screaming her name."

"Until she stopped," Hannah recalled. "She just...stopped."

"It took three grown men to pull her off of Emma's body," Joseph said.

Ladeaux's attention jumped from Georgiana to her parents, and back to Georgiana again. And this time, when he made eye contact with the girl, Georgiana's lips pulled away from her teeth.

"That's what I can't unsee," Hannah said.

"Emma jumping," Ladeaux concluded, but Hannah shook her head.

"No," she said. "Not that. I can't unsee Georgie's face when they finally pulled her free." Hannah's fingers trailed across the curve of her bottom lip, as if recalling that terrible moment. "She was grinning," Hannah whispered. "Smiling as though her dead little cousin had told her the funniest joke."

And it was then that Georgiana began to laugh.

TWENTY-SEVEN

JESSE HEARD LouEllen's approaching footsteps as he typed the final line of the passage he was working on.

...Georgiana began to laugh.

A moment later, he snapped his laptop shut.

Lou stepped into the living room, slowing her steps when he looked her way. She was carrying a plate in one hand, a glass of water in the other. Hesitating, as if reconsidering her approach, she eventually completed the distance and placed a sandwich next to her husband's elbow—ham and cheddar on white bread, cut diagonally, just like he liked it.

"Figured you were hungry," she said. "Sorry if I distracted you ..." She turned and began to walk away.

Say something, he thought.

Maybe this was Lou's way of trying to mend the bridge, to extinguish at least some of the flames that had been lapping at their delicate bond. But he didn't speak, and he didn't get up to follow her. Something held him in place, silent and unmoving. It was an uninvited yet somehow reassuring weight, reminding him that his work, this story, was the most important thing. LouEllen would be there later. Inspiration, though? That was fleeting. So fleeting that it could vanish in an instant, never to return. He had to stay the course.

He turned back to his computer, but that single moment of distraction had been enough. Staring at the plate Lou had delivered, his mind went blank. He grabbed half a triangle of the sandwich and took a bite. Still nothing.

Georgiana was punishing him for wavering.

She had evanesced, refusing to tell him more.

"Great," he murmured, then pulled himself out of his seat and moved to the hall. He considered seeking out his wife, but that seemed like a bad idea. Because now, with his rhythm disrupted, that familiar spark of aggravation began to smolder again. It was the same annoyance that had pushed him to unpredictability with Shawn Gregory. Even after kicking Shawn out of class, Jesse continued to think about tracking the kid down and laying into him, if only to teach him a lesson.

It's why he didn't trust himself anymore. This anger? It didn't make sense. It wasn't a sensation he was used to. Jesse had always been an amicable kind of guy. He'd never been in a physical fight in his entire life. He'd only ever gotten into a serious verbal altercation maybe half a dozen times. The buzzing tension he was feeling so often now was alien to him, like poison flowing through his veins.

It was that odd, amped-up feeling that kept him from wandering down the hall to find his wife and son. He knew as soon as he showed himself, Lou would give him an annoyed look, and that look would be enough. His irritability would kick in. He'd say something stupid and make things worse. Tense words would spiral into a full-fledged argument. They'd yell in front of the kid.

Stepping into the bathroom, he cranked the tub faucet to hot, peeled off his clothes, and stepped into the shower for the first time in days. Maybe a shower would wash away his annoyance. He ducked under the stream, closed his eyes, and tried to bring Georgiana back from wherever she'd gone.

Georgiana, standing in a grassy patch of dandelions, peering up at her cousin Emma as she balanced along the barn's roofline.

Emma, shouting down to her.

Reed and Casey, a pair of tightrope walkers precariously balancing on top of Georgiana's house, shouting down at Jesse.

It was becoming more evident, now. There was an invisible line connecting Georgiana's experience to his own. The day Georgiana had become "different," her cousin Emma had leaped from a barn roof. Casey's personality had shifted after he had watched Reed tumble over a farmhouse balustrade. And now it was Jesse's turn, edgy and temperamental, plagued by hallucinations and nightmares, all of which had hit him full-force after Casey had taken his life.

Except that doesn't make sense, he thought. *Because there's real life, and then there's the story you're making up as you go.*

Of course, Jesse's story echoed his own experience. He was the one writing it, after all, weaving his own reality into the tale. The fact that Georgiana had become affected after witnessing a suicide, or a tragic accident, or whatever it was little Emma had been doing up there on top of that barn...that was no coincidence. It was a way for Jesse to subconsciously work through his own grief. Georgiana was a catalyst.

But if *that* was entirely true, then why that smile? That creepy little girl squall.

Hey, Georgie! Catch!

Why the low, rumbling laughter; the same laughter he swore he'd heard in his dream when Hannah had rushed down the stairs to call Doctor Ladeaux?

He pressed his hands to his face as water jetted against the back of his neck. Maybe he needed to step away from the computer and get out of the house for a while. He rinsed the soap and shampoo from his skin, cut the water, toweled off, and made his way across the hall to the bedroom. Lou wasn't there. And while the anger he'd been feeling just a few minutes ago had mostly passed, he decided to give them both some space regardless. Sometimes, it was best to let a fire burn itself out.

He dressed, bundled up in his coat, pulled a beanie over his still-damp hair, and clucked his tongue at Winston as he approached the front door.

"Let's go, Dubs," he said. "Time for a walk."

Winston clumsily scrambled to his feet when he saw Jesse approach, but it wasn't to meet his master on the front mat. It was, instead, to take a few backward steps. Winston issued a muted snarl, and Jesse sighed. This was getting old.

"What's with you?" he asked, crouching to come eye-to-eye with the dog. Perhaps, if he got down to Winston's level, if he reasoned with the beast, the dog would come around. But Winston backed away even further, and this time he exposed his teeth.

Jesse gaped, unable to help his surprise. This, coming from a dog that neither he nor LouEllen had batted an eyelash at when they discovered they were pregnant. Some folks worried that their dogs would get jealous of a new baby, but when it had come to Winston, it hadn't even been a consideration.

And yet here he was, snarling at his owner, wanting no part of whatever was out there in the cold. Even when Jesse held out Winston's leash, shook it, and asked, "want to go?"—*Come on, dog; I just need some company*—Winston continued to sneer. No, Winston didn't want to go. As a matter of fact, the dog was so opposed to going anywhere that, rather than continuing to protest, he stalked out of the living room in search of some peace and quiet, leaving Jesse crouched beside the front door with the dog's lead in his hand.

"Whatever, suit yourself," Jesse murmured, hanging the leash back up beside the door. He grabbed his keys from the hanger instead, trying not to feel offended by Winston's slight, but it was tough. Suddenly, the dog he'd raised from a puppy was wanting less and less to do with him. It was a bitter pill.

Not that it really mattered. Walking a dog in weather so cold would have been nothing short of madness. So, rather than freezing his ass off while dragging Winston around their dying neighborhood, Jesse decided to crawl into the car and take a drive to clear his mind.

He had no idea where he was going as he guided the Altima onto the highway. With the heater cranked to high and the stereo booming, he passed Speedy's and the local Thriftway, the Mister Frosty and Warsaw High. Before he knew it, he was guiding the car onto the rutted drive that would lead him up to that terrifying relic hidden among the trees, not having realized he'd been driving toward the house until it was right in front of him.

He felt outside of himself as he crept closer, imagining the stoic and stone-faced Doctor Ladeaux—curious, if not slightly apprehensive about the girl he'd been called to meet. Jesse turned down the drone of 90's hits until it was almost muted, but not quite. He left 4 Non Blondes to play themselves out if only to save himself from deafening silence.

...what's going on?

The car rolled to a stop in the middle of the road, and with his foot on the brake, Jesse tried to picture the scene: Doctor Ladeaux gathering his things, slowly exiting the vehicle. Georgiana flying out the front door, stumbling down the front steps. Hannah Ecklund staring wide-eyed at Ladeaux with a look of horrified distress.

Oh my God, do I pray...

He tried to imagine what had transpired upstairs to have sent Hannah skittering to the telephone. What had Georgiana been doing to cause such a racket overhead? He imagined raging screams and hissing snarls. And just as he was about press his foot to the gas, those noises came to him as vividly as if they were coming from the backseat of the car itself.

Jesse's pulse whooshed in his ears. For a moment, he was afraid to look back, reminded of the ghost stories he'd believed in as a boy. Stories about uninvited backseat passengers. Ghosts you only saw when you glanced into the rearview a second before they grabbed you by the neck and squeezed. But that thought just unnerved him more, and he found himself twisting against the driver's seat to peer into the back.

No ghost.

Nothing but Ian's car seat and an abandoned plastic teether shaped like a giraffe.

You're losing it, Wells.

He faced forward and stared down the length of the dirt drive, still too far away to see the house clearly. Though, if he squinted hard enough, he could make out a few peaks of its multi-tiered roof. Nothing but a silhouette in the dark.

I should turn around, he thought, but a voice whispered inside his head—or was it against the shell of his ear?

But we've come too far.

It's what Casey had told him when Jesse had suggested they leave the place that waited for him in the distance now. Though, if Casey's ghost thought Jesse was going in there tonight, he had another thing coming.

No, he'd just pull forward until he hit the roundabout in front of those broken porch steps. He'd get another look—a refresher so his writing would be more vivid—and get the hell out of there. No big deal.

Except, the closer he got to the building, the stronger its pull became. Jesse couldn't look away from it as he approached the crooked steps, the broken windows that stared out at him like empty eyes. Its eaves and finales became all-the-more intricate as the distance between it and Jesse's car dwindled. For a moment, he swore he saw a flickering of light somewhere inside, like someone igniting an oil lamp. Or maybe they were lighting a fire in the great room.

He eased around the central island and stopped in the same place Casey had parked his Impala two weeks before, then looked to the steps he had tripped down while scrambling toward safety. He shut his eyes again, trying to bring his thoughts back to Georgiana. But instead of seeing the girl, he saw Casey leaning against the top floor's banister, appearing doleful and tired, as though he'd killed himself a thousand times since his funeral, all for the betterment of Jesse's understanding. But this time, Jesse knew what was coming. In his mind, he approached Casey with an outstretched hand.

Please, don't.

Casey canted his head in response, like a curious dog eyeing a friendly stranger. An unnerving smile settled into the corners of his mouth. Finally, he reached out for Jesse's hand. But rather than stepping away from the banister, Casey jerked Jesse forward, moving out of the way in time for Jesse to go tumbling over the railing in Casey's place. And as Jesse fell, the laughter returned, low and rumbling against his ear.

One to go.

Jesse jolted at the sound. It was impossibly real. So real that he could swear he felt breath against his earlobe.

And when his eyes shot open, that's when he saw her.

There, standing at the foot of his bumper, was Georgiana in her dirty white nightgown.

Her hair tangled and matted.

Cheeks sunken and face gaunt.

Her lips cracked and bleeding, wearing a smile so depraved it stopped his heart.

He screamed. His foot came off the brake. The car jerked forward and he cried out again. But there was no thump of a body, no feeling of hitting something solid but soft. She was there one second, gone the next. And as soon as Jesse managed to get the pounding of his heart under control, he whipped the car around the circular drive and put that farmhouse to his back.

And this time, he didn't dare glimpse the rearview mirror's reflection.

No, he was far too terrified to take a chance like that.

TWENTY-EIGHT

BY THE TIME Jesse pulled into his driveway, he'd reasoned the whole thing away. Everything he had seen had been a result of his overactive imagination, a visualization made even more vivid by relentless insomnia. He'd done next to nothing but sit in front of his laptop since Casey had been put in the ground. He'd spent nearly two weeks thinking about that crooked, hollow house.

But the fact that he'd imagined the girl—so vivid, so real—didn't make things any better; if anything, it made matters worse. Because this was why LouEllen didn't want him writing about that place. This was the very thing Missus Augusta had warned him about: focus on the negative, and negativity will inevitably consume you.

But that was nonsense, right? Surely, if he wrote about Georgiana and the Ecklunds, it wouldn't bring them back to life. They were fictional characters, and that house was a dead place, just like Reed and Casey were dead people. Just because Jesse thought about both their suicides a dozen times a day didn't mean he could bring his friends back from the grave.

But that girl.

Jesus Christ, he thought. *She had looked so awful. So real.* But again, it was just a manifestation. *It was Georgiana,* he told himself. *It was her, or, what she had looked like in the end...*

That thought brought on another bolt of inspiration. His dark muse was reaching out and brushing her dirty fingers across his temple. Jesse pivoted toward the steering wheel, then glanced up at his own home, the windows glowing in the dark. Lou had probably heard him pull up. She was most likely peeking around the curtain, wondering what he was doing out in the car. She may have decided that he'd run off to the bar again. Or maybe she was wondering if he was going to bother coming in at all, what with alcohol on his breath.

The bar hadn't crossed his mind until just then, but once it did, Jesse wasn't sure whether he would go inside or book it to the crappy joint down the road. For a long while, he couldn't remember how he'd gotten into that driver's seat or why he'd left the house in the first place; just as he couldn't recall why the hell he'd driven north toward the farmhouse or what had compelled him to park in front of those broken front steps. The past few hours felt out of his control, just like his flashes of anger. Just like his resurfacing itch to drink.

Maybe this is what they call a mid-life crisis, he thought. The tension. The dissatisfaction with his career. The overwhelming need to write a book, as though producing a novel would somehow bring meaning to a life that struck him as wasted and unfulfilled. Or maybe it was none of that, and all he needed was a good night's rest. Perhaps, after all that had happened, he just needed to sleep.

"Where did you go?" LouEllen posed the question as soon as Jesse stepped inside. "I was worried," she said. "You left your phone."

She motioned to his desk, and there it was, his mobile lying next to his computer. Funny, he hadn't realized it had been missing. And that was strange in and of itself, because Jesse had as bad a smartphone habit as anyone—email and social media, Google twenty times a day. He shook his head at the phone, both baffled and amused. But LouEllen didn't find it funny.

"You can't just disappear like that," she told him.

He shrugged out of his coat, then plucked off his beanie.

"This isn't how this works, Jesse," she said, determined to get a response. "You can't just vanish. You have to talk to me. How long is this going to last?"

He turned to her, giving her a questioning look. "How long is what going to last?"

"This." LouEllen motioned toward him as if to say *You; how long are* you *going to last?*

"I don't understand the question," he said, moving around her and away from the door. But he understood it perfectly. Jesse had taken what Missus Augusta would have called *a dark turn,* and

155

LouEllen wanted to know when the old Jesse would be coming back. She wanted to know how long she had to put up with this new, ornery man who seemed to have an interest only in being evasive and writing that damned book.

He walked away from her and out of the living room, but he only did it to gain some distance. What he wanted was for *her* to leave so he could do what he wanted, which was to sit down at his desk and start writing again. He needed to type out what he'd seen out there along that circular drive. Though, he doubted he'd ever be able to unsee that unhinged smile, that cracked and sickly face. She had been hideous. A waking nightmare.

He pulled open the fridge and frowned into its fluorescence, wondering how long it would take LouEllen to clear out of his workspace. That was another thing about this house; had they held out for a bigger one, maybe he'd have a proper place to grade papers, a better spot to write when he was so inclined. Of course, now he was stuck working in the living room with no escape from Ian's fussing. In less than a year, that fussing would be replaced by the drone of toddler TV; cartoons about numbers and the alphabet, the incessant yammering of Spongebob Squarepants and Paw Patrol.

Staying after class was an option, but the idea of spending even an extra minute under those buzzing lights gave him a headache.

He could hit up Java Joe's on the way home. The thoroughly unimpressive coffee shop was one of Warsaw's only spots with reliable WiFi. But talk about replacing one diversion with another. If it wasn't the scream of the burr grinder or the hiss of a steamer wand, it would be an overzealous barista screaming out random names and impatient customers complaining about their drink orders being wrong. Warsaw was middle-of-nowhere, but when it came to coffee, assholes were everywhere. Besides, Java Joe's was clear on the other side of town. If he was going to drive that far, he might as well motor it in the opposite direction toward...

He blinked at the mere thought of it.

The house?

What was he going to do, drag his laptop over there with him and build up the courage to creep past the front door? *Fat chance.* Or maybe plant himself in that rotten old chair on the third floor? *Right. That'll happen.* Or perhaps he'd buy himself a small desk from the second-hand furniture shop next door to the Mister Frosty and create a workspace in front of the great room's fireplace. Hell, why not just trudge up to the fourth floor itself, where he'd have the perfect vantage point from where both Reed and Casey had leaped, where he was sure Georgiana's room had been?

No way. Reed smirked inside Jesse's head. *You're too much of a jellyfish. A gutless wonder, remember? You wouldn't even go upstairs when I—*

"Jesse."

Jesse veered around, the refrigerator door's handle still in his grasp. He felt dazed as he stared at LouEllen, who now stood at the mouth of the kitchen, her arms crossed over her stomach. But her posture wasn't defensive. Her arms were pretzeled in a far more helpless gesture, as though she was trying to comfort herself since nobody else was up to the task.

"Where did you go?" she asked, reminding him that he hadn't answered her question, assuring him that she hadn't forgotten he'd gone missing without so much as telling her he was leaving. If she suspected the bar, she hadn't marched up to him and stuck her nose against his lips. She was giving him time to explain his unacceptable behavior, and she deserved an answer. But Jesse wouldn't, *couldn't* give her the truth.

"School," he said, then immediately busied himself at the fridge so she wouldn't catch his lie. He pulled the door open again, then squinted at an endless selection of condiments.

"Why?" she asked.

"I'm behind on grading. It's easier to think there."

He could feel her hovering, which only made his thirst that much more intense. He reached into the fridge and grabbed a cherry cream soda.

"Essays?" she asked softly.

"Yeah." He twisted the top off the bottle and flicked the cap toward the trash can. It pinged off the rim of the bin and jangled to the floor. He sighed and shuffled to where it had landed, leaned down, and swept it off the linoleum. When he turned, Lou was gone, her scent still lingering in the doorframe when he passed back into the front room.

It was only after he sat down at his desk that he grasped the fact that she knew he was lying, no matter what story he spun. He hadn't gone to school to grade papers, because there, between the wall and back leg of his desk, was his messenger bag—the one that housed all his student's assignments. The one he never went to school without.

TWENTY-NINE

JESSE FELT terrible about lying to Lou, but the guilt wasn't enough to keep him from staying on his computer all night. By the time he noticed the hour, the house was dark save for the droopy task lamp on his desk. He snuck down the hall and peeked inside the master bedroom. Both LouEllen and Winston were asleep—Lou wrapped mummy-tight in the comforter, Winston snoring on his pillow. But rather than slipping into bed beside her, he stood in the hall and listened to Ian's white noise machine thud the sound of a heartbeat through the nursery door. Jesse was waiting for Lou to sense him standing there, but she didn't. It meant the coast was clear.

When he ducked into the kitchen, rather than heading to the fridge, he opened LouEllen's baking cabinet. The thing was chock-full of odds and ends, from a bag of coconut flour to electric blue decorating sugar. But there was also supposed to be something else, something that he doubted she realized he knew about.

She only had a few bottles, and she'd always buy it reluctantly because having alcohol in the house was against the rules. But sometimes a recipe needed cherry kirsch or coffee liqueur—not really stuff Jesse would choose to get drunk off of, but if it wiped that fuzzy feeling from his tongue, it was good enough. Except, even before he opened the cabinet door, he was sure she'd removed those bottles after his slip-up. They had been there less than a month ago. He'd spotted them while seeking out some walnuts for his cup of vanilla ice cream. But now, they were gone, LouEllen perpetually three steps ahead of him. He pictured her pouring that expensive liqueur down the sink the night he came home smelling of booze.

Besides, what the hell he was thinking? Was he really going to get hammered while his wife and child slept just down the hall? Shaking his head at himself, he grabbed a bottled water from the fridge. Flint was less than sixty miles away; close enough to have LouEllen spooked and buying an endless supply.

Back at his desk, he brought up Casey's videos again. He wasn't sure why he couldn't stay away from those things. Before the farmhouse visits, he found Casey's work to be pretty dull; just footage of a guy walking through abandoned buildings and occasionally finding an interesting artifact. Big whoop. But those farmhouse videos, especially part four...Rather than replaying the episode in its entirety, he just watched the moment Casey pointed the camera down the stairwell and caught that mysterious blotch darting out of frame.

Jesse couldn't remember doing it, but he was sure now: he *must* have told Reed about what he'd seen in the window. After his friends had pranked him and Jesse had run down the road in a full-blown panic, he had spilled it all to his best friend in a whirlwind confession. And Reed had gone behind his back and told Casey, because of course he had. They had been eleven-year-old boys who couldn't keep a secret to save their lives. If one of them had claimed to have seen a ghost? That secret would have lasted an hour, tops. The most likely scenario: Reed had told Casey right after the trio had split up to go to their separate houses. Those two had probably been gabbing about it on the phone that very night.

Except, if Reed had told Casey about the figure, wouldn't Casey have said something, even if it was only to make fun of Jesse for thinking he'd seen a phantom out there? Wouldn't both Casey and Reed have taken the opportunity to harass him with Reed's ridiculous *jinkies* and Scooby Doo *zoinks*? Hell, wouldn't a pale and horror-stricken Casey have brought it up after Reed had plummeted through the center of the farmhouse's stairwell? And yet, Casey had said nothing while both he and Jesse had sat locked in his car. Meanwhile, Reed lay on the broken floorboards, unmoving and alone.

It all led Jesse to the seemingly impossible question: what if Reed *hadn't* told Casey about the girl? What if Casey—drawn back to that farmhouse the way Jesse had been lead to it today—had gone back and seen her for himself?

"Reed told him about her," Jesse said softly. "He must have." Because no matter how wild, a story of a phantom girl pushing Reed to the brink of madness made more sense than Reed just having been depressed. It made more sense than Reed deciding he had experienced enough living at seventeen years of age. *Anything* made more sense than that.

But the similarity between Reed and Casey's deaths was undeniable. It was a cycle, whether Jesse wanted to believe it or not; a sequence that hadn't started with Reed, but with Georgiana's cousin, Emma: two fictional people that had never existed. Yet somehow, that didn't matter. At that very moment it made sense, and what Jesse desperately needed was logic, however unsound. Because among all the things he didn't know, he knew one thing without a doubt.

The cycle was repeating.

And he was the only one left.

THIRTY

THE NIGHTMARES refused to stop, which was part of the reason why Jesse started sleeping on the couch.

During one of his dreams, Georgiana was sitting in the farmhouse's living room watching Doctor Ladeaux take notes in his little notebook. And as she listened to her father tell the story of her cousin Emma's accident, she dropped to the floor and began to convulse.

In another, he'd see Georgiana folded over Emma's body while friends and family rushed toward both girls. A few men caught Georgiana by her arms to pull her free of little Emma. When they did, rather than crying, Georgiana grinned up at the sun, basking in unspoken triumph.

In a third, Georgiana was strapped to a four-poster bed, thrashing and squealing as if being skinned. And yet, any time someone would step into her bedroom—be it her mother or father, or especially Ladeaux—she would go deathly silent, pausing her thrashing to watch her visitors with a wide-eyed stare. That was, except if it was Jesse. When *he* stepped inside, she'd arch her back and let her tongue roll over her dry, cracked lips. Lewd noises would escape her throat as she spread her knees wide, inviting him in.

That one was a reoccurring dream, one where he'd either flee the room in disgust or inch closer to the mattress, as though genuinely considering climbing into her bed. He'd managed to stay asleep long enough to let that happen only once. It resulted in jolting awake and a scream sitting heavy at the back of his throat.

He decided to start sleeping on the couch after that.

And then there was the laughter, low and rumbling, yet somehow simultaneously, inexplicably childlike. He heard it in his dreams, but sometimes he could swear it lingered beneath the dull roar of the shower or the drone of the car radio, too. Once, he heard it in the middle of class during silent reading, so close to his ear he swore he could feel breath on the back of his neck. It had made him jump enough to knock a stack of papers off his desk. His students sat there, watching him from behind their copies of *Lord of the Flies* with muted fascination. Because not only was he startling at nothing, but he looked terrible. The dark circles under his eyes were so distinct, he hardly recognized himself when he glanced in the mirror. It was disquieting. He began to avoid his own haunted gaze.

By the time the one-month anniversary of Casey's death was on the horizon, Jesse had lost the ability to keep track of time. He'd stand up to address his second-period students only to dismiss fourth period to lunch. He was sleepwalking through his lesson plans, and while he could tell the kids had noted his exhaustion, they didn't altogether mind. A sleepy teacher was an inattentive one, and that suited most of them just fine. Sometimes, when Jesse would look up from his desk, he'd see a sea of glowing blue faces, heads bowed over cell phone screens. Once, phones were forbidden in class. Now, Jesse couldn't have cared less. His students recognized his indifference and took advantage. Silent reading devolved into time to check Facebook, post selfies, and scroll through celebrity Instagram feeds.

The days bled one into the other, each one an echo of the last. Get up, drive to work, go home, try to write; all of it followed up by passing out on the couch and waking up terrified. Even when the nightmares began to shift, to involve Casey and Reed—Reed jumping, Casey folding himself over his unmoving body the same way Georgiana had leaned over Emma—the fear felt routine.

LouEllen began to search for the perfect combination that would jolt Jesse out of what could only be described as a fugue-like state. But the only thing that shook him from his trance was that fucking laughter.

It's what startled him as he walked down the school hallway, his shoulders jerking and every muscle going tense. It happened in the wrong place at the wrong time; right before lunch and directly in front of Principal Garvey's office. Garvey was standing in his open office door, hawk-eyed as students shuffled past him. That look quickly zeroed in on Jesse, taking note of his reflexive startle.

"Mr. Wells," Garvey said, both eyebrows arching high on his forehead. "Just the man I was hoping to see."

Jesse was tired, but not tired enough to keep the swell of dread from filling his chest like a balloon. Both students and teachers had noticed Jesse's state. Sam had been kind enough to not bring it up—continuously feeding Jesse a string of peanut butter crackers at every lunch, like a kid feeding an injured bird. But Jesse had noticed all the sidelong glances. The kids. The teachers. Hell, he'd heard the whispers.

Is he all right? Should he even be here?

Then again, that may have been his imagination. It seemed that these days, nearly everything was.

But in the end, all roads led back to Garvey, and that man was now motioning for Jesse to come talk to him. He'd noticed the change in Jesse, same as everyone else. It was his school, and he was concerned.

Jesse stepped inside the office and took a seat in front of Garvey's desk. Meanwhile, Garvey finished addressing a couple of rowdy students in the hall. A moment later, Jesse heard the door shut. The noise of the hallway was dampened, and Jesse rubbed at his left ear. That laughter was back, mocking him.

Wide awake and you can still hear it. How does that feel? Isn't it strange?

It was sleep deprivation. He'd Googled it. Auditory hallucinations weren't common, but they weren't unheard of. He'd seen the way Lou had been watching him over the last few days like maybe she should call someone, like perhaps he should be committed. But Jesse didn't need a shrink. He just needed some nightmare-free sleep.

Garvey took a seat behind his grandiose desk—ridiculous for the school he was governing. If you judged Warsaw High by the heft of mahogany, it was a private school for the gifted, not a failing middle-of-nowhere institution. Garvey's suit was just as out-of-place. It was navy blue, the color crisp against his white shirt and emerald green tie. The man dressed to the nines, as though he was in the habit of dining at Michelin-star restaurants after school. And maybe he was. What did Jesse know? His own reality had become so bizarre, he wouldn't have been surprised to learn the man was secretly a millionaire who sucked down Australian oysters at every given meal.

Garvey folded his hands across his desk blotter, tapped his thumbs against the tops of his hands, and cleared his throat. He was stalling, possibly unsure of how to ask Jesse what was wrong. That, or maybe he'd never fired a teacher mid-semester before.

"Jesse," he finally said, cutting through the formality. "You don't mind if I call you Jesse, do you?"

"No," Jesse said.

He waited for Garvey to say something akin of *excellent, then call me Stan*, but the man didn't extend such pleasantries. Garvey was just Garvey, preferably either Principal or Mister. He didn't bend his authority for anyone. One *hey Stan* in the hallway could bring the entire house of cards tumbling down.

Yo, Jesse!

"Jesse," Garvey said again, this time with a bit of a sigh. "What's going on, son?"

Jesse lifted his gaze from his hands to take in the man before him. Was Garvey actually old enough to be Jesse's father, or was he being condescending? Garvey noted the questioning look, but his stern expression didn't waver.

"Are you feeling all right? There's been some talk," he said.

"Talk?" Jesse asked.

"About your..." Garvey hesitated again, pausing to choose the right word. "...state," he finished.

"My state?" Jesse asked.

Sure, he knew what Garvey was getting at, but he wasn't about to make this easy. If Garvey wanted to play armchair psychologist, fine. Jesse would go along with it. Hell, maybe it would do him some good. But shrinks weren't paid the big bucks for nothing. Garvey was going to have to work for the answers he wanted. And if Jesse didn't get anything out of this impromptu therapy session, he'd at least get to watch Warsaw High's main man squirm in his seat.

"You look tired," Garvey said. "Though, of course, I haven't forgotten what you must be going through."

"I don't understand," Jesse said.

"Your friend," Garvey told him, seemingly particularly uncomfortable with the subject. Jesse raised an eyebrow, as if having forgotten what friend Garvey could possibly be talking about. "Mr. Richmond?" Garvey asked.

"Ridgemont," Jesse corrected.

"Yes, that's right. Ridgemont. From what I understand, Jesse, you were there when it happened?"

Jesse frowned. Of course, Garvey had heard. Everyone knew.

"Jesse, if you don't mind me saying so, you aren't looking very well. Some of the students are worried about your health. They feel that maybe you need more time to..." He lifted his right arm and made an almost delicate motion with his hand, like a bird unfurling long tailfeathers before taking flight. "...gather yourself, I suppose. To regain your bearings. To get back to your old self again."

"There's nothing wrong with me, Mr. Garvey." The words escaped Jesse's lips before he could stop them, as did the smile—like Georgiana speaking to Ladeaux. "I'm perfectly fine. Just a little tired, that's all."

Garvey didn't like that response, and he certainly didn't like the slow creep of Jesse's grin. He shifted his weight in his seat, as if suddenly wanting to cut their meeting short. Perhaps he had been expecting Jesse to be thankful that someone had noticed his sad state, that someone was going to suggest a few extra days off on top of the ones he'd already taken. But an additional few days at home weren't going to do anything but make the tension between Jesse and LouEllen worse. Besides, he'd already used his paid time off. Another week would destroy his paycheck, and the name-brand diapers and special formula that Lou insisted Ian have weren't cheap.

"I understand that may be how you feel, Jesse," Garvey countered, "but that's not the impression I'm getting from seeing you now. I mean no offense by that, you understand," he added, trying to smooth over feathers he may have ruffled. "I'm not here to judge you, Jesse. I'm just here to help."

Jesse imagined this was the talk Ladeaux and the Ecklunds had with Georgiana before she ended up strapped to her bed. *We just want you to be safe. Healthy.* This was the part where Garvey grabbed Jesse by the arms and dragged him down the hall before locking him in the boiler room, wasn't it? *This is for your own good, Jesse. For the good of the kids.*

"Jesse?" Garvey leaned forward, noting his lack of response.

Jesse blinked, then forced another smile. "I'm fine," he said. "I understand your concern, and I appreciate it."

Garvey scowled, not sure whether to buy it.

"Honestly, I'm just tired," Jesse reassured his boss. "But that isn't going to last. I'm planning nothing but sleep for this upcoming weekend," he said. "I have the wife and kid going out of town." Christ, wouldn't *that* be nice? "They're even taking our dog." Winston, that traitor. Jesse was still sore about that stab in the back.

Nothing from Garvey, though Jesse could make out the slightest twinge of relief in his face.

"You're right," Jesse said, sure one more affirmation would seal the deal. "I've been under a lot of stress. This suicide…" He shook his head, clenched his fists in his lap. "It's been hard. I think about it a lot. My sleep has been compromised. But everything is under control."

"So…" Garvey squared his shoulders, trying to decipher Jesse's assurances. "You're just tired," he finally said, echoing Jesse's first excuse.

"Exactly." Jesse nodded. "Just tired."

"Okay." Garvey finally gave in.

Jesse breathed a sigh of relief, but he kept it quiet. He didn't want to come off as too appeased. "Thank you," he said, rising from his seat. "Again, I appreciate the concern. Really, I do." He inched his way to the door, not wanting to be trapped in that office any longer.

"But I want you to be aware," Garvey said, stopping Jesse before he was able to make his getaway. Jesse looked back, waiting for the inevitable ultimatum. "I'm watching you, Mr. Wells. This school is a far cry from Ivy League, but we're determined to give our students the best shot they've got in this little town."

Jesse nodded. "Sure, of course," he said.

"Get some sleep," Garvey said. "And close the door behind you."

It was only when Jesse ducked out of the office that he realized he'd been holding his breath. The last time he'd had such an awkward conversation with a principal, it had been during his senior year. He'd sat in that very office, though back then, the principal had been a tall twig of a man named Albert Herman—a guy most of the students referred to as Pee-wee behind his back. Pee-wee had called Jesse into his office after Reed's death, then offered to excuse Jesse from classes for the rest of the semester if he submitted his assignments on time. Jesse had taken Herman up on his offer, and that had been the beginning of the end. Not having to sit at a desk all day, Jesse ended up blowing all his cash at Speedy's on Snicker's bars and booze.

He imagined the situation would be similar if he found himself with extra time off now, or, God forbid, if he flat-out lost his job. Because what would there be for him to do but sit at his desk, write, and dull his senses? Walking back to his classroom, Jesse pinched the bridge of his nose at the possibility of another downward spiral. Not at all paying attention to where he was going, he didn't notice Sam until he nearly ran into the guy just outside his classroom door.

"Hey," Sam said, stepping out of Jesse's empty classroom. "I was just looking for you."

"Here I am," Jesse said. "Live and in person." He was trying to sound upbeat, but he doubted it was working. Something about the walk from Garvey's office back to his classroom had zapped what little energy he had. Suddenly, all he wanted to do was sneak out to his car and sleep.

"Yeah," Sam said. "In the flesh."

Jesse didn't meet his coworker's gaze, but he could hear it in Sam's voice—Sam didn't like what he was seeing. The drooping shoulders, the disheveled hair; Jesse knew he looked like death warmed over, but he'd used up his supply of bullshit excuses only minutes before. Sam would be allowed to jump to his own conclusions.

"Listen, I wanted to talk to you about something," Sam said.

"Yeah?" Jesse shouldered past Sam to step into his room. Sam followed.

"Yeah. I mean, I don't know if you want to talk about it here, but you know how you wanted to find answers?"

Collapsing into his desk chair, Jesse rubbed his face with his hands. Jesus, he was tired. He wasn't sure he'd ever felt exhaustion this intense before.

"It's not the best time, man," he murmured. "I'm cruising on fumes, here."

Sam stood motionless in front of the open classroom door, one hand clasped around the top of a brown paper lunch sack, the other pressing a history book to his chest like a shield.

"Yeah," he finally said. "I gotcha. Maybe when you're feeling better. You should call me," he suggested. "We'll go have lunch or something. On me."

"Sounds good," Jesse said, and it honestly did sound appealing. Maybe going out to eat was precisely what he needed. Perhaps it was the very thing that would smooth things over between himself and Lou. A night out. A nice dinner. Just like old times.

"Okay," Sam said, still hovering, reluctant to leave. "Just text me and let me know."

"Will do," Jesse told him, finally glancing up to give his friend a nod. Sam nodded back and pivoted to go, then paused and turned again.

"Almost forgot," he said, approaching Jesse's desk. He reached into his lunch sack and brought out a pack of peanut butter crackers.

Jesse gave the cellophane pack a sad smile as Sam made his final retreat. Because those crackers? They felt like the last thread of normalcy in Jesse's quickly disintegrating life.

THIRTY-ONE

IT WAS SNOWING when Jesse stepped out of the school building and into the parking lot. A good quarter of an inch had accumulated on top of the Altima's hood during the last few classes of the day. He climbed into the vehicle and huddled in his coat, waiting for the heat to kick in. And as he did so, his stomach began to roil with anxiety. Because he had to drive beneath that overpass on his way home; the one where he swore he'd seen someone standing with their arms outspread, taking in their final moment.

The story of the Warsaw jumper never made it into the news, which meant it hadn't happened. If someone had leaped onto the highway in a town that size, every person within a twenty-mile span would have been talking about it. But the memory of what Jesse *thought* he saw still made his stomach churn.

Needing some distraction, he woke his phone, navigated into his music app, and scrolled through his playlists. A moment later he was typing 'Eminem' into the search field, unsure what was compelling him to do so. After Reed had died, he'd avoided the rapper's music the way a cat avoided water. Even hearing as little as the first few beats of any track off *The Slim Shady LP* brought him back to that night, to the sound of bottles rolling around beneath Casey's seats. It brought him back to Reed rapping along with the lyrics and laughing. Back to Casey's pallid, terrified face. To the way he had sat behind the wheel and sobbed into the palms of his hands.

Jesse hesitated when the available albums appeared on his screen. Any other day, he'd have thrown his phone into the passenger seat and proceeded to fight off the lump of emotion that was doing a slow crawl up his throat. But today was different. Something about hearing the opening chords of *My Name Is* was too compelling, like hearing the voice of an old friend. He synced his phone with his car stereo and pressed play. Five seconds in, he cranked up the volume. When the track came to an end, he played it again. He looped it all the way home. He even remembered some of the lines.

By the time he pulled into his driveway, he was oddly invigorated. Maybe it had been the hard-driving beat. Or perhaps it was the fact that finally, for once, he'd been thinking about the good times he'd spent with Reed and Casey rather than the tragedy that had erased them from Jesse's life. Whatever it was, the commute had left him feeling encouraged. *Alive* again. Jesse had spent the last few weeks feeling as though the world was against him, but the more he thought about it, the more it seemed as though he was pulling out of his funk.

Garvey had given him a break. Sam had invited him to lunch. Lou was still at the house with Ian. Thomas had lent him support about the book, about his desire to move. Perhaps all that was missing was an extra push of effort. Maybe if he tried a little harder, things would be okay.

Stepping inside the house, Jesse spotted LouEllen waiting for him in the din of the hall. Draped in a dress he hadn't seen in years, her arms were loosely looped around her own waist. She had pulled her hair up and off her neck, and she'd put on what she called her *good makeup*—the stuff she only ever used for special occasions. His gaze paused on the sparking tennis bracelet he'd given her as a push present the day Ian had been born. The cubic zirconia was nothing but a sad excuse for the diamonds she deserved, but she had fawned over it regardless. A tennis bracelet hadn't been the most practical gift for a new mom, however. Ten months later, he hadn't seen her wear it until now.

"Hi," she said as Jesse closed the door behind him.

"Hi," he echoed, giving her a questioning look. "You look...amazing." He hesitated only because he was trying to decipher the occasion. Their wedding anniversary was in July, not January. And it certainly wasn't either of their birthdays.

"What's happening?" he finally asked, waiting for her calm expression to grow cold, for the contours of her features to harden in an I-can't-believe-you-forgot kind of way.

"Nothing much. I just thought since it's Friday, we could spend some time together," she said. "You know, go out. Get something to eat. Maybe see a movie?"

"And Ian?" Jesse asked, unable to help looking across the living room to his desk chair. He'd intended on working on his book all evening.

"Carrie Mae picked him up a few hours ago," she said. "She's keeping him through tomorrow so that we could have some time together." That's when LouEllen dropped her hands to her sides and moved across the room to meet him at the door. Her fingers drifted across the front of his zipped-up coat. "We've had a hard few weeks," she said. "I'm so tired of fighting with you, Jesse. Maybe we just need to get out of the house, you know?"

Exactly what he'd been thinking just hours before.

But now that he was standing there, so close to his desk, it called to him from the corner of the room just as his laptop had been whispering to him all afternoon. *Sit. Write.* The plan had been to come home and bury himself in his work until tomorrow night, *then* get out of the house. But here was Lou, dressed to the nines, already having made plans for them both.

Part of him was relieved. If he was going to put in more of an effort, what better time to start than now? But the other half of him was aggravated, because she could have at least asked if he had scheduled anything for after class. Screw the writing. What if he had wanted to go out with Sam?

"Jesse?" Lou's smile faded a notch. She was coming to realize that despite all her carefully laid plans, he was already zoning out, already thinking about something other than her. "Why don't you go change into something a little more dressy?" she asked, catching the zipper of his jacket between her fingers and giving it a downward tug. "I made a reservation at Marcello's."

"Marcello's?"

It was an expensive Italian joint out in Detroit. They'd only gone there once, and after suffering sticker shock, they'd agreed not to go back. From what Jesse remembered, their dinner menu started at a good thirty-five bucks a plate. *Do you know how much pasta we could make at home for thirty-five bucks?* He'd complained about it during the forty-five-minute drive home. Eventually, they ended up laughing about the bill before crawling into bed together, Lou mewing about how she wanted him to cover her with thirty-five dollars' worth of linguine.

"Marcello's," she whispered against his cheek, remembering the same thing that had just crossed his mind. "I've heard they have fantastic pasta." Pressing herself against him, she nipped at the curve of his jaw. "But they won't let you in wearing those khakis," she told him. "So class it up, buddy." And then she slapped him on the ass and took a sidestep away.

Jesse did as he was told. He took off his jacket and found himself standing in front of a closet full of stuff that was either too casual for a place that charged exorbitant prices, or it was stuff he hated to wear. And the more he brooded, the less he wanted to go.

Sure, Lou had a point; the last few weeks had been hell. Not only had Casey been wiped out in a near-exact rerun of Reed's own end, but now Jesse's marriage was on the rocks. He couldn't remember the last time he'd slept in his bed—had it been Tuesday? Maybe Monday. And he looked so bad that he wanted to obfuscate every mirror he came across if only to avoid seeing his own haggard face.

But none of that mattered. What was important was that LouEllen was trying to make amends. She was trying to make things better.

No, she's trying to keep you from your work.

He furrowed his eyebrows at the stray thought.

She's distracting you from what's important: Georgiana and your book.

He tore a dress shirt off its hanger and flung it onto the bed, then pulled a pair of black slacks off the closet shelf and tossed those as well. That was it, then, wasn't it? LouEllen was manipulating him. After all, she'd been the one who had gone to Garvey after Casey's death. She's the one who insisted he stay home from work without ever asking what *he* wanted to do. And who knows what she had said to Carrie Mae at that awkward birthday party. Hell, she had just sat there while her own mother crawled up Jesse's ass for wanting to do something creative for once.

For a second, Jesse was so pissed he was ready to march into the kitchen or living room or wherever LouEllen was waiting for him and tell her that he was on to her. *I know what you're doing.* And how dare she, when *she* was the one who had started all of this in the first place? Or had she forgotten that part? Because he hadn't. He couldn't. He remembered this was her doing every fucking day.

Jesse glared at his crumpled clothes, those stray but overwhelming pangs of anger needling him. He knew his annoyance was overblown, knew that he was twisting this whole thing up to make Lou into the enemy. Hell, he should have been happy that she still wanted to spend time with him at all. But he couldn't shake that feeling of betrayal, that sense that she'd forsaken him. This was just a ruse to convince him to forget the novel, to settle on teaching, to push everything but the promise of a bi-weekly paycheck aside, happiness and a brighter future be damned.

"Don't be stupid," he whispered to himself, because LouEllen wasn't that kind of person. His brain told him that he was being ridiculous, but that strange, unwavering aggravation remained rooted deep within his chest.

"Just try," he spoke toward his laid-out outfit. Perhaps tonight was the night they mended their relationship and Jesse could celebrate his creativity's homecoming. There was, after all, the possibility that she wanted to go out not to steer him away from his inspiration, but to tell him that she'd been wrong. *I want you to be happy,* she'd say. *I'm so glad you're writing again. I can't wait to read what you've composed.* Because that's what the old Lou would have said. That's the kind of steadfast and unwavering support the girl he had married would have given.

"Okay," he said, tugging his sweater up and over his head. If LouEllen wanted to go to Marcello's, he'd take her. He had to believe that, in the end, she wanted the same thing for their family as he did: betterment, happiness. He was desperate for her to understand that he had to do this, that this story wasn't a choice—at least not anymore. Maybe tonight he could finally explain to her that he had to write it to get those nightmarish images out of his mind.

He had to write it, if only to get *her* to leave him alone.

THIRTY-TWO

MARCELLO'S was the kind of place where waiters dressed in tuxes and held wine bottles over their forearms as they poured. Jesse remembered enjoying himself during their first visit—at least before they were hit with the bill. But this time he felt like an imposter. Half the menu was in Italian, mocking anyone who thought they could correctly pronounce the names. Cioppino, bresaola, pizzaiolo, and guanciale never sounded so intimidating.

Once the overdressed waiter left them with their ciabatta and olive oil, LouEllen reached across the small table and caught hold of Jesse's hand.

"Are you okay?" she asked.

"Yeah," he said, pulling his hand away to pick up a piece of bread. Lou watched him in silence. He could feel her studying him; studying, much the way a psychologist examines their patient—the way Ladeaux had analyzed Georgiana from across a fire-lit room.

"Are you sure?" she questioned. "You seem—"

"Lou, I'm fine," he told her. "I'm just not sure I should have ordered the lasagna."

She appeared puzzled for a moment, then gave him a faint smile. "I'm sure it's going to be delicious."

"Oh, I'm sure," he murmured. "And expensive."

LouEllen exhaled a breath. "Please don't worry about that, okay? Let's just try to have a good time. We've earned it."

Jesse wasn't sure how he wasn't supposed to worry about the check—he was the one paying the bill. That emergency family leave he'd taken had gouged his pay. And how either he or Lou had "earned" anything was unclear. As far as he was concerned, he hadn't earned a damn thing yet, which was why he should have been back home, at his desk, working. Because that book wasn't going to write itself.

Don't get yourself started. Just try, he reminded himself, then gave his wife a nod.

"You're right," he said, "we've earned it," and she relaxed.

Lou made light conversation while they waited for their food. She talked about Carrie Mae's plan to trade in her car for a red Mazda3. She mentioned Pop-Pop's determination to finally get to see a Superbowl in person—the next one was in Miami, and not only did Pop-Pop have friends in The Magic City, but he had accrued enough points on his credit card for a round-trip plane ticket to get himself there and back, free of charge. Jesse listened without saying a word, waiting for her to bring up the book or the farmhouse or Casey or Reed, but she didn't. And when their food finally arrived, he was struck with such an overwhelming sense of nausea, he just about excused himself from the table.

LouEllen peered at him as she picked at her mushroom risotto. Meanwhile, Jesse just stared at his lasagna like a petulant child glaring at a plate of Brussels sprouts. It looked incredible, but he couldn't bring himself to eat.

She leaned across the table and whispered. "What?"

"Nothing," he said.

"Oh, come off it," she jabbed back. Her pleasantries were suddenly spiked with irritation, as though she'd been bottling up that annoyance the entire time. "You've been acting weird all night."

"I just thought you wanted to talk," he told her, the confession making him feel far more vulnerable than he was used to. But that was all part of "trying," right? He had to open up, had to expose his doubts and fears.

"We're talking," she said, her features twisting up in a *what's your problem* sort of way.

"No, I mean about..." He hesitated, then shrugged. *About things that matter,* he wanted to tell her, but he knew that wouldn't come off well.

Meanwhile, LouEllen's face had gone dark. Jesse didn't need to say what he was thinking. She read him loud and clear. He wanted to talk about the things she wasn't willing to discuss. She'd decided that part of their life was over, that they'd moved on. After all, they were at Marcello's having a good time. They were fancy. A perfect couple on a Friday night.

Within a span of a few seconds, Jesse watched a variety of emotions flash across her face: indignation, frustration, exasperation. Because her plan to reestablish normalcy wasn't working. Jesse was still stuck on that house, on that stupid book.

"You can't just drop it, can you? Even for one night?" she asked. "We aren't allowed to enjoy this?" She motioned around Marcello's with a hand. *Look at this place,* the gesture said. *Look at how nice. And you're spoiling it, Jesse. Just like you're ruining us.*

"I'm sorry." He grimaced down to his plate of food. "I just want to be on the same page about this."

"The same page," she repeated.

"I don't want to feel like you're against me, Lou," he told her. "Against this project. I don't know why you can't just be supportive."

"I'm not supportive?" She laughed. It was a cold snort, like he'd just said the stupidest thing she'd ever heard.

He frowned at his complaint, at the sound of her disdain. Because she was right. She was his rock, his everything. Had it not been for her support, he'd probably be lying six feet beneath the carefully manicured Cedar Grove lawn. And that was more than likely where her anger was stemming from. She'd put so much effort into maintaining their relationship, especially during these past few weeks. But she'd had it.

He heard her sigh.

"Look, I know this is hard," she said. "It was hard last time, too, remember? But back then we were kids. Now, we're adults. You should be better able to cope."

He couldn't help it. The question left his lips before he could swallow it down.

"Are you serious?"

"Why wouldn't I be serious?" she asked.

He stared at his food. He thought their conversation had been kept to a hush, but he could feel eyes on them. Other patrons were eavesdropping. Wives were eagerly whispering to their husbands. *Oh, an argument!* Trouble in paradise. The ultimate in Friday night entertainment.

Their waiter noticed the tension. He rushed back to the table, doling out concern.

"Is everything all right?" Pensive, he wrung his hands, waiting for a response, as though his job depended on their satisfaction alone.

"Sure," Jesse said after a moment, then let out a quiet laugh. Because this was ridiculous. If Lou wanted to talk to him about coping, why bring him here? They should have ordered pizza, stayed home, and hashed it out where they could have yelled and cried if they needed to. But instead, they had to pretend they could afford to eat here, pretend that they were just like the couples that came to Marcello's on the regular.

And what was this nonsense about coping *like an adult?* Was she suggesting that Jesse's inability to push through such trauma made him a child? What did she expect him to do, forget about Casey? Forget what he'd seen? Move on, just as Blaire had told him to? Jesse was discovering that he couldn't do that, and was that really so bad? He hadn't dealt with his grief after Reed's death, so it was only natural that he'd have a hell of a time dealing with it now.

"Maybe some wine?" the waiter asked.

Jesse felt LouEllen go stiff. He saw her in his periphery, ready to respond, determined to force Jesse into a box she insisted he fit into—a box labeled *good dad, good husband, sober human being.* All at once, it reminded him of how she always answered for Ian. No, Ian didn't want any juice. No, he couldn't open that drawer or rummage around in that cabinet. No, it was not okay to eat nothing but Pirate's Booty and Cheerios for lunch. And that was fine and good when it came to a baby. LouEllen was not, however, Jesse's mother, and Jesse wasn't a goddamn child.

Suddenly, the sadness that had been welling up inside him shifted to that now-familiar aggravation. It came back to him all at once, and this time it returned with a vengeance, leaving room for nothing other than retaliation.

She wanted to push him? Fine. He'd push right back.

"Wine? Sure," he said, answering the waiter before Lou could jump in.

He watched her in his periphery. Her mouth snapped shut. Her eyes grew wide. She sat so statuesque on the opposite side of the table it was a wonder she hadn't petrified right there in her seat.

"Might I suggest a red?" the waiter asked. "We have a Chianti that pairs beautifully with the Bolognese."

"Sounds good," Jesse said. "I'll have that."

"And for the lady?" The waiter turned to regard a stunned LouEllen. "I have a lovely Pinot Noir that will bring out the earthy notes of your risotto. Or, if you'd prefer white, might I suggest a lightly oaked Chardonnay?"

She didn't respond. Quite frankly, Jesse wasn't sure she'd heard the waiter's suggestions at all. She was staring across the table at him with a look of disbelief, as though he'd not only ordered a glass of wine but had thrown it in her face as soon as it had arrived. And in a way, he had done exactly that.

"Ma'am?" The waiter offered them both a nervous smile.

Jesse couldn't help it. He felt a twinge of satisfaction at her indignation. She looked the way she had made him feel at Miss Augusta's dinner table. Incredulous. Beyond floored. Double-crossed.

"You know what?" LouEllen finally spoke up, her attention darting from Jesse to the waiter at her elbow. "I just realized I'm not hungry."

The waiter gaped, then blinked at Jesse for help. *Is she serious?*

"Yep." Jesse lifted his napkin off his lap, crumpled it in his fist, and dropped it onto the table next to his glass of water. "Me neither. I guess we're just going to go. Imagine that."

The waiter lifted a hand to his breastbone, rendered speechless for the first time in his career. His focus darted from Jesse to LouEllen to their nearly untouched plates of food. "Shall I box these up for you?" he stammered.

"You bet your ass you should," Jesse said, leaning back in his seat. "It's almost thirty bucks a pop, right? I'm not one to throw money away, and just between you and me? We can hardly afford the bill."

A few female patrons stirred at that. Oh, the gossip they'd have for their girlfriends during Sunday brunch. The waiter, on the other hand, blanched and quickly whisked their plates away. When Jesse turned back to his wife, LouEllen had placed her fork down and shut her eyes, as if trying to contain herself.

"What?" he asked. "You said you weren't hungry, so we're going home."

She lifted her hands and pressed them together over her mouth, staring down at a spot of oil she'd dripped on the white tablecloth. Finally, she rose from her seat.

"I'll wait for you outside," she said softly. She gathered her coat and purse and pivoted away from him, then made her way toward the front of the place with her chin held high.

Watching her strut by all those gawking women reminded Jesse of exactly why he loved her. She was phenomenal. A class act.

But she was also, at times, impossible.

With the tip, the bill came out to nearly a hundred bucks, all for service that had hardly been provided and for food that would go cold. By the time Jesse gathered their leftovers and paid the check, LouEllen was shivering next to their Altima in the snow.

She said nothing when she saw him coming. She only waited for him to unlock the doors before climbing inside. Jesse knew, however, that her silence would be short-lived. Not that long ago, Jesse had been an expert at keeping his emotions buried, but LouEllen had always been the opposite. She brought up any little thing that irritated her. It was only a matter of time before she went full Hollywood and blew her top.

"So, I guess the movie is out, then," he said after a minute.

"You think?" LouEllen shot back, her tone razor-sharp. Because she'd planned the perfect evening, and Jesse had fucked it up. "Not that I'm surprised," she muttered. "Or, maybe I am, and that's what makes me such an idiot. Surprised that I thought all it would take was a fancy dinner and a movie and a decent screw to get your head on straight."

There it was. The classic movie reel monologue.

LouEllen snorted at a thought. "But I guess if it were that easy, there wouldn't be such a thing as divorce," she finished, and that word stopped his heart cold.

"Divorce?" He shot her a look. "For what, cutting dinner short?"

LouEllen laughed the same cold laugh she had emitted in the restaurant minutes before. It was a sound Jesse wasn't sure he'd ever heard her make until tonight. Lou wasn't the type to chortle in anger. If anything, she crumpled into a heap and cried out of frustration when things became too much. But that smirk...it reminded him of the disconcerting rumble of laughter he knew all too well. Goosebumps rose up along his arms.

"Please, don't do that," he said.

"Do what, divorce you?" she asked.

"Laugh like that," he said. "It sounds bad. Evil."

"*Evil?*" She didn't like that one bit. "I swear, sometimes I want to knock you right across the side of your head. You're ridiculous, you know that?" She glared at him. "*Ridiculous.* And what you pulled back there...ordering wine, if only to spite me..."

He wasn't about to argue that one, because she was spot on. It's precisely why he had done it—a stupid, mean-spirited, accomplish-nothing move that had made everything between them worse.

"The things you've been pulling for weeks," she said. "Staying up. Sleeping in the living room. Doing God only knows what on that computer. Vanishing off the face of the Earth."

"Doing God only knows what?" Jesse asked. What did she mean by that? Now she was accusing him of, what, spending hours watching pornography while camped out on the couch? Or maybe he'd found himself a girlfriend on Match.com...

"I looked at your computer, Jesse," she said.

"What?"

"You heard me. I've seen how much you've written."

"You're *spying* on me?"

It wouldn't have been hard to do. He left his laptop on his desk when he wasn't dragging it with him to class. His password was the same for everything: Winston555. It was a password LouEllen knew by heart, the same one they used for their bank account login. That, and he never closed out of Word. The file was right there, open and at the ready, just waiting for someone to pry.

"So, we're violating each other's privacy now?" he asked, but she didn't bother answering. She was too busy staring out the window, more than likely coming up with her next verbal blitz.

But Jesse was suddenly compelled to reel it in. *Try.* Sure, they could sit there spitting fire at each other, but what good would it do? That word—divorce—was still rattling inside his chest like a spooked coal mine canary. Was she serious about that? Had it really gotten so bad? And what would happen with Ian? How often would Jesse get to see him?

After a tense beat, he slid the key into the ignition and started the car. Guiding the Altima out of the parking lot, he pulled onto the street and pointed them toward Warsaw. The silence that settled between them was heavy, oppressive. Eventually, he was the first to bend beneath its weight.

"Did you think it was any good?"

Focused on the road, he could sense that she was watching him in the dark. She stared at him for a long while, as though trying to decide what she thought about what he'd written. After a long silence and no critique, Jesse glanced at her. He found her peering at him, her expression was far less annoyed than it had been a minute before. If anything, she appeared dumbfounded. Hopelessly confused.

"Three hundred words," she finally said. "That's hardly enough to judge."

Jesse focused back on the road. It was his turn to be perplexed.

"Three hundred words in how many hours?" she asked, her tone hushed, as if asking herself the question rather than seeking out a genuine answer.

He'd been trying to keep tabs of the time he'd spent on his project, and he was pretty sure it had been at least forty hours, maybe more. But it *hadn't* been three hundred words. Closer to thirty thousand from what he remembered. So, what was she talking about? Was she saying three hundred to scare him? Was she intentionally trying to freak him out?

"You're sacrificing your family, and for what?" she asked softly, but he hardly heard her, too busy spinning worst-case scenarios inside his mind. What if she was telling the truth and it really *was* three hundred? What if he hadn't saved the file correctly and had lost all his work? Then again, this could have been another one of her power plays—it seemed to him that she was full of them these days. Maybe she was pushing his buttons, determined to get a rise out of him.

"—and the thing with the wine," she said, still not over that jab. But her tone had softened. She was no longer fuming. Now, she was little more than a concerned partner issuing delicate reminders. "You know it only takes a little, Jesse. One beer here, a glass of wine there…"

It was a slippery slope, sure. But Jesse hadn't drunk a drop since his slip up. He hadn't ordered that Chianti with any intention of consuming it. She was blowing things out of proportion.

"I don't care about the novel," she said after a long while, her fingers toying with her bottom lip.

He wanted to snort at that.

Yeah, you've made that abundantly clear.

But it felt like anything he said would only add kindling to an already raging fire.

"If you want to write it, fine. Write it. But while you do that, I'm the one left trying to save us."

Jesse said nothing. He was afraid to speak, sure that she was backing him into another corner.

"When was the last time you took Winston for a walk?" she asked.

"Winston doesn't want to go for a walk," Jesse muttered. Winston was a sore subject, anyhow. "Like he has anything to do with anything." It was one thing to be at odds with his wife, but his *dog?* Dogs were supposed to be loyal. Winston's cold shoulder was a stab in the back.

"He has to do with plenty," she said. "He has to do with the fact that you've completely stepped away from your life. You've stepped away from *us.*"

Three hundred words.

Speaking of stepping on anything, all he wanted to do was step on the gas and do one-twenty down the highway back to the house.

Three hundred words.

Impossible. He refused to believe it.

"I love you, but you're lost, Jesse." The anger had seeped out of her voice, replaced by sorrow. "I don't know what to do anymore. I thought that maybe tonight...but as soon as you walked through the door, I could see it."

"See what?" he asked, not bothering to look in her direction this time, guiding the car down the freeway at a good twenty miles over the limit.

"That haunted look. All you wanted to do was sit in front of that computer again. That's the only reason you come home anymore, you know. To sit at your desk and obsess over this..." She paused, shook her head. "*This.* Whatever this is."

"Whatever this is," he echoed beneath his breath.

She was being dismissive again. The book didn't matter. His passion didn't matter. Reed and Casey didn't matter. Nor did Jesse's emotional state, his need to grieve.

He narrowed his eyes at the tarmac and pressed the gas pedal to the floorboard. LouEllen shot a look at the speedometer.

"What are you doing?" She looked out the window in time to catch their exit blow by. "You missed the—wait, where are we going?"

Her questions only made him angrier, that much more determined. She didn't understand a damn thing, which meant it was up to him to explain it, to *show* her.

She was judging him, pissed at him for being distant and removed. But this wasn't his fault. *She* was the one who had made him go along with Casey's stupid request. Lou was why he'd been there, why he'd seen what he'd seen, why his childhood nightmares were triggered, why he could hardly sleep anymore. Yes, it was Casey who had sealed Jesse's emotional fate, but had it not been for LouEllen's encouragement, Jesse would never have been there. Had it not been for her bolstering his hope that perhaps that creepy old house would lend him some much-needed creative inspiration, Casey would have been left to go it alone.

"Jesse!" LouEllen was nearing panic now, as if realizing that the man driving their car wasn't her husband, but someone she'd never met. "Slow down and pull over! I want to go home."

"No," Jesse said. "You need to know what *this* is."

Lou stiffened in her seat, and for a second Jesse was sure she was about to pull the door open while they did ninety down the road. But she shoved her hands between her legs and tried to keep herself from crying instead.

"I'm going to show you," he said, "so you can understand."

Because maybe if he took her to the place that was haunting him, it would haunt her too.

THIRTY-THREE

HALF-WAY TO the farmhouse, Jesse's mood shifted again. His determination to take LouEllen to the place where his two friends had ended their lives was replaced by the hope of being pulled over for speeding thirty-five miles over the limit. But there was never a cop around when you needed one. Save for a random car traveling in the opposite direction, the highway was abandoned. It was just Jesse, LouEllen, and a broken white line unspooling down the center of a black ribbon of road.

He considered pulling over and cutting the engine, thought about sitting there in darkened silence before telling Lou how sorry he was about his behavior. He couldn't explain why he was feeling this constant simmer of anger, but perhaps if he talked to her about it, she could point him in the direction of an answer. Hell, maybe the answer was *see a shrink*. Perhaps it would help him get to the root of the problem. A psychologist would at least give him leads.

Maybe it's the constant sense of abandonment you've felt since Reed ended his life, they'd say. *Or perhaps the anger comes from Casey needing an audience, and now you're stuck dealing with the fallout.*

Yeah, *that* could cause a bit of anger.

Maybe it's that you don't feel supported.

Because Lou could say she supported him all she wanted, but her words didn't match her actions. Hell, it may have been something as simple as Winston turning his nose up at an offer of a walk, or the fact that Ian was too young to confide in. Or it could have been

Garvey and the suggestion that there was something wrong with him, something wrong enough to take him away from his work.

And then there's the simple truth that the longer this goes on, the more fractured you feel. It's like you're split into two; the old Jesse, who loves his wife and child, and the new Jesse, who is always on edge, ready to snap his teeth at any little thing.

It could have been any of those things, or all those things at once.

But by the time he had considered the possibilities, he was pulling onto the road that would take them to that crooked farmhouse's crumbling front steps.

LouEllen, who was sitting tensely beside him, finally spoke.

"What is this?" she asked, her eyes wide as they passed the no trespassing sign. "Jesse, where are we going?" Her voice pitched toward panic again. For a split second, he imagined it was what an abductee must have sounded like while pleading with a predator.

Please, pull over. Please, let me go.

But did Lou really think Jesse would hurt her? He'd never laid a hand on her in his life, so why would he do it now?

Because you aren't yourself.

Because there's something darker at play, here.

It's got you, Jesse. The same something that had snaked itself around Reed and Casey, and now it's got you, too.

He could hear that low, rumbling laughter in his ears. Could feel the heat of the fire, the tension in the room as Georgiana's mouth twisted into a snarling sort of grin.

He wanted to hit the brakes. To forget this whole thing. But something kept him from stopping the car just as it had days before, when he had found himself in this very spot, alone and revisiting this nightmarish place.

The car kept rolling, and the house came into view from behind a copse of leafless trees. Lou covered her mouth and shrunk back into her seat, repulsed by their destination.

"Oh my God," she whispered past her fingers. "Jesus, Jesse, why are we here?"

Jesse didn't respond because he had yet to figure that out. All he knew was that it felt right to take her there. He *needed* to be there. It's where he belonged.

They pulled around the roundabout and stopped in front of steps leading up to a weatherworn door. The police and paramedics had taken it off its hinges weeks ago. LouEllen was weeping now, scared and confused. Because what if Jesse got out of the car? What if he made *her* get out? What if he left her there so she could understand how it felt to be there alone just the way he had been as a kid; the way he had been when Casey had hanged himself?

Glancing up those steps and toward the front door, Jesse was overwhelmed with a need to do just that. To get out. To go in. Something about that building was calling him back inside.

Come in. See what Casey saw. See what Reed had found.

He'd imagined this place in his mind's eye so many times, the way it appeared in his head, the way it looked in Casey's videos, and the way it stood in reality. He'd walked through those rooms at least a hundred times. They were sometimes moonlit and covered in cobwebs, sometimes filmed in the whites and greens of a night vision camera, and sometimes illuminated in warm yellow light. Perhaps now he could tell Lou about the evil laughter that caressed his ear. He could confess that he'd come here alone only to see a figment of his imagination become real; that girl standing with her bare knees against his bumper, her cracked lips pulling away from her teeth.

"What are we doing here?" LouEllen asked again, her words hitching in her throat.

She was still hiding behind her palms, but he could tell she was trying to calm herself. Her voice no longer warbled with terror. It was only tinged with a buttoned-down sort of distress.

"Why are we here?" she asked, more forceful now.

Jesse had to look past her as he regarded the house beyond her window. He wondered what it would look like in the spring. Peaceful, inviting, with vines of ivy and wild clematis climbing up the house's splintering sides. To him, it seemed the epitome of rural tranquility, nothing at all like what folks who came here seeking restless ghosts thought about it. Haunted. Terrifying. A skeleton of its former self.

"Why don't you go in?" LouEllen asked. Her hair was covering her face, having replaced her hands, which were now in her lap. She wasn't crying anymore. As a matter of fact, her tone was strikingly calm. "That's what you want, isn't it? That's why you drove all this way, to go inside?"

Jesse turned his attention from the building to his wife. Her suggestion struck him as strange. If he went in, he'd have to leave her alone in the car—not something she'd be okay with, especially not out here in the dark.

"Come on," she said. "Hurry up. Take me with you if you're too scared."

It was a proposition she would have never made.

He reached up, jabbing his fingers against the dome light above the dash. There was something wrong. Maybe he'd pushed her too far.

It was then, as soon as the light clicked on, that LouEllen looked up at him. Except it wasn't her.

The ashen-faced girl stared at him with her sunken eyes. She smiled, exposing broken teeth and blackened gums.

Jesse's heart jumped into his throat. Reflexively, he grasped for the door handle to get out of the car.

Hey, Jesse! Catch!

The words were an earsplitting shriek.

Hey, Jesse! Catch!

Growing louder with each repetition.

Hey, Jesse! CATCH!

He screamed and tumbled out of the car, then scrambled away only to watch the girl undo her seatbelt, his name slithering past her spittle-slicked lips.

Jesse. Jeeeesseeee.

She began to climb out of her seat and across the center console, her movements eerily serpentine. A moment later she was slinking through the open door, her bare feet stepping onto the snow-covered road.

Desperate to put more distance between them, he cut through the car's high beams as he ran to the opposite side of the vehicle. But she kept coming.

Jeeeesseeee.

Kept moving toward him.

Jeeeesseeee.

Before he knew it, he was sprinting up the house's crooked stairs in search of safety, because where else was there to go? Running in the opposite direction would leave him in the middle of a dead highway, dark and unlit, cold with no shelter. It would throw him back into the past. Eleven years old. Scared. His friends nowhere in sight.

Jeeeesseeee.

His name caressed the curve of his ear, disembodied.

Come upstairs.

He darted past the propped-up front door and into the foyer, his knees threatening to buckle as soon as his sneakers hit Reed's divot. The broken boards bit at his ankles, threatening to split apart and pull him underground.

Jesse! A voice, this one different, coming from above. A voice he'd recognize anywhere.

He stood motionless, mouth agape, shivering against the cold despite the warmth of his coat. Every movement—however minuscule—was accentuated by floorboards groaning beneath the soles of his shoes.

Jesse, come up here! Reed called out from endless darkness. *Come up, bring Lou!*

Lou. That name rattled him, because who the hell had he seen inside his car? What had happened to his wife? Where the hell was she?

Torn between wanting to see if Reed was upstairs and his need to know what had happened to LouEllen, he spun around where he stood, looking to the door that would take him back outside.

He nearly screamed when he found her standing there, her face a mask of confused terror.

"Jesse!" she yelled. "Jesus, what is it, what's wrong?" She reached out and grabbed him by the sleeves of his coat. "Why did you leave me out there?" she demanded. "What—"

But he didn't let her finish. He crushed her to his chest in a fierce embrace. And then, without a word, he rushed them both out of the house's foyer and back to the car.

THIRTY-FOUR

THEY HARDLY spoke during the drive home. Jesse watched the unlit highway while LouEllen slumped in her seat, the fingers of her right hand curled against her mouth.

He imagined what the scene must have looked like to her; the way he had stumbled out of the car, completely freaked out. Sprinting up the front steps of a dilapidated building, terrified of God only knew what. Of his own wife. He had probably come off as raving, like a man who had finally lost hold of even the slightest shred of what was real.

All the while, he'd left the keys in the car. She could have driven away. Hell, maybe she *should* have. And yet, she'd gone in after him. Despite their arguments, the tension between them, and the crap he'd pulled just that night, she hadn't given up on him yet.

They pulled onto their unlit street. It was only then that LouEllen broke her silence.

"Jesse." Her voice was quiet, almost as though she wasn't sure she wanted him to hear her. "I'm scared," she confessed, then went quiet once more.

Jesse guided the car into their driveway and cut the lights, but left the engine running to keep the heater on. He wanted to tell her everything, wanted to ask her about all the things he didn't understand. Was it possible for Casey to have seen the same girl Jesse had as a child? Was that why Reed had become obsessed with the house? Could it be that when Reed died, his infatuation had somehow remained very much alive; can something like that be passed on from one person to another, like some sort of dark disease? And was that why Reed's mania had eventually taken over Casey's life; and now that Casey was gone too, that preoccupation had needled its way under Jesse's own skin?

And yet, the same force that had kept him from turning the car around when the farmhouse had come into view was preventing him from talking about his nightmares, from telling her about the laughter that was plaguing him more and more. Something was blocking him from speaking—a hand reaching up from the pit of his stomach, invisible fingers tightening around his throat. He could hear a low rumble just beneath the blast of the heater, a muted growl like the ones Winston had grown so fond of during the past few weeks. It was a warning. *Tell her, Jesse. See what becomes of her then.* His silence remained steadfast, but he hoped she could sense that he was scared, too. He had to trust that she could.

"Please," she said, "just take a break, okay? I know this is important to you, but just for a few days."

She reached across the center console and caught his hand in hers, then gave his fingers a squeeze. When Jesse looked down from the dashboard to his lap, she took it as a sign that she wouldn't be getting a response. She undid her seatbelt and slid out of the car, taking their bag of expensive Italian leftovers with her. Jesse watched her vanish inside the house from the driver's seat, and just like that, the cautionary rumble inside his ears subsided. The sensation of someone tightening their fist around his windpipe went away.

While thankful for that momentary reprieve, he didn't get to enjoy it. All at once, he remembered what LouEllen had said about his computer, his work.

Three hundred words. It's hardly enough to judge.

He yanked the keys out of the ignition and shoved open his door, then marched through the cold and into the house. Inside, a startled Winston snarled, then scrambled into the kitchen. LouEllen peeked out from around the threshold, then squinted at the dog in confusion. But Jesse was too caught up in the moment to acknowledge Winston's bizarre behavior, to tell Lou that yeah, Winston acted like a lunatic all the time now...or to realize what he was about to look like himself—an obsessive drawn to his computer even before pulling off his coat.

He threw himself into his desk chair, his fingers tapping the tabletop as he impatiently waited for his laptop to rouse. When it finally did, he clicked the minimized Word document at the bottom of his screen. And there it was, plain as day. Three hundred words. Two hundred ninety-six, to be exact. LouEllen hadn't been screwing with him. She'd been telling the truth.

"...it can't—" He rose from his seat, repelled by the number. His chair skittered backward against the living room floorboards, then toppled over with a bang. "No," he said. "That can't be right."

He leaned over the computer again, trying to scroll through a document that was only half a page long, desperate to find the missing pages he was sure he had produced. But the longer he stood stooped over his computer, the less he understood what he was trying to find. Was there a particular scene he could recall having written that was now gone? No. Did it appear as though someone had purposefully deleted ninety-five percent of his work? It didn't. The longer he skimmed, the more he was sure he was losing his mind. Because it was there. It was all there. And yet if that was true, what had he been doing all those late-night hours? Where was all the work he was sure he had done?

Still in your head, he thought. *In your nightmares. In your mind.*

He veered away from his desk only to find himself staring across the living room at his wife. She seemed more distressed now than ever, her arms tightly coiled around her waist. Still wearing her pretty dress, her makeup was smeared from all the crying she'd done in the car. Her hair was disheveled, as though she'd been caught in the middle of taking it down. She looked like a reveler after a long night out, like the girl he'd lusted for in high school and fallen in love with in college; the one he used to dance with at cheap Detroit nightclubs and buy drinks for at seedy bars. She looked like his bride, sweaty and unkempt after their wedding reception. The girl who had danced barefoot in the grass for three straight hours to the likes of No Doubt, U2, and Counting Crows.

LouEllen let her arms fall to her sides.

I've lost you, haven't I?

Her body practically screamed the question into the space between them.

I've lost you, and yet you're still here.

IF YOU SEE HER

Jesse closed the distance, propelled forward by the need to stop this, to get back to the way things were. He pulled her into his arms, and she melted into the soft down of his coat with a choking sob.

"I'm sorry," he murmured against her ear. "I'm sorry, Lou. I'm so fucking sorry." Because LouEllen had been right. This whole thing was a mistake. "I'll stop this," he said. Because he had to. If not for her sake, then for his own.

He had to stop it, or it would steal him away.

And from how he felt now, he was already half-way gone.

THIRTY-FIVE

FOR THE FIRST time in nearly three weeks, Jesse finally slept in his own bed. Miraculously, the nightmares were gone, as though apologizing to his wife had atoned him of his sins, purging him of the darkness that had been shadowing his every move.

Easy peasy. Just like that.

When he woke, he found LouEllen nursing a cup of black coffee at the kitchen table. She was flipping through a mailer for a kid's retail outlet and listening to a Portishead album he hadn't heard in years.

"I thought we could go get breakfast," she said, glancing up from the colorful junk mail before her. "Maybe do a little shopping."

Jesse had never been the shopping type, but a strong espresso and a couple of hours milling around a department store full of baby stuff felt like just the thing to get his mind back to where it belonged: on his family and far away from the crumbling building north of town.

After picking Ian up from Carrie Mae's place, they got waffles, then wasted nearly twenty minutes searching for a space in a crowded mall parking lot. LouEllen spent an obscene amount of time inside Baby Gap and Brookstone while Jesse and Ian marveled at the crap they were pawning at a few of the mall kiosks—jewelry and hair straighteners, knock-off Detroit Lions memorabilia and squishy stress ball-like toys Ian refused to put down.

They grabbed lunch at their favorite Tex-Mex place, where Ian shoved a sliced jalapeno into his mouth, then froze with saucer-wide eyes as his chubby face turned red. They hit Kercheval Place, one of LouEllen's favorite shopping spots. She never said as much, but Jesse knew if they ever did leave Warsaw, she'd pine for a house out in Grosse Pointe, just like Carrie Mae. Not that he'd ever be able to make that happen—at least, not without a kickass literary agent and a lot of luck. But after last night, he was ready to give up on the book. Hell, he had to be honest with himself. There *was* no book. Just three hundred words of random drivel he'd vomited onto the keyboard while half-asleep.

At Ann Taylor, he sat in a wingback chair and messed on his phone while Ian napped in his stroller. Left to little more than his wandering thoughts, he couldn't help but wonder what was going to become of his family. The past few weeks had been draining, but they'd also left him feeling like a loser who couldn't achieve a single creative goal.

Once upon a time, he'd been the type to scoff at peers who insisted writing a ten-thousand-word essay was next to impossible. He'd been the young man who could start a novel on a whim, write it in a fury, and have a first draft banged out within a couple of weeks. But now, all he could manage was to stare at Ian, searching for answers in his son's sleeping face. Because no matter how he tried to explain it to himself, it didn't make sense; how had thirty thousand words dwindled down to three hundred? And those forty-some-odd hours; where did that time go? Where the hell had *he* gone?

Maybe Garvey was right and there was more to it than just being tired. It was becoming glaringly evident; Jesse was losing time. And it wasn't just while he was sitting at his desk. There had been moments in class when he knew he hadn't been present. His first-period class morphed into altogether different students. He'd blink while sitting at a cafeteria table, his tray of food untouched, then blink again and find himself in the teacher's lounge with Sam talking about some history lecture he'd just given or how the school library was next to useless. *They may as well have a 1950's Encyclopedia Britannica in there.*

But this outing with LouEllen and Ian, it was a good way to help Jesse feel at least somewhat like his old self. Hell, he and Lou had been so busy jumping from one store to another, he'd hardly thought about Georgiana at all. That was, until he heard that goddamned laugh.

With his cheeks flushing hot and his heart thudding hard in his ears, he swiveled around in his seat to find a smiling sales girl folding shirts behind him. She gave him a grin, one that struck him as almost too sly, too wolfish. He offered her a strained smile of his own and turned around again, his pulse fluttering against the hollow of his throat.

It's just my imagination. It's impossible. This shit isn't real.

But he failed to convince himself, because somehow, he could see Georgiana in that salesgirl's face. Jesse suddenly needed to move. He gathered himself up and pushed Ian's stroller through the store.

"We should get going," he told LouEllen, anxious to get back to the car.

She nodded and shook a blouse at him. "I just want to try this on first," she said, then retreated to the dressing rooms at the back of the store.

Jesse dared to look the salesgirl's way. She was focused on the stack of colorful shirts before her, but she was laughing, probably at a lame joke or gossip about a coworker who was out sick. He remembered those sorts of on-the-job exchanges from his stint at Mr. Frosty's well. But from where Jesse stood, the salesgirl seemed to be laughing at *him*, amused by his anxiety's sudden spike.

Two down...

He pushed Ian's stroller to the glass double doors, as though approaching the exit would somehow make Lou hurry it up in the dressing room. Had it not been snowing again, he would have opted to wait outside.

He kept glancing at the salesgirl, making sure she was where he could see her. And she kept chuckling to herself.

Like it matters where I stand, Jesse. I'm already precisely where I want to be.

When LouEllen finally surfaced from the back of the store, the girl dared to meet Jesse's gaze. She winked, and a shudder scurried up his spine. He held his breath while Lou paid for her shirt.

The drive home was terrible. There was an accident on I-94, which slowed traffic to a crawl. Ian woke mid-drive, and LouEllen shimmied into the backseat to spare their ears from his screeching. Meanwhile, Jesse fixated on the driver to his left—a young girl in a black hatchback, her long hair framing her face.

Eventually sensing that she was being watched, the driver peered out her window, her eyes meeting his. But rather than diverting his own stare, Jesse found himself unable to look away. She smiled, and when she did, he swore he could see her lips cracking against the strain. That low, rumbling laugh hit him again; a premonition over Ian's inconsolable cries.

His heart lurched.

His foot stabbed against the brake.

Lou yelped in the backseat as the car jerked to a stop from its lazy forward roll. Even Ian went silent for a few seconds, stunned by the sudden jostle.

"Jesus," Lou murmured. "Are you trying to kill us?"

Jesse had stopped mere inches from the bumper of the car in front of them. Half a second longer and they'd have been I-95's accident number two.

Thirty minutes later, having finally broken free of traffic, Jesse drove fast down the highway and through Warsaw's sleepy streets. His nerves were rattled. He couldn't unsee the salesgirl's serpentine grin; couldn't erase the driver's rotting, blackened teeth. He knew what he'd seen hadn't been real, knew that if Lou had watched those two girls the same as Jesse, she wouldn't have seen what he had.

It's getting worse, he thought. *She's following me, now.*

When they arrived home, he felt entirely different from how he'd felt at the start of the day. Hours ago, seated at the breakfast table with Lou, he'd been optimistic, sure that he could put this whole Georgiana thing behind him. He'd had a spark of hope that maybe he was finally ready to move on, to push through the guilt and grief that were causing his nightmares, his hallucinations. And yet, now, stepping through his own front door, an oppressive heaviness hit him head-on.

It could have been the sudden recollection of Blaire explaining how Casey had changed. Maybe it was the flash of memory to when Casey sat on Jesse's couch, looking exhausted and terrified. It may have been the sight of his laptop; a reminder that he could avoid it all he wanted, but it would always be standing by, patient and unwavering. Or it could have been Winston, who growled as soon as Jesse unlocked the door—a sign that all was not well, that things were just as he had left them. Assurance that freeing himself from Georgiana's jagged-nailed clutch would take a lot more than a few hours of distraction.

"Winston," Lou scolded. "What the heck is wrong with you?"

But it wasn't Winston's fault. Suddenly, all the blame he'd put on the dog, the betrayal he'd felt…it all came clear. Winston wasn't growling because he'd decided he didn't like Jesse anymore. He was only lending assurance that something was clinging to Jesse's aura, something dark and ugly and unseen. Something that was changing him from the inside out, making him see things that weren't there, making him do things he couldn't control. No amount of waffles or shopping or wishful thinking would change that. That house had marked him. He'd lost a piece of himself there.

That sense of foreboding became so completely consuming, he had to steady himself against the wall.

"Jesse?"

He pivoted away from his desk and looked to his wife, only realizing he'd been staring at that laptop when he caught a glimpse of her face. There wasn't any doubt that his intense focus had spooked her all over again.

"Are you alright?" she asked, looking skeptical.

"Fine," he said. "Just a little lightheaded."

"I'm going to start Ian's bath," she said. "Could you grab the stuff out of the car?"

"Sure," he said, then glanced to Winston, who was watching him with what could only be interpreted as suspicion.

I know, Jesse wanted to say. *I feel it too, Dubs. I just don't know what to do about it. I don't know how to—*

"Just put it all in the bedroom," Lou said, bouncing Ian against her hip. "After you're done, come join us at the tub."

LouEllen disappeared down the hall with the baby. Meanwhile, Jesse stood motionless, staring at his dog.

"Dubs," he whispered to the Bassett Hound. "Maybe you should finally strike."

Winston didn't like being spoken to so directly, whispering or not. He let out a grumbly woof and stalked out of the living room on his short, stubby legs. There would be no attack. The dog knew the limits of his power, which made him smarter than his master. He knew no amount of snarling would scare away the thing that had hijacked Jesse's shadow.

Jesse went out to the car to retrieve Lou's shopping. But rather than taking the bags into the master bedroom and then heading to the bathroom where Ian was splashing around, Jesse placed the bags next to the front door, crossed his arms over his chest and regarded his desk. He had thought he could escape it, but writing wasn't an option. Willing it out of his life wasn't going to work.

Standing next to the front door, he could hear the pop of gravel beneath Ladeaux's tires. He could smell the singe of firewood as it burned in the great room's fireplace. He could see the yellow wallpaper that Hannah had plastered to the walls of that odd, oversized home to lend it a bit of warmth. There was something about that story, that house, those people...

Jesse stepped across the room, paused at his desk, and drew his palm across the laptop's surface in an almost gentle caress. Could he do it? Could he abandon Georgiana and the Ecklunds? And what about Doctor Ladeaux? There had been something intriguing about him, something enticing that gave new promise to the story Jesse had just begun.

Three hundred words.

And so what? He could start over and make it that much better, couldn't he? He'd started over on plenty of stories back when he was younger, when he couldn't stop himself from writing if he had tried.

His fingers curled against the computer's top as if trying to pull something invisible out of the machine. To give up on this story was to give up on ever finding closure when it came to Casey and Reed. It was, in a way, giving up on the man he hoped he could become; to deny himself something he knew he needed, even if that something demanded too much of the life he had now.

"Jesse, are you coming?" LouEllen called from down the hall.

She was checking up on him, and who could blame her? Because there he was, his palm atop his computer like a priest swearing upon a Bible. Like a junkie eyeing the needle. A user needing another hit.

Just this one last time.

"Coming," he called back, but rather than heading in her direction, he swept the computer off his desk, tucked it against his chest, and slipped out the front door.

Once outside, he thought about hopping in the car and driving away. The laptop was warm against his chest, like a lover promising to shelter him from the cold. He could drive to the corner store, pick up a bottle of something, and head to the farmhouse, where he'd creep past the front door. The blue glow of his screen would soothe him while he deciphered the mystery of Georgiana Ecklund. He could sit and drink and work because nobody would seek him out there. Lou wouldn't dare go back on her own.

But rather than giving in to what felt like an unquenchable desire, Jesse gnashed his teeth against that overwhelming urge.

"No," he said aloud, denying Georgiana the one thing he was sure she wanted: his undivided attention, his devotion, for him to forget everyone but her. "No, I told her I'd fight." Except, the 'her' wasn't Georgiana. It was LouEllen.

It was wrong to make his wife compete against his desire of finally becoming a writer. He had to love her first. She was his best friend. His partner. *She* was his muse.

He stashed the laptop in the trunk of the car—as good a place as any.

Out of sight, out of mind.

If it wasn't sitting on top of that desk, it would be less of a temptation. He owed it to LouEllen to try to stop this, just as he'd promised, no matter how much his palms itched, no matter how thirsty he became, no matter how long he stood there staring at the trunk after he'd slammed it closed...considering, still considering...

I could go back. Just get in the car and drive.

Because the farmhouse was no longer a place that he feared.

If he was right, if he'd really had lost a piece of himself there, that meant it was home.

THIRTY-SIX

THAT NIGHT, the nightmares resurfaced, and they were more vivid than ever.

It started with his car, his trunk. Something was banging around in there while Jesse stood mesmerized, staring at the tailgate. When he finally found the nerve to open it, he found Georgiana inside. Her nightgowned body was twisted like a pretzel, her face frozen in a soundless scream. It was only after he tore his gaze away from her that he realized she hadn't been knocking on the trunk lid to get out. The banging had come from her wrists and ankles, which were shackled to the upholstered floor.

Jesse staggered backward and away from her. When he did, he found himself not in his driveway, but in a bedroom. The hardwood floor was scuffed with age. The same yellow damask wallpaper he'd seen in the farmhouse's grand room covered the walls. This was Georgiana's room, the same fourth-floor bedroom he'd stood inside in so many of his dreams.

With the car now gone, a four-poster bed replaced the trunk. Georgiana—who had been dead only moments before—screamed in distress as she struggled against her restraints. Her wrists and ankles were raw and bleeding where the manacles bit into her flesh, and as she thrashed, her hair flew around her face, smudging her features like a blurry photograph. Jesse glanced away from her struggle to a cross on the wall. Of all the times he'd visited this room, he'd never noticed the crucifix hanging there before.

Behind him, the bedroom door swung open. Jesse pressed himself against the wall, as though doing so would somehow disguise that he was there. But his effort was unnecessary. Doctor Ladeaux didn't notice him, and neither did the man who accompanied him inside. Jesse's lack of religious background rendered him dumb when it came to the difference between a priest and a pastor, but he'd seen enough men of the cloth to recognize a man of the church.

"This is how she's been since last I saw her," Ladeaux said. "Hardly anything will calm her. We've been considering insulin. Given enough, it should put her to sleep. But the mother insisted I call you first."

The priest regarded the thrashing girl. With his hands clasped behind his back, he leaned over her much the way a zoologist would loom over a new species of lizard or snake. "I see," he said, then looked to Ladeaux with concern. "She's thin."

"They say she won't eat," Ladeaux explained.

The priest's focus roved the walls, pausing upon the cross before turning back to the girl. "You've already attempted shock treatment?" he asked.

"Under her father's request," Ladeaux said. "It did nothing. She's only grown more violent. I've never seen anything like it." He paused, looking to his colleague. "Father Baker, I don't think this is a typical case. If I did, I would have her committed. I wouldn't have called you here."

"A demon?" Father Baker asked.

"The mother thinks so," Ladeaux recalled. "You noticed the crucifixes? She's the one who's lined the walls with them. The first time I was here, I didn't see any. Now, not a single room has been spared."

"I assume the girl has gotten more violent since then," Father Baker mused.

"She has," Ladeaux confirmed. "The father still wants to believe it's psychological, but the mother..." He paused, recalling Hannah Ecklund's haggard expression, remembering what she'd told him over the phone: *Please come as quick as you can. It's here.*

Father Baker pivoted back to Georgiana. But she hardly took notice of anyone in the room, busy trying to pry her wrists out from under thick leather cuffs.

"At first I was taken aback by her assertion," Ladeaux continued. "You don't often expect a family member, let alone a parent, to be convinced of, well…"

"And now?" Father Baker asked.

"I don't know, Father," Ladeaux confessed. "That's why you're here. Hopefully, God will give us the answer."

"She's strong for how small she is," Father Baker observed.

"Yet another reason I think this is more than of-the-mind, Father," Ladeaux said. "I've spent forty years of my life caring for patients, but this strikes me as different. There's an aura about her. Can you feel it?"

"The crosses will do nothing," Father Baker explained. "They're little more than decoration. They need to be blessed."

It was then that he reached into a pocket hidden away in his robe. A moment later, he brought out a rosary—long and beaded with a silver crucifix glinting at its end. That's when the frantic Georgiana ceased her struggle. Eerily silent, she turned her head to watch both men. A helpless look crossed her face as she parted her lips to speak; so wholly defenseless it made Jesse's heart ache to see it.

"Save me," she said, suddenly homing in on Jesse's eyes. "Don't abandon me here. We've come too far."

Father Baker began to pray while Jesse stared at the girl. It was then that her countenance began to twist, as though a horde of beetles was writhing beneath her flesh. Her mouth widened, pulling up at the corners, tugged by invisible hooks. Her lips cracked, then began to bleed into the gutters of her teeth. Georgiana's vulnerability vanished, replaced by a dirty and lecherous grin.

"Hey, Jesse." She said, her tone sweet despite her monstrous sneer. "Catch."

He jolted upright in bed, his heart pounding and his t-shirt covered in sweat. He shot a look at LouEllen, but she was sleeping, facing the wall. For a moment, he was compelled to grab her by the shoulder and pull her onto her back if only to make sure it was her, not the phantom that had stolen her body while they had sat parked in front of the farmhouse. But that idea only pushed him to flee the room entirely. He threw back the covers and snuck into the hallway, his fingers twisting against the fabric of his sweat-dampened shirt.

The house was cold again. He reflexively paused at the thermostat and adjusted the heat, then stepped into the living room. It was all in order despite the darkness, just the way he remembered it.

He sank into the couch and pressed his hands to his face. That dream was still so vivid, replaying itself against the backs of his eyelids. Georgiana had been thin and frail when Ladeaux had first arrived at the Ecklund place, but in this dream she'd been different. Emaciated. Little more than a skeleton wrapped in skin.

How long had Ladeaux kept her tied down in her room like that?

And had her mother really been attempting to feed her, or was Hannah too afraid to approach her daughter in such a state?

But it doesn't matter, Jesse thought to himself, *because it's not real, remember? None of this is real...*

Georgiana was a figment of his own making, as was Ladeaux, and now Father Baker.

"This needs to end," he whispered to himself. "Stop thinking about it. Get it out of your head." He dropped his hands to his lap, let his head fall back against the couch, and tried to lull himself back to sleep. But he knew sitting there like that would only send his mind reeling again. At this rate, he'd be up all night. He needed a distraction. A movie. Something light. The opposite of what was going on inside his mind.

He reached out and clicked on the side table lamp. It bathed the living room in a soft saffron glow. There, on the coffee table, was a small stack of DVDs. They were LouEllen's high school favorites. *There's Something About Mary. Rushmore. Election.* He grabbed one at random and made a move to the Blu-ray player nestled in the entertainment center beneath their TV. But before he could get the DVD out of its case, something caught his eye.

He froze as he stared at it in disbelief. Because it couldn't be. It was impossible. *Not real.* And yet, there it was, as real as anything else in that room. His laptop, which should have been in the trunk of his car, was back on his desk.

Back as if to say, *you want this to end, then finish the story.*

As if to say, *two down, one to go.*

THIRTY-SEVEN

WHEN JESSE woke slumped in his desk chair, his laptop was open and he had a wicked crick in his neck. He squinted at the screen, too bleary-eyed to understand exactly what he was looking at or where he was. But the realization came quickly. The light that filtered through the window was soft and gray. Pale sunlight was reflecting off a fresh blanket of white. It was morning. He'd been at his desk all night.

He pushed away from the computer, the legs of his chair scraping against the floor planks. But before he rose from his seat, he rubbed the blur from his eyes and squinted at the word count at the bottom left-hand corner of his screen. Still three hundred. He had lost time again.

A bang sounded from the kitchen. When Jesse reached the threshold, he found LouEllen standing at the counter. She was fumbling with wet baby bottles, trying to stack them like Jenga blocks on top of a drying rack. She sensed him and turned, her eyes rimmed with red. Having found herself alone in bed again, when she'd gone to seek him out, she'd discovered him exactly where she thought he would be. In front of that fucking computer.

"Lou…" He didn't know what to say, didn't know how to explain. Because he literally didn't understand what the hell was happening. How had he ended up in front of that laptop again? He couldn't recall any of it. All he remembered was the nightmare.

"Don't," LouEllen said, diverting her gaze. She'd had enough of his excuses. She'd lived through this before, after all. It was like his drinking problem all over again. Tears shed. Promises made and broken in a single breath.

"Lou, please..." The plea escaped him despite her desire for silence. He was at her mercy. *Just tell her,* he thought, then moved further into the kitchen, as though proximity could accentuate his sincerity. "I woke up," he said, "I had a nightmare, so I went into the living room."

She didn't look at him and didn't speak. She continued to stack bottles like a millennial hiker balancing an impossible tower of river rocks. Something about that clear plastic pillar cranked Jesse's anxiety up to eleven. They were going to fall, crash to the floor. And even if Lou decided to stack them up all over again, the structure would never be the same. That precariously leaning tower of bottles was a one-of-a-kind creation. Like the events that made up a life. Like tragedies that could make it all fall apart.

"I was going to put in a movie to get my mind off of it," Jesse said, glancing away from the drying rack. "But then I just—" He stalled, searching for the right words. "I've been seeing things, Lou. A girl."

"You mean Georgiana?"

LouEllen's inquiry nearly bowled him over. He hadn't seen it coming, hadn't expected to hear that name leave his wife's lips. He must have appeared dumbfounded because she shook her head and smirked.

"The girl from your story, right?" she asked, reminding him that she'd read the measly three hundred words he had written. "Jesse, you're obsessed." Her tone no longer held a beseeching air. Instead, it was tired and angry, because he had made her a promise that he had immediately rendered a lie. Again. "You're obsessed," she repeated, as if to make sure he understood. "It's sick."

"No, I swear..." Jesse shook his head at her, insisting that she was wrong about this. She just had to listen, had to give him a chance to explain. "I put the computer in the car," he said. "Last night, before I came into the bathroom."

LouEllen stared at him, unimpressed by his false-hearted fast-talk.

"I admit it, it has a hold on me," he said. "But that's why I locked it in the trunk, Lou. I put the damn thing *in the trunk.*"

"And what?" she asked. "It just showed up on your desk again?"

"Yes!" He moved closer to her, which only made her cross her arms over her chest. "I know it sounds crazy, but I woke up freaked out. I went into the living room. I was going to watch one of your movies, so I turned on the lamp."

There was proof of that. The lamp was still on. He'd abandoned the movie he'd grabbed off the coffee table on top of the entertainment center. Hell, Lou was a fan of true crime documentaries. If she only went to see for herself, she'd see all the evidence. The forensics were sound.

But LouEllen wasn't in the mood for investigation. She looked as though she was waiting for the punchline, but her sour expression assured him she was far from enjoying the joke.

"It was there," he said. "On my desk."

"Like magic," she said, unfurling her arms and making jazz hands to say, *poof!* "And then, like magic, you found yourself sitting in your chair, typing away on that magical laptop. Is that it?"

When he failed to answer, she turned away from him again.

"You know, I've really had it," she murmured. "You being bedeviled by that place is one thing, but—"

"Bedeviled?" Jesse asked.

"Yes, *bedeviled*," she said, challenging him to say otherwise.

There was something about that word that made his stomach clench, a truth to it that she couldn't have possibly known. He imagined Blaire saying the same thing to Casey. *Obsessed. Bedeviled. You're sick.*

Sick. Like a disease. A contagion you catch from the already infected.

"Why would you say that?" Jesse asked softly. "Why that word?"

LouEllen blinked at him, as though convinced that her husband had finally lost his grip.

"You're questioning my *word choice?* I'm telling you that you have a problem and you want to talk vocabulary, Jesse? Are you *kidding* me right now? It's like you've lost sight of everything important here."

Her tone of voice, the animosity reflected in her face…it was too much. Because he was trying, goddamnit. He'd put the fucking computer in the trunk of the car and walked away. He *knew* he'd been lucid when he'd done it, and yet here he was again, defending himself even though he didn't understand what the hell was happening to him, to his life.

"I would have never gone if you hadn't told me to!" The words spilled out of him in a helpless shout, like a protest from a kid tired of taking the blame. He was lashing out, pointing the finger in a different direction. Because it was too much. She was unfair.

"Jesus." She rolled her eyes. "*This* again?"

A cry sounded from down the hall. They'd woken Ian.

LouEllen pushed away from the kitchen counter with a glare, momentarily closing the distance between them.

"Lou," he said, desperate for her to listen. "Please, I swear…"

She paused, her gaze meeting his. For a moment, his heart leaped into his throat, elated. *She can see it,* he thought. *She knows I'm telling the truth.* But that blip of euphoria was little more than a cruel joke.

"No, you're right, Jesse," LouEllen said, her tone cold. "This is all my fault. You have nothing to do with it."

"No, I—"

She held her hand up. *Just stop.*

"Keep blaming me and do whatever," she said, stepping around him on the way out of the room. "Because you know what I just realized? I no longer give a shit."

IF YOU SEE HER

THIRTY-EIGHT

LOUELLEN TOOK the car. She didn't say where she was going or when she'd be back. She simply stuffed Ian into his winter coat, threw on a jacket and scarf, and slammed the front door behind her.

Jesse watched her pull out of the driveway from the front room window. Winston, on the other hand, kept his attention locked on Jesse from the corner of the room.

Chewing on the pad of his thumb, Jesse sank back into his desk chair, still focused on the tire tracks Lou had left in the snow. He was alone, lost and struggling. Lou had had it, no longer determined to help him through this mess, which meant she wasn't going to save him. This time, he needed to save himself.

He turned to the laptop on his desk—the thing that had made this situation so much worse; the thing that had somehow made its way back into the house while he had stood in Georgiana's room, watching her writhe and kick and scream.

None of it made sense. That farmhouse was just a house. There was nothing special about it. And who the hell was Georgiana anyway? Little more than a figment of his imagination, a person he'd made up who had somehow managed to crawl out of his skull and into his actual life.

Maybe he really was going crazy. Reed's death had triggered his spiral into darkness. Perhaps Casey's suicide had flipped some permanent switch in his brain. Because it was worse now, so much worse. He kept staring at those tire tracks, trying to summon some telepathic power to will LouEllen to think better of it, to veer the car around and come back home.

It was then, sitting in a dead-silent house, that Jesse suddenly shoved himself away from his desk, stood from his seat, and grabbed his computer in both hands. He studied it for a moment, reconsidering. But before he allowed himself to change his mind, he lifted the laptop over his head and slammed it to the floor.

The machine bounced against the planks with a nerve-jostling crack. Winston scrambled off his dog bed and onto his feet, his eyes wide and tail drawn between his legs. His spooked reaction didn't stop Jesse from swiping the laptop off the floor and slamming it down again. Each lift and throw was a release. Every new crunch of that computer brought an inkling of relief.

But rather than becoming calmer, Jesse felt himself grow more frenzied. Before he knew it, he was using his desk chair to smash through the laptop's lid. He yelled as he brought the desk's back leg down against it, over and over, determined to pulverize the machine into little more than plastic dust.

Winston whined before vanishing from view; a good idea, seeing as to how, a moment later, that chair went flying across the room and into a wall. A framed photograph of Ian fell from its hanging spot and hit the floor. Glass shattered. But Jesse was too preoccupied to worry about the repercussions that would come from destroying the living room. He was too busy dropping to his knees and prying the laptop's lid from its body with his bare hands.

When he managed to pull the screen loose, he flung it across the room like a Frisbee. It boomeranged past the couch and clotheslined the side table lamp—the light still on from the night before. Both the lid and the lamp fell to the floor. The lightbulb exploded. The screen skidded to a stop against the baseboard, just shy of the hole the chair had left in the drywall.

Sitting on the floor, Jesse blinked at his handiwork. The computer was nothing but a keyboard now; a useless bit of electronic waste. He coiled his arms around himself and stared at the gouge he'd left in the floorboards. LouEllen would be pissed about that, right along with the lamp's now-bent shade, Ian's shattered portrait, and the wall that needed to be repaired.

And what would he tell her when she asked what happened? A frenzy wasn't a good look. He needed to put together a story, something less damning, less unhinged than smashing his computer to pieces with the leg of a chair. But at least the laptop was gone now, right? It couldn't come back. Lou wouldn't be able to help but be happy about that. Because he hadn't just erased the temptation. He'd altogether obliterated his ability to continue what he'd begun.

Fuck that house, he thought. *And fuck that girl.*

Letting his forehead rest atop his knees, he tried to steady his heartbeat. But a moment later, he felt something slide up behind him and brush against his right arm. His head jerked up. He spun around where he sat. It was just an empty room, just the giant mess he'd made.

But there was that laugh, low and ominous, slithering along the curve of his ear.

Oh, if it were only that easy…

And then, just beyond his periphery, he caught a glimpse of something.

A wisp of white disappearing down the hall.

THIRTY-NINE

JESSE CLEANED up the living room and tried to smooth the dent out of LouEllen's lamp shade. There was, however, no easy fix for the hole he'd made in the wall. Not that it mattered. Lou would notice every misplaced detail as soon as she walked through the door. Regardless, he hung up Ian's picture where it belonged minus the broken glass, which he swept up and tossed into the bin outside. He would have gone out and bought a replacement frame, but the car was gone. So, instead, he curled up on the couch and tried to compose himself, tried to rest.

But rather than finding some semblance of quiet comfort, he instead found himself back in Georgiana's room.

She was still tied down, though someone had moved her from a prone position to sitting propped against the wooden headboard of the bed. The curtains were pulled aside, allowing winter light into the room. Soft tinny-sounding music drifted through the open door from downstairs. A woman was singing about stormy weather, her voice a soulful echo of the past.

Georgiana's head lulled back and forth to the slow sway of music, as if enjoying the song. But her face told a different story. She looked cadaverous, as though she hadn't eaten in weeks. Her cheeks were sunken. Her eyes bulged from the hollows of sockets that appeared impossibly deep. There was crust in the corners of her chapped lips, and her hair was a tangled mess of darkness. And her wrists? They were so thoroughly bruised they were blue-black beneath her restraints.

Hannah Ecklund swept into the room with a tray in her hands, and while she wore a smile, Jesse could see it was strained.

"Time for lunch, Georgie," she said, her chipper tone an eerie contrast to the scene at hand. There was a plate of food on the silver tray she'd brought with her—something brown and slathered in gravy; perhaps meatloaf or Salisbury steak. Next to it, peas and carrots, mushy and almost certainly from a can. It looked just like the lousy school lunches he'd grab on the regular, complete with a glass of milk he wasn't sure how Georgiana would manage to drink.

"You have to eat," Hannah told her daughter, then forced a smile. "We need to show our visitors that you're keeping up your strength."

Hannah placed the tray on a small bedside table, then pulled up a chair to sit next to her daughter. When she took a seat, Georgiana began to fight, as if repelled by her mother's presence; a caged animal trying to flee her captor.

"Georgie, *please*," Hannah begged, but it didn't make a bit of difference. Georgiana's fingers clawed at the mattress as her mother lifted the plate of food off the tray.

Hannah tipped her chin upward and patiently watched the girl before her, waiting for her to settle or tire, whichever one came first. It reminded Jesse of the way Ian sometimes thrashed against the five-point harness of his high chair, kicking and bucking while he turned red with rage. Jesse slid down the wall to sit on the floor as he watched the duo. He wondered how long Hannah would give her daughter, considered what she would do if Georgiana took too long and tested her mother's patience. It didn't take long to get an answer.

"I'm sorry," Hannah said softly, "but you have to eat." She then took up the spoon that was half-buried beneath a pile of diced vegetables. With her free hand, she caught Georgiana by the chin and pushed the spoon into the girl's mouth. Georgiana sputtered. Orange and green mush spewed across her bottom lip and dribbled down her chin.

"I'm sorry, Georgie," she said again, her voice warbling with emotion. "You're wasting away." She tried again, this time holding Georgiana's nose so that the girl had to swallow.

With her mother's fingers still pinched against her nostrils, Georgiana gave her head a vicious shake, freeing herself from Hannah's clutch. As soon as she was loose, she spit a mouthful of half-mashed peas and carrots into her mother's face. Hannah gasped and dropped the plate of food onto the tray with a clang, and for a moment Jesse was sure she was about to give up. But rather than rising from her chair and rushing out of the room, Hannah calmly wiped herself off with the corner of her apron, then fixed her gaze on Georgiana, baring her teeth like a dog about to bite.

"You will not take my daughter from me," she hissed, then slammed her right hand into the brown gravy slathered upon the plate. With a fistful of meat in her grasp, she squeezed Georgiana's nose shut once more. Jesse's stomach lurched as Georgiana fought to keep her lips sealed, but her need for air eventually won out. As soon as her lips parted to gulp air, her mother shoved the food into her mouth.

Jesse winced and turned away as Hannah smeared gravy across her daughter's cheeks and chin. Some of the stuff made it into her hair. It was awful to witness, especially when Georgiana began to choke. Thankfully, both Doctor Ladeaux and Father Baker stepped into the room before Hannah could stuff another helping past Georgiana's lips.

"Miss Ecklund!" Ladeaux exclaimed. Jesse whipped his gaze back to Hannah. It was just in time to see a geyser of vomit spew from Georgiana's mouth, hitting Hannah square in the chest.

Both men gawked as Hannah shot up from her chair in a backward stumble, her clothing dripping in bile and undigested lunch. Surprisingly, it was Georgiana who broke the silence. With food slathered across her face and vomit covering the front of her nightgown, she threw back her head and cackled, as though the situation was the funniest thing she'd ever seen.

Doctor Ladeaux and Father Baker blinked at one another, coming to some sort of unspoken understanding.

"I see it now," Father Baker said softly. "My God, it can't be true."

And Jesse could see it, too. He didn't want to admit it, but they were right. Georgiana was no ordinary girl. This was something else. Something beyond understanding.

This was wicked, whatever it was.

FORTY

JESSE ROUSED from sleep only when he heard the front door unlock. He sat up, bleary-eyed, and found LouEllen standing on the doormat, a sleeping Ian slouched against her shoulder. It was hard to tell what she was thinking, but she looked less than happy as she surveyed the room.

Jesse held his breath as she moved past the broken-framed portrait and the gash in the wall. He knew better than to hope she wouldn't notice. The woman had an uncanny ability to sniff out even the most minor out-of-place details, and that ability didn't fail her now. She paused in front of the wall and stared at the portrait for a long moment, then looked to her husband. When Jesse didn't say anything, she continued walking, pausing at the lamp with a now-dented shade.

He waited until she moved down the hall toward the nursery, then peeled himself off the couch, wracking his brain for what to say. While relieved that she'd come home, her body language did little to dispel his anxiety. The wannabe-writer needed to think up some fancy words pretty quickly or things were likely to implode.

But before he could come up with an apology, LouEllen ducked into the kitchen. Jesse rose from the couch, freezing when he spotted her standing at the kitchen table. Her brows were furrowed, her features twisted in a confused sort of wonder. Her attention was fixed upon the mangled pieces that had once been his laptop, now reduced to an abstract dinner party centerpiece.

When she sensed him standing there, she glanced up.

"I broke it. So now I can't use it anymore," he explained, in case Lou was under the impression that the pile of electronic waste was somehow still in working order.

She looked back to the computer, taking it all in. For a fleeting moment, Jesse hoped that his willingness to destroy the thing that had been facilitating their problem was enough to prove that he really was sorry. He was trying to make things better. He was trying to change.

And yet, the longer they both stood there, the more it dawned on him: LouEllen wasn't going to give him a smile, and she wasn't going to step out from behind the table and throw her arms around his neck. From what he could see of her expression, which was half-hidden behind her hair, she was the opposite of pleased.

She was using her sonar to picture his meltdown, as though his rage had left a psychic scar on the house itself. And Jesse's suggestion of intentionally breaking the computer? She knew it was a lie. He hadn't destroyed that machine with some higher purpose. He'd trashed it because it had finally happened: he'd completely lost control.

Finally, LouEllen met his gaze, but Jesse knew his excuse had failed before their eyes ever met.

"I'm going to keep Ian in our room tonight." She didn't offer an explanation as to why, only that it was happening. There was nothing he could do about it. "I need you to sleep on the couch."

Jesse turned back to the broken pieces of his computer.

"Please get rid of this," she said, motioning to the pile of junk, and then walked out of the room.

Jesse was left to stand there, alone again, fighting off the slow crawl of a new emotion. Not fear or aggravation. Not confusion or even a sense of foreboding. No. This was hopelessness. It was despair.

FORTY-ONE

JESSE MADE up the couch, but he didn't bother lying down. He merely sat there and watched the shadows shift along the walls of the darkened living room while trying to cobble together the strange story that was unspooling inside his mind.

He kept seeing Ladeaux's black car pulling up to the house in the snow, kept seeing the girl thrashing while tied up in her room. Jesse pressed the heels of his hands into his eye sockets as he tried to purge his mind of those images, if only for a few minutes of peace. It was, however, no use. He kept seeing it: Hannah shoving food down her daughter's throat. Georgiana vomiting. Doctor Ladeaux and Father Baker watching the girl they were now sure was possessed.

And those pictures? They felt real, not like fiction at all. They felt alive, and he didn't understand how that could be. They were as real as the dark things that had bled their way out of his nightmares and into his reality. That low, rumbling laughter. Georgiana standing in front of his bumper. LouEllen sitting in the passenger's seat while wearing Georgiana's face. Casey telling him about a girl he shouldn't have known about yet somehow did. Casey claiming that Reed hadn't jumped. That he'd been pushed.

Hey, Jesse! Catch!

And now, the more Jesse replayed Casey's suicide, the more confident he was that Georgiana hadn't been far away that night. He hadn't made her up yet, but somehow she'd already been inside that house with them both. Because he'd sensed something just before Casey had leaped. He'd felt it intensify after the rope had gone taut and jerked Casey back, as if God himself had reached down and tried to reverse Casey's downward trajectory, attempting to launch him into heaven with a single forceful pull. Jesse had smelled the stench of ammonia and vomit, had seen black vapor drift down from Casey's dangling feet to where he had stood beneath him, so close to the spot where Reed had died that he may as well have been standing on his best friend's grave.

Yes, Jesse had felt something.

Inexplicably, he'd felt *her*.

By six that morning, Jesse had downed three cups of coffee while scribbling notes in a tiny field notebook. They were things he'd seen and heard and felt in real life rather than fiction. And the more he recalled those details, the more haunted he felt.

At seven, he left his desk and headed toward the master bedroom, needing to get ready for school. When he found his clothes and toiletries outside the bedroom door—carefully folded and stacked as though delivered by hotel housekeeping—his heart twisted within his chest. The message was loud and clear: Lou didn't want to see him, even if it was just to let him take a shower and brush his teeth. But that pang of sorrow only lingered for a moment. He needed to get moving. Garvey would notice if he was late.

He took a shower in Ian's bathroom, which was full of toys and foam letters that spelled out garbled nonsense on the tile above the tub. He dressed in the living room, grabbed his keys, and drove all the way to Java Joe's. His exhaustion was all-consuming, but he couldn't let Garvey see his fatigue. After all, he had lied and told him a story about a lovely, relaxing weekend. And now, here he was, sleep deprived and more tired than ever before.

He ordered a large black eye—but rather than two shots of espresso, he requested four. The girl at the drive-thru gave him a look of concern when he pulled up and handed her his credit card. It was as though she was sizing him up, wondering if his heart could take all that caffeine. *Little girl,* he thought. *You have no idea what I've been through.* Hell, maybe if he had a caffeine-induced heart attack, the trouble would finally be over. That, however, was a laughable notion. If anything was going to stop his heart, it sure as hell wasn't going to be this.

By the time he pulled into the school parking lot, half his coffee was gone, and his nerves were sizzling like livewires beneath his skin.

He muscled his way through his first handful of classes, concentrating on students who acted up at the back of the room. Playing disciplinarian took his mind off LouEllen. Though, when he barked an order of *'sit down'* at a fourth-period kid, he cranked back the dial. The anger was back, and it felt even more volatile.

He left campus for a sandwich and another coffee. He wouldn't make it through the day without a second cup, and he didn't trust himself to keep his cool among those gossiping assholes he called coworkers in the teacher's lounge. That's how he found himself in a sticky booth inside a place called Hooper's—a mom and pop shop that was half little grocery store, half walk-up deli counter—staring at a turkey sandwich he didn't much feel like eating.

Going back to work felt like a bad idea, but he knew if he skipped, Garvey would be down his throat. There was a chance he'd lose his job, and he couldn't let that happen, not with how things with LouEllen had panned out the day before.

When he returned to campus, there was chaos in the hallway. A couple of girls were sparring, fists and hair flying in the middle of a ring of cheering teens. He recognized them both. One was a blonde-haired girl named Ama. He had her during third period. She was a tough girl; the type that freely threw glares at her classmates from across the room. The other was a dark-haired underclassman. Jesse wasn't sure of her name, but every time he saw her, she reminded him of that lone art-inclined student stuck on an island of cheerleaders. She was an outsider. The one that didn't belong. If he had to pick sides, he's put his money on the underdog.

Fights weren't rare at Warsaw High. Just the month before, Elliott Winestead—another kid who didn't quite fit in—had been beaten up outside the gym by a couple of Warrior linebackers. Elliott had been lucky to walk away with nothing but a broken nose. That fight had served to remind Jesse just what life was like for a kid growing up in his hometown. It was a quaint and wholesome farming town on the outside, but beneath that bucolic façade, it was a hateful place.

"Goddamnit," he murmured, then shouldered his way through the huddled group of kids. He had to physically move a few people to get to the front of the crowd, then glanced to the student next to him. It was James Jones, the kid who'd launched the snowball at him from down the hall a few days before.

"Hold this," he said, handing James his cup of coffee. Before James knew what was happening, he was grasping a paper cup in his hand and watching his English teacher step into the ring.

"Stop," Jesse said, trying to keep his composure. As long as he stayed calm and asserted himself, the girls would declare temporary peace, right?

Wrong.

They continued swinging.

Ama grabbed a fistful of the art girl's hair and yanked, causing her opponent to stumble forward and crash to her knees.

"Jesus, *stop!*" Jesse yelled. "That's enough!"

But the girls hardly noticed him, let alone complied with his demands. Instead, they came at each other again, complete with wildly waving arms and high-pitched screams. The dark-haired girl was bleeding from the corner of her mouth while Ama had a couple of scratches down her right cheek. That, and the crowd wasn't helping. All that cheering and whooping gave the entire scene a *Lord of the Flies* vibe.

The girls refused to separate, so Jesse grabbed Ama by the shoulders and gave her a backward pull. She reeled around, her fist pulled back, ready to sock whoever was coming between her and victory square in the mouth. But rather than throwing a punch, she went ashen when she realized it was a teacher. Her opponent, however, wasn't as easily deterred.

Before Jesse knew up from down, Ama was crashing against his chest. Her forehead slammed into his chin, and they both lurched backward into a bank of lockers. The crowd's jeers shifted to something closer to joyful shock. *Holy shits* flew left and right.

Jesse winced against the throbbing of his jaw. His vision went blurry, as though someone had slid Vaseline-smeared glasses onto his face. The kids were keeping their distance, but they were too invested to leave the scene. He could see the glow of their phones bobbing above their heads as they recorded the fight, possibly live streaming it to the social platform of their choice.

Ama pushed away from Jesse's chest with uneven steps, her hands pressed against her forehead. And then, just as Jesse thought it was over, the art girl charged. Ama yelped and skittered out of the way just in time to save herself, but Jesse was too dazed to react. Having succumbed to her own momentum, the art girl was unable to change her trajectory in time. She stumbled through her lunge, and that's when he finally caught a glimpse of his soon-to-be-attacker's snarl.

Pale and hollow-eyed.

Lips cracked and bloody.

A sneer pulled across that ugly mouth.

He let out a yell, then caught her by the biceps and swung her around. Georgiana's face went blank when her back hit the lockers, as if not understanding the mechanics of how she'd gotten there. But rather than letting her go, Jesse yanked her forward and shoved her back again. Georgiana's head hit the blue-painted doors behind her.

"Fuck you!" Jesse spit the words at her. "Fuck you, you hear me? I'm tired of this shit. You aren't real, goddamnit. Get the fuck out of my life!"

The crowd gasped.

The jeers and hooting stopped.

An unsettling silence fell over the hallway. Meanwhile, Jesse continued to shake the ghost before him, as though shaking her hard enough would somehow scare her away. That's when Georgiana opened her mouth and screamed.

"Get off of me!"

She struggled, stronger than Jesse expected her to be, prying her way out of his grasp with a couple of yanks and twists.

His hands fell away from her, the silence behind him now a deafening roar. For a moment, he was sure the crowd of students was gone. The school had vanished. Everything he knew had disappeared and the dilapidated house with broken floorboards and peeling paint was all that was left. But when he finally gathered up his courage to look over his shoulder, the kids were still there. Their faces were cloned grimaces of disbelief. Their phones remained in their hands; freelance reporters in the time of instant news.

He didn't have to see the dark-haired girl's face to know the truth. Just like the time in the car with LouEllen, Georgiana wasn't there. She had *never* been there. And yet, she absolutely had been. She had been. She had...

FORTY-TWO

THE POLICE came, just as they had the night of Casey's death; as they had when Jesse had seen Georgiana screaming into the wind.

Garvey sat behind his desk, his arms crossed and his face stern. The dark-haired art girl was named Savannah Hudson, and Savannah was now speaking to the police in the nurse's office, where she and her parents would be allowed to press assault charges against Jesse if they saw fit. And Jesse knew, they'd see fit. Money was a rare Warsaw commodity. Lawsuits were a not-to-be-missed opportunity.

He knew he wouldn't escape unscathed. Even if the Hudsons decided to spare him, there were videos taken from dozens of vantage points. There would be no denying it, no trying to explain it away. It didn't matter that he had seen someone else coming at him, that he'd thought it was a girl from his nightmares rather than a girl he passed in the hall every day. What mattered was that he had attacked her. He'd hissed profanity at a child through his teeth. It was over for him. Career. Reputation. Marriage. Done.

After a long silence, Garvey finally spoke.

"Do you want to call your wife?"

Jesse looked up, not understanding the question.

"She'll probably have to meet you at the precinct," Garvey explained. "This is your first offense, I hope."

Jesse frowned and looked back to his lap. He prayed he wouldn't have to spend the night in jail, but he'd definitely be slapped with a fine before the day was through. Then, there would be a hearing and even more fines he couldn't afford. And now, after this, there was a possibility that Casey's suicide would be viewed in a different light. Hell, maybe Reed's death, too. Anyone in their right mind would wonder.

He attacked a kid. Clearly, he's out of control. What really *happened with those two guys at the farmhouse? How can all this be a coincidence? There should be an investigation. What if he—*

"Jesse." Garvey cleared his throat and leaned forward, his chair squeaking beneath his weight. "You do understand that I have to suspend you."

Not only did Jesse understand it, but he was already predicting the future. Most assaults were misdemeanors, but in his case, he'd attacked a minor. It could turn into a felony. And whether it did or not was beside the point. His ability to continue teaching was gone. And yet, despite the circumstances, he couldn't help but smirk at the realization.

"Something funny?" Garvey asked, not sounding the least bit amused.

"Yeah," Jesse murmured. "Just the other day I was thinking about quitting my job," he confessed. When he looked up again, Garvey's eyebrows were in a high arc upon his forehead. *Oh really,* his expression read.

"I guess I can stop thinking about it now," Jesse said, then emitted a single, dry laugh. "She took care of it for me. There's literally nothing left to do. Now, I *have* to write the fucking thing."

FORTY-THREE

THEY TOOK his fingerprints and his mug shot. Soon, Jesse's photo would end up in a city database, accessible to anyone who felt like perusing Warsaw's criminal elite. He gave it less than a week before every student had his glamour shot saved onto their phone. Forget making a name for himself as a novelist. Now, he'd be the man, the myth, the legend: Jesse Wells, the teacher who was about to kill a girl in a high school hallway. The one who'd lost his mind.

The police didn't keep him overnight—thank God for small mercies—but they did tell him not to leave town. An officer dropped him off in the school parking lot so that he could retrieve his car. Jesse left town a minute later, driving twenty minutes north instead of heading home. He parked a good eighth of a mile from the farmhouse in the middle of the derelict drive. From there, he could only see the home's severe silhouette in the rapid onset of dusk, but it was enough to bring him a strange sort of comfort. It stood to assure him that, no, he wasn't insane. This place? It was real. And the things that were happening to him were real, too.

When he finally arrived home, it was after nine. He found LouEllen sitting on the couch, the TV glowing in the darkened living room. When she twisted where she sat to look at him, her face said it all.

"You're on the news," she said flatly. It appeared that the Action7 newscasters had done Jesse a service. And here he thought he'd have to fumble through an awkward play-by-play of his day. *So, today was strange.* But Lou had a firm grasp on how a man who had had a job just that morning was now not only unemployed, but also unemployable beyond his high school burger-flipping gig.

Jesse hung his coat on the hook beside the door, then shuffled further into the room and stopped to survey the small gash he'd made in the wall beneath Ian's broken picture frame. The damage he'd caused within that room had seemed severe when he'd done it. But now, the frame, the lamp, it all struck him as trivial. This, however—LouEllen's emotional state, her unwavering stare—*this* was severe.

"They showed, like, four videos of it," she said, finally turning away from him. "You attacked a child." Her voice broke. She pressed her hands to her cheeks and took a shaky breath.

He stood motionless, waiting for her to speak again, not offering any words of his own. He knew trying to give the whys and wherefores of what had happened would be pointless. She wouldn't want to hear it, and even if she listened, she wouldn't believe him or understand. It was best to stand there, silent and stoic, waiting for the inevitable fallout.

"Carrie Mae is on her way."

And there it was. Swift. Unsparing.

"We're going to stay with her for a while." Lou swiped at her tear-streaked face, then pulled in another broken breath.

"That's probably for the best," Jesse said softly.

"Jesus, Jesse." She shook her head, at a loss. "What were you thinking?"

He lifted his shoulders in a half-hearted shrug. *I don't know anymore.* But rather than giving her a non-answer, he strived for something better. A moment later, he met her gaze with his own.

"I amplified the negative," he told her. "Just like your mother said I would."

FORTY-FOUR

LOUELLEN LEFT with Ian, and Jesse remained within the unbearable silence of an empty house. He kept the television on to cut through the quiet, drank coffee at the kitchen table and frowned at his hands, wondering how his life had become so fractured. His nightmares had finally given way to something even bleaker than themselves—a cold bed, a vacant crib, a soundless home, and damning isolation.

Was there a way to fix this disaster, to repair the damage? He wanted to believe there was. But his thoughts of how to mend the ruin quickly spiraled in a direction he resented. The black car. The broken porch steps. Georgiana stumbling into the snow.

No, those specters hissed. *There's no fixing it. This is what you have left.*

He squeezed his eyes shut, trying to block out the visions, but they kept coming. Georgiana's terrified mother. A concerned Doctor Ladeaux. Georgiana screaming. The priest with his rosary beads.

Your old life, they whispered. *It's gone, Jesse. This is what you have left.*

"But why?" He asked the question aloud so that Georgiana could hear, so that she could answer if she chose. "What does any of this have to do with me?"

Had it all stemmed from that childhood autumn afternoon? If Georgiana *was* real, had Jesse's seeing her sealed his fate? No, he refused to believe that. It had been nearly thirty years since then. She would have come for him sooner, would have resurfaced long ago.

And that was, perhaps, the most maddening part of it all. He couldn't piece together the connection; couldn't decipher why he'd started seeing images of the farmhouse at all. Sure, he'd always be tied to the house after what he'd lived through, what he'd witnessed. But what did that have to do with Georgiana? Why was she replaying her misery like an old movie reel every time he closed his eyes? What did she want, and why had she chosen him?

He leaned back in his chair, his fingernails scratching at the surface of the table much the way Georgiana had fought for purchase while tied to her bed. He looked across the kitchen, past the darkened hallway, and into the empty living room—empty and dark, like the rooms of the Ecklund farmhouse.

A scream sounded from the flickering blue darkness. An actress was yelling on TV. But rather than shrugging it off as nothing but background noise, it forced another image to the forefront of Jesse's mind: a picture of Georgiana wailing as her mother turned away, leaving her manacled to the bed.

Jesse blinked at his hands, a new understanding dawning on him as the screaming kept on. This was all by design. He was alone here, just as Georgiana had been alone there. She wanted him to experience the same misery, the same loneliness, the same helplessness she had gone through all those years ago. And maybe *that's* why she had picked him. He'd spotted her in the window when he had been overwhelmed with betrayal. She'd watched him as panic seized his heart. She knew that he was familiar with those emotions, with the things she had felt, too.

But she's not real, Jesse, he reminded himself. *You're forgetting, she's a figment of your imagination.*

He rose from the table, unable to sit still any longer. Stepping into the living room, the hysterical sobs of the TV actress grew louder as he approached the couch. His attention drifted to his work desk, to the spot where his laptop used to sit. What he wouldn't have done to have his computer back, if only to rewatch Casey's videos, to try to find the answer to the puzzle just one more time.

And even if she did *exist, she can't do this, can't take over your life.*

He sank onto the sofa and pulled YouTube up on his phone. But the connection was terrible. The videos would play for half a second before buffering and reloading. He shoved the device into his pocket and moved to the front door, grabbed his coat off the hook and pulled it on. He only stopped to glance at Winston, who was now resigned to sharing the house with the one person he no longer liked.

"Dubs," Jesse said, taking a step toward the canine. Winston didn't like that. He immediately tensed, then emitted a muffled grumble. *Stay away.*

"Okay," Jesse said, holding up his hands. "I get it." He moved back into the kitchen, poured the dog a bowl of kibble, and left it on the floor beside the stove.

Part of him resented Lou for leaving him with Winston. If Jesse was such a danger, why wouldn't she have taken the dog to Carrie Mae's as well? But another part of him was glad, because at least Winston was a tether. If he hadn't been around, there would be no reason for LouEllen to consider coming home.

Winston lifted his head when Jesse stepped back into the living room. "Food is in the kitchen," he told the hound. "I'll be back in a bit." It almost felt like he was saying it not to the dog, but as a reminder to himself.

You have to come back.

You can figure this out.

And yet, simultaneously, he could hear that whisper of a new mantra repeating itself on a loop.

This is all that that there is, all that ever would be.

This is it, Jesse. Just us. You and me.

FORTY-FIVE

HE DROVE to Warsaw's one and only library, but at three in the morning, of course it was closed. Sitting in the car and staring at the building, he wondered where the hell he could find access to a computer or some decent Wi-Fi at such an hour. Any other time, he would have been able to head to school, let himself in, and use the computer lab, no matter how ill-equipped it was. But Garvey had taken Jesse's keys. The only way to get in there was to break in, and that would certainly result in immediate jail time.

The only place he knew was open was Speedy's, but there was no hope of accessing the Internet there. Only just recently the owner had begrudgingly started taking credit cards. An old behemoth of a cash register still sat on the counter—an eighties relic if Jesse had ever seen one. Wi-Fi? Not a chance.

He leaned against the Altima's steering wheel and tried to think, but a shift of light somewhere ahead of the vehicle distracted him from his thoughts. Looking up, he caught a glimpse of white fabric in his periphery.

His heart thudded hard against his ribs, because while he couldn't outright see her, he knew she was there; standing statuesque and half-hidden by some shaggy boxwoods near the library's front doors. Every so often, the wind would grab fistfuls of snow off the rooftop and send it spiraling to the ground. When those snowflakes scattered across Jesse's windshield, he could see the corner of Georgiana's gauzy nightgown whipping in the gale.

She was following him, assuring him that he couldn't get in his car and drive away. They were connected. They always had been. He had wanted a muse, right? *Careful what you wish for.* Georgiana had made her appearance and was here to stay.

At least until I figure this out, he thought to himself. *At least until I save her, the way she asked.*

Because that was the answer, wasn't it? She needed help. If he did what she wanted, she'd be done with him. She'd go her own way.

Jesse peeled out of the library's parking lot and pointed the vehicle in the direction of the farmhouse, but half-way there he had a change of heart. Because there was no magic bullet, at least not there. If there had been, he'd have found it by now. If there was an answer to all this, he'd have to search for it elsewhere. But where?

"Blaire," he said, suddenly struck by how obvious it was.

Of course. If anyone would know what to do, he had to believe it was her.

Blaire lived in an enormous custom-built home on a vast swath of land. There was a gate at the entrance to the driveway. Jesse knew the code from all the times Blaire had invited him and LouEllen over. He punched it in, then considered that it might do nothing. Codes were easy to change. And after what had happened with Casey, Jesse wouldn't have been surprised if Blaire had opted for heightened security, for extra privacy rather than unexpected guests. But the gate swung open, and Jesse pulled through onto the tree-lined road.

The house was an impressive stone and shingle colonial that looked like a picture postcard decked out in its holiday best. It was nearly February, yet there were wreaths hung in every window, a perfect match to the massive one hanging on the grand front door. A giant garland decorated in red ribbons and baubles was draped from the top of the front porch, shining even in the dark. Those holiday decorations served as a reminder that Jesse wasn't the only one suffering. Somewhere inside that mansion, Blaire was lost in her own grief. Time was standing still for her, just as it was for him.

He slid out of the car and walked up Blaire's front walkway, climbed the front steps and furrowed his eyebrows at the door. There was no doubt Blaire was sleeping. If he knocked, she'd be alarmed and possibly call the police. But he had to try.

Save me, Georgiana had pleaded.

That was the plea Jesse had to make to Blaire now.

He pressed the glowing button of the doorbell and listened to it chime from behind the door. A light clicked on somewhere in the house. A minute later, he spotted a silhouette. He bowed his head, hoping that when the door swung open—*if* it swung open—it would be Blaire standing there, not that sallow-faced girl he'd come to know so well.

The front door opened a crack, and an eye appeared.

"…Jesse?" Blaire sounded unsure, hesitant to take the chain off its slide.

"Blaire," he said. "I'm sorry. I know it's late. I just, I didn't know where else to go."

"Are you alright?" She sounded concerned, but the question was still posed from a safe distance. The door remained between them.

"No," he said. "I need to talk to you."

"…right now?"

She seemed baffled, and for a second Jesse thought about taking his leave. *No,* he could have said. *Of course, not right now. It's three in the morning and I'm losing my mind.* But he heard Reed's voice whisper against his ear—*we've come too far*—and he nodded instead.

"Yes," he said. "Right now, if you'll let me." And then he looked up at Casey's widow. "LouEllen left me," he told her. "Can I come in?"

A few minutes later, Jesse found himself sitting in a living room five times the size of his own, staring at a Christmas tree that must have been a good nine feet tall. It was unplugged, as were all the decorations, from the oversized wreath hanging above the fireplace to the garland draped along the mantel. Those festive embellishments only made the place feel that much more empty. Undoubtedly, they were a constant reminder of a holiday that would never be the same again.

Blaire came into the room with two steaming mugs of coffee. She was unsure of herself, but she was making a go of being a good hostess; old habits really did die hard.

"I hope you're okay with black," she said. "I'm all out of cream. Haven't bothered with the grocery store since…" She paused, shook her head, then handed one of the mugs to her guest. Taking a seat across from the couch, she rested her own cup on her robe-covered knees.

"Thanks," Jesse said, then peered into the steam of his cup, wondering if Blaire would break the tension and ask what the hell was going on. But that wasn't the way Blaire worked. Jesse had come knocking on *her* door, not the other way around. If there was talking to be done, Jesse would be doing it.

"Blaire..." He began, then stopped, sensing something shift in his periphery. His chin jerked upward.

Blaire frowned. "What's wrong?" Her own gaze drifted across the night shadows that clung to the corners of the room.

Georgiana could have been behind the Christmas tree, watching them both through baubled branches and bits of tinsel. Perhaps she was standing in one of those dark corners, that maniacal grin little more than a slash of teeth across her face. Yes, she knew this house. She was familiar with these rooms. She had been here before.

But Jesse's newfound certainty only brought a new question to the forefront. Casey had said he'd seen her. In his videos, he'd mentioned that he'd been drawn back to the farmhouse time and again. Blaire had mentioned that Casey had taken to sleeping on the couch, had screamed himself awake on more than a few occasions. Did that mean that Casey had been having these same visions? Had Casey stood in Georgiana's room, same as Jesse? Had he watched her thrash against those restraints? Had Georgiana asked *him* for help?

Jesse snapped his attention back to Blaire. "Was there a girl?" he asked. Because if Casey had lived through what Jesse was dealing with now, if he had been haunted in the same way, that changed things. Perhaps Casey—spurred on by his love of things forgotten— had promised Georgiana he'd help her. Maybe, when Jesse had lost Casey, Georgiana had lost him, too. That would explain why Georgiana was beseeching Jesse, right? With Casey gone, his promise was left unfulfilled.

"A girl?" Blaire canted her head to the side, not understanding the question.

"For Casey," Jesse said, trying to clarify without saying it outright. "Before his...before what happened."

"A girl..." Blaire echoed.

"Did he ever mention someone?" he asked. "Or talk about any dreams he may have had?"

"Are you suggesting Casey was having an affair?"

Jesse blinked, realizing that his line of questioning sounded far more scandalous than it was. But of course, how could Blaire have not jumped to such a conclusion? He was making it sound suspicious, like something it wasn't.

"No, I—" He stammered, but she cut him off.

"Jesse," Blaire squared her shoulders and looked down to her coffee mug. "As I told you before, Casey and I weren't really on speaking terms toward the end."

"But before that," he said, pleading for her to dig into her memory, to excavate some small piece of recollection. Because if Casey *had* promised Georgiana that he'd help her, that was the answer. She was just searching for someone to fill Casey's shoes.

"And as I mentioned before," Blaire continued, her posture stiff, no-nonsense. "I don't talk about what happened anymore. I don't want to *think* about it anymore. After what happened with Reed, I thought that you, of all people, would have respected my privacy when it came to this."

Jesse looked away from her, suddenly ashamed of his late-night intrusion. She was right, this was madness. He'd pulled her out of bed to ask her questions about her dead husband as though he was somehow owed the information. Regardless of what he was going through, that made him an asshole. He should have thought it over before he had come barging up Blaire's front steps.

"I'm sorry," he said softly. "But, Blaire, I need to know. When he and I went to that house—"

"Don't."

She held up a hand to stop him, but Jesse couldn't allow himself to be silenced. She was going to kick him out. That was becoming clearer with every second. He could see it in the way her mouth tightened into a tense line, in the way her shoulders pulled up to her ears. But he'd roused her from bed, and he'd already brought up a sensitive subject. The least he could do, before she told him to get the hell out of her house, was say what he needed to say.

"Casey said that before Reed jumped, there had been a girl."

Blaire rose from her seat, her expression full-on bitter now. He could read her thoughts. *How dare you?* But he refused to let them stall his questioning. Because this was important. Blair had lost Casey to this. Now, it was Jesse's family on the line.

"Casey said there had been a girl in the house the night Reed had jumped, but he hadn't seen her until it was too late. He told me that maybe he hadn't seen her at all until after he was replaying the whole thing in his mind, over and over the way I'm replaying Casey's suicide in mine."

"I'd like you to go," she said.

Jesse placed his mug on the coffee table and rose, just as she had. "I will," he said, "and I'm sorry I came here and brought all this up. But something is happening..."

"Something," she repeated, her voice softening.

"Something bad," he said. "To me. To my family. And I think it might be the same thing that happened to both Reed and Casey. There's a girl, and she'd been there since we were kids..."

Blaire offered him a tight-lipped smile. "Okay," she said, then motioned with her hand for him to take his leave. *Time to go.*

"I think she died in that house," he explained despite being led toward the front door. "They mistreated her, and she...I think that's why she's back. We used to ride our bikes to that place as kids. I saw her in the window once. I told Reed. Then Reed became obsessed with that house, the same as Casey had after Reed died." He paused, watching Blaire pull open the front door. "Don't you get it? If I don't help her... I don't..." His words became soft, almost inaudible. He was speaking more to himself now than to the woman a few feet away. "I don't know what will happen to me."

"Jesse," Blaire said. He glanced up at her. "You're talking about ghosts."

"I know." He nodded. "Yes, I know, but—"

"There is no girl," she said. "There's only the truth, which is that you watched Casey kill himself."

Jesse winced. He looked away again, but Blaire pulled his attention back, her hand falling upon his arm.

"I told you, you need to move past this, or it will destroy you," she said. "You need to accept that bad things happen. Reframe your life. Allow yourself to live. Neither Casey nor Reed were your fault."

"But it's not about Casey or Reed," Jesse whispered. "It's about her."

Blaire nodded faintly. "I'll call LouEllen in the morning, okay?"

"It's about her," he murmured while Blaire guided him onto the front porch. "It's not about them, it's about *her.*"

"Goodnight, Jesse," she said, beginning to shut the door behind him.

"I think her name is Georgiana," he said, imploring her. "Did Casey ever mention the name Georgi—"

But Blaire closed the door just then, and he doubted she had been listening, doubted that she'd heard.

FORTY-SIX

HE DROVE back home in a daze, unsure of what he was going to do when he got there. Perhaps he'd try to sleep again. Maybe he'd have another vision, something that would make this puzzle all come clear.

He pulled into the driveway and reached for the handle of the driver's side door. But he stalled in exiting the vehicle when his phone chimed a notification tone. He tugged his phone out of his pocket with worst-case scenarios spiraling through his head. He imagined it was Lou. She was sitting sleepless at Carrie Mae's house, finally texting him to tell him it was over. Texting to inform him that Blaire had just called and told her about Jesse's late-night intrusion. Reassuring him that, yes, she wanted a divorce. It was her, breaking the news that she'd decided he was out of his mind, that she'd be filing for full custody, that she wasn't sure she wanted him anywhere near Ian at all.

It was her, telling him that no matter how much she tried to understand it, she couldn't figure out how all this had gotten so out of hand. Because only two months prior, Lou and Jesse had been happy and anticipating their first string of holidays with their baby boy. They had driven two hours into the wilderness and cut down their own Christmas tree, Griswold-style. Jesse had even bought an old-fashioned metal-railed sled on Amazon, unable to shake the desire to pull little Ian behind him like something off a Norman Rockwell postcard. Only a month before, they had rung in the new year, excited about all the possibilities it held. The night before Casey stopped by the house, they had lied in bed together, their limbs intertwined. She had still loved him then.

But that was a lifetime ago.

He sighed into the darkness of the Altima's interior, then unlocked his phone and braced himself for bad news. But it wasn't a text from Lou. The notification was a junk email pinging his inbox. There was, however, something else: a message he'd missed from Sam hours before.

HEY, MAN. I HEARD ABOUT WHAT HAPPENED AT SCHOOL. CALL ME. WE NEED TO TALK ASAP.

He stared ahead at his house. It was the last place he wanted to be. Winston was in there, and he'd snarl and cower as soon as Jesse stepped through the front door. It would remind him that there was something very wrong, something that needed to be fixed, that time was running short. Blaire refused to help, but maybe Sam...

His finger hovered over the CALL button. But rather than ringing Sam up at four thirty in the morning, Jesse reversed out of the driveway and drove. If Sam's place appeared to be asleep, he'd wait for sunrise—anything to stay out of his own house for a few hours, to give himself time to think.

It took him less than ten minutes to get to Sam and Stella's place. It was like every other Warsaw residence—plain and small and somewhat run down. Stella tried to keep it looking pulled together with pruned boxwoods out front and English ivy growing along the fence. A wooden knee-high grizzly bear was sitting next to the front door, holding a welcome sign and half-buried in the snow. The light next to the door was on despite the hour, not that it meant much; Lou had a habit of leaving their porch light on all night long herself. But it wasn't the porch light that spurred Jesse to exit his vehicle, it was the light shining through the drawn curtains of the front room. He saw a figure move inside. Someone was awake. Maybe Sam was pulling an all-nighter, grading papers. Or, perhaps it was Stella, and as soon as Jesse knocked on the door, he'd come off as a lunatic.

But it was a bit late to worry about such things. After all, there was no doubt the majority of Warsaw knew what had gone down at school the day before. And despite the ungodly hour, Jesse didn't want to sit in his car until the sun came up.

ANIA AHLBORN

He trudged up the front walkway and knocked on the door. It took a moment, but Sam eventually answered. Wearing a pair of well-loved sweatpants and a Red Wings jersey, he was startled to see Jesse standing on his front doorstep. Jesse didn't regard his surprise. He had expected as much.

"I saw your light on," Jesse said. It was as good an excuse as any.

Sam raised both eyebrows before stepping aside—an unspoken invitation to come in.

"Sorry," Jesse said as Sam closed and locked the door. "I saw your text, and I didn't know where else to go."

"Did they fire you?" Sam asked.

"Suspended. But it's inevitable," Jesse said. "No way they'll have me back."

"What the hell happened?"

Jesse lifted his shoulders at the question. *I thought I saw a ghost* didn't strike him as a reasonable answer, so he didn't respond at all.

"I need to show you something," Sam said, then moved through the tidy living room into a study that put the Warsaw public library to shame. "Here, sit," Sam said, pulling an extra chair up to a desk that reminded Jesse of his own. Covered in books and papers, it even sported the same style of task lamp that Jesse had back home. Sam took a seat in his office chair and adjusted the lamp, which drooped same as Jesse's did.

"After I heard what happened, I couldn't sleep," Sam confessed. "Look." He searched around on his desk, then located the printout he was hunting for. It was an old article from the Warsaw Herald, dated summer of 1932.

"I nearly missed this," Sam said as he handed it over. "It's such a small mention, but I'm almost positive they're talking about your house."

Your house. Is that what it had become? The sentiment gave Jesse the creeps, but he didn't say as much. He took the article from Sam and frowned at the text.

The title read: WARSAW'S NEW FAMILY. Below it, there was a single paragraph detailing how a Mr. Joseph Ecklund of South Bend, Indiana had purchased thirty-five acres of land north of town and was planning on building a house "grander than any Warsaw has ever seen."

Jesse's heart just about seized at the sight of that name, because it was impossible. He had made Joseph Ecklund up, hadn't he? Unless he'd seen the name somewhere before. Unless, without even knowing it, he'd heard of this man as a kid and had filed the name away in some dusty corner of his mind. He'd heard of things like that happening—mundane details trapped in the wrinkles of the brain, waiting to be excavated; details that, when they came back up, were so strangely specific that their recollection seemed almost supernatural.

"Once I had a name to go with the property, it got easier," Sam explained while handing over another printout. This one had been procured from the Lansing public library.

"You went to Lansing?" Jesse asked. Hadn't Casey done that, as well?

"No. I've got access to the archives online, but the physical copy is in Lansing," Sam explained. "Again, had it not been for the last name, this would have been almost impossible to find."

Jesse took the computer printout and studied the grainy photo to the left of the article. It was a picture of the farmhouse. Above it, the title: WHAT'S HAPPENING ON OLD MILL ROAD?

"There's no verifying the validity of this," Sam said, nodding to the article Jesse now held. "To me, it reads like old-timey gossip, stuff to sell papers on a slow news day."

And it did. The article was short, but it would have undoubtedly captured Warsaw's interest. There was talk of Joseph Ecklund, his new farmhouse, and Mrs. Ecklund, who was placing emergency calls to a fancy Detroit physician. It spoke of Mrs. Ecklund and her daughter; nobody had seen them since the family had come home from a family event in Indiana, which had been months before. And then the article spiraled to assumptions: bronchitis and pneumonia, maybe typhoid, tuberculosis, or scarlet fever.

Sources state that the only time Mrs. Ecklund is ever seen outside the home is on shopping days when she visits Jasper's Grocers. Her purchases have become sparse, and her demeanor is temperamental. She appears to have not slept and is losing weight. Perhaps it's true, then, that the much-admired Ecklund Estate is a case of the grass being greener on the other side. What's happening on Old Mill Road, what are the Ecklunds hiding, and why?

Jesse's mouth went dry. He swallowed against the lump that had grown at the back of his throat, then handed the articles back to Sam.

"What else did you find?" he asked, his voice sounding foreign to his own ears, as though he hadn't heard himself speak for weeks.

"There were a few more blurbs about the Detroit physician," Sam said. "But it doesn't seem like anyone knew his name or why he was visiting. Just more kindling," he said with a shrug. "It greased the wheels of gossip, I guess."

"And then?" Jesse asked.

"And then they got bored of it. I figured that was it, no end to the story. But then they published *this* thing…" Sam pulled something up on his laptop, pointing the screen in Jesse's direction.

Jesse leaned in to read.

ECKLUND GIRL FOUND DEAD IN HOME.

Responding officers found Miss Georgiana Ecklund unresponsive in the foyer. She had either jumped or had been pushed from an upper floor. Her wrists and ankles were lacerated and bruised, as if by restraint. Despite an emergency call coming from inside the home, there was no sign of Mr. Joseph Ecklund or his wife when officers arrived. Police are attempting to locate the Ecklunds, though are doubtful they will succeed.

"Jesus Christ," Jesse whispered, leaning away from the laptop.

Sam reached over and scrolled down the page to stop on a photograph.

It was Georgiana.

"Jesus *Christ!*" Jesse nearly yelled the incantation as he staggered out of the chair and onto his feet. He veered away from the desk, diverting his gaze from Georgiana's face. The photograph was of a smiling girl, her dark hair perfectly combed. She looked just like the girl he'd seen in his head, the one in the family portrait that hung above the mantel in that grand yellow room. Though, he knew that when the police had found her, she hadn't resembled her photo. No, she had been far different—different enough to cause her parents to abandon her body, to flee.

"I need a drink," Jesse whispered. "*Christ*, I need a drink."

Sam rose from his desk and caught Jesse by his coat sleeve. He led him out of the study, through the living room, and into the kitchen. Popping open the fridge, he motioned for Jesse to help himself from a menagerie of bottles—water and Fantas and a couple of beers. Jesse grabbed a bottle and leaned against the kitchen counter, then pinched the bridge of his nose.

"I take it this actually means something to you, then?" Sam asked after a moment's pause. "It isn't just random facts and Warsaw gossip?"

Jesse didn't know how to answer that without coming off as completely mad.

"I mean, growing up, there were always stories," Sam said. "But that was kid stuff. I remember hearing all sorts of mythology about that place."

And so did Jesse. There were tales of ghosts, of lights blinking off and on despite the property having spent decades without working electricity. There was a story about someone being murdered there. Another about a cannibalistic family moving in after their victims had been discovered buried in Ohio, or West Virginia, or upstate New York, or wherever. There was never any rhyme or reason to those fantastic narratives. Their sole purpose was to scare and fascinate. But after the summer of 2000, after Reed, those stories were replaced by only one: the place was haunted by a restless suicide. Enter at your own risk.

Jesse took a drink, then placed his bottle on the counter and rubbed his face.

"Are you okay?" Sam asked. "You want to crash on the couch, or...?"

"What about a priest?" Jesse murmured the question past his palms.

"A priest?"

"Yeah." Because he'd gotten everything right, hadn't he? Somehow, he'd gotten the entire fucking story right, so where was the priest?

"I didn't see anything about a priest," Sam said. "You mean after the girl died?"

"He came with the physician," Jesse said, grabbing his bottle off the counter. "Father Baker. Can we look that up?"

Sam seemed puzzled for a moment, watching Jesse step out of the kitchen and back toward the study. "Yeah, sure," he finally said, catching up to his former coworker. "If you're sure that was his name."

Jesse was sure.

Stepping into Sam's study, he moved aside as Sam took a seat at his desk once again. Sam logged in to some sort of library database and began typing into the search field. FATHER BAKER didn't bring up any results. Jesse nearly sighed in relief at the dead end, because maybe he was wrong. Maybe, just like with the Ecklund name, he'd heard this wild story during his childhood. He had filed it away only to have it manifest into a waking nightmare. But Sam wasn't deterred. He continued to type into the search bar, continued to hit enter, waiting for results to pop up on his screen.

"Never mind," Jesse said, suddenly wanting nothing more than to believe this was all a phenomenal display of his long-repressed creativity. It was a symptom of grief magnified by a writer's mind. It had to be.

But Sam kept searching, now typing in FATHER BAKER along with the year of Georgiana's death, tacking on WARSAW and MICHIGAN for good measure. And that did it. It brought up a single, solitary result.

"Bingo," Sam said, "Check it out." He pushed the laptop away from himself, triumphant.

But Jesse didn't want to check it out. On the contrary, all he wanted to do was back out of that room and leave, to forget he'd ever come to Sam for help. Sam, the guy who was diligent enough to find even the tiniest grain of sand in an ocean of public records; Sam, the history buff who had made it his personal mission to find an answer to the question of *what's happening on Old Mill Road?*

"Father Alexander Baker, 1934. He was the pastor at Saint Mary's out in Zion."

But that wasn't an answer. The answer Jesse needed was yet to be discovered, and it wouldn't be found in any computer database.

Jesse drew in a slow breath. "Okay," he said. Because he no longer had a choice in the matter. Hell, he'd *never* had a choice. This whole situation had always been out of his hands.

"Okay, what?" Sam asked. "What's with the priest?"

"I'll tell you later," Jesse said. "But for now, I have to go."

"Go?" Sam asked. "Go where?" he asked, following Jesse out of the study and back to the front door.

"To Zion," Jesse said.

And it was only then, standing in front of Sam's door, that Jesse glanced down and saw what he held in his right hand. He had sworn he had grabbed a bottle of water, but what he was grasping tight in his hand wasn't a bottle of Evian. It was a nearly empty bottle of beer.

FORTY-SEVEN

BY THE TIME Jesse arrived in Zion, it was nearly six in the morning. Yet, despite the hour, the sun would not rise for another hour and a half.

Pulling into Saint Mary's parking lot, he doubted the place was open. But there was an old pickup parked around the side of the building. He could see the end of its rusty red tailgate, and something about it struck him as familiar, though he couldn't put his finger on why. Regardless, its presence compelled him to get out of the Altima and check the large wooden double doors. To his surprise, the right one unlatched as soon as he gave it a firm pull.

Saint Mary's was a small place that smelled of melted wax and faint traces of frankincense and myrrh. Jesse hadn't set foot in a church since he'd been a kid—the Wells' had never been much of a religious family. But he couldn't deny the subdued beauty of the church's interior and the odd comfort of that warm, earthy scent. Dark-stained wood beams supported a vaulted ceiling. Ornate pendant lights hung above each side of the center aisle. A massive cross stood behind the pulpit.

Whittled out of wood, Jesus's face was angled down toward the altar in sorrow, his crown of thorns sitting heavy upon his head while a long white drape hung from his outstretched arms. Jesse considered that cross for a moment, unsure whether to step further inside. Because, while his brain assured him that this was precisely where he needed to be, that this was where the answer to his question lied, his mind screamed *run*. His body told him to flee.

"Good morning."

A voice filled the empty space between the pews, leaving Jesse to search for its source. His attention finally settled upon a man standing next to an open door on the right side of the room, one that more than likely led to a small office or rectory.

"May I help you?" the man asked. Jesse was given the opportunity to politely decline. But running would leave him in the same position he was in right now; no idea what to do, feeling hopeless, his life falling apart. If anyone needed guidance, it was him, and the time was now.

"Hi," Jesse said, lifting a hand in greeting. "It's early. I'm sorry."

"It's never too early," the man said, motioning for Jesse to step deeper inside the nave. "Would you like some tea?"

"Sure, thanks."

The man ducked into whatever hidden room was behind that door, leaving it open for Jesse once he made his way across the length of the church. When Jesse finally reached the door, he stepped into a surprisingly modern-looking office. The man was standing next to a small table. A Chinese teapot sat beside a couple of little cups.

"I hope you don't mind green," he said, pouring two servings. "Personally, I can't stand it. But the doctor says it's good for my heart, so here I am." He then looked up and gave Jesse a smile. "I'm Father Donner."

"Jesse," he said. "Jesse Wells, from Warsaw." He added the last bit to assure the man that there was no need for brochures or open invitations to Sunday mass. Father Donner took the hint, gave Jesse a nod, then motioned for him to take a seat at his desk.

"Okay, Jesse Wells from Warsaw," Father Donner said, placing Jesse's cup of tea in front of him, then moving around to his own office chair. "What can I do for you?"

That was a great question, one that Jesse wasn't sure how to answer. But this felt like his last shot, his final opportunity for concrete answers. He only hoped Father Donner wasn't an avid watcher of the nightly news. Otherwise, Jesse was screwed.

"I'm a teacher..." he said, immediately feeling weird about stretching the truth. *The first thing you do is lie to a priest,* he thought, but he had to finesse the details. If he didn't, he doubted he'd get very far. "I've been doing some historical research on a building near our town. I found a name that links to this church back in the thirties."

Father Donner nodded, encouraging Jesse to continue. He lifted his little cup and took a sip of his steaming tea before wrinkling his nose at the taste.

"Foul, really," he murmured to himself, then placed the cup down again. "The thirties, you say?"

"1934," Jesse clarified. "A pastor by the name of Father Baker."

"Was it that recently?" Father Donner grinned, satisfied with his odd little joke. "And what building is this?" he asked, prodding for details Jesse wasn't sure he should reveal.

Because sure, the farmhouse felt like it belonged to Warsaw, but after Casey's suicide, he had landed at the Zion police station. That meant the place was just as close to Zion as it was to his own hometown. There was a good chance the Zion kids were just as fascinated with that old place as the Warsaw kids were. And if Father Donner had grown up anywhere near this area, he had most likely been one of those kids himself. Jesse wasn't sure whether that would give them some common ground, or if Donner would shake his head and ask him to leave; just another nut job obsessing over a bunch of ghost stories. But he had to answer the question. And so, he came out with it, because what did he have left to lose?

"It's an old farmhouse north of Warsaw, so it would be south of here," he explained. "It belonged to a family by the name of Ecklund."

"Oh, I know it," Father Donner said, lifting his cup once more. "Quite well. And what on Earth do you want with a place like that?"

Jesse lifted his shoulders to his ears. *Oh, no reason.* "Just tracing the roots," he said. "Nobody knows much about it, so I decided to take it upon myself."

Father Donner threw the rest of his tea back into his mouth like a seasoned drinker slamming a shot of hard liquor. He then gave Jesse a stern look before rising from his seat. Stepping back to the small side table where he'd left his Chinese teapot, he lifted it by its handle and brought it over to the desk.

"So," Father Donner began, "it has nothing to do with the recent tragedies that occurred there?"

Jesse's heart clenched into a fist. Meanwhile, Father Donner arched a skeptical eyebrow over one eye. Retaking his seat, he poured himself a refill of the stuff he claimed he didn't like.

"I know who you are, Jesse Wells of Warsaw," he said, his voice as calm as an altar bell. "Zion is a small town, too, you know. And Officer Watson is one of our most celebrated gossips."

Jesse shook his head, though he wasn't sure whether it was to deny knowing what Father Donner was talking about, or whether it was to soothe his own frazzled nerves. He'd come here for help, but instead, he'd been caught in a lie. Either he came completely clean now, or Donner would tell him to get the hell out of his church, and rightfully so.

"Officer Watson?" Jesse asked, his throat suddenly parched. He fumbled for his tiny cup of tea and took a drink. Donner was right. It tasted terrible.

"Strange fellow," Father Donner said with a low chuckle, "though, a good guy overall. He's a bit obsessed with cults; swears the Satanists are taking over Detroit." The priest scoffed to himself, amused by the notion.

Officer Watson. Jesse emitted a quiet laugh. He didn't know the name Watson, but Donner's description revealed enough. *Bad Cop Mel.*

"It's okay to seek answers, Jesse," Father Donner said. "Especially after such a traumatic event. Not knowing the reasons for something can be torture, can't it?"

Jesse hesitated, because Donner was smiling a weird sort of smile, as if thoroughly enjoying this conversation, as if relishing in the knowledge that Jesse had been there when both Reed and Casey had passed. But Jesse nodded anyway. Strangely, Father Donner's request for full disclosure brought him some relief. Finally, he could tell *someone* about what was going on.

"My friend, Casey Ridgemont," he began, "the one who hanged himself...he was infatuated with that place. As was my best friend, Reed Lowell, who killed himself inside that house when we were in high school, back in 2000. I was there both times."

Father Donner shifted his weight in his chair. He folded his hands, then unfolded them again, as if not knowing what to do with them. Finally, he fiddled with his small cup of tea once more. His movements struck Jesse as strange, almost mechanical; a puppet with invisible strings.

"Something was going on in that house in 1934," Jesse explained, choosing to ignore the anxiety that was starting to churn deep within his guts. "A physician was repeatedly called out to the house. Eventually, the family called a priest as well."

"Sounds like someone was gravely ill," Father Donner said, flicking his gaze up at Jesse.

"The Ecklund girl," Jesse said. "Georgiana."

Speaking that name seemed to spark the static electricity that hung heavy in the air. He felt the hair on his arms stand up. The back of his neck prickled with gooseflesh. When he peered down to his hands, he discovered that he was squeezing them into tight fists. He pulled in a steadying breath and tried to relax. After all, Father Donner had asked for this information. Finally, someone was taking the time to listen. Someone actually wanted to know.

But when he finally glanced back up to Father Donner, it felt off, as though something within the room had shifted. Or, perhaps, it wasn't within the room at all, but within the structure of Donner's face. An eye, the slightest bit askew. Or his mouth, just a little farther up than it had been a moment before. Whatever it was, Jesse was overcome with the same sense of dread he'd come to know every time he visited the Ecklund house—a feeling of overwhelming apprehension, a sensation of needing to run before something came crawling out of the woodwork, or out from beneath Father Donner's skin.

"I'm assuming she died," Father Donner said. It was then that his mouth turned down in an almost comical sort of frown, so exaggerated it was nearly grotesque. Again, Jesse was struck with the strangeness of it. It wasn't the response a normal person would give, especially not to the subject at hand. "Just like both of your friends, isn't that right?"

Jesse rubbed his mouth with his left hand, as if attempting to wipe Donner's grimace off his own face. He searched the room, though he wasn't sure what he was looking for—a clock, maybe, or another way out other than the door behind him.

"I think I've taken up enough of your time," he said softly, incapable of keeping a nervous warble from peppering his tone. He stood, unable to sit there for a second longer, because there was something wrong here. It was time to make a retreat, because that all-too-familiar feeling was back, the one that screamed *get out*. The one that told him, *run*.

And that pleasant scent of church incense? It was gone now, replaced by the faintest trace of something putrid. Rotting trash. Or vomit. An open sewer. Or maybe a dead rat decomposing in the walls.

"You said you were there when your friends died," Father Donner said, not moving a muscle otherwise. "There were three of you the first time, but only two the next."

Jesse furrowed his eyebrows at the man before him, not sure how he had such information. He supposed it was included in police reports, but why would someone like Father Donner go digging through those? Maybe it was Bad Cop Mel—he could have mentioned that Jesse had been there in 2000. That he'd been there again, nineteen years later, watching another one of his friends off himself. *Devil stuff.* But even if that was the case, he still wasn't sure what that had to do with anything.

"I'm sorry," Jesse said, "I need to get back…"

Get back. Get back to what? An empty house. A wife that had left him. His son's room, silent and empty. A dog that acted as though he was a stranger. *Whatever,* he thought. *Just get out. Just go.*

He began to make his way toward the door, toward the nave and that huge cross, when Donner's voice stalled him.

"Have you heard the story of the dark trickster, Jesse?" he asked. "His best friend is the Devil, and his favorite pastime is to prank the living."

Jesse coiled his arms around himself, wanting to book it out of there, but despite his unease metastasizing into pure dread, he knew he'd regret it if he bolted. He needed to hear whatever it was that Father Donner had to say, because he still didn't know what Georgiana wanted. He didn't know why she had chosen him. And from how he was feeling now, he needed that answer fast.

"Two down, one to go," Donner said. "You were the only one it could turn on, Jesse. It leaps from person to person, you see. It's a game. Nothing but a bit of fun."

A game. Like tag.

"Did you know that the most dangerous of the Devil's friends disguise themselves as the innocent?" Father Donner asked. "As virginal girls and small children, as visions draped in white."

Draped in white.

Jesse's thoughts jumped to the long white cloth that hung from Jesus's arms, reaching down toward his feet, down toward hell. And Georgiana's nightgown. It had been so dirty by the end of her life it may as well have been brown, but it had started out as white; as pure as the smile she wore in the portrait that hung above the Ecklunds' fireplace. As innocent as the photo printed in the paper when her body had been found.

"People think the Devil is afraid of God." Donner's voice went deeper, tinged with dark amusement. "But the Devil loves God. God gives the flock a false sense of security, assuring them that they can avoid damnation if they spend their Sunday's on their knees. Or, say, by hanging hundreds of crosses on their farmhouse walls."

Jesse bit his bottom lip to keep himself from screaming.

Get out. Get out get out GET OUT.

"I'm sorry," he said, the words nearly inaudible, sticking in his throat. "I'm sorry, I have to go."

"Okay," Donner said, offering Jesse a faint shrug of the shoulders. "I'll see you around, Jesse Wells from Warsaw."

But Jesse hardly heard the priest's farewell. He was already marching out the open office door and running down the side aisle past the pews and out those double doors. And while Donner didn't follow, Jesse swore he could hear the man laughing. And that laugh? It was similar to the one he'd heard all this time.

Similar, if not altogether the same.

FORTY-EIGHT

HE DROVE away from Saint Mary's and toward Zion's town limits, but mounting hysteria forced him to pull over. He guided the Altima into a gas station parking lot, pulled around the side of the building and parked next to a door marked RESTROOM. There was a sheet of paper taped to the door, wrinkled by rain and snow: PAYING CUSTOMERS ONLY.

Jesse slid out of the car and stepped over a small snowbank to tug on the door. It was locked. He scanned the lot, not a single car but his own present so early in the morning. And yet, the isolation did little to offer any sense of security. He needed a door, a lock, a barrier between himself and the world. Feeling about a minute shy of vomiting the contents of his empty stomach onto the icy sidewalk, he rushed around the front of the place and stepped inside.

"Bathroom," he said, regarding the pimple-faced kid that sat behind the counter. The kid was screwing around on his phone, probably playing Angry Birds or killing time on Snapchat.

"Gotta buy something," the kid said, hardly looking up from his screen. "Bosses orders."

"I don't need anything." Jesse croaked the words, reaching into his back pocket for his wallet. A few more seconds and his knees would buckle beneath him. His jacket suddenly felt eight layers thick. Had he not known better, he would have sworn he was on fire. Or maybe he was having a heart attack. Regardless, he needed to go outside again, needed to suck arctic air deep into his lungs.

"Sorry," the kid muttered, "I'll get fired if—"

"Just give me the goddamn key," Jesse demanded, tossing a dollar bill onto the counter. "It's an emergency."

The kid managed a smirk despite his surprise. Jesse could see the teen sizing him up, probably wondering what Jesse had eaten that would have made him so desperate for a disgusting gas station bathroom so early in the day. But the kid knew better than to ask. He swiped the dollar bill off the counter and replaced it with a key attached to a foot-long piece of scrap wood. On the wood, someone had scrawled BRING BACK TO COUNTER in black Sharpie. Jesse grabbed the thing and pivoted away from the register, shoved the glass door open and inhaled a chest full of cold wind.

The bathroom was as disgusting as he had imagined, not a chance in hell anyone had cleaned it in the last few weeks. Needless to say, the place had seen its share of emergencies; war stories half-told by splashes of dried urine, wads of wet toilet paper, and a sea spray of random liquids decorating the bottom half of the crooked mirror that hung above the sink.

Any other day, Jesse would have backed out of that bathroom as soon as the stench him. But today wasn't that day. He let the door thud closed behind him, then locked himself inside. Tossing the key into the sink, he grabbed the sink's porcelain sides and squeezed his eyes shut so hard he saw stars. He willed the nausea that was crawling up his throat back down into his chest. And as he stood there, he whispered the mantra he'd taught himself after he'd had his panic attack at eleven years old. "You're okay, everything is fine. You're okay, everything is fine."

Except it wasn't fine, because what the hell had he just run away from? What was the deal with Father Donner? Had what Jesse just experienced really happened, or had he imagined it; like the girl folding shirts at Ann Taylor, or the driver in the car next to him on the freeway, or Georgiana standing in the middle of his street in the dead of night, or the guy on the overpass with his arms spread wide.

"I don't know." The words left his throat in a hush. "I don't know, I don't know…"

"…what to do anymore." Hannah Ecklund finished Jesse's sentence.

She was wringing her hands while standing in the corner next to the toilet, Joseph's arms wrapped around her in an attempt at comfort. Next to them was a door, but it wasn't the bathroom door

Jesse had used to enter the room. It was Georgiana's bedroom door, and beyond Hannah's worried words was a cacophony of noise—screams and yelling, roars and shouts. Jesse blinked at the Ecklunds only to be distracted by another cry. When he spun around to see where it had come from, the bathroom was gone. He was in Georgiana's room again.

She writhed upon her bed, her wrists and ankles tied to the bedposts. Doctor Ladeaux and Father Baker stood over her like two executioners. Ladeaux held her down as Baker drew a cross onto her forehead with his thumb, then pressed a crucifix against her chest.

Georgiana snarled, the sound akin to something a wild animal would make during its last fretful moment of life. Her back arched before she slammed down onto the mattress. It bent again, this time at a more extreme angle. The restraints around her wrists and ankles creaked against the strain. When it arched a third time, she was all but lifted off the bed, held aloft in an impossible bend. Nothing but her knuckles and the tips of her toes touched the dirty sheet beneath her. She remained that way for what felt like an impossibly long time—her tangled hair cascading down toward her sweat-stained pillow, her filthy nightgown tattered and half-unbuttoned, her arms and legs a collection of blue and purple bruises. Her eyes were nothing but dark hollows, open as wide as her mouth, which seemed to unhinge as she prepared to scream again.

But the scream didn't come. Father Baker cut it off with a string of aggressive-sounding Latin. He thrust the crucifix down against her chest once more, as if trying to sink it through her ribcage and directly into her heart. The girl collapsed back onto the bed, silent and motionless, her gaunt face becoming an unnerving mask of peace. Slowly, a round spot of wetness bloomed over her crotch. The scent of ammonia hit Jesse all over again.

"Georgiana?" Ladeaux leaned in toward the girl. "Can you hear me?"

Father Baker continued to quietly murmur his prayers.

"Georgiana?" Ladeaux dared to touch her, shaking her by a shoulder, but she didn't stir. A second later, Ladeaux grabbed his physician's bag and drew out a stethoscope. He hooked the device onto his ears and pushed the small drum against Georgiana's chest. A long moment passed before Ladeaux straightened and turned to Baker. Father Baker issued a defeated sigh.

Jesse blinked at both men. "What?" He turned to Georgiana's motionless body, then back to them again. "What happened?" As if they could hear him. As though he were really there.

Father Baker nodded at Doctor Ladeaux in unspoken understanding.

"You killed her." The words left Jesse in a confused sort of exasperation, unable to believe the stoicism both men were able to maintain. "You fucking killed her!" He yelled at them—a meager attempt at muscling an emotional response from the duo.

Of course, they didn't hear him. Rather than startling at Jesse's bellow, Ladeaux pivoted away from the bed and move to the door. He unlocked it, stepped into the hall, and regarded Georgiana's parents by placing a hand onto Joseph's shoulder.

"She's free now," he told them, then stepped around them and began to move down the stairs. Father Baker followed shortly after, his head lowered either in prayer or penitence—it was unclear as to which.

Hannah tore herself out of her husband's clutch and ran into the room.

"Georgie?!" The name was a desperate plea as she crashed onto her knees next to her daughter's bed. "Oh my God, Georgie?!" She ducked her head against the dirty sheets, succumbing to a weeping scream.

Joseph didn't enter the room to comfort his wife. He hovered outside the door, then descended the stairs.

"Not my Georgie!" Hannah sobbed into her daughter's side. "Don't take her," she said. "Come back! Take me instead! I won't fight. I promise I won't fight."

Jesse swallowed as he listened to the woman bargain with her daughter's lifeless body. He watched her undo Georgiana's restraints, as if freeing her would somehow help the girl find life.

"Don't take her," she repeated, convinced that an invisible force had snatched her daughter away. Undone by despair, she couldn't bring herself to think that, perhaps, death had come by other means. It could have been that Georgiana had been restrained for so long, or that she had refused to eat. Perhaps it had been exhaustion, or maybe dehydration. But in the end, it didn't matter what had caused Georgiana's surrender. She was gone, and that was all.

"No." Hannah sobbed. "Come back..."

Having seen enough, Jesse was just about to turn away when he stopped short. He took in the girl's pale, skeletal-looking face. Maybe he was hallucinating, but he swore he saw something dark swirling just above Georgiana's lips. It was as though her breath had come back, dark and looming, like octopus ink. He gaped at the smoke-like tendrils. Because he couldn't really be seeing what he was seeing, could he?

"Bullshit," he whispered to himself. "There's no way."

But then Hannah noticed the dark swirling mass creeping past her daughter's lips as well. She gasped and staggered away, stumbling directly through Jesse, stealing his wind like a punch to the gut.

His breath heaved out of him, and suddenly Hannah and Georgiana were gone. He was back in the gas station restroom, surrounded by stench and filth.

Pivoting away from the empty corner, he glanced up to meet his own gaze in the mirror.

"I'm okay." The words eked out of him, weak and unconvincing. "I'm okay, I'm..." That mantra faded to nothing as he swallowed hard. Because there, behind his reflection, was something he couldn't begin to understand or explain. There, behind him, was a swirling mass; black vapor surrounding him like an aura. The shadow reached forward and draped itself over his shoulders, the weight of it seizing him from behind.

Jesse gaped, struggling to find air as the load bore down on him, growing heavier with every second. He tried to yell but couldn't, tried to move but was frozen in place. The shadow slithered forward, that black vapor sliding across the front of his neck like a noose. And as he gasped for air, it came: that laughter, deep and malicious. It was so overpowering that, had he been standing with his toes at the edge of a fourth-floor banister, he would have pitched forward and taken flight.

That darkness kept growing heavier, as if trying to push his legs through the bathroom floor. And all the while, Jesse's thoughts rushed back to LouEllen and Ian, to his own house—currently silent and empty, but safe; so much safer than here.

"Take me."

The words felt involuntary, snatched from the depth of his diaphragm by the shadow's invisible hand. But they were his, because he was imagining going home. He was picturing Lou and Ian there, knowing that this phantom would follow him until he could no longer take the strain.

"Take me," he repeated. "I promise, I won't fight anymore."

And just like that, the fluorescent light above the mirror brightened.

That dank, dirty smell returned.

Just like that, the swirling darkness was gone.

Jesse stared at himself in the mirror, then looked down to the sink, because he finally had his answer.

There was no winning this.

All he could do was salvage what was left.

FORTY-NINE

WHEN JESSE found himself behind the wheel of his car again, he was driving toward nothing and nowhere. All he knew was that he was driving as far away from Zion, the gas station, and Saint Mary's Church as he could get. He was running from the things Father Donner had said, the things he didn't want to believe.

He would have happily dismissed the whole experience at Saint Mary's as nothing but another hallucination, but even if Jesse had only seen and heard Father Donner's words inside his own head, he knew there was still truth in the things Donner had said. The way he had spoken of the Devil and his best friend, the way Donner had *looked* at him, as though they had met before. It made his skin crawl, but it also made him want to veer the car around and head back to that church. He imagined pummeling the priest with whatever he could get his hands on—a lamp, that Chinese teapot, a cross off the altar.

You mean, like Baker thrusting a crucifix against Georgiana's chest?

That overwhelming anger was back, filling him up the way Father Donner had filled those tiny teacups. He pulled onto the side of the road and tried to calm his thudding pulse, because there it was again: that low rumble of laughter, a flash of Georgiana's cadaverous face, the image of her arching her back and all but levitating above her bed. These were reminders that he wasn't alone, assurances that no matter how the words had come to Jesse—by way of reality or delusion—Father Donner knew what he was talking about. It was

257

real. All of it. And as quickly as his anger had come, it melted into panic. Because it was then that it dawned on him.

The truck. He'd seen it at Casey's funeral.

But the driver had been a little old lady, he reminded himself. *She had been sweet, had encouraged you to press on, to write...*

Except, Donner had said so himself; the Devil takes on many disguises.

And the thing about the Devil not being afraid of God...It had seemed like a random statement at the time. But now it came clear.

The priest, Jesse thought. *If the Devil isn't afraid of God, it can disguise himself as a fucking* priest.

Casey had been right. There was something dark inside that house. All the kids who had double-dog dared themselves to drive out there by cover of night, the ones who were ballsy enough to creep in through the front door, the once-brave who had bolted to safety; what if they had all seen the same thing Jesse had—the girl in white, the one that lived on the fourth floor? What if she...no, *it* had been waiting for children to come galivanting up the stairs, and the only difference between them and Jesse, Casey, and Reed was that the Three Musketeers had been stupid enough to delve further inside the building than anyone else?

Reed had admitted he had gone into the farmhouse alone. It was silly to assume he'd stood in the foyer and nowhere else. After all, he'd told Jesse *I want to show you something* before bounding up the stairs, as though he'd done it a hundred times before. He had wanted to show Jesse something because he had known what lurked up there.

And Casey? He was the professional, the one who did it for money. He had pushed himself further than anyone ever dared, had walked in too far and roused a sleeping beast. It had tangled itself around his ankles. He had taken it home with him. And once it got bored of Casey Ridgemont, it encouraged him to bring someone else into the fold. Someone else to tag.

You're it.

And what better way to prank a living soul than with sudden, unexpected death? What better way for wickedness to quench its dark appetite than to snatch away a friend?

One to go.

"No." Jesse squeezed the bridge of his nose, refusing to entertain such a ludicrous idea.

Because people didn't die of demonic possession. That was nothing but Hollywood Linda Blair bullshit, right? That stuff didn't happen in real life, and if it did, wouldn't it occur somewhere more appropriate? Someplace like Louisiana, where the trees hung heavy with Spanish moss, where Voodoo was at play? Certainly, a demon wouldn't choose a middle-of-nowhere place in Michigan to do its bidding.

But that thing Donner had said—Jesse couldn't get it out of his mind. The Devil and its disguises. The manipulation of innocence. Cloaking himself as children jumping from barn rooftops. As virginal girls bowing over their dead cousins. As best friends motioning for you to follow them upstairs and old cohorts pleading for company and comfort.

And then there was that woman at Casey's funeral. That sweet little old lady who had praised his writing. The one who had climbed into a red pickup that...that had been parked behind Saint Mary's Church. The church where a demon had awaited Jesse's arrival.

You're a wonderful writer. You should write a book.

"Holy shit."

He began to tremble, unable to control the quaking of his body.

He pictured Casey bowed over Reed same as Georgiana had bowed over Emma. He imagined that swirling darkness creeping past their dead lips and around their attending companion. He remembered it descending from Casey's body as Jesse stood frozen, unable to move. It had snaked itself around his sneakers, hadn't it? No, he'd imagined that. He'd imagined it, same as he'd imagined everything else.

Is that why the newspaper articles exist?

Jesse pressed his hands against his eyes. "Oh, shit shit *shit.*"

Not knowing what else to do, Jesse grabbed his phone, pulled up his contacts, and tapped his finger against LouEllen's smiling face. He waited, but after four rings it went to voicemail. He knew what that meant. She'd glanced at her phone and declined the call. But he wasn't going to give up that easily. He needed to talk to her, needed to tell her about the hallucinations, the way Winston had been acting so strangely. He'd explain the nightmares, the visions, how they matched up to the information Sam had discovered online. He'd even tell her about Father Donner and the twisted way he had smiled at Jesse from across his desk, as though a man he'd never met had been expecting him to arrive at that tiny Zion church.

Because he had been. He had...

And after all was said and done, Jesse would beg LouEllen for her help. Because she'd saved him before. Maybe, just maybe, she could save him again. But he had to get through to her first.

He dialed Carrie Mae. She didn't answer either, but he tried again. Goddamnit, if he had to call both Carrie and Lou a hundred times while sitting along the side of the highway, he'd do it. Because what else was he supposed to do?

You know the answer to that, he thought. *The house. You have to go back.*

The idea of going there gave him an immediate headache, as though Georgiana was sitting in the back seat, squeezing his skull between her dirty palms. He lowered his phone to his lap. That was when he heard a small voice speak up.

"Hello?"

At first, he was sure he was hallucinating again. Was the laugh *speaking* to him now? He caught his lip between his teeth, afraid to look behind him, but finally forced himself to crane his neck toward the backseat.

"Jesse?"

There was nobody there.

"Jesse, are you there?"

Finally, he peered at the phone in his hands. Carrie Mae had answered. He put the phone to his ear and exhaled a breath.

"Jesse? What the hell is going on?" Carrie Mae sounded irritated, having zero patience for phone calls from her sister's estranged husband. But Jesse had to tell LouEllen that he loved her. If something terrible happened at the Ecklunds', she had to know that no matter what, he'd been devoted. She and Ian, they were his everything.

"Carrie," he said.

"Jesus, Jesse. What, you're placing creepy mouth-breathing stalker calls now?"

"I tried to call Lou," he said.

"Yeah, I know," Carrie responded, non-plussed about the whole thing. "And she has no interest in speaking with you right now. You should be smart enough to figure that out when she didn't take your call."

"I need to talk to her," Jesse said. "Please. It's important."

"She'll talk to you when she's ready," Carrie Mae shot back, because Carrie wasn't the type of sister to vacillate when it came to picking sides.

She was team LouEllen through-and-through, and what Lou said went. It had been the same with Lou when Carrie had guy troubles. Once, Carrie had spent an entire week at their house all to avoid a guy who kept driving by her place; a *mouth-breathing stalker*, as she would have called him. Finally, LouEllen had done the unthinkable—a move that had launched one of her and Jesse's biggest fights. She'd gone to Carrie's place, waited for the guy to roll by, and marched out to his car to give him a piece of her mind.

The dude could have been a serial killer. He could have thrown her in his trunk, driven out to the woods, and murdered her. She should have known better, what with her endless true crime documentaries. But rather than being afraid, LouEllen told him to screw off or she'd do her worst. Those were the type of sisters Lou and Carrie were. If one put up a wall, the other decorated it with loops of razor wire until it resembled Guantanamo Bay.

But this time, Jesse didn't have the luxury of waiting for one of them to let their guard down. He had to get Carrie to listen. Because the last thing he wanted was for Lou to be where he had ended up during that final summer—without closure, not able to understand what he could have done differently, trying to decipher what he may have done wrong.

"Listen," he said, "I need you to tell her something."

"Oh, a message?" Carrie snorted into the phone. "I'm not your secretary, pal."

"Carrie…"

"No, Jesse. I'm not getting involved."

"You're *already* involved," he argued.

"Semantics," she smirked.

Jesse pinched the bridge of his nose. The anger was creeping back.

"You made your bed," she continued. "Lie in it, Jesse. Don't get me wrong, I'm sorry about Casey, okay? That's…well, it's just terrible. But ignoring your own family? Your wife and—"

"Would you just shut the fuck up and *listen?*" he snapped.

The line went dead.

For a moment he was sure that, in her surprise, Carrie had hung up. Because how dare he speak to her like that? But when he pulled the phone away from his ear to glance at the screen, the call remained connected. She was still there, sitting in stunned silence.

"I need you to tell Lou I love her," he said. "I need her to at least know that no matter what, I always have. I never wanted any of this to happen. I tried to stop it, but it just kept coming at me."

More silence. He didn't know if Carrie had heard any of that, but there wasn't anything more he could do. He'd said what he needed to say. It was time to end this once and for all.

"I've got to go," he said. "Hopefully, I'll—"

"Jesse, wait." Carrie finally spoke. "You're freaking me out. You sound like you're saying goodbye." That's when her voice cracked. There was genuine fear there, something he wasn't sure he'd ever heard from the likes of LouEllen's boisterous and confident little sister.

"Well, I hope it isn't what it sounds like," Jesse said, all the anger gone as quick as it had come. "But I can't let this go on. It's too dangerous. It's—"

"Wait, what are you talking about?" Carrie asked.

"Nothing," Jesse said. "Never mind. Just tell her, okay? I have to go."

"Wait, Jesse," Carrie was desperate to stall him now. "Wait, okay? Go *where?* What's dangerous? What the hell is going on?"

But Jesse didn't have the energy for more talk.

"Bye Carrie," he told her. "Give Ian a kiss."

He hung up.

His screen went black.

That was when he found himself staring a pale sunrise so bleak it felt as hollow as darkness. As though it could swallow him and make him invisible. As though he, Jesse Wells, hadn't existed since the night Reed Lowell fell four stories down.

FIFTY

JESSE STOPPED the car on the road leading up to the farmhouse and leaned back in his seat. It was there that exhaustion finally hit him, lulling him into a trance-like state, visions as vibrant as real-life blooming against the backs of his eyes.

Sitting there, silent and focused on keeping his composure, he felt the air around him shift. The cold became less so. The smell turned from the familiar scent of his own sedan to something different, something sour, like faint traces of vomit and sweat. She was there with him. She'd been waiting for him to come home.

He could hear her gasping through her tears. Could feel something tighten around his own ankles and wrists. Could make out the murmur of quiet prayer beneath it all—a woman in English, a man in Latin. Words he'd heard before—*I won't fight, I promise*—unmistakable in their desperation.

When he pulled up to the front steps, those once-crooked risers were now straight and varnished. They gleamed wet in the grey morning light, freshly shoveled of snow. Lights illuminated the windows and the curtains were pulled aside to let what little sunlight there was inside.

He slid out from behind the wheel, walked around the front bumper, and looked toward the front door. It was now back on its hinges and securely shut, as if never having been pulled from its jamb.

A wail sounded from upstairs—a cry for mercy—but this time Jesse didn't look up to the fourth-floor windows. He knew he would see her up in that turret, knew that it would rattle his nerves. He couldn't allow himself to get spooked. This time, he *had* to go in.

His legs began to move almost of their own accord, guiding him up the steps and toward the door. He stepped inside and took it all in; the foyer bright with its yellow wallpaper, a fire roaring in the great room. The photographs that had lined the staircase were, however, gone. They were replaced by a mismatched array of crucifixes instead.

He understood those crosses now. Hannah Ecklund had swapped family pictures for religious relics in hopes of chasing the monster that had moved into their home away. She'd even removed the family portrait that had hung above the fireplace. A large cross hung there now, so big it hardly fit in the space above the mantle, as though the more prominent the cross, the more Jesus would bless her home with His mercy and love.

But the crosses hadn't worked. Despite the warm glow of those rooms, there was a sinister unease lurking beneath it all. Electric, like lightning. Something continued to linger there, creeping from corner to corner, from room to room. Because, as Donner had said—so plainly stated it may as well have been fact...

...*the Devil loves God.*

That false sense of security—the idea that God would protect them—had lowered their guard and done the Ecklunds' in.

Jesse traveled through the foyer and up the stairs much the way a body moved through water—slow and smooth, dreamlike. When he reached the third-floor landing, he paused and pointed his attention upward. He heard a door open. Someone rushed out.

Hannah ran to the upper banister and yelled down to the ground floor. "Joseph!" A moment later, she was careening down those risers, taking them three at a time, so fast it was a wonder she didn't stumble head-over-feet. The soles of her brown shoes clopped against the stairs as she continued to yell her husband's name. "Joseph. *Joseph!*" She whipped past Jesse, who stood motionless against the wall.

Joseph appeared in the foyer before Hannah reached the first floor.

"What is it?" he asked, his tone somber.

It was only when Jesse saw the grief upon the man's face that he understood the timeline. This event wasn't occurring before everything had spiraled out of control for the Ecklunds, but after Doctor Ladeaux and Father Baker had left, after both Hannah and Joseph had learned that their only child was dead. The doctor and priest had left them to cope with the bizarre and unfathomable reality: something unexplainable had taken their daughter, something beyond their understanding. And nobody—not Ladeaux, not Baker—had tried to explain it away.

"Georgie," Hannah said, manic. "You have to come. You have to *see.*"

"See what?" Joseph asked, his body language easily read; the last thing he wanted to do was go up to that room again. He didn't want to see his daughter's lifeless body, didn't want to believe the nightmare to be real. But Hannah shook her head, insistent, refusing to let him stand there and brood.

"Something's happening," Hannah said. "You have to—" And before she gave herself a chance to finish her own sentence, she pivoted where she stood and bolted back up the stairs.

Joseph reluctantly followed. When he reached the third floor, Jesse tailed him up the final staircase. His shoulder hugged the wall as he climbed the risers until he reached the fourth story. It was where Georgiana's parents now stood. Stepping behind them to witness what they were seeing, he spotted her through the open bedroom door.

Georgiana sitting upright, bare feet firmly placed on the floor. Her chin tipped down. Her tangled hair obscuring her face. Fingers digging into the mattress beneath her. Not dead. Not even close.

"Sweet Lord." The words left Joseph in a whispered rush.

Meanwhile, Hannah clasped her hands over her mouth, as if worried that any sound they made would scare Georgiana back to the other side. And Jesse—invisible and standing between them—could do nothing more than gawk at what he was seeing; a skeleton of a girl resurrected. Motionless, sure, but resurrected regardless.

"God Almighty," Joseph said, then turned to his wife. "We need to leave."

"*What?*" Hannah's countenance bloomed with disbelief.

"Can't you feel it?" he asked. "This isn't right, Hannah. This—"

"It isn't *right?*" Hannah's tone went cold. "It's a *miracle,*" she told him, then pushed him aside as she moved into Georgiana's room. "I prayed to God and—" She paused because that's when Georgiana slowly tipped her chin up.

Prayed to God? Jesse thought. *No, you prayed to whatever had taken her. I heard you.*

And Georgiana had heard it, too. That was, perhaps, why she was canting her head at her mother, giving her a slow smile. It was the same lecherous grin Jesse had seen so many times—her lips cracking as they pulled taut, her teeth impossibly rotten where healthy teeth had once been.

"Jesus..." Joseph gasped.

And as he did, Georgiana sprang to her feet, as if spurred on by her father's call to a higher power. She lunged, just as she had jumped at Jesse in the hallway of Warsaw High. She flew at her mother in a half-stumbling run. Hannah emitted a startled cry and staggered backward.

"Georgie!" Hannah yelled the name just before Joseph yanked her out of Georgiana's way.

Georgiana had built up too much momentum to stop herself by then. Her bare feet scuttled as her pelvis crashed into the waist-high balustrade. Hannah exhaled another cry. She even reached for her daughter's emaciated frame. But it was no use. Georgiana flipped head over heels into the empty space of the farmhouse's towering stairwell. By the time Hannah rushed to the spot where the girl's feet had touched last, Georgiana was lying on the foyer floor four stories below.

"We need to leave," Joseph repeated himself, and this time he wasn't taking no for an answer. He clamped a hand around Hannah's bicep and dragged her forward. Hannah didn't protest. She couldn't. In her renewed grief, the woman seemed to be choking, unable to draw in a sustaining breath.

Jesse watched them descend the stairs, forever aware of the spot where Reed's body had lied on that muggy summer night. And it was only then that he fully understood what Father Donner had meant when he had said this was a game.

Over the handrail and down the stairwell.

Like Georgiana. Like Casey. Like Reed.

"Like Emma," he said, remembering the story Joseph had told Doctor Ladeaux about the wedding, the tragedy, the fact that little Emma had asked her cousin to catch her before jumping to her death. It had been the moment that darkness had snaked its way into Georgiana's life. She had folded herself over Emma's body, and it had passed from one girl to another. It's why Georgiana had changed.

And how did Emma come to be involved in this dismal Ring Around o' Rosie? There was no way to tell. Who knew how long the game had been going on; years, decades, centuries? One thing, however, was now abundantly clear: the moment one host was gone, another had to be found. And from the way Joseph was pulling Hannah toward the door, he was quick to make the connection. He wanted out of that house, even if it meant leaving with nothing. Even if it involved abandoning their child.

When the couple finally reached the first floor, Hannah managed to tear herself free of Joseph's grasp. But it wasn't to rush to her daughter's side. If it had been, she would have been pulled into the game. *Tag, you're it.* But Hannah ran out of view. A moment later, Jesse could hear her on the phone, crying out to the switch operator to call the police. Within a few seconds, Joseph grabbed her again. He dragged her out of the place while she screamed for reprieve.

Standing just shy of the fourth-floor banister, Jesse watched the Ecklunds' pickup ramble away from the farmhouse as fast as it could. The sudden stillness of the place made his ears ring. And as he tipped his chin down to cast a final glance at Georgiana's body, he watched a dark mist rise from beneath the folds of her nightdress. That inky blackness drifted upward, coiling like incense smoke, draining the color from the house as it ascended.

The yellow wallpaper went gray with age as it climbed. The crucifixes vanished, one by one, leaving nothing but cross-shaped shadows upon the wall. The banister's glossy varnish faded until the wood splintered and cracked. And when that mist reached where Jesse stood, he found himself in the Ecklund house not as it was before, but as it was now: a hollow shell of what it had once been. Empty, but far from abandoned. Infected by the Trickster whose game had stalled.

But somewhere in that house, Georgiana was watching him just as she had watched Reed, waiting for him to brave the stairs and cross the threshold into her room. She'd lead him here, just as she'd led

Casey and his camera. And now that Jesse was where she wanted him, like with the others, there was no way she'd let him go.

Jesse coiled his arms around himself. He balled his fists against the cold that was snaking its way through broken windows and the unhinged front door. The house's warmth was gone, replaced by a cold winter numbness.

Had this been weeks ago—hell, had it been only a few days prior—Jesse would have reeled at the fact that he was standing where he was. And yet now, he no longer cowered at the dread that cocooned itself around him. Standing amid the ruins of the Ecklund home, he was reminded of why he needed to be exactly where he was.

LouEllen, laughing at one of his jokes while she sat across from him at the kitchen table. Ian, giggling as he squished boiled carrots between his chubby fingers. Winston, lying beneath the table, waiting for veggies to fall to the floor. Jesse, happy again, because despite his absence, his family would be mended. This nightmare would finally be behind them. He'd be gone, but at least they could all move on.

This game would end with him.

"Where are you?" He yelled the question into the pale morning shadows that clung to the corners of the stairwell. "I'm here," he told her, spreading his arms to accentuate the point. "You wanted me, so here I am."

But there was no response. No sound. No flash of white running from one room to another. No foreboding sense of a dark figure standing over him, trying to drill his legs through the floor. And for once, rather than taking solace in the silence, all it did was leave him unnerved.

"You're okay," he whispered to himself. "You're okay, just wait her out." But how long would that take, and would he freeze to death before it happened? He winced against the cold and tucked his hands beneath his arms. He pulled his shoulders up to his ears and began to move, if only to keep his blood from crystalizing in his veins. But rather than pacing the upstairs hall, he found himself making a bee-line for Georgiana's long-abandoned room—the one place he wanted to avoid.

Jesse?

He tried to block out the cold, block out the voice he heard coming from somewhere below him.

Jesse!

Footsteps. She was coming for him, but not in the way he had thought she would. He'd been wrong. All those visions had been part of the plan. Georgiana hadn't been helpless. She hadn't been searching for companionship or understanding, hadn't been hoping for someone to join her in death so that she was no longer alone.

Jesse!

It had all been a ruse. A trick. She had lied to him, just like Casey had lied to Jesse to get him to come here the night he had died. And if Jesse waited for her to appear, she'd finally have him. She'd wriggle her way inside him just as she had snaked her way inside Casey and Reed. And that was all part of the game, wasn't it?

It leaps from person to person. Nothing but a bit of fun...

And then what, game over?

No, Jesse thought. *Game on.*

She'd make him go home. She'd infect his every waking hour. She'd destroy his life beyond what she'd already managed. And then, when she grew tired of him, she'd make Jesse bring someone new into the fold. Someone like Sam. Or Carrie Mae. Or LouEllen.

But not if he stopped it first. Not if he called a permanent time-out.

Jesse turned away from Georgiana's vacant room and moved back to the top railing of the stairs, his fingers curling over the dry wood. He felt himself lean forward, and despite trying to convince himself to let go, his breath hitched in his throat. Reflex took over. His grip tightened. He caught himself mid-wobble, his frozen digits hardly able to hold on as he twisted away from the four-story drop.

...just in time to see Georgiana running toward him.

Her nightgown billowing in slow-motion.

Her hair flying like a tangle of Medusa's snakes.

Jeeeesseeee.

The name left her in an ominous hiss.

There was no time for panic, only for his heart to somersault once, flipping in perfect unison with his body as he tipped backward. Back into the gaping void.

He hardly felt himself hit the splintered boards, but he knew he had when his heart crashed against his spine, his face flashing hot despite the cold.

Jesse?! JESSE!

He blinked, his lashes fluttering, fascinated that he was still alive, hypnotized by the pain that was beginning its slow outward bloom from the center of his chest.

Oh my God...

Riveted by the fact that he didn't see Georgiana's snarling grimace, but his wife's face twisting in horror. She was playing tricks on him again. She'd stolen LouEllen away from him the night he had driven her up here, if only for the briefest of moments. Now, he was bringing her back in one final act of cruelty. Because how *dare* he ruin her game? How dare he bring it to an end? This wasn't supposed to happen. He was supposed to die *after* he'd been infected. He was supposed to be the new "it."

"Oh my God, *oh my God,* Carrie!" LouEllen crashed to her knees beside him, the vision of her so real that he could smell her—the coconut shampoo she used, the faint scent of her favorite lotion.

"It's okay," LouEllen said, her hands fluttering across the top of his coat, unzipping it with a furious pull. "Jesse, it's okay. You're okay. Holy—why...I..." But he knew there was something more, something she wasn't telling him. He could tell by the way her gaze roved his body and stopped on a certain spot before widening. "No, it's fine," she whispered more to herself than to him. "It's fine. *Carrie!*"

Jesse's attention shifted, but his body didn't move. He saw Carrie Mae step through the unhinged front door of the house. That's when he knew, when it hit him full-force.

This wasn't a hallucination.

Lou and Carrie, they were really there.

And then his stomach pitched because there, in Carrie Mae's arms, was Ian bundled in his winter gear.

Jesse tried to speak.

Get out.

Tried to yell.

Get out!

Tried to tell them to go.

GET OUT!

Because Georgiana was still inside the house. If she didn't come for him, she could come for somebody else.

But he only managed a wet, gurgling sob, and it was then that Lou began to cry.

"Hold on," she told him, scrambling to her feet. "I'm calling, I'm—" She looked to her sister as she fumbled for her phone. "Shit," she said. "*Shit!*"

"What?" Carrie asked.

"Stay with him," Lou said.

"Wait, where are you going?" Carrie sounded panicked.

Jesse listened to scrambling footsteps, unable to see Lou or Carrie as they moved out of his line of sight. He tried to turn his head, but he couldn't. He tried to yell again, but it didn't work. That gurgle changed into a choking cough. He could taste blood at the back of his throat, could feel it splash warm and wet across his lips and chin.

"No reception," LouEllen said. "I need to find—I said *stay with him!*" she screamed, only to be joined by a child's frightened howl.

Jesse knew that cry. Ian was still inside that fucking house, and he was afraid.

But at least it had worked, right? He had leaped before Georgiana had transformed him into something beyond himself. Lou or Carrie would have to go up to the fourth floor, now, just like Reed and Casey had. Because that's where she was waiting. It's where she lived.

Unless those hallucinations, that laughter, the hours he'd spent doing nothing in front of his computer...

Unless that had been...

Unless he was...

No, he thought. *If that were true, I would have asked someone to come here with me. I would have set it up, just like Casey and Reed had.*

And it was true that he'd come here alone. But hadn't he attempted to call LouEllen just an hour before? Hadn't he dialed Carrie Mae's number over and over until she had answered? If anyone had known where to look for him, it would have been his wife. Carrie had passed on the message, just as Jesse had known she would.

When they had first started, the visions he'd been having of the farmhouse had started to come out of nowhere. He'd thought they were his imagination, the writer in him stepping up to the plate. But that hadn't been it. Not in the least. Georgiana hadn't been showing him anything. They were memories. A part of her, which had now become a part of him.

Suddenly, all he wanted to do was scream. He squeezed his eyes shut as tight as he could and willed it out of himself—a guttural roar born out of desperation and fear. He hoped it was enough to scare Carrie Mae out of there, to at least force her and Ian onto the porch.

But rather than listening to footsteps rush away from him, he heard the opposite. He blinked up at his sister-in-law, a crying Ian still clutching tight to her chest. Jesse tried to speak again, but he couldn't draw in air. His vision began to blur, and so he looked away from them both, unable to cope with his son's tear-streaked cheeks. And out of the corner of his peripheral vision, he caught a glimpse of a blip of white upon the stairs.

He could see her dirty fingers coiled around the spindles of the banister.

Could make out her hair, dark and tangled around her face.

And when she met his gaze with those hollow black eyes, he could hear her against his ear.

One to go. One to go. One to go.

EPILOGUE

IT WAS A beautiful day out, perfect for pedaling; not too hot, not humid, and cool enough for a light jacket until you broke a sweat, which Ian had done over a mile back. He now traveled with his windbreaker cinched tight around his waist.

His bike was a Schwinn, just like he'd seen in the photos he'd found in the back of his aunt's armoire. Organized in a thick album that documented his parents' childhoods, Ian had spent a lot of time staring at those pictures, particularly the ones of his dad at the age he was now. That's where he first saw photos of his father's bicycle. And while he often wondered who those two other boys in the photos were, he never asked. He didn't want to blow his cover, didn't want his Aunt Carrie to know that he snuck into her room to view those snapshots every chance he got. And so, with nothing else to call them, he dubbed the trio of boys the Three Musketeers.

Ian had lived with his Aunt since as far back as he could remember. His dad had died when he was a baby, and the incident had pushed his mom to some sort of brink. At least that's how Grandma Auggie told it. There's a limit to what people can handle, baby, she'd once told him. Everyone's got a breaking point. Sometimes, to shut out the pain, you've got to shut out the world.

But living with Aunt Carrie wasn't so bad. She wasn't super strict, unlike Grandma Auggie. Ian's grandmother, on the other hand, was convinced some terrible tragedy would befall him while crossing the road or riding his bike along Warsaw's dreary streets. I have a feeling, he'd heard her say, once. I just have this awful feeling. Ian was just a week shy of his twelfth birthday, but his grandma treated him like he was two.

Aunt Carrie understood that he wasn't a little kid anymore, however. They had an unspoken understanding. Ian could do pretty much whatever he wanted as long as Aunt Carrie knew where he was. She had even given him a cell phone. It was old and scratched up, but there were a few cool games on it that he could play. He'd asked for a new one for his birthday, but he wasn't sure he'd get it. Then again, maybe Aunt Carrie had told his mom, and Ian's mom was a wild card. You never did know what LouEllen Wells had up her sleeve.

His mom lived out in Detroit. Ian and Aunt Carrie would make that trip within the next week even though Aunt Carrie hated the drive. He hadn't noticed it when he was younger, but now he saw it every time; she'd start crying before they reached the place where Ian's mom lived. It was a boring-looking building that, on the inside, smelled like a hospital but seemed more like a weird hotel.

Ian didn't see his mom all that much, but that was okay. His mother was never excited to see him, anyway. Sometimes, she'd turn away from him as if disturbed by his appearance, as though she were seeing a ghost. But Aunt Carrie stuffed him into her sedan and made the obligatory trip into the city at least three times a year anyhow— always for Christmas, Mother's Day, and his birthday; sometimes for Thanksgiving and Easter. Ian wasn't crazy about the trips, same as his aunt, but he could hardly complain. His mom had gifted him his beloved bike, which was one of the best gifts he'd ever received. And now, on the first truly warm day of April, he couldn't help but think of his mother as he pedaled down the side of a quiet highway toward his destination. If she did get him the phone he wanted, he could take some photos of where he was going. Not that he'd ever show anyone but his best friend, Quin. Even Aunt Carrie would give his current destination a hard pass.

He'd seen the house plenty of times before, set off a good distance from the road. There was a sign posted at the entrance— probably something about trespassing, but it was so old and faded it was hardly readable; a good excuse as any that he "didn't know" if he got caught.

The house was in bad shape. It leaned at a weird angle, as though a good gust of wind could bring it crashing down. As a matter of fact, any time Warsaw was hit with a decent storm, Ian would worry about whether the house would withstand the gale. Because unlike everyone else in town—who only saw the place as some creepy haunted mansion—Ian knew better. He could imagine the way it had once been, and it was a pretty place. Yellow wallpaper: that's what he kept seeing. Yellow wallpaper with some sort of delicate design.

Aunt Carrie always noticed the house when they drove past, as if searching for someone in the windows. He was pretty sure his aunt had no idea he knew it's where his dad had died. Nobody had told him as much, at least not beyond that jerk Clive Morris at school. He'd looked it up at the library after Clive had jeered at him in the cafeteria earlier that year.

Your old man haunts that creepy old place, you know. No wonder you're so weird.

After learning about his father, his fascination was suddenly peppered with newfound urgency, as though he had to go there before the house collapsed in on itself. It felt like a duty, a preservation of his father's memory.

Despite his personal connection, Ian knew there was no way he was the only kid in town who wanted to creep through the door and see what was inside. Quin had mentioned how cool it would be to sneak inside. Heck, maybe if it was really cool, Ian and Quin could come out here together next time. But at the moment, there was more to his visit than a thirst for exploration. Perhaps, if it wasn't too babyish to believe in ghosts, it could have been his dad beckoning him to visit. Calling out to him from beyond the grave.

But it is babyish, Ian decided.

Believing in ghosts was dumb, right? Loving spooky books and making up his own stories, however, was a different matter. He'd found a few folded up sheets of paper between the pages of his parents' photo album when he'd first found it hidden away at the back of Aunt Carrie's armoire—an innocent enough discovery, since she'd told him to rummage around in there for a pair of winter gloves. The papers were nothing more than snippets of stories, but they had been creepy enough. And he knew they'd been written by his dad, since he had dated and initialed the printouts—JW—as if to tell the world these are mine, don't touch.

His dad's stories were tantalizing because Ian had always loved scary novels. Maybe, even though he never knew his father, the love for spooky stuff had been somehow passed on. You know, like in his

DNA. Heck, he didn't know. Maybe he was just grasping at straws. But he'd just finished another Goosebumps book a few days before his teacher had assigned the class a short story to write, and that's when Ian was struck by inspiration. That house where his dad had died? That's what he'd write about. Quin would think it was cool, and maybe if the story was really good Clive Morris would shut his stupid mouth.

Though, really, the why of it didn't matter when it came to that old place. What mattered was that his English project was due on Monday and that house was at the heart of Ian's story. He just needed a closer peek to get his creative juices flowing. Fiction sometimes required a bit of research, after all. At least, that's what he'd heard.

Aunt Carrie's house was clear on the other side of Warsaw, so it took Ian over an hour to get to where he was going. When he finally arrived, he pulled onto a road that was so overgrown it was hardly visible—just two tire tracks that cut through what was now nothing but a field of wildflowers and weeds. And at the end of that long, invisible road was the house, creepy with its tall tower and slanted roof. He'd imagined an old black car driving down that road, once. It had been neat, like something out of an old-timey film.

Unable to ride his bike along the ruts and weeds, he walked the Schwinn past the rusted warning sign. He peeked over his shoulder a couple of times, just in case someone had noticed him, but it wasn't likely. Hardly anyone used the highway that ran along the property. He'd only passed three or four cars during his entire journey there.

When he reached the house, he leaned his bike against the warped front porch railing and stepped back to get a good look. Vines were growing up the front facade, vibrant and green now that the weather was warm. He imagined them snaking their way through the broken windows and decorating the interior walls. It didn't seem all that scary to him. If anything, it was kind of nice. Maybe there was a treasure or two in there—something his dad had left behind for him to find.

However unlikely that was, Ian couldn't help but entertain the possibility, especially after the reoccurring dream he'd been having. It wasn't anything spooky, really. Just his dad motioning for Ian to follow him up the stairs.

Come on, his smile seemed to say. *I want to show you something.*

"Dad?" It felt silly talking to no one, but who would know? "Are you here?" he asked, allowing his attention to drift across each window, seeking out his father's face. Of course, he saw nothing. At least not until he reached the top turret windows. That's where he swore he caught a glimpse of something shifting out of view, like someone stepping away from the glass, afraid to be seen.

Ian narrowed his gaze, then pivoted to the front door. He'd go in, if just for a minute. He'd get a good look for his assignment and leave. At least that way, he could stop wondering what it was like.

Taking a few steps toward the warped front steps, his pulse picked up the pace. Despite his determined curiosity, something about this whole thing begged him to reconsider. Because what if there's a dead body in there? After all, this was where his dad had passed away. It was creepy to go exploring in there, right? Morbid, as Grandma Auggie would say. But he hadn't ridden his bike all the way out here for nothing.

"You've come too far," he said, carefully placing one sneaker after the other onto the porch steps as he climbed.

When he reached the front door, he paused, steeling his nerves.

"You're okay," he whispered, and then took another forward step. Because sure, the house could collapse at any moment, but there wasn't a breath of wind that afternoon.

Almost like he was supposed to be there.

Almost like it was meant to be.

ANIA AHLBORN

ent ti as:

ACKNOWLEDGEMENTS

This book is an exercise in dogged determination. It's been a long, hard road, and it often felt like this novel would never be complete. After finishing the first draft, I had a baby. It took over six months for me to find my way back to Warsaw, Michigan. I guess you could say I was a lot like Jesse Wells for a while—unable to write, with Georgiana never all that far from my mind.

My biggest thanks go to my husband, Will, without whom I'd have probably given up on ever finishing this book. Your encouragement and belief in me carried me through to the end, even during days when I needed as many naps as the kid. To my bestie, Dani Jaeger, you know I couldn't have made it through this without venting, and venting, and venting about…everything. Babies. Publishing. Babies. More babies. You are the best listener, even if you're only listening half the time. (Don't lie.) To my kiddo—Beebo, you're still way too young to understand how motivating you are despite demanding every second of my day. Every effort is for you. Also, please don't trespass inside creepy old houses when you're older. And if you absolutely must do it, take Mama with you. At least that way, the ghosts will get me first.

To Ashley Sawyers, Johann Trotter, and Sadie "Mother Horror" Hartmann, thank you so much for agreeing to beta read an absolutely terrible version of this book, as well as for your steadfast and tireless social media cheerleading. Sadie, you've always been my champion. I'm so glad this process has made us friends.

Speaking of social media, to my Instagram pals and the Bookstagram community: there are too many of you to name individually, but know that I appreciate every post, every review, and every recommendation you put out onto the world. To Jeroen Ten Berge, I'm so happy we were able to reconnect after so many years and come up with an incredible cover together. And of course, to my readers, some of which have been with me since Seed; you guys are extraordinary. Your support and enthusiasm never cease to humble and amaze me. The best way to sincerely thank you is to keep writing, right? So, that's what I'll do.

ANIA AHLBORN
Greenville, South Carolina
May 7th, 2019

DID YOU ENJOY THIS BOOK?

Help spread the word about Ania's work! Please share your thoughts with other readers by posting a review on Goodreads and Amazon.com.

Find Ania on social media, read her blog, and connect with the author via her website, WWW.ANIAAHLBORN.COM.

Made in United States
Troutdale, OR
09/09/2024

22685531R00176